THE
IMRATI
TRIALS

THE
IMRATI
TRIALS

LIZZY GAYLE

CITY OWL
PRESS

THE IMRATI TRIALS
Sisters of Magic and Shadow, Book One

CITY OWL PRESS
www.cityowlpress.com

Cover Design by MiblArt. All stock photos licensed appropriately.

Edited by Tina Moss.

For information on subsidiary rights, please contact the publisher at info@cityowlpress.com.

Deluxe Hardback Edition ISBN: 978-1-64898-514-0

Paperback Edition ISBN: 978-1-64898-513-3

Digital Edition ISBN: 978-1-64898-515-7

CITY OWL PRESS
Escape Your World ● Get Lost in Ours

To all who dream of being part of something bigger. I see you.

PROLOGUE

Alone in his chambers, the king paused, sneering at the room's ostentatious finery, for none of it compared to his greatest treasure securely hidden from all but him. It was the very prize which called to him now, deep in the marrow of his being. Ready, he knelt beside the enormous fireplace laden with ash. The harsh weather of the Night Kingdom often called for keeping the hearths lit, but for the present, reaching inside and tapping the right place with his scepter was far more vital.

Rising, he waited as the marble slid aside almost soundlessly, revealing the spiral staircase down to his private dungeon. He trusted no one with the knowledge of this chamber's existence, for what he possessed was too powerful, too tempting not to turn even his most loyal subjects against him. Certainly, his daughter would never find out. Not until it was her time to join his collection, and that he hoped would be far in the future. Not because he carried a soft spot for her—she was too weak to deserve his admiration. He ignored the knowledge that this was by his own design as he snapped, igniting the single torch on the wall, and flooding the small round room with light.

His gaze roved over the set of gilded doors. Each one was fitted with a stone of power spelled to keep its occupant in a dream state. Only one of the three sat open, and the sudden memory played in his mind of the day his queen gave the last of her power. She'd opened her big golden eyes like she hadn't done in so many years—though only for moments—before the light slipped from them forever. Despite what she'd thought, despite it not being enough, he'd cared for her in his own way. Perhaps that was why he'd made sure never to grow too attached to their child. No need to torture himself with useless regrets again.

The king's attention shifted to the door at the opposite end of the row. He raised his scepter with the powerstone inside. Violet light erupted from the nucleus of the crystal, surging into the similar stone that sat behind a magical force-field on the room's center podium. When the light hit, the stone glowed as well, and he mentally directed the beam to the correct space. Unlike the center door, which had yet a third stone embedded and forever lit in its center, this one was unadorned. Its occupant was important, but not worthy or in need of extra protection. The center door would remain sealed until he had all the stones. Only then would he be strong enough to face Her without fear of wrath.

The woman inside the now open chamber blinked as she woke, eyes fluttering like tiny wings. She was attractive for an elf, but that wasn't his purpose in keeping her. When she saw him, she thrust her arms forward, meeting only the restraint of the iron chains that bound her to the wall. Unable to attack, she focused all her anger into her gaze, wishing she could hurt him back. But wishes were made of dust, and only those who seized power could mold the future.

He chuckled softly as she spit out a trail of colorful language in a raspy, rarely used voice. He lifted his scepter, and the sound stopped, though her lips kept moving. It took her a good while to realize he'd silenced her. She threw her head back against the stone, causing her long wild hair to slip back and reveal the points of her ears.

"I trust you've had a good nap, Miyal." He said it to irk her as he enjoyed watching her struggle. Knowing it was futile to fight against her bonds, that once he'd gotten what he needed, she'd be back asleep until the time came for clarification once again.

She curled her lip in a silent growl, daring him to try to make her. He smiled.

"I felt the shift in energy. The gods awaken." He stepped forward until he could reach out and lift some of her hair just to make her strain against her bonds again. "What must I do in order to collect the final two stones before it is too late?"

The fight drained out of her as he set the surface of the crystal in his scepter against her stomach. The remainder of her dress had long since burned away from the first of these sessions. He watched with fascination as her body arched against it, the pale purple light traveling up her chest to her throat and then over her head like a glowing hood. He'd have to recharge his magic when he was done here, and that meant a visit to his daughter sooner than expected. It couldn't be helped, though.

"And while you're at it, how long will my current energy source last?"

With one last tiny shove against Miyal, he released her voice so the deeper one with little affect could answer his query. She was poorly behaved, but she made a good personal seer. Quite accurate.

"The Imrati must be called. It is time to meet your destiny, Balram of Centos." He liked the sound of that, although he wished whatever spirits spoke through the woman would address him as king.

"The Imrati? You're sure?" He'd avoided the sacred tournament designed by the gods since he'd won the last one as a young man. Even the divine beings had been too shortsighted to envision someone like him could manipulate the balance of power they'd designed. He smirked, stroking his dark beard as he considered the fact that he'd outsmarted the gods.

"It is imperative to your destiny," the voice repeated, then continued, "Your source fades as she expends too much magic. She is like a star— bright but burning too quickly."

"How do I prevent this?" he hissed.

"You cannot. Though if she marries the Astrodonian combatant, you will receive the next stone. And if they provide an heir, a new source will be born with even more magic."

He nodded, calmer. Sooner than he'd have liked, the princess would be part of his collection, but it couldn't be helped. "And what of the other two stones?"

"One resides in the sky palace. But you will not access it until the princess' betrothal, though you will try."

"And the other?" he asked, tamping down the anger simmering below the surface. He knew the answer would be the same as always.

"The other is in the possession of your nemesis. Beware, for your foe is closer than you realize."

"As always, I will ask you again then, who do you name my nemesis?" The oracle had never given the name, and he often took his rage out on the useless bitch it spoke through. But he'd keep trying until he found the one she spoke of, or at least a new receptacle for the oracle. One that could answer *all* his questions. At least she'd added the warning this time. Whether the news was welcome or not, only time would tell. He would have to tighten his security, though he couldn't imagine anyone able to penetrate the fortress he'd created of Centos.

"His name must not be spoken," the seer proclaimed.

Rage broke free and flooded the king's system as his hand clenched around the scepter, trembling. "Speak it!" he demanded.

"I cannot."

"So be it," he whispered, then drew back the staff to swing.

ONE

NYAH

I t had started as a whisper—a breeze flowing through the Night Forest. It'd reached me as I'd sat on my favorite perch atop the citadel, alone beneath the dual moons of Centos. A normal gust, no matter how cold, shouldn't have stood out, but when the rest of the wind and clouds blew in the opposite direction, well, it didn't take a sorcerer like the wretched king to figure out magic was involved.

What it'd meant, I had no clue. Still, the ominous feeling stayed with me for days as the shiver it had produced resurfaced at strange moments, raising gooseflesh on my arms and the back of my neck beneath the hair tied there. Each chilled caress on my skin brought a mix of confusion and certainty. Confusion as to where this strange type of magic originated and the certainty that whatever it was trying to impart was dangerous.

Now, days after the first time I'd sensed it so high above the kingdom, I hid deep in the shadowed corner of a tavern. I thought I could avoid the skin crawling sensation in the shelter of a building. Yet it had found me once again, like a spirit trailing an icy finger down my spine, even as I sipped at the bitter ale I'd swiped from a table before. Huddling beneath the hood of my cloak, I scanned the room as usual. Nothing else was different from a few moments earlier when I'd propped one leg up on the bottom of a dusty shelf and contemplated whether I ought to interfere on the behalf of the waitress being cornered by three of the King's guards.

Avoiding the ghostly shiver was impetus enough to move. With a sigh that issued deep from my bones, I kicked back from my seat and stood. I always seemed to choose to involve myself, despite the danger of being discovered. Why bother remaining alive if I didn't do my best to counter the evil that spread through the kingdom like a disease which sprouted from the black-hearted royal bastard himself?

"I have to serve—" The young woman, probably just a couple years my junior, far bustier, yet barely of age, stammered around the beefy arm of the biggest brute.

His bicep flexed, making the skull inked on it sneer. I'd have recognized Rufus' markings anywhere. He was the worst of them as he thought being captain meant he had some sort of say over anyone of a lesser rank. He preferred to ignore me, since I technically outranked him.

Then again, almost everyone ignored me. I stopped being offended years ago and used it to my advantage now, watching from the sidelines.

One learned much while staying hidden in plain sight. It was how I trained with the sword at my hip. And how I knew about all the important goings-on in Centos. The constant darkness and my choice of black clothing didn't hurt either.

Making a scene now wasn't necessary, even though I planned to intervene and help the poor barmaid pressed against the wall as the others jeered.

"Your job is to serve me," Rufus said. Ugh, I could only imagine the rancid breath that wafted over her face.

"Fuck you," I whispered as I released my meager magic. It was nothing compared to my sister, but it was enough to send the table beside them into his hip.

The idiot stumbled and fell, knocking over a neighboring table and two full mugs on top. The men who lost their beer stood red-faced as the girl slipped away.

I smirked as I downed the remainder of my own drink, then hugged the dark outskirts of the massive brawl I'd started on my way out the door.

The cold air hit my face, forcing a more natural shudder than the mystical one that had been plaguing me. In response, I pulled my cloak further around my shoulders. My boots barely crunched in the snow. I was an expert at sneaking and avoided leaving evidence of my presence, sometimes with the help of a bit of magic. But I'd used enough to tire me already tonight and decided that leaving my footprints at a busy tavern wouldn't raise suspicion.

I wound a path through the streets, keeping to the thin tree line where I was most at home. The skeletal trunks and thin branches sagged, sickly versions of those in the Night Forest beyond the thirty-foot walls. Whoever decided the boundaries of the citadel long before I was born seemed to have arbitrarily cut off some portion of the great wood.

Above, the double moons shone bright, yet didn't manage to break through the dense darkness that lingered over the land no matter the time. Instead, the dual light diffused, adding an eerie yellow glow that followed me like two hungry eyes watching from on high.

Sometimes, in dreams, I flew over far away land and sea, the golden sun warming my face with a kiss of life and promises of a beautiful future. I had no idea how I could know what sunlight would feel like, let alone why my mind bothered to wish for it when it only made the reality of my world feel colder and lonelier upon waking.

Legends told of days long ago when the sun rose and sunk beyond the horizon in a cycle round the world. Those same stories also proclaimed ridiculous things like dragons, elves, and mechanical beasts used for travel.

I snorted, head down, as I followed the crooked path toward the palace. But when I'd climbed the hill and finally arrived, my heart dropped. The imposing mass of dark gray stones reached into the sky with towers curling and clawing at the moons. All of that remained as expected. The drawbridge, however, was raised, cutting off access across the murky water. *That* never happened.

I drew my sword, Stealth, which I'd stolen from the armory over a decade earlier. Then I assessed the situation, gaze moving around to take in every bit of my environment. I heard nothing amiss, nor did I smell or feel anything—not even the strange breeze. All good signs for certain. But there had to be a reason for closing the castle.

Has Father discovered my wanderings?

Heat warmed my chest and face as my breath sped up. *No.* He would take my freedom if for nothing else than the pleasure of my suffering. But I would never be like Leuruna. I'd rather die.

Leuruna. What if this had something to do with my sister? *Shit, I have to get in.* Pumping my legs, I ran around the perimeter of the intimidating structure. I'd used this route when I first started sneaking into the city and before I'd become bold enough—and adept enough—to leave through the front doors.

I found the gnarled tree with fat twisted limbs that sprouted long before the palace intruded on its habitat. A practiced leap took me to the lowest branch. I swung my legs up to the next and continued climbing like an animal. By the time I reached the branch that hung far enough over the moat, I was out of breath but smiled from the adrenaline rush of climbing so quickly.

Tucking some of my stray hair back below my hood, I spread my arms to my sides and scurried forward, balanced above the poisonous water churning and bubbling below. When I reached as far as I dared, I focused on the stone gargoyle across from me and aimed for the snout filled with sharpened teeth. Then, I sprang, grabbing hold and clambering up to the stone balcony above me, finally vaulting over the side of the balustrade and landing in a crouch.

The leaden glass doors were open, allowing the cold air access, but that didn't surprise me. Leuruna longed for fresh air and didn't care if she had to keep the fire in the hearth roaring to counter the temperature. The thick emerald curtains swayed inward with the direction of the breeze, and I crept to the thin part between them to cock an ear.

Other than the crackling of the fire, I made out nothing. No voices. No crying, which could have been either a good or bad sign. Reaching for the opening, I readied to find the princess in her catatonic state, retreated inside of herself—the only place she felt truly safe. It tore me apart when she did that. It felt like he'd won in those times, even though I also felt stronger. Rage brought me strength, and seeing her that way...well, the anger was difficult to control. But inevitably she came back. Thank the goddess, she always did.

With a deep breath, I pushed through and found her seated by the flames...smiling.

My shoulders eased as she rushed to embrace me. I nuzzled against her snow-colored hair that smelled of what I imagined sunshine to be like, so different from my own dark and dirty locks I always kept tied.

"You came the old way," she said, backing up a bit so I could look into her crystalline eyes, not quite blue and not quite green. It was the one trait we shared, which I found strange since father's were dark like oil, and he was our biological link.

"Rune, the drawbridge was up," I said, examining the room for anything amiss.

"Nyah," she grabbed my hand to regain my attention, "I'm okay. Father hasn't even visited today. He must be busy with something."

"You're saying the palace being closed off may be a good thing?" I challenged, amused by the thought.

She shrugged her delicate shoulders, and we shared a laugh. I loved this carefree version of my sister. Lately, I seemed to find her less and less often when I visited.

Shaking off the thought, I settled with her before the fire, where she leaned her head on my shoulder. We stared into the flames for a bit, enjoying the peace.

"What's bothering you?" she asked, startling me.

She was the one person I could never hide from, not even what was on the inside. I hadn't wanted to worry her, but I found myself reporting on the phantom breeze that plagued me.

In response, she hummed and sat up, pulling her knees to her chest. "It is a sign."

"For what?" I asked, wondering if she'd at last share some secrets of her own power with me. She never liked to talk about it, but I was forever curious. Normally, she would laugh and tell me I was so much better off not troubling myself with such things.

"Tell me a story like you used to." Her big eyes pleaded so I could neither ignore nor be angry with for changing the subject. This was Leuruna.

"Which one?" I asked, turning to face her. The flickering flame and shadows played across her face, making her look so pale, so fragile.

"The Shadow Hand." A playful smile appeared at her request. I should have known. It was her favorite.

"Long ago, when humans had access to all the magic of the gods, a child named Illio was born." I recited the tale from rote as I had so many times over the years. I'd read it while hiding in the back of the great library. I'd spent countless hours in the dusty, neglected shelves discovering treasures to share with my sister—and only friend.

"It was apparent from the start that Illio had a strong connection with magic in all forms, particularly that associated with the goddess Revka, as he could create grand illusions almost indistinguishable from reality." I paused, knowing Leuruna liked to pipe in at this point.

"Like my magic," she said, as expected.

"Like yours," I agreed. "But Illio didn't stop there. He also controlled the ocean waves and all the elements of the earth, creating storms of fire, rain, and earthquakes when he was angered, which caused everyone around him to walk on eggshells and cow to all his requests."

"So, he became self-important and spoiled," Rune said.

"Indeed. He grew to think his wants should be everyone's and his word became law. When someone dared to stand up to the young man, he used his mind magic to dreamwalk, making sure they would either never wake again or become subservient to him if they did."

"It's a shame someone like him became so powerful. Magic like that is dangerous," Rune muttered almost to herself as she turned back to stare into the hearth's flames.

"As Illio grew, so did his power, and he managed his greatest feat." I used my fingers to add a bit of flare to the story, knowing this was her favorite part.

"He made a Shadow Hand."

"That's right. He created a whole new version of himself that walked among the people, like he was made of flesh and blood, and reported back to Illio of any who whispered against him. It wasn't until an assassination attempt against Illio that it became clear what he had done, as his Shadow Hand intervened and slaughtered those that had come to kill his master."

I slashed through the air with an imaginary sword as Rune appeared horrified.

"It was then that the gods interceded, for Illio was on his way to becoming their equal, and they did not want someone with no empathy to wield such incredible power. And so, all three of them, Revka, Darvol, and Zariah, surrounded Illio and used crystals to separate his power into three stones, draining him and ending his reign of terror. Once a sobbing and defenseless Illio was all that remained, the gods each took one crystal, corresponding to their favored abilities, and gifted it to a different kingdom so that the humans there would only have access to that type of magic. Then, they put some of each into a fourth crystal and devised a plan to ensure that the fourth power crystal would be passed from hand to hand every few years so as not to allow such an imbalance of power to fall into a single human's hands ever again."

"Until the current king, anyway." Leuruna scowled.

"Yes," I agreed, settling back to rest on my elbows. "But at least he doesn't have them all."

"Do you think the gods would destroy someone again if they had all three?" Rune asked, eyes glittering and wide as she leaned over me.

I shrugged, thinking of the evil king. "We could only hope."

Rune's countenance changed as if I'd flipped a switch. She buried her face in her palms, letting her cloud of hair fall over her like a curtain. I scurried over to her, grabbing her hands and standing.

"It's okay," I said, waiting until she peered up at me. "One day, he will no longer be around to hurt you." If I could make that day come sooner, I would.

A small smile answered me, but it was short-lived as the color drained from her skin and her hold on my fingers tightened almost painfully before she released me to back up toward the upholstered chair near the hearth.

I didn't have to ask what happened. I'd seen it too many times to count.

He was coming.

Part of me wanted to wait beside the door and stab Stealth through his neck when he entered. But aside from being flayed by his bodyguards or burned at the stake for treachery, I had my doubts it would kill him. The man was as wily as a stone lizard and as slippery as the eels in the moat. He would probably just laugh as I was murdered instead.

"Hide," Leuruna hissed so low it was almost inaudible. But it was enough to break me from my reverie as I slipped back into the shadows behind the curtains, watching from the balcony as the knock sounded on her door.

"Come," she said solemnly, staring into the fire, now seated and clutching the arms of the chair.

I doubt they heard her through the thick wood, but it swung open, banging against the stone wall and making her flinch. Still, she didn't turn to look even as two pitiless guards entered and flanked the doorway. Our father stepped inside.

His dark eyes narrowed as he searched the corners of the room. The golden circlet on his slicked back hair, thick leather armor, and staff with the ornate gilded top and sacred inlaid crystal couldn't disguise the darkness that followed him. What Leuruna's mother ever saw in him, I could not fathom despite his physical prowess. I harbored no doubt that whoever my own mother was, she went unwillingly to his bed. I couldn't imagine it any other way. He might have been objectively handsome with a fit body and strong chin, but one look at his oily eyes and his true nature was obvious.

As I peered through the curtains, my breath hitched when his gaze stalled on the opening. But other than a too-long moment of hesitation, he continued around to face my sister.

"Stand before your king," one of the guards commanded, gesturing with an iron spear in his grip.

Leuruna did without so much as a glance toward the man. Her head lowered as Father stepped closer. She wouldn't meet his eyes. Was it cowardice? Or did she suspect he'd mesmerize her with his magic? I swallowed back the lump in my throat.

"There has been a proclamation," he said, voice echoing around the room. "In a month's time, the ritual of Imrati will commence."

Leuruna's face darted up as her mouth dropped open. But she lowered her gaze back to the floor in the space of a moment. I understood her shock. I felt it too. The ritual trials hadn't been allowed since her mother —Queen Tenara first fell ill. He forbade it.

I'd always assumed it had to do with his refusal to relinquish control of the stone. If another kingdom's representative were to win the trials, their ruler would take possession of the power crystal, as was the gods' original intention. The competition was supposed to take place every few years so that no one king or queen could upset the balance of such power by holding the key to all three forms of magic. But no one dared challenge

King Balram's hold. Not since he'd demonstrated what no one else had since the stone was created by our gods—more than one type of magic.

Have the gods themselves finally demand he relinquish it? My throat grew thick as he continued speaking.

"You are not becoming younger," the king said, pacing past her to peer into the fire. One arm braced against the mantle. "Nor am I."

What is he doing? I shifted slightly, causing the curtains to sway, but no one noticed.

"You will attend the ceremony with me," the king declared. He turned to face Leuruna and away from me as he planted his staff against the floor, making another loud bang. "And the winner will be your betrothed."

Leuruna's face shot upward to meet his gaze. The fear in her eyes had me clenching my fists. "Father, I've never left the castl—"

Father's hand flew faster than the words could leave her mouth, and he struck with no mercy. Rune crashed to the floor, sprawling before the fire, palms splayed against the thick gold carpet. He leaned over her, flames dancing on his twisted face.

"There is only one appropriate response," he lectured.

"Yes, Father," she said, thin shoulders slumped and arms shaking with the effort to hold herself up—or maybe from fear.

"Rise," he ordered, standing tall. The guards moved to help her, but he stayed them with a hand.

So, this is his game. I should've known better than to hope for divine intervention. If someone outside of Centos won, he'd remain in control of the crystal by default if they were betrothed to his daughter. A clever plan to look benevolent while continuing to cheat fate.

Still...the drawbridge, the wind, and the sudden shift in Father's concern about appearances told me something had happened to unsettle the complacency he'd enjoyed for so long. Perhaps, it signaled a way to dethrone him at last. I'd have to find out what that was.

Inside, Leuruna seized her chair and hoisted herself into it. Her bottom lip split and trembled as blood trickled down her chin and onto the thin fabric of her pastel gown. It was petal pink, like a child's dress. But that fit her perfectly. Despite his sudden concern for her age, he'd never allowed her to grow up.

"I am displeased with your lack of manners and understanding of the ways of the world. There are no excuses. You have tutors and access to the finest library in all the realms. I only keep you confined for your own safety, but one day you will no longer have that luxury." Father paced to the wall closest to my hiding space. I could no longer see him, but I could almost feel him leaning against it, arms crossed as he shook his head pityingly. "The winds of change are upon us, hastening the timeline. Your lessons will be doubled starting now."

"But—" she leaned forward, gripping the armrests again until her fingertips turned white.

"*All* of them," he said, then crossed to her. "Leave us," he commanded the guards without taking his eyes from her.

They marched from the room, pulling the door shut behind them. I tensed, hand on the hilt of my sword. I knew what was coming and so did Rune.

The king lowered his staff until the inlaid crystal, which had been clear like glass, lit up from inside with a lavender glow. Leuruna whimpered, then touched her forehead obediently against it. I turned away as the flash of light engulfed the room, making me wince. My muscles tensed, then released as I sunk to the ground with my own energy weakened. I could only imagine how it felt for her to have her power drained.

Slowly, the light dimmed until the darkness returned, somehow even more oppressive than usual. I peeked through the curtain again and found Leuruna slumped in the chair, chin to chest as Father raised the staff, the crystal in it now glowing a deep purple. He patted her head and lifted her face with his index finger and thumb.

"We have to make you appear as normal as possible if you are to travel from the castle. We don't want any accidents endangering your image. People mustn't be frightened of their future queen. Pull yourself together. I shall send in Serano soon for your behavior and magic lessons."

Releasing her so that her head drooped again, he marched from the room. I rushed inside, sliding onto my knees at my sister's feet. But she would not wake for at least an hour, and then, the lessons would begin.

Two

I left the way I came, leaping across and scrambling down the old tree to slip into the shadows. I refused to stay and watch her struggle to recover. I'd done so too many times, and the pain of being unable to intervene was too much if I wanted to retain my sanity. I hated that man, so much so that it was hard to believe the sheer force of the emotion didn't cause him to turn spontaneously to ash.

If only I had that kind of power.

Then again, if I did, he'd have treated me like my sister and never let me be.

I picked a path through the outskirts of the city toward the wall, wishing as always, I had the strength to leave. Light shone from stone cottages and wood cabins in the distance, the flickering specks from their windows mocking me with stories of families and love. Smoke puffed from their chimneys as they fought to stave off the constant cold of their surroundings, but inside they possessed something so special. Yet, they seemed hardly to be aware of the gift they'd been given.

The urge to run overtook me as it had so often in my life. I lived like a shadow, a wraith on the outside, never belonging. The craving for more had me looking anywhere and everywhere else. Forbidden or not, the lands beyond the citadel could not hold worse. I'd take my chances with the mythical creatures in the story books I always consumed, if I could just escape from the one monster I called Father.

Whenever I felt trapped like this, I tried to remind myself of my sister, who had it so much worse. Locked in her rooms in the palace, she remained, except for the rare occasion the king allowed her in the throne room or to a feast to prove to his subjects she was still alive.

I was lucky to be the ignored one. The one with little magic or pedigree, and therefore, not worth Father's attentions. I'd been gifted with the ability to avoid the palace at all times, which I took full advantage of unless visiting my sister. I could—and did—slip out, explore or come up to the top of the citadel and at least daydream about freedom.

A small voice inside argued with me when I thought about staying for Rune. It whispered encouragement to slip away, down the outer walls of our barriers, and into the forbidden lands beyond. To truly escape. But my conscience was stronger. My feelings about my sister might have been complicated, but she was my only friend, and I hers. I could not, would not, abandon her.

And yet...inside I hated the way she cowered before our father. I loathed her for her weakness. *Am I any better?* Not when I refused to jump in and intervene. Together, perhaps we could do it. But the one time I suggested it, she'd sunk to the furs before her fire and cried so hard I thought she might never stop.

Even now, the sick feeling in my stomach returned at the memory. I tried not to blame her. Truly I did. Our father had tortured her body, mind, and soul. He'd broken her long ago, surely on purpose, so she wouldn't fight back. For she was the only one who could have challenged his power.

If only I had the same.

As usual, I made it quickly to the top of the citadel to perch among the stone guardians, so high above the watchtower that there was little chance they'd notice me creeping about.

Staring at the Night Forest, I strained to make out the peaks in the distance, where moonlight reflected off the snowy tips like a beacon. My imagination had taken me beyond their border countless times. The desire to explore was the secret that drove me. Deep into the night as teenagers, we used to whisper and plan our escape to distant worlds of elves and dragons. I'd never let that dream go, even though Rune refused to discuss it anymore.

It couldn't happen, of course. Not if I wanted to protect my sister. The shame of not defending her, of leaving her again, stabbed me through the heart as sure as a blade. But if I truly did run, she would be left with no one, save the oppressive evil of our father.

Yet, I yearned to discover what lay beyond our sight borders. And I would pretend the possibility existed, no matter how unlikely.

I knew, of course, as all Centos did, about the other two human lands, but it had been so many years since we'd had any interaction, and even then, only with Tromodia, the seafarers. As far as the sky dwellers of Astridon, they felt almost as mythological as the elves that were said to inhabit the in-between lands. Still, they remained in our history books. At least the ones neglected in the rear of the royal library, where I'd received my education with my nose in a tome. And in small shards of pottery hidden in the backrooms of the old museum, no one seemed to visit but me.

It had started with a desire to find a spell for Rune to help her escape her situation. I'd brought her several that might use her powerful illusions, but each one had been turned down. Waking Nightmare to frighten him, she'd argued would only fuel his anger. Silent Sentry, she said could do no more than intimidate, and Father was immune. I'd given up after suggesting the one in her favorite story, The Shadow Hand, at which she'd recoiled and begun to cry. I assured her she could never be as evil as Illio in the story, but privately decided never to bring it up again.

The outcome, however, had been that I enjoyed learning about the past and reading stories in which heroes ultimately won, even if my sister never would try. I'd spent almost as much time exploring the library and museum as I had trained with my sword.

Yet now, here I was, with nothing but a wish to bring down my father and no means to enact such a feat.

Glancing up toward the double moons, I couldn't help but squint, hoping for a glimpse of something, anything that might hint at the presence of one of the Astridonian flying beasts or chariots from the stories. But whether fiction or the result of the dome of gloom, a fortress of fog courtesy of the king's magic, I found nothing but stars and lazy clouds drifting away toward the mountains.

Nyah. My sister's strained voice tore through my head, and I grasped the sides of it in pain.

"Rune?" I whispered as loud as I dared. The watchtower guards had wards set up to detect any unusual sounds or movement. Usually easily avoidable for me.

Take it. Go. He must not have it.

The scream that ripped from my throat couldn't be avoided, but the second the words stopped reverberating in my skull, I was up and moving.

Take what? I wondered as I ran the length of the turret and leaped. The drop in my stomach as I flew across to the lower wall might as well have been from her message. The lights of the tower flared to life, focusing on my vacated post. But I was already scurrying down the familiar hand and footholds of the far wall.

When the brightness nipped at my heels, I dove for the thin trees of the forest, pulse thumping in my ears as I crouched among the brambles and a semi-sturdy trunk. Good thing I was slight, or some part of me would surely show.

Leuruna had never contacted me that way before, yet there was no doubt in my mind that it was her, and it worried me more than her words. *What has he done now?* I let the anger consume the fear as I glared toward the castle, rising past the tree line. The moment the light moved away toward the outside border, I ran, determined to do whatever was needed to protect her.

It took far too long to get back to her, with the echoing emptiness in my mind left behind by her assault. I'd have traded comfort for the pain, if it meant knowing she was still alive and well. Surely the king would never cause her permanent harm, right? She was his heir, his hold to the strong magic he shared with her mother.

Stories of the queen's slow deterioration and disappearance flooded my thoughts as I rushed up the tree across from Rune's room. The accounts said she'd died of homesickness and lovesickness. She'd apparently loved another from her seafaring home but was betrothed to our father for political reasons. Even so, she'd had her daughter, and though I didn't know much about mothers, it seemed impossible that she wouldn't have struggled through whatever she felt to be there for Rune.

I silently stopped to catch my breath as I landed on the balcony. Gripping the stitch in my side, I leaned forward to find the glass doors closed. My heart beat so loud I was sure I'd be found, but I had to see inside. I focused my magic on the curtains behind the door and, with a small shove, I moved them to the side enough to peek through.

Rune sat in her chair by the fire, hands gripping the arms as she stared into nothingness, unblinking. I'd seen her withdraw before when the pressure and pain from our father was too much. But something felt different this time. I searched for an answer as I observed her.

The doors opened behind her and my father's advisor and magic instructor, Serano, entered, his black cloak swishing around his ankles. There was something about the wizard that made my stomach turn whenever I was in his presence. With a disgusted face, he wrenched her head toward him and shook her.

My hand clenched over Stealth's hilt, but he released her and paced, coming so close to the glass that I held my breath and dipped out of sight for a count of five. When I peered in again, he was lifting her hand by the wrist and examining it. He didn't seem to notice what I had, that her other hand moved, finger lifting slightly. Suddenly, I heard what Serano was saying.

"...withholding your power. He will find it, you know, even if he has to break you open to get to it."

Serano paused, watching her face intently for a reaction. When he received none, he dropped her wrist and sneered.

"You think you can protest the betrothal this way?" He snorted. "Your father will marry you off even if all that's left is a corpse, so I suggest you make this easy. You have only one recourse if you wish to be left alone. Release the power to me instead, or I will force you. You know I am strong enough."

He lunged before I could work out his meaning, long fingers pressing into the sides of her face and temple. I stood to withdraw my sword when her eyes snapped to me.

"Run." The word was spoken out loud, but with it came a blast of bright purple, the color of the poison berries that grew on the vines along the wall of the citadel. The blast shattered the glass between us and hit me full force with a sensation like a hundred stinging insects.

Both Serano and I froze in shock for a few precious seconds. But as my sister's eyes blinked closed, and she slumped in the chair, determination to protect whatever magic was so important to keep from the king and his crony forced me into motion. Serano bared his teeth, and I leaped onto the railing, then across to the tree. Barely touching the bark, I scrambled down, dropping from a far higher spot than I would normally have dared.

"Stop!" he shrieked from above, and I dodged to the left out of instinct, avoiding a blast of power that shot dirt and rocks in all directions.

I wove a chaotic path to the trees, pumping my legs even faster than I did on my sprint to the castle. But there was no chance he'd try to climb down, and the drawbridge would take a good five minutes to lower enough for anyone to leave. Whatever had the king so paranoid cost him dearly.

The sound of hoofbeats thundering across the bridge proved me wrong. I didn't count on a magical assist. I swore through heavy breath as I darted between swooning trees to reach the wall. The idea of pausing to recover when I set hands on the rough stone was dismissed by a volley of arrows. Several landed far too close for comfort as I reached for the well-worn divots I knew by heart.

I thought I was going to make it to the top when three uniformed watchmen peered over the edge, pointing at me.

"I surrender!" I shouted. "Just let me get up there the rest of the way so you can take me down an actual ladder."

One of the three aimed a bow and arrow at me but didn't move to fire. The other two motioned for me to finish climbing and helped hoist me over the parapet.

"Thanks," I said, bent double as I collected myself.

When I rose, Stealth was in my hand, ready.

"Don't kill her. The king wants her alive." The man beside the one with the bow stopped him with a touch.

"Well, the bastard isn't getting me." I adjusted my stance as the horses below came to a stop at the bottom of the wall with a thundering of hooves. "So, move aside unless you want to fight me. I might look small, but I wouldn't recommend it."

I took in the men before me. The one in the center was the shortest and a bit stocky. His weight wasn't centered, and he was either forgetting or not bothering with a defensive stance. He would be easy to take down. The one with the bow and arrow looked as young as me, tall and willowy with long dark hair. His features read confusion as he glanced between the others and me, lowering his weapon to his side. The last of the three would be the hardest. He was prepared for me, gripping the handle of the short sword at his side as he widened his stance, sinking his weight. He stood behind the others slightly, putting them at risk to give himself enough time to assess my style. I'd seen it before. It seemed Rufus had trained him.

I remained still. I would not make the first move. These men did nothing but their jobs.

"Come on then, let's get you to the palace," the middle one said, relaxing a bit. He reached for me.

I accepted his hand with my free one and yanked him off balance to the ground, using the momentum to leap at the biggest threat. By the time the man in the rear reacted, I had the tip of my blade at his throat and my hand over his on his hilt.

"Let me repeat that since you are obviously hard of hearing," I said, glaring at him while the young bowman rushed to aid his fallen friend. "Don't make me hurt you. I'm leaving and you're staying quiet."

Below us the sounds of men dismounting slowed and stilled. The creak of the oaken doors to the ladders told me I had little time left. I refused to take my eyes off the threat as I backed away toward the outer wall. The minute I was far enough, the man I'd threatened drew his weapon and charged. I'd hoped he wouldn't but knew he likely would. I turned and ran, pushing off from the ground as I focused my attention on my destination. I needed to make it to the top of the balustrade so that I could climb down the other side.

Behind me, the man lunged. I felt him brush the heel of my worn leather boot, knocking my aim astray. But even as the sound of soldiers climbing the ladders grew closer, and the unforgiving stone floor raced toward me, something inside my chest ignited. As though my heart had grown wings, a fluttering took hold of me and spread throughout my body as a buoyant gust of air had me rise instead of fall.

I kicked back at the man scrabbling for my ankles and heard a satisfying crunch as I floated higher and farther toward the edge of the citadel wall. My heart seemed to soar into my throat as I glided past my goal, stretching, desperate to find purchase, but barely able to scrape the rough surface with my fingertips.

Stealth clattered to the stone floor as I passed beyond the border of Centos and began a descent down the opposite side of the wall.

"Shoot her!" the fallen man barked at the boy with the bow, but I already knew the bigger danger was the speed I gained as I plummeted toward the ground of the Night Forest.

When I hit, I aimed for my shoulder and rolled across the hard dirt, coming to a stop on my back and breathing hard.

I didn't have time to recover, as the arrow peeked over the edge high above me and the boy took aim. I scrambled to my feet and ran for the much thicker tree line even before I was completely upright. The twang of an arrow planting in the ground behind me let me know the boy's aim was off, whether due to his nerves or lack of training I wasn't sure. Either way I was grateful as I ducked beneath foliage I'd never seen up close before.

I watched, clutching my knees as my chest burned with my efforts. If they came, I'd do better to hide than run. The guard never forayed into the forbidden lands before, but was that born of need or fear? *Would the king's command force it?*

The second he heard Rune had transferred whatever the hells this was to me, I'd be his sole focus, so it was in my best interest to get as far from Centos as soon as possible. My best hope was Serano's fear of disappointing my father. If he delayed telling him and hunted me himself, I'd be able to get more distance between us. I trusted Rune. Whatever Serano imagined of his great power, he was nothing compared to my sister.

But what has she done exactly? I stared at my hands as though they might give up some sort of hidden secret. My body trembled from the rush of adrenaline coupled with the cold air as my breath fogged before me. Clutching my cloak tighter, I huddled against a tree that was far larger in person than it had appeared from high up on the wall. If only I had some idea how to wield whatever she'd given me.

Soon the arrows stopped, and the night fell silent. Suddenly, I was far more aware of my circumstances and surroundings than I had been minutes earlier. The lack of sound unnerved me worse than any scream could, as I peered around and through the strange forest. Here, it wasn't simply the one I rested against, but almost all the trunks were as thick as a building, knotted roots curving up from the moss-covered soil. Leaves larger than my head rustled, as once more, the familiar cold breeze rose, forcing the hair on my neck and arms to stand at attention.

It stopped as quick as it began. I swallowed, reaching for a sword that wasn't there. And the reality of my situation fell heavy upon my shoulders. I had nothing but the clothes on my back and the knowledge that my sister had hidden something within me, which sooner or later our father would stop at nothing to gain back.

Three

"I'm a wanted criminal." The reality of what I'd done hit harder than my landing on the outside of the citadel. Even if I hoped to help my sister, I'd never be able to set foot on castle ground again —never re-enter Centos. Although I'd dreamed of the freedom of the lands beyond the citadel, now that I was here in the midst of the unfamiliar forest only the hollow loss of it burned deep in my chest. A tremor of uncertainty had me to clenching my fists in an effort to get ahold of myself.

Refocusing, I took several deep breaths. I'd spent the entirety of my life sticking to the shadows and avoiding all but my sister. I was capable of handling this situation—better suited to it than anyone else in truth, having been self-taught in defense and survival, skills that Father would never have voluntarily taught his daughters.

First order of business was to find a water source near which to make camp. So, I set off in the opposite direction of home and those that would hunt me, carefully eyeing the moisture of the soil. The recollection of the path I'd flown over the parapet, instead of crashing, played on a loop in my mind. Whatever magic Rune had given me had to be accessible then. If only I'd had any magical training, I might have been able to use it to overthrow my father.

The laugh that bubbled from my chest felt unreasonably loud in comparison with my silent surroundings. *Overthrow the king? Am I mad?* I couldn't even try to defend my sister when he hurt her. If she, who had this all her life and had been trained to wield it couldn't overthrow him, what chance did I have?

Hours passed as I hiked on uneven ground and twisted roots, alone with my thoughts. The same heavy fog of darkness I'd spent my life with pressed down on me through the canopy of leaves, somehow even more oppressive. Strange, I mused, that loneliness should bother me more out here than it did all my life as I shied away from others, or more accurately, they'd avoided me. Only Rune had been there to share my thoughts as we'd comforted each other.

And I let her down.

I wiped at the corner of my eye with the back of a fist as the first sounds of rushing water met my ears. Faint though it was, I perked up and adjusted course toward the promise it held. But as I neared a clearing, voices began to emerge, just detectable against the backdrop of a small waterfall.

Once again, my hand fell to an empty sheath, making me curse under my breath. I darted from tree to tree until I skulked in the shadow of a bent branch, where I could make out the scene without being noticed.

A group of men in strange clothing, much lighter in color, sparser, and tighter fitting than the normal villagers wore in Centos, gathered at the edge of a pool of water where the falls spilled over a small rocky cliff about ten feet above. From my vantage point, it was difficult to see into the pool itself as it was several feet down a sloped embankment. Only the far side was visible, but the water sloshing toward the muddy roots made me think there were others bathing inside.

That meant at least a half a dozen of them, varying sizes and all with plenty of dark, bronzed skin on display. I scanned for weapons and found most of them were armed with at least a dagger, if not a sword—and that was what was visible. Then, I noticed the pile of clothing and goods to the side of the pool, about half-way between me and the nearest of the men. In it, I caught the glint of at least one blade. My pulse sped up as I calculated the odds of being able to snag it and return to the tree line before they noticed.

Waiting was a gamble. It was possible they'd make camp and sleep, leaving only one or two awake to guard. On the other hand, they might finish up and take the goods away to somewhere I'd never get ahold of them.

"I'm going to use mine to buy a wife," one of the men said, catching my attention.

A tall lanky man with a long nose and bangs that fell in his eyes took a swig from a shiny tankard after speaking. He swayed a little on his feet and stumbled when his shorter, stouter companion shoved his arm.

"Like money would be enough for a good-looking one to go for a fisherman. You smell of grouper. Unless you were Darvol himself, you'd have better luck catching a mermaid."

Darvol. I rolled the name through my mental archives and recalled a studded shield in the museum. It depicted a three-headed god with many more tentacles rising from the sea and holding out a hand with an aquamarine embedded in his palm. These men were Tromodians then.

"Well fancy him or not, she won't be able to help it if her father says yes," a third man, whose back was to me, added. I crept forward a step, straining to hear him over the other's laughter. "If Idox here wants to dream about getting his cock inside some spoiled bitch after the mission, let 'im."

My stomach bottomed out. I fought against the urge to snatch the blade and drive it through the man's heart from behind. A fourth man climbed from the pool, stark naked and dripping wet. I'd seen male bodies before, especially the king's guards who could have cared less who saw them whether they were taking a piss or fucking a scullery maid. But the way this man's wet hair clung to his scarred chest made me recoil, despite the lean, wiry muscle that spoke of physical work.

He shook himself like an animal and snatched up a pair of the same kind of light brown pants the others wore. It seemed to stretch to fit him as he tugged it on, finally covering his limp cock.

The others had stopped joking the moment he appeared, and when he brushed back his long hair, a thick beard and pockmarked face glared out at the others.

"Talking a big game, are ya?" he asked, a strange accent coiling his words. "We'll see which of ya makes it past tomorrow."

The man stalked through the center of the group, scattering the others back several yards as though he'd bodily shoved them. He looked each one of them up and down, past their flowy shirts that opened in a deep V and screwed up his face in derision.

"It'll be a challenge that's for sure. Let's get back to the campfire then," the burly man, who'd shoved his friend and said foul things about buying a bride, piped up. "We'll need a good bit of rations if we're hiking the rest of this gods' forsaken forest tomorrow. Besides, it'll be about time for the craves to come out hunting."

"Maybe killing a cravenbeast would be good practice for people," Idox said, falling into step with his companion as they circled toward the other side of the pool.

My stomach rumbled with hunger at the mention of rations, and my cold limbs cried out for the warmth of my own campfire. But as far as cravenbeasts, I'd never heard of them.

How are these men able to bathe, and not wrap themselves in furs, and avoid freezing to death? And why are they out here in the Night Forest speaking of earning money?

The tall one, Idox, scooped up some of the items from the pile I'd been eyeing, and I instinctively curled against the trunk of the tree, pulling my dark cloak tighter.

The pockmarked man grabbed hold of a shirt from the same and then tucked the blade I'd been wanting into his belt before taking a long drink from a canteen. What was left was a couple pieces of clothing and a longsword, curved and wicked looking lying on the ground abandoned. The hilt was polished obsidian, carved with runes etched into it. I couldn't read them from where I spied.

It was huge. Even if I grabbed it, I'd have hells of a time wielding it. The tall one was possibly the only one among the bunch I could even imagine using such an enormous and daunting weapon.

Then, another man climbed from the pool, dripping wet and nude. My mouth dropped open at the sight of him, and I had no doubt that he was the owner of the weapon I'd been looking at.

Enormous and built like a sculpted god, his copper skin gleamed even in the diffuse moonlight. His hair was long, and his face was just as beautiful as the rest of him, down to the scruff on his cheeks, chin, and neck. His dark eyes searched like a hawk, circling prey, sharp and deep, and everyone within a few feet of him backed away as he strode toward the remaining belongings in the pile.

Gods help me, but something low in my belly clenched at the sight of his rear end when he bent to retrieve his pants. I'd never seen a specimen like him working in the palace. Though Rufus might challenge him in size, he couldn't hope to match him in perfection.

"No one's getting paid until we finish the mission," he announced, voice like rich velvet. He didn't yell, nor even speak very loudly, but it carried across the clearing, and I had no doubt every man heard him and was ready to obey.

Hells I was ready to obey, and I didn't even know what the mission was. I shifted against the bark of the tree and his gaze whipped toward me. Freezing like a rabbit in the crosshair's sights, I held my breath. There was no way he should be able to see me from this vantage point.

The other men began trekking into the woods on the opposite side of the clearing, but this man's eyes lingered, unblinking as he sheathed his enormous sword over his broad shoulders. Without another word, he turned and headed off in the same direction as his men.

I waited until he'd disappeared into the opposite tree line. Then, I clung to the shadowy outskirts and thick foliage. When I reached the other side, I crouched to examine the tracks they'd left and nearly missed the glint of silver, half buried in leaves. Someone had dropped a trap, and as the sinister breeze lifted the hair on the back of my neck, I suspected it was meant for something other than edible prey.

He'd left it for me.

Scanning the now quiet woods ahead, I narrowed my eyes and tilted my head slowly. Sure enough, a tripwire as thin as a spiderweb slanted across two trunks. He'd been fast and stealthy in his trappings, but I could be better.

The size of the trees made it an easy climb, and the thick branches left little concern I'd fall as I leaped from one to the next then scurried across the side of the path the men had clearly taken. Before long, voices rose along with the crackle and scent of an enormous fire. And something else...something that made my mouth water and stomach rumble once again, letting me know my instincts to follow them had been right and not a waste of an extra hour's time.

The light from the flames made shadows dance in the treetops as I approached from above. When I was close enough to see the entire campsite, I lay on my stomach and surveyed the situation.

The trees here thinned, becoming more varied in size and species. Tents made of animal hides and various crates of supplies ringed the campsite. In the center, the fire crackled, wider than if the leader had laid on the ground from foot to head. It was encircled in stones, and above it, a large animal roasted on a spit that the one named Idox turned with a long handle to the side. This was more than just a roaming band of knaves. There seemed to be at least some planning and money behind this group's purpose.

Scanning the camp, I counted eight men in total, those visible outside of tents. The pockmarked man sat to the side, furthest away from the others, brooding as he sipped from a tankard, his other hand resting on the hilt of his weapon. The large, impressive man stood on the other side, arms crossed, watchful. His gaze skimmed across the space, over his men, and past into the woods.

Is he looking for me?

"I'd say this Wylar's as ready as she's going to get," Idox announced.

The others crowded around and waited as he and the burly, smaller one pulled it off the fire and used a short sword to slice into it and hand out chunks of meat. I couldn't help but lick my lips. I honestly couldn't remember the last time I ate, other than the ale I'd had at the tavern which felt like days ago. I'd have to forage once I was sure these men were asleep. I didn't know if they were dangerous, but being as I had no weapons and no clue who they were or their business here, I wasn't about to risk letting them know about my presence.

Staying still I watched as they feasted, talking and laughing at boorish jokes.

"Eh, Rivven!" One shouted after a bit, and the man I'd been hoping to learn the name of dropped his arms to his sides and approached. "Why don't you have a drink with us?"

Rivven remained stone-faced. "I'd rather someone keep their wits about them, thank you."

"There's no one out here, sir," Idox said, brushing the bangs from his face. "If you had a drink with the men, and relaxed, maybe we could earn a bit of camaraderie."

"I'm not paying you to be drinking buddies," Rivven answered. "And I've learned to be prepared for anything. I'll take first watch. You get some sleep. Tomorrow, we move."

As they slowly dispersed to their tents, drunk and full, I started planning to pilfer supplies, including food and weapons I could use to survive while I figured out my next move. The pockmarked man was smoking now, blowing rings out from a glass pipe I'd seen some of the wealthier people use in the keep. He and Rivven were the only ones left awake, and I hoped one would retire soon.

"Get some sleep, Skipper." Rivven nudged the man in the side with a toe of his leather boot.

"I do what I want with my time," Skipper snarled back. "Why not let me take the first watch?"

"Because I trust you least of this lot," Rivven answered, and my ears perked up.

"Then why'd you hire me?" Skipper's lips stretched into a thin smile, one that felt more like a challenge than anything.

"Because of your reputation. You've never failed, and your ship and your name are feared by all near the sea. But your methods? Those I don't agree with."

"Then again, I ask you, oh righteous one," Skipper stood and blew a smoke ring out that floated to Rivven's face, "If you're so disgusted by my methods, why did you hire me? Seems a bit hypocritical."

The only sign that Rivven had heard him was the bob of his throat as he stared the man down. "That's why I didn't hire your captain, and only took his first mate. As long as you stick to my rules and only kill those who attack you, we have no problem."

Skipper nodded and settled as he pulled at his pipe.

"But," Rivven said, unmoving, "if you do one thing outside of those parameters, I will kill you. Now go to bed so I know you are rested and at your best for tomorrow."

"You aren't my captain," Skipper growled.

"No, but I am your boss on this mission." Rivven held his gaze until

Skipper's upper lip lifted in a derisive snarl. But the man shouldered past the larger one and disappeared into a tent with his pipe.

I watched as Rivven walked toward the fire, cut a chunk of meat from the half-ravaged carcass and set it on a tin plate a few feet away. He straightened, searched the surrounding trees, then went back to the carcass of a long dead tree and sat, folding his arms once again.

Is that meant to lure me out?

I wasn't an animal, but perhaps that's what he thought was trailing him and his men. Now that his attention was focused on the lure he'd set and the others were out of the picture, I should be able to easily circle around and drop down behind him. He was one man. How hard could it be to take him out? Yet it felt like such a shame to spill the blood of this beautiful and intriguing man. It was refreshing to find someone who seemed to have some morals, no matter how thin.

This would be easier if I had a blade.

As the plan formed in my mind, I crept across the treetops to the other side of the encampment and shimmied down, dropping silently into a crouch behind one of the tents where the men had retired close to an hour earlier. But before I could sneak inside, rustling caught my attention. I stilled, watching as Rivven stood and walked off into the woods, sword drawn.

He must have heard something—probably an animal for real—and gone to investigate. This was a fortuitous turn. I wouldn't have to approach the sleeping men at all, or kill the big one.

With a grin, I skirted the tent, searched the forest, and then darted out to grab the meat he'd left for me. I nearly groaned at the smell of it this close. I should wait though and take advantage of the moment.

With nothing but the crackling of the enormous fire, I scanned the ground until I found a set of daggers discarded beside a canteen and a pair of boots. *Perfect.*

I snuck over to the pile and helped myself to the remains of the canteen before tucking the daggers into my belt. This time, when the hairs on the back of my neck stood on end, I didn't feel the accompanying breeze. Whipping around, food forgotten and the hilts of my new weapons in each hand I faced Skipper, who stood with a creepy smile on his bearded face.

"What have we here? I was hoping to catch a certain man unawares, but you be an even better surprise." He tilted his head, drinking me in from head to toe and licking his chapped lips. "I think the gods have gifted us a little entertainment before our battle." And before I could react, he whistled so loudly, I cringed as several birds flew from the treetops. By the time I recovered my wits, the sounds of tents opening and men awakening surrounded me.

A loud crunching sound behind me had me whipping around and stepping with my back to the fire as three new men closed in. Okay, at least it wasn't all five of the others. I sank my weight ready to fight as they spread out around me. The fear was a distant thing, speeding my pulse and forcing a surge of adrenaline through me. Instead of causing panic, it cleared my mind like the sky after a storm. There was nothing but this moment and my attackers, and I was hyperaware of their every movement and twitch of their bodies.

"Stay back or I will kill you," I warned.

A couple of the men glanced at each other unsure, but when Skipper laughed, the others joined in and pulled their swords.

"Drop the toothpicks, doll," Skipper instructed. "If you relax, you might enjoy the rest of the night. But if you accidentally draw blood, we'll be sure you don't."

"I'm no doll," I said, my new daggers at the ready. "Fuck you."

"But she'll be fun to play with anyway, eager little cunt," one of the others said, and they all laughed.

I slashed out in an arc, forcing them to back up several steps as I lunged forward. The laughter ceased and they glared, raising their weapons before them. *Right. Four to one.* I could do this. I just wished I had Stealth, which felt more like an extension of my own arm than these daggers I wasn't used to. Flipping one, I caught it by the tip as I staved off one man's sword with a well-placed slash of the other.

"She's feisty," the man said, pulling back.

"I like it when they fight back," Skipper shouted. "Come on, doll. Let's get on with it. I want every minute I can wring out of you."

I was happy to oblige as I let the upside-down dagger fly, embedding itself in the shoulder of the center man. I feinted right, then dipped left, sliding beneath the sword arm of one of the three helpers and cutting a gash in Skipper's leg as I skidded past on my knees. By the time he turned, crimson soaking his torn pants, I was on my feet and backing toward the tree line.

"Get back here you little cunt." Skipper lunged, waving the others into action. I ducked as one slashed at me, kicking out and tripping him to the ground. But now, another man had come out of his tent to join the fray. He knocked the remaining blade from my hand with the hilt of his broadsword, and someone tackled my ankles at the same time, sending me down hard. I coughed at the dirt that flew in my face as I was dragged backward toward my attacker.

When he wrestled me onto my back, straddling me, I was pinned down and facing Skipper's pockmarked face. I punched at him, but my wrists were caught by two other men who fought my arms back above my head and to the dirt. I was left breathing hard, glaring into the dancing flames that reflected off evil dark eyes. Struggling got me nowhere, so I spit in his face.

The answering smack came fast and hard, sending bursts of light through my vision, and stopping my efforts to escape while the pain bloomed along my cheek. A second punch stole my breath, and I fought to stay conscious as hands tore at my clothes.

"Give me that dagger," Skipper ordered, and the tip of the blade I'd wielded moments before grazed my stomach as he sliced apart my tunic.

Icy air and calloused hands assaulted my skin. Too many hands to belong to only one or two men. I swore loudly, thrashing against the onslaught, but still unable to do more than lift my head. Then, the blade slipped beneath my waistband and my heart thundered as the rest of my clothing fell away. The reality of the situation crashed over me, and panic seized me.

I reached for the magic that had come to my rescue at the parapet, but nothing answered as someone pinched me hard and laughed.

"She drew blood," Skipper said somewhere above me as he backed off and others pulled my legs apart. "I say we repay the favor."

If Rune's magic wouldn't help, I'd have to use my own.

With a burst of energy, I sent the men holding me down flying off in every direction, leaving me alone on the ground, the epicenter of an explosion that had drained whatever magic of my own I possessed. But I was free, naked and beaten, but free, so I scrambled to my feet, teetering from a wave of dizziness as the surrounding men recovered as well.

My gaze fell on a discarded short sword at the same time as the man who'd knocked the dagger from my hand. We both dove for it, and though I punched, bit, and kicked, between the five of them, they had me restrained—albeit more upright this time—in moments. My hands were held behind my back, my ankles held together. I wriggled, suspended in the air as Skipper gazed down from above once again.

"Bend her over the log and hold her down. We'll take turns until we fuck the fight out of her."

He reached into his pants as I screamed, dragged over to the dead tree Rivven had sat on not an hour before. Tears streaked down my face, the only heat in the freezing air around me and I glared at Skipper, promising his bloody death before they could turn me over the trunk.

As I pictured all the ways I was going to murder him, a large, curved sword swung silently from behind, lopping off his ugly head which flew toward the feet of those holding me and rolled to a stop, leering up at me.

The men dropped me, and I scooted away from the head as they ran at Rivven, who stood looming over Skipper's fallen body like a glowing god. Four armed men rushed him, and he easily evaded each one, parrying and moving with such grace and precision that it was like he barely moved at all, until every one of them lay dead at his feet.

Removing his blade from the last one's chest, he lowered the bloody sword and strode to where I crouched, naked and dirty on the ground, gaping up at him. He paused, then reached out a hand.

I stared at it, then curled in on myself further until he dropped it and crouched beside me. He was so close I could see the faint scar skimming his right eyebrow. His dark eyes glowed slightly, as though flecks of fire blazed inside them. I blinked. It had to be a reflection. I had been hit pretty hard.

"I'm sorry it took me so long to get back to you," he said in that deep, luscious voice. "I'm sorry they hurt you as well. I'd offer to kill them again, but that's impossible."

Part of me, deep down, wanted to laugh hysterically, but that was likely the panic and adrenaline, that were also probably responsible for my body's trembling. Instead, I just stared at him and waited.

He cocked his head. "My name is Rivven."

I swallowed the dryness in my throat. "Nyah."

The corner of his mouth quirked up. "You've been trailing us."

I nodded.

"That's a problem." He stood again but didn't raise his sword. *Is he not planning to kill me? Or does he think it's not necessary to overpower me?* I wanted to trust this man that saved me, but trust wasn't something that came easily to me. "You're shivering," he pointed out, "Let's get you some clothing before I wake my remaining men."

Keeping an eye on me at all times, he rummaged around in some crates and tossed me the same kind of form-fitting pants they all wore. I tugged it on quickly, wanting to cover my body from his prying eyes. The pants were as soft as they looked, some sort of animal skin, and felt like they melted against my bruised body. They were long, so I rolled up the bottoms quite a bit.

"Thank you," I managed.

"You're welcome. I don't tolerate that sort of behavior from my men." He glared at the remains of the five assailants.

"But they were your men. And you killed them." The idea of it still mystified me.

He shrugged. "Less money I have to pay out. That, and I didn't like them much."

He wiped the sword on the shirt of one of the fallen men and sheathed it. Then, he pulled the shirt from his own back, revealing oh so much more muscle and delicious copper skin before tossing it to me.

I pulled the shirt over my body, then wrapped it around myself, tying it at the waist like a jacket. He was so huge compared to me that it covered everything important yet slid off my shoulder to my upper arm.

"Thanks for the shirt," I said, turning from him, "I'll be going now."

Rivven froze in the middle of checking over one of the bodies and lifted an eyebrow at me. "No. You won't."

And there it was, just when I was on the verge of trusting.

"Threatening me is hazardous." I gestured around vaguely. "These guys wouldn't take no for an answer. And now you're doing the same thing. I don't want to have to hurt you after all you've done for me."

He smiled, showing off practically perfect white teeth. "I assure you, there's no danger of that. But allow me to explain. I see from your former clothing you are from Centos." He held the remnants up to demonstrate.

"And you are from Tromodia." I nodded.

"Very astute for someone who I doubt has ever been farther than the falls. In fact, I am surprised you ventured out this far. Which leads me to suspect you are a spy as no known person has either voluntarily left or escaped from the walls of the Night Kingdom other than the few the king sends to do his dirty work. And I cannot allow you to report back to him because that would cause a potential problem for me."

"A spy? You think I'm a spy?" I snorted in disbelief. Nothing could be farther from the truth.

Rivven considered me. "Precisely what a spy would say." He looked up at the moons and frowned. "We need to clean up. The spilled blood will attract the cravenbeasts which stalk at night. We'll still be safe by the fire though if we dispose of the bodies."

"You won't distract me with nonsense." The words slipped out on instinct. "It's always night and I've never heard of such a beast." I crossed my arms over my chest and planted my feet.

The hearty laughter that shook his massive chest sent flames up the back of my neck. "Night and day still exist outside the confines of the wicked king's magic, little spy." He pulled back the flap of a tent, summoning the remaining two men, Idox and the burly one, who came scurrying out.

"What the fuck happened?" Idox asked, glancing around at the bodies and then at me. "Did she do that?"

"I have no doubt she could have if she'd had the right weapon. Five armed men—and she seemed to have taken a chunk out of several of them." Rivven's eyes crinkled at the edges, as though the thought amused him.

I appreciated the compliment, but I still wasn't sure what he planned to do with me. At least I was fairly certain he wouldn't rape or murder me, which was a positive.

"So...who killed them then?" the burly one asked.

"I did," Rivven said without hesitation.

"You killed your own men?" Idox's voice cracked as he said it, then he stepped away from Rivven.

"You've nothing to fear unless you try to attack her," Rivven said. "Now get this mess cleared. Throw them as far from camp as possible so the craves don't disturb us."

The men set to clearing the various bodies and pieces thereof from the campsite.

"Come on then." Rivven stalked toward me, covering the distance in three massive strides, as the others carried the first of their dead colleagues out of sight.

I glared up at him, trying not to be mesmerized by the sparks in his eyes. "Where?"

"The fire."

"No. I'm not going anywhere unless it's of my own free will."

Heaving a sigh, he scooped me up and tossed me over his shoulder, clamping down on the backs of my thighs so I couldn't escape. I beat on his back with my fists, shrieking my outrage, but he seemed not to notice as he marched me over toward the fire.

"Put me down!" I demanded.

He dropped me onto the ground at the base of a tree. The trunks here varied more than those closer to Centos. The one I landed beside was far thinner than the massive ones I'd passed so far. Still, it was sturdier and healthier than those inside the kingdom's walls.

I scooted back against it and away from my infuriating captor.

"Now what do you plan to do with me?" I asked, though I had to admit that the heat from the massive fire already stung my frozen limbs, alerting me to how bad off I'd been. He was right—this was the best place to be if I didn't want to end up freezing to death. Besides, the way the light danced over his smooth, copper skin was hard to look away from.

He squatted before me, tilting his head and scratching at the scruff on his face. "Good question, little spy. What *do* I do with you?"

I remained silent, waiting for whatever he had planned. He killed his own men to spare me after all, even if he thought I worked for my father. I wanted to know more. If I convinced him I was on his side, perhaps he'd be an asset in traveling through the forbidden lands.

He sighed, slapped his thighs and stood. "Are you hungry? I saw no supplies with your clothing, so I expect you left your own campsite on the other side of the stream."

"I have no supplies," I said carefully, glancing at the good meat I'd dropped to the dirt out of necessity.

"A shame the king doesn't teach his spies to ration."

"I'm not a spy."

"Wasn't that exactly what you were doing since our bath this afternoon?" He raised a brow. "Did you like what you saw?"

Furious, I opened my mouth—but no words came to my defense, so I settled for a cry of frustration. His tone changed yet again as he too considered the fallen meat. "Come on and have some food. You must be hungry. There's more left over from earlier. If you're good, I may even offer some bread from our village. It's the best in all the lands even stale."

"I'd rather die than accept a handout from someone as arrogant as you." I didn't even know if I meant it; I just had the urge to stab him, and since I was without a blade, I used the words I had.

He set his hands on his hips. "Very well. I'll have to bind you then."

"Excuse me?"

"I can't risk you running off, and if you're more comfortable as a prisoner, I shall oblige. I'd rather not run you through after all that trouble saving you." He scooted right up to me, angling his head down to meet my eyes.

I supposed he meant to be intimidating, but the damn oaf smelled of cedar and tobacco, and the definition of his body, all the peaks and valleys so close had me mesmerized. Swallowing my next barb, I straightened my back against the tree.

"What no argument? Now there's a good little spy." He flipped open a wooden box resting by the nearest tent and snatched up a fair amount of rope. When he squatted by my side again and held it up, I considered striking even without a sword.

"Feel it," he said, holding it out. It was the color of eggshells and surprisingly smooth to the touch, nothing like the roughhewn cord I was familiar with. He leaned in close, and I froze as he whispered over my ear, warm breath tickling my neck. "I want you to know my goal isn't to sacrifice your comfort, merely to stop you from spoiling my plans."

Focusing on his words was difficult while distracted by the heat and scent of his body, and by the time I worked it out, he'd looped the bonds around the tree and my wrists, pulling them taut behind me. He knotted it so quickly and well that I could barely move, let alone try to wriggle free. Then he sauntered over to the fireside and began helping himself to dinner.

My stomach rumbled loudly, and when he glanced over, mouth filled with meat, I turned my head away in protest. I didn't hear him move, but when I turned back, he was sitting beside me with a tin plate filled with wylar meat and stale bread, which he continued shoving into his mouth like a beast.

"Want some?" he mumbled around his latest mouthful.

I scrunched my nose up. "Pig."

He laughed, mouth filled, and I leaned away. To think I'd thought him attractive. But he swallowed it all and tilted his head at me. "What were you looking for out here?"

My brow rose. Was he starting to believe me? I opened my mouth to ask, and he shoved a piece of meat inside.

"It isn't poisoned," he said when I nearly spit it back out.

But the flavor of the juicy bite on my tongue nearly made me moan. My stomach cramped in response. I was ravenous. I chewed and swallowed, pressing my eyes closed so I wouldn't have to see him watching me.

"Good girl, little spy," he whispered.

My eyelids snapped open, and I curled my lip. "Stop talking to me like I'm a dog."

"I'd never," he said. "A fine horse perhaps, but not a dog."

I struggled against my bonds, which remained immovable.

"Have some more food." He stuffed some more in my mouth which I chewed as I glared at him. Why waste it if I needed my strength?

"Don't you dare call me good girl," I warned as he lifted another bite. "In fact, why not just let me out? I'll take a plate of my own now that I think about it."

His gaze lowered to where the circle of rope tucked beneath my breasts. "I think I prefer you tied up after all." He met my eyes again. "Less chance of you bashing my head with a rock while I sleep."

I grabbed the food from his fingers with my teeth, just missing his flesh, and continued chewing.

"When you're ready to talk, let me know." He put the rest of the meat to my lips, then stood as I followed the bread left on the plate with a hungry gaze. But he stuffed it into his own mouth before speaking around it. "Mmm. Too bad you don't deserve this. You'd have liked it."

By now, Rivven's men had finished hauling off the carnage and were approaching the campfire, eyeing me warily. Then, most frustratingly of all, they left me bound and alone in the middle of the Night Forest to retire to their tents.

FOUR

T couldn't believe the bastard had actually left me there while he slept in his tent. If some sort of beast had come, I would have been helpless to defend myself. For what felt like ages, I tried to find a way free of the bonds he'd secured me in. They loosened a fraction, but they never enough to matter, and I grew tired of struggling after a time.

I'd been through a lot since I'd last rested, and though I was accustomed to staying awake far longer than normal, I wasn't immortal. So despite fighting the heaviness of my eyelids, I couldn't resist for long.

Complete darkness surrounded me, save for the glint of something in the distance. My footsteps echoed as I moved toward it—the sound the only backdrop as the source of the light grew larger. Was it a window? No—the silvery, reflective surface was that of a mirror. And there was a girl on the other side, with long frost-colored hair and pale skin.

We reached out at the same moment, touching the surface, which rippled in response, slower than water, but not solid. Leuruna stared back at me, mimicking my movements. It was like peering into my own eyes.

"You're awake," I said, chest warming with the relief of seeing she wasn't in one of her withdrawn episodes.

"You're doing so well," she answered, a tiny smile gracing her lips.

"What? Running away? Being captured?" I snorted, ashamed. But she waited patiently for me to look at her again.

"You've gone farther and done more than I ever thought possible. You can do this, Naya. Keep going. Take it far from father's clutches."

"What did you do to me?" I asked, the words echoing back louder than I'd intended.

Her mouth drew into a tight line, eyes seeming to shimmer with apprehension. It was a feeling that threatened to drown her on a regular basis. She'd told me as much many times. Her fingertips touched the surface again, and she waited until I sighed and reciprocated.

"You have my power, Nye. Don't be afraid of it. Don't you always tell me that it's about the heart of the one who wields it?"

"But how do I wield it?" I asked, desperate for answers. Desperate to be what she needed, what I wanted to be—anything but the coward I was.

"You claim it."

My sister's words echoed in my mind as the scraping of crates through the surrounding dirt seeped into my consciousness. My head hung forward, my chin resting on my chest, and it was none too pleasant to readjust, my neck hurting something fierce from the position. My fingers were numb from the bonds, and I had a horrible taste in my dry mouth. I clung to the memory of the strange dream that felt like so much more. Why had Rune never talked to me this way before? Was it because I could only do it after she'd shared her power?

Once I'd gotten upright again, I focused on the now familiar giant of a man loading up a cart I hadn't seen anywhere when we first arrived. I blinked as all my senses came back to me.

"Where did that come from?" I asked hoarsely.

Rivven glanced over at me as he tugged some rope over the top of his bundled tent. The fire was out too, covered with dirt, trails of gray smoke curling upward, all that remained of the roaring blaze. My pulse ratcheted up. Was he going to abandon me here? I kicked harshly at the ground, grunting as I fought my way free all over again.

"Settle down there, little spy. Don't want you to hurt yourself. This is our supply cart. I had five extra men to help me pull it before yesterday, so I'll probably have to hide it here until my business is done. There's an earth cloaking spell on it." He stepped back and snapped his fingers, making the entire thing fade into piles of earth and moss indistinguishable from the rest of the forest.

"You're an earth spinner?" I asked, awed by the strange magic.

"Me? No. That's not my talent. This spell was purchased from a merchant in my village."

"Why did you kill your own men?" I asked, watching as he checked around for missed items.

Rivven stopped and looked at me. "I am an honorable man, little spy. I know that's unheard of in the rule of the wicked king. But I will never be like him."

"Yet you tie me to a tree while you sleep and leave me for the beasts of the Night Forest?"

"I told you the fire protected us. I would not have let you die."

Shaking my head, I tried a different tactic. "Those men were hired to help you with whatever your business is. Now they're gone. You only have two remaining."

Rivven nodded. "She can count!"

I glared until he answered, stepping away from the mound of supplies.

"I'd been considering releasing them with payment. It had become apparent long before yesterday that they were not the men I should have hired."

"I saved you from having to pay." I smiled.

This time, when Rivven laughed, a burst of pride rushed through me. I said no more, watching as he came over and pulled his sword. I didn't flinch as he swished it down, severing the ropes around the tree and releasing me at last.

Standing, I stretched and shook out my tingling hands as he re-sheathed his weapon.

"Since you no longer have all of your assistants," I said, stepping close to him as he had to me before. "The smart thing to do would be to head back to Tromodia."

"Actually, you, Horis, Idox, and I will be headed in the opposite direction, little spy. In fact, they've gone ahead to clean up once more after last night. And I am not leaving until I've done what I've come to do." He closed the distance between us, the heat from his body warming me like the now dead fire from the pit.

"And what is it you came to do?" I whispered.

The corner of his mouth ticked up as he stared unabashedly into my eyes. His dark ones held tiny flecks of amber that must have been what gave the appearance of flame the night before. His nose was slightly crooked, and I couldn't help wondering if he'd broken it at some point in his past. Suddenly, I wished to discover where the scar over his brow had come from, too. I wanted to learn everything about this strange and infuriating man —and yet I feared what that might mean. Especially why I was so drawn to him, when I should be searching for a blade to run him through and make my escape.

"Wouldn't you like to know?" he challenged just as softly.

Determined to prove his size would not intimidate me, I stepped close enough for our bodies to brush. A thrill of danger raced through me. "You won't let me go, so at least tell me what the plan is. I deserve a fighting shot at not dying along the way."

His throat bobbed as he swallowed, still peering down at me. I couldn't help but feel as though his eyes were attempting to pry me open and see everything inside. Perhaps he was as thirsty for my secrets as I was for his. Perhaps...

"I'll trade you answers for answers," I said my voice steady. "Truth for truth."

"And what guarantee do I have that you'll speak truth?"

"Do you answer every question with another question?" I cocked my head in challenge. My hair, wild and tangled, spilled over my bare shoulder where his too large shirt had slipped down. His gaze snapped to follow before darting back to my face.

"Fine. Answer this then—what were you doing alone and unarmed in the Night Forest?"

I stepped back, hugging myself. "I ran away."

"From?" His eyebrows rose, highlighting the thin white line of his scar.

"Your turn. Why are you here?"

With a deep breath, Rivven threw back his head and glared up at the treetops for a moment. "I've come to rid the world of the evil king of Centos."

He watched me, waiting for a reaction. I kept my expression neutral, though inside, my heart pounded like a prisoner desperate to escape.

"That's impossible," I said, my voice cracking and betraying me.

"Not so. It merely hasn't been done—yet." Rivven grinned and puffed out his massive chest. As impressive as it was, brawn would be no match for my father's magic.

"Only a sorcerer stronger than him can hope to defeat the king." Anger flared in my chest, hot and sudden, like a match struck to kindling. I began to pace, my steps sharp and restless.

"Again, not so. Only if he sees me coming." Rivven voice was laced with the arrogance of a man who hadn't seen true horror. He hadn't seen the king turn a blind eye when his guards beat and raped prisoners at will. He hadn't watched a father rip the magic from his own daughter to use for his pleasure—what the king would surely do to me if he caught me. It stoked my fury into a blaze, the heat of it rising to my cheeks.

"You won't even get past the citadel, let alone inside the castle. Don't be foolish."

"You know nothing of what I'm capable of." His rage met mine, stroke for stroke, as he leaned in toward me.

"I know a fool with a death wish when I see one." I narrowed my eyes at him, my tone low and pointed.

"Then what's the problem, little spy? You'd be rid of me in no time."

My mouth snapped shut as I regarded the man before me. He'd slaughtered his own men to save me, even though he seemed certain I was a spy. Then he gave me the shirt off his back. He tied me to a tree...but he also fed me. The man was more confusing than anyone I'd encountered. Even with the king, I always knew where I stood. But Rivven? He was as unpredictable as a skalimog in heat. And yet. the thought of him wasting his life this way frustrated me to the point of wanting to knock him on his ass.

"Well?" he prompted.

"If you drag me with you, I'll be trapped or dead as well," I answered, smacking the tree beside him. "Be as foolish as you like, but don't save me from one terrible fate to force me into another."

"And what are you running from?" he asked in a low rumble.

"Where are the rest of my clothes?" I countered, hoping to avoid the question as long as possible. The truth was, I wasn't happy about running —not after everything that had happened. Part of me longed to stay and fight, even if it meant risking everything..

"I burned them."

"What?" My eyes rounded with shock.

"There wasn't much left and if you escape me now, it won't be as easy to slip back inside the walls. The guards will see traitor's clothing."

The urge to scream and scratch him was almost overwhelming. Instead, I strode around him to the cart, digging through it until I found a pair of trousers closer to my size. Still, they were too big for me. I frowned at them.

"Look, I want the bastard dead too," I said. "But what you're proposing is a suicide mission. Even with an army at your beck and call, you'd still be unlikely to succeed."

"If you truly want the king dead, then prove it."

I paused while wrapping some string around my waist to hold up the garment. "How am I supposed to do that?"

"Help me. Give me information that will make this easier." He towered over me, arms folded so that his biceps bulged.

"I doubt you'd trust anything I had to say." I finished tying off the string and proceeded to bend and roll up the length of the legs. The material almost melted in my fingers, and not for the first time, I wondered what animal it came from.

"Try me." Rivven bent to be eye level with me and waited.

"Okay. Here's the truth. If you take me back there and I'm captured, he'll gain something that will make him even more powerful—something I've given everything to keep from his hands. I may have lost the only person I ever cared about to protect it. And with it, any life I've ever known. I'm no spy, Rivven. I hate him more than anyone could, even you."

Rivven stood, back stiff, gaping at me. I waited as he stroked his beard, then scratched at it, as if deciding what to do with me.

Folding my arms, I stood. "If you take me back there, you're handing over exactly what he wants—and signing your own death warrant."

"You have nothing on your person," he said after a moment. "What could you hold that he wants so badly?"

"It's in here." I thumped a fist on my chest between my breasts, willing him to believe me.

Rivven shook his head. "Then I'll just have to be sure he doesn't get ahold of you, whether because you are a spy or a runaway. The result is the same."

"Are you insane?" I hurried to keep at his heels as he strode forward. His damn legs were so long, I was practically running while he strolled. "Of course you are. Just let me go on my way. I'll head in the opposite direction. I swear on...Darvol." The name of his people's god had to carry weight.

"You don't answer to Darvol," he said, spinning on me and forcing me back a step. His eyes lit like embers, and there was no mistaking it now. Perhaps he was filled with lava after all.

"I'm simply trying to get through to that thick skull of yours that I mean what I say. I am not, nor have I ever been, a spy. I hate the king, and while I'm all for you or anyone else running him through, I've had the unpleasant experience of growing up in his keep. And I've seen so many perceived enemies dispatched, it's disgusting. Those were just people who he *thought* were out for his life or throne. You actually are." While speaking, I'd approached him again, going so far as to set a hand on his arm, which proved hard, smooth, and warm. We both stared at the point of contact for a moment.

"And you wish to save me from a terrible fate, despite the fact I tied you up and kept you prisoner last night?" he asked, though the fire had faded from his eyes and voice. He looked at me like a puzzle he couldn't quite solve—the same way I looked at him.

I shrugged and pulled my hand back. "You saved me. We'd be even I suppose."

A small smile tugged at his lips, and my heart did a flip-flop. Damn him for being so alluring. Perhaps it was part of his people's magic.

"I appreciate the concern, Nyah."

He used my name instead of branding me a spy. Praise the goddess.

"But unless you give me something specific, I will continue with my task. This has been a long time coming, carefully planned. I've trained all my life for this. A seer I know well has read the stars. Change is upon us. It is time to act. She said I'd meet my destiny if I left when I did, and I don't plan to put everything I've worked for in jeopardy because you're scared."

I sucked in my bottom lip as I considered his words. *Change is upon us.* Perhaps that was what the curious breeze that haunted me these past days was trying to impart.

"Come on, little spy. We are wasting precious time." Rivven grabbed my wrist and yanked me forward alongside him. Though it certainly wasn't a sign of affection, he was careful not to hurt me just the same. I had no choice but to stumble along until I found my feet.

We were back to "spy" now.

"We're going the wrong way," I tried.

"We're headed to Centos," he answered, watching the trail ahead.

"Exactly." I wracked my brain as my pulse pounded. I couldn't waste this kind of time. Surely my father would send someone after me if he wanted what I had. And he did. I knew it in my bones.

But as we approached the clearing by the falls again, Rivven stopped short and tugged me into the trees. I fought to peer around him and threw a hand over my mouth to stifle a gasp.

No, no, no, no.

Both Idox and Horis knelt in death, their bodies bent over large rocks. Their hands were bound behind their backs, and their severed heads rested on the ground before them—shock and fear carved forever on their faces.

FIVE

ells. As much as I'd welcomed seeing the other men cut down by Rivven, these two hadn't deserved the same fate. And they hadn't been granted a fair death either. They'd been tied and executed with no trial, no regard for who they were or what they'd planned. There was little doubt it was my father's men who'd done this—and they were after me.

Those men were dead because of me. The ones Rivven had slain last night deserved what had befallen them. But, as far as I knew, Idox and Horis' only sin had been speaking lewd comments. If that deserved death, Centos would have few occupants left standing.

A rushing filled my ears as I stared at the blood still dripping from the gaping necks. I'd seen executions before, so why did this one make bile rise in my throat?

A noise to the left had Rivven pulling his sword and shoving me against a tree. His hulking frame acted like a shield, but that only sent panic needling through every inch of my skin. I'd trained my whole life for this situation, but in truth I'd never slain a man—maimed perhaps—but never killed. Not that I had any compunction about doing so to defend myself. Whoever had so easily murdered these men deserved my blade.

All the shock and outrage—and even the strange emptiness their deaths had caused— sharpened, mixing with the adrenaline of the moment. The roaring in my head cleared. At last, here was a chance act.

The problem was that I not only needed a weapon, but also needed to see what was happening if I was going to defend myself. As chivalrous as Rivven thought himself, right now he was a hindrance.

The familiar yet unwelcome breeze whispered against the back of my neck, and I shuddered, pushing at his mountain of a body to see the threat. The next thing I knew, he was stepping aside and tucking something into my hand.

I almost laughed with delight at the small sword he'd handed me as the branches shook and parted. Out of the woods came three men, all dressed in the gray and dark red of my father's guard. The second they spotted Rivven, the front man lifted his sword and the two behind him pulled theirs.

I recognized the man in front. Krosis rivaled Rufus in cruelty. I'd caught him in the dungeons, beating prisoners for sport when he thought he was alone. Unlike Leuruna, I didn't shy away from exploring the darkest depths of our father's kingdom, Seeing it only made me hate him more. Krosis was no exception to the evil that thrived in Centos. He took pleasure in inflicting pain. Sometimes, in the village closest to the palace, I'd seen him leave a whore in an alleyway unconscious and bleeding on the ground with a handful of silver coins on her stomach.

"The first one's mine," I said, stepping next to Rivven.

"There she is," Krosis said, honing in on me. "So you have some rebel helpers. That explains how you're still alive out here. Come on back now, and I won't kill your friend. At least, not yet." He smiled, revealing a gold tooth where Rufus had knocked his out during training a few years back.

"She won't be going anywhere with you," Rivven said before I could respond. His deep voice was low and threatening.

Coward that he was, Krosis motioned for the guards to attack. They converged on him, lunging at Rivven, who parried one easily and tripped the other with a well-placed foot. Krosis moved toward me, and everything seemed to tunnel, leaving only him and me in focus. He didn't expect me to know how to fight, and I wasn't planning on getting into a head on battle. I knew where my talents lay, and they relied more on agility and surprise than brute strength.

I spun away from his strike and slammed the hilt of my new weapon into his back as he fell forward, missing me. He stumbled, and by the time he turned and righted himself, I was poised to stab the vulnerable spot in his neck armor. Sadly, he was relieved of his head from behind before I could finish him. I stared as it rolled to the foot of a tree, his body still swiping at the air with his sword where no one stood.

"What part of *mine* don't you understand?" I demanded as Rivven shoved the body over and strode past me to the clearing.

I joined him as he stared down at his two decapitated men, anger almost steaming from the hunch of his massive shoulders. Dipping my head in respect, I knelt and gently drew a hand over Idox's open eyes to shut them forever.

We didn't speak as Rivven trudged forward along the trail toward the Night Kingdom. After the fight, he acknowledged that I'd been telling at least part of the truth, but it did nothing to dissuade him from his goal of single-handedly invading an impenetrable kingdom. The moment I thought about running, he seemed to sense it, and now, my wrists were tied with more of his soft rope as he led me forward by a length like a leash.

Instead of looking for an escape, I started pondering ways to get through his thick skull. A sudden thought made me laugh, which caused him to stop and stare back at me. Maybe I had gone mad.

"What?" he asked.

"It's just," I smiled, "you'd be really good at the Imrati. Too bad you'll be dead before you can partake. Not that you want to be related to him anyway."

"What did you just say?" He marched up to face me, forcing me to crane my neck to look up at him.

"I said you'll be too dead to participate."

"Before that, little spy. Did you say Imrati?"

"Yes. Are you hard of hearing?"

Rivven's nostrils flared as he looked right and left. "The Imrati hasn't been fought in decades."

"Wait. You haven't heard?" I blinked, thoughts flashed through my mind so fast I could barely keep up. Of course he hadn't. How would he if he'd been traipsing through the wilderness for weeks? Excitement shot through me like a lightning strike. "That's how you can get to him."

Rivven licked his lips as though I'd whet his appetite. "If you are purposely trying to delay again, I will bind, gag, and carry you over my shoulder." He bent so that his hair framed my face.

"It's perfect. Whoever wins can get close to him without his whole kingdom as a shield." And I didn't have to be thrown back to the wolves I'd barely escaped from.

Rivven scratched at his beard as he thought on it. "Come on." He tugged me forward again, but this time, he veered off in a third direction through the woods, giving me hope.

"Where are we going?" I asked, rushing alongside him.

"To the closest place where I can verify that information. If you are correct, you will rest in comfort. If not…" His gaze darkened as his words trailed off. A shiver traveled down my body—disturbingly born of equal parts fear and curiosity.

"I'm not lying," I said, holding my chin high.

"We shall see. If you are right, then you have little to worry about. If you're not, I'll have to think of a way to make sure you won't deceive me again."

SIX

I couldn't be sure, but I suspected Rivven moved slower than his normal pace since untying me. Even so, after half a day—assuming it *was* a day, given the perpetual gray mist that hung over everything —I could barely keep up. I consoled myself that at least we were headed away from Centos. Tromodia made sense as a destination, but I wasn't married to the idea, so long as wherever I ended up, I could go into hiding.

Still, I wondered what other inhabited kingdoms might exist beyond those I'd heard of or read about. No one had left Centos for ages, as far as I knew, and I wouldn't put it past Father to hide anything he felt might pose a threat or give his people hope. The farther we came, the more excitement stirred in me. I'd never imagined traveling under the current circumstances, yet this was everything I'd ever dreamed of.

"You grew up in the evil king's keep?" Rivven asked, as he drew his sword to cut a path through some overgrown brambles. His muscles tightened, glistening with moisture from the surrounding mist while he swung his blade like it was an extension of his hand.

"I did." I followed his trail so as not to trip, picking my way through the underbrush and avoiding the leftover thorns.

"Are you going to make me pry everything out of you?" he asked over his shoulder.

I'd like to see you try. Another unwelcome shiver passed through me at the thought, and I smiled to myself. I'd never let him know my wicked musings. They were my own small rebellion against him. Yet, if he insisted on acting as a captor, at least I could enjoy the view. My gaze dipped to where his pants hugged the curve of his rear end and thick thighs.

"What do you want to know?" I asked aloud.

"What was it like being a servant in his castle?" He slipped his sword back into the sheath at his hip as we pushed our way into a clearing.

I did not correct his assumption that I was a servant. "Most everyone ignored me. I learned to slip by unnoticed, for the most part."

"Let's sit in the grass, little spy. I reckon you need a rest."

Rivven led the way to where the tall blades tickled the sides of my thighs through my clothing. He motioned for me to sit as he removed his cloak and dug into his satchel. In moments, he was seated across from me, handing me a canteen.

"Thank you." I took a good long drink.

He watched me warily, his dark eyes flashing with what appeared like flames. It almost felt like they gave off heat based on the way my body flushed. Then he took his turn with the water. I wished he'd return the weapon he'd lent me when we fought the guards.

"There should be another intersection with the stream ahead aways," he said, stowing the canteen in his bag and pulling out some cured meat, which he divided between us. "We can refill there. The temperature should be warmer too, so you'll have a chance at a bath. It might be a good idea to clean up a bit before we reach the Deadlands."

"What are the Deadlands?" I asked, curious as I tore a bite from my meal.

His eyebrows rose again. "I forget you don't know much beyond the walls you were raised in. The Deadlands are what they sound like. A desert that stretches a good fifty miles in all directions. We want to head dead center toward the Cloud Peaks." He gestured vaguely to what I thought was north. But I couldn't make out the mountains from the depths of these enormous trees.

"You promised me a bed," I said. "Now you say we have to cross fifty miles of desert?"

"I promised you a good night's sleep. No bed was mentioned, little spy. And it would take us several days or more to cross the deadlands on foot."

My heart sank. If anyone else was following my trail, there would be few places to hide in a barren desert. And where would we refill his skins while there?

"I thought you said we'd find a village."

"We will. Trust me."

"Why would I trust you?" I challenged, rising to my hands and knees to face him. "You kidnapped me."

"If you spoke the truth about the Imrati, I will release you at the village. You have my word. And I've been true to mine so far, haven't I?"

I thought about that. "It isn't like you've promised much."

His self-righteous expression made me want to wipe it off his face. *Patience, Nyah. You'll have your opportunity.*

"I'm going to rest," I announced, lying back in the soft earth and closing my eyes. There was a rustle, and then a heavy cloak was laid over my body. Without peeking, I turned on my side and nestled in the thick fabric. I fell asleep to the scent of cedar and tobacco.

I woke what felt like moments later to a sharp jab in the ribs. My answering exclamation was muffled by a large, calloused hand pressed over my mouth—and a matching body eclipsing mine. Rivven's hot breath tickled my ear as he whispered, "Don't move." Guiding my head slowly upward, he added, "Cravenbeast."

At the edge of the clearing, through the tall stalks of grass, I made out a hulking form striped with bright scarlet and black fur. Its body had to be twice as wide as the man pressed against me, and pure muscle rippled beneath its skin as it snuffled against the ground.

It raised its head, staring in our direction as though it sensed me watching it. Rivven's hand muffled yet another profanity. The thing's pig-like snout wriggled above two enormous, wickedly sharp tusks that protruded upward from its bottom jaw. One had the bloody remnants of some poor animal's muscle tissue still staked there from its last meal.

"Stay put." Rivven slowly released me, moving through the grass on his elbows and belly away from both me and the beast.

The monstrosity's head jerked toward the movement, and it snorted, a cloud of steam bursting from its nostrils. My heart pounded as I watched

Rivven, wide-eyed. He was still progressing slowly toward the satchel on the ground. Then I saw it: the glint of silver beside the bag that proved the idiot had removed his sword.

Fear turned to outrage as I decided Rivven might just deserve to be speared by those tusks for such a mistake. But when the cravenbeast reared back on its thick legs and charged straight for him, all thought drained away as I sprung to my feet with a shout.

"Look out!" I screamed, but was I already moving and waving my arms to get the animal's attention.

"Nyah!" Rivven cried, and I noted with some satisfaction that he'd used my real name when it counted and not *little spy*. But I couldn't focus on him. I had to keep my eyes trained on the beast. It had stopped, glancing between us both in confusion.

"I taste better!" I taunted as I danced around trying to keep its attention.

It worked. Despite Rivven's loud swearing, it focused on me. I gathered my magic as it charged, waiting for the right moment. When it was far enough from Rivven and almost too close for comfort, I leaped to the left and sent it onto its side, skidding to the right.

The blast of magic winded me, and I bent to grip my knees and recover, while the animal did the same, climbing awkwardly to its clawed feet. If it was possible for it to look even scarier, it did as it pawed at the ground and lowered its head to charge.

But now, I was out of magic, and I still had no clue how to access what Rune had given me, or even if I should. What if it sent up some sort of flare to my father?

The cravenbeast charged, and I sank into my fighting stance, not knowing what else to do. There was no way I'd outrun it or climb quickly enough if I even managed to reach a tree. Besides, I had no idea what the thing was capable of. What if it could climb as well?

Before it managed two feet forward, a wall of fire erupted before it, forcing it to rear up to avoid the new hazard. It hadn't yet settled back on all four legs when Rivven's sword plunged through its flesh, slicing through its thick hide. The beast collapsed before the inferno, and the flames shrank and melted into embers before dying, leaving only a six-foot strip of burnt grass in their wake.

Rivven rested the hilt of his weapon on his broad shoulder as he stalked toward me, chest glistening with sweat and eyes lit from within. When he reached me, he raised a hand, then dropped it to his side. "That was foolish."

"I'm sorry, *I* acted foolishly?" I challenged, poking him in his reckless chest. "You're the one who left his sword—"

"You're right," he said, stopping me mid-tirade. "I opted to warn you before retrieving it."

All I could manage was a shriek of frustration as I threw up my hands. The bastard laughed as I shoved at him, which of course had no effect whatsoever.

"You...you...," I stammered. Then, the reality of what I just witnessed hit me, and I stopped, breathing heavily as I stared up at him with understanding. "You're a fire wielder."

"She catches on quickly." Rivven strode to where the rest of his belongings lay and scooped them up. "Now I really can't allow you to get that information back to your king."

My frenzy fizzled into a glower as he swung his sack and cloak back on his body. Then he joined me, still shouldering his sword, as I stared down at the dead beast.

"It seems such a waste," I said. "Are they edible?"

"If you like things that taste like vomit and are impossible to chew." Rivven shook his head at the body and moved off toward the opposite tree line.

I hurried to catch up with him. "For not wanting me to get away, you aren't doing a very good job at keeping me in your sights all of a sudden."

"You doubt I could catch you?" he asked with a sideways glance. "Besides, I think you may just be stuck on me, little spy."

"Excuse me?" I asked as I climbed over an excessively large hump of dirt and root.

"I can't blame you," he added. He must have enjoyed riling me up, so I silently vowed not to give him the satisfaction of reacting again. "But aside from my magnetic charm, I suspect you want as much information as you can gather. Either that," he paused, waiting for me to catch up again, "or you aren't a spy at all, and you've been telling me the truth all along. In which case, it *is* my magnetic charm."

I bit down on my bottom lip in my attempt not to break the vow I made mere moments ago. "May I suggest an alternative explanation?"

He motioned for me to continue as he picked his way forward.

"I am telling the truth, and you are an oaf who happens to know his way to another village where I can find safety and some semblance of a normal life."

He paused again, facing me. "I guess we will see when we reach the village of Elvenloft."

"Elvenloft?" I repeated, tasting the word. "As in elves?" I bit back a laugh when he met me with such a serious expression.

"I never said it was a human village." He turned back to the path we'd been carving. "I estimate another few hours. Are you up to it or do you need to rest again?"

"What? You can't carry me if I get too tired? I thought your strength was endless."

"If you prefer." He lifted me from my feet so quickly I let out only a tiny squeak before he tossed me once again over his shoulder—me on one side, his sword on the other—as he pushed forward at an even faster pace.

This time, I was aware enough to realize my ass was beside his face, and mortification swelled. "Put me down! I was joking."

"You shouldn't joke if you wish to be taken seriously, little spy. Besides, I owe you for distracting the crave."

"This is not repayment!" I shouted. "This is...," I struggled to find the words to encompass the feelings flowing through me, "it's demeaning."

"Then perhaps next time you will think twice before doing something so dangerous when I've gone out of my way to protect you."

He dropped me onto my feet and backed me into a tree trunk.

"If you'd retrieved the sword first, we'd both have been safe far sooner."

Rivven grunted and turned to continue down the path, leaving me to follow in his wake. Was that agreement—or dismissal? The man was one huge infuriating contradiction.

Thinking about my companion—my captor—hurt my head, so as we marched onward, my mind wandered back to Rune and the way I'd flown over the parapet. Witnessing Rivven wield fire had sparked something in my subconscious. What type of magic hadn't already been accessible to our father through the sacred stone? Flying didn't feel like the power siphoned through our goddess, Reevka. That felt more like air magic: elemental, physical, and the body-centered magic of the Tromodians through their god, Darvol. But even so, Father had already demonstrated his strange ability to wield both of those types of magic. So what was it that Rune was so desperate to keep away from him now?

According to the history books I'd studied in the back of the library, magic had once been accessible to everyone. But Illio, like my father, had gone too far, and the gods had deemed it too dangerous for mortals to wield it freely. So they divided it up among the three main kingdoms. Our goddess, Revka, held the power of the mind and senses. Rune was a master of illusion. My father could withhold others' sight, hearing, and more. I had a minor ability to enhance the sense of touch to the point I could send immense force toward a person or object for a short time. I could shove a table or an attacker—or a cravenbeast. But the power was weak compared to stronger wielders and it burned out quickly.

From my readings, I also knew that Tromodia's god held the physical elements in his grasp. Their people had wielders like Rivven, who controlled fire to some unknown extent, while others used earth, water, or air. Astridon, on the other hand, had a goddess, Zariah, who used the power of spirit, and rumor had it their abilities were tied to dreams.

The gods had stored their respective magics in two crystals. One they broke into three pieces, gifting each shard to the kingdom whose wielders matched its type. The other crystal was the one that passed hands through the Imrati every three years.

And now I was back to the strange edict of the king. He already had the last in his possession, along with the shard of the first stone from Revka secured in his scepter. *So why now? What had Rivven said?* That his seer had read the stars, and that it was time for change. No stars were visible from Centos, so what had my father read that prompted him to act?

Behind us a familiar cold breeze whispered across my back, sending a shiver to my toes.

"Rivven," I said, grabbing hold of his elbow to stop him. "Did you feel that?"

He furrowed his brow as he studied me. "The wind?"

"That isn't a normal wind. I've been sensing it for weeks." The words were hard to find, and I fumbled to express my thoughts properly.

He put a hand on my shoulder, warming my now cold body. "My people say the wind carries warnings to those coming to a turning point."

I drew a deep breath, my frustration ebbing. He'd taken me seriously. I smiled in relief and decided he deserved it. Perhaps if I rewarded his good behavior, he'd be less of an ass.

"We're near to the desert," Rivven said, jerking his head toward the ground.

On closer inspection, I noted a thin layer of sand. And as my gaze trailed onward, I found less and less tufts of grass marking the way.

"Is the village far?" I asked, anticipation growing. He'd been right about the craves. Maybe—just maybe—I'd meet an actual elf by the hour's end.

"Not far. But, before we enter, you should know a few things."

"Such as?" I asked, folding my arms impatiently.

"Such as you should never speak of the evil king in their presence. They believe to speak of something is to call its attention."

"Okay." I nodded, finding the information fascinating. "What else?"

"They will test anyone who enters their village. If they find you worthy, you may enter."

"And if they don't?"

"You will die painfully." He patted my shoulder, nearly knocking me off balance. "But don't worry, if they don't find you worthy, then I know you're a spy. And I shall vouch for you so that I can question you further."

"Not that I am a spy, but is your word truly worth my life?" I challenged, sensing another of his boastful teases.

"Those in Elvenloft owe me for a favor I did long ago. If I say you are my betrothed, they will let you be." He grinned then spun to keep moving forward.

"Hold on a second. I am not your betrothed."

"Certainly not," he agreed without looking back. "But they don't know that. And if we say so, they will not think twice about us sharing a room."

"What if I don't want to share a room?"

Rivven stopped at the foot of a hill made of boulders that seemed to spring up in his path. "Too bad, little spy. Come to think of it, we shall do that no matter what. How else will I keep an eye on you?" He gestured for me to climb the mountain of stone. "Ladies first."

"How thoughtful," I muttered as I examined the rock for potential footholds. Then I tested the sturdiness of the first one with a foot.

With a smirk, I climbed, hopping from stone to stone until I reached the top. Rivven's swear followed me, and I knew I'd impressed him with my agility. But the grin was wiped from my face when I peered over the top of the incline before me and a new world opened.

SEVEN

"Amazing to see the real world, eh?"

I didn't notice Rivven beside me until he spoke. I'd been too enraptured by the desert spread before me. Open, flat land appeared to stretch to the foot of the mountain peaks in the distance, though it was hard to tell through the glinting sunlight that reflected off the far away ground in a blinding display. It was like the rock barrier we'd climbed had been the edge of a box, holding in the night and fog—and suddenly, inexplicably, I had my first glimpse of true daylight.

With what I was sure was a stupid grin on my face, I glanced over at my companion, then half slid, half sprinted down the far side to the hardened ground. When I made the final leap, a cloud of reddish-brown dust spun up around my boots, settling over and clinging to the leather. I ran my fingers through the earth, then stared at the skin that came back warm as though I'd been huddling by a fire. By the time Rivven hopped down to join me, I was shading my brow and trying to see the elusive sun in the sky. The sky was the color of my favorite painting in the museum entitled *Spring*, the same captivating, brilliant blue. How had the artist known the truth of it?

How had my dreams?

"You can't look directly into it," Rivven said with a chuckle. Then he tugged my wrist to get my attention. "You'll go blind if you stare into the sun."

"That's hardly fair." I pouted, but it only lasted a moment before my heart felt light enough to fly again. I threw my arms out and spun. "I can't believe this is real. It's like a storybook come to life."

Rivven's laughter deepened. "Most people do not get this excited about a seemingly endless desert named the Deadlands."

"Why not?" I asked, genuinely curious. "It's incredible. It's...it's warm." I removed the cloak he'd given me during the last stretch of our trek and handed it over to him. But he shook his head and pressed it back to me.

"You'll want it, even in the heat. It will protect you from the sun. You're so pale you'll probably boil like a lobster if you aren't covered. You look like a damn Night Dweller."

I blinked, conjuring up an image of the alabaster skinned, pointy fanged, blood suckers I'd seen in a book. "Are those real too?"

"I haven't met one, but it wouldn't surprise me. If I hadn't known you were from the Night Kingdom, I would have guessed you to be one. Now come on, let's get on with this."

He strode forward, but it was easier to keep up on the flatland. I glanced around, taking in everything from the spiny, bulbous plants that stuck up from the ground on occasion to the random scurry of small, flat, yet colorful creatures that darted across the path ahead.

"What are they?" I asked in awe.

"Garro Lizards," Rivven answered, set on a spot ahead. But when I followed his gaze, I saw nothing but the distant mountains.

"It'll take days to cross. Do we have enough water?"

"We aren't going all the way across. Not yet, and not if you turn out to be what I think you are, little spy. Almost there."

Perhaps the cravenbeast had gotten in a strike I hadn't noticed— because there was nothing ahead at all but more ground and...and...

I stopped, tilting my head to change perspectives. The air about fifty yards out shimmered slightly, as if some sort of magic warped the light, creating an appearance of movement like waves across the expanse.

When Rivven reached the spot, he waited, brows raised for me to join him. The closer I got, the more obvious the distortion was, and yet, I couldn't imagine what it meant. Reaching out, my fingers slipped through the strange light show and an unpleasant buzzing had me drawing away.

In answer to my questioning look, Rivven stretched out his own hand and pressed it flat against the brightest spot. A wave of golden light swept over his forearm, brightening before it gradually subsided. When the light withdrew, a rectangular door opened in the center of nothing, revealing a slender woman with reddish skin, almond-shaped eyes, and pointed ears that poked through sandy brown waves.

She regarded Rivven for a moment, then broke into a smile before jumping into his arms, kicking her feet in the air behind her. For his part, Rivven spun once, then set her on her dainty, slippered feet and grinned right back.

"Elora," he said in a low, rumbly way that spoke volumes including sentiments like, *I missed you* and *we've shared good memories.*

"Riv. You've returned."

The heat must've been getting to me because my neck and chest felt warm and uncomfortable as they stared at each other. I cleared my throat.

"El, this is Nyah," Rivven said, motioning toward me.

The way she narrowed her eyes into slivers as she looked me over from head to toe had me squirming.

"Um, hi," I said with a small wave.

"Why did you bring a stranger?" Elora asked, folding her arms across her chest.

"Nye is my..." It was Riv's turn to clear his throat as he rubbed the back of his neck. "Betrothed."

Her head snapped around to face him, mouth ajar.

"I didn't expect you as guard," Rivven said awkwardly.

"Clearly." She snorted. "Well, I'm glad I found out firsthand. Come here, human."

Rivven nodded toward me, and I took a few reluctant steps forward.

"Turn around," Elora commanded, pulling a sharp, black spike from somewhere behind the door that shouldn't be there.

"Why?" I demanded.

"She's going to test you and make sure you are an honest person," Rivven said, smirking.

I glared at him as I turned. "This better not hur—"

Stars exploded in my vision as my body went rigid. The tip of the spike had struck dead center on my back, barely scraping the skin, but the anguish that ripped through me was unlike anything I'd ever experienced. Cold fingers of pain slid up my spine, prying at my mind like they were sifting through a pile of trash in search of a pin-sized treasure.

"S...s...stop," I pleaded, falling to my knees.

Rivven dropped to my side and yelled something back at Elora, but his words might as well have been gibberish as all I heard was the pain in my skull.

I pictured the fingers poking around my mind and grabbed hold of them with my own hand of fire, forcing them back and away as though they were real.

Suddenly the pain halted, and Elora's scream was the first thing to burst through from outside myself. I dropped to my hands on the ground, gasping for breath, while Rivven rushed behind me. He was back moments later, helping lift me beneath the arms and setting me on my feet. His grip remained until he was sure I was steady. Then he let go and ran both hands through his wild, dark locks.

A glance at Elora showed her cradling a blistered hand against her stomach as she stared at me. The black stake lay smoking at her feet, still smoldering like the embers in Rivven's eyes when his power rose.

My gaze snapped to him. "Did you—"

"That wasn't my fire," he bit out.

"You should have warned me she was a wielder," Elora cried.

"You should have treated her with more kindness just knowing she was with me," Rivven roared, aiming his anger not at me, but at the elf in the doorway.

She visibly swallowed whatever she'd wanted to say, then looked at me again —her gaze sharper and more menacing than the black weapon she'd used on me— before she finally spoke.

"She is welcome." She spit the words at the ground as though I was anything but, spun around, and stalked inside the darkened entrance, leaving the door open behind her.

"What just happened?" I asked as Rivven joined my side.

"We will discuss this in private where it's safe," he whispered under his breath.

I could tell he was angry by his stiff body posture, but what I didn't know was what exactly I'd done. That couldn't have been me. I didn't wield fire. Even whatever Leuruna hid in me couldn't do that.

Can it?

Completely confused, I trailed after Rivven as he climbed through the doorway.

I stood on a wooden platform above a bustling city built into a circle of layers with stairs running between them. Small buildings with windows and archways filled each level. I counted five in all. Elves of all ages and sizes hurried around, going about their business. At the bottom appeared to be an enormous door fashioned from logs likely hewn from the giant trees of the Night Forest and trimmed in gold. Several guards stood around it, still and serious with helmets and long black spears that resembled the small one Elora had tested me with.

Turning back, I found the elf there, dabbing at her injured hand. She must've closed the door, because all I saw was the inside of the wood structure.

"She said I was welcome," I repeated, something dawning on me as I glanced at Rivven. "That means I passed the test."

Elora perked up. "What test?"

"The test to be admitted without having to vouch for her," Rivven explained, taking my elbow.

"Did you not expect her to?" Elora asked, once again narrowing her eyes.

"He—" I started but was cut off by Rivven's mouth swallowing mine.

I froze as he took my face in his hands. Surprise melted into something else when his firm yet tender lips pressed against mine. His scent of cedar and tobacco swirled around me as the heat of his mouth coaxed a sigh from me. When I opened my lips to release it, instead of pulling away, he swept his tongue inside, tracing it along my own. Currents of pleasure sparked to life, racing down my body and into my core as he tilted my head back and deepened the kiss.

I'd never known kissing could be like this. I responded to his movements, letting my own desires take charge as I wrapped my arms around his neck, and he lifted me off my feet.

"Okay, I get it. Just go to your rooms and stop doing that in public," Elora said from somewhere far away.

Rivven set me down and stepped back. I swayed on my feet, pressing my fingers to my swollen lips in wonder. What else did he know how to do that might make me feel that good? I wasn't naïve to sexual acts, having witnessed countless among the people of Centos, especially the soldiers. But even in my wildest imagination, I hadn't conjured the extent of what that kind of contact could feel like.

Keeping his eyes on mine, Rivven muttered an apology and took my hand to lead me down the stairs to the next level. I followed mutely, still trying to wrap my head around what just happened. After walking half the circumference of the city, Rivven pulled me into a darkened alcove and through a hefty door. He slammed it behind us and backed up against it, watching me.

We both started speaking at the same time then snapped our mouths closed in unison.

"You first," I said.

"You cannot say anything about the magic you demonstrated."

Okay, that was not what I expected. "Is that why you kissed me?"

Rivven, who was raking his hands through his hair again and murmuring to himself distractedly, turned my way and blinked several times.

"I had to stop you from telling the damned truth somehow." He pushed away from the door and strode past me, gesturing so that a large fireplace roared to life, illuminating the space.

He paced in front of the enormous bed that dominated the room. Below him and before the hearth lay a scarlet rug with black stripes, clearly fashioned from the hide of a cravenbeast. A small, roughly carved, round table sat on the other side of the room with two wooden chairs and an unlit candle, half melted in a frozen cascade over the copper holder. To my left, a silver tub stood on clawed feet, tarnished with time, alongside a basin and looking glass.

"Is this your home?" I asked, confused.

Rivven stopped his pacing and sighed. "No. There was a time I spent a few years here studying elven magic and fighting styles."

He gestured at the wall to the side of the bed. I turned to find a rapier and short sword hung in a cross pattern. I didn't know much about elves, who I'd assumed were mythical until quite recently, but if I remembered correctly, the books said their magic worked differently than that of our gods.

"So...where is my room?" I asked, wanting nothing more than to throw myself on the mattress and lose consciousness.

"We stay here. Please focus."

"On what?"

Grabbing my arms, Rivven led me to the table, kicked out a chair, and sat me in it. Then he dropped to his knees before me, so we were eye level. "I need to know everything, Nyah. How do you wield fire magic?"

Good question. I would've loved to know the answer myself. But I wasn't sure I should share even that with Rivven. His mixed signals confused me as far as his intentions, and I knew better than to trust easily. I leaned back in the seat, letting out a breath.

"I don't."

"Clearly that's untrue." Rivven stood, the embers in his eyes flashing the color of lit coals. He ran his hands over his head so many times it was a wonder his fingers didn't get stuck in all the tangles.

Watching him pace fascinated me. He was angry, there was no doubt, but he didn't aim it at me, which earned him points toward trust. Wanting to kill the damn king also showed promise. But taking me prisoner? That kind of balanced things out. When he finally stopped and turned to face me, he seemed to have steadied himself.

"I didn't do it on purpose," I admitted quietly. "All I know is I was in more pain than I'd ever felt, and that bitch was trying to tear open my mind. Then it just...happened."

Rivven grimaced at the name I used for his elf lover—or whoever she was. But he wanted truth, and she was most certainly a bitch, no matter how good she was in bed.

"I believe you," he said after a moment. Then he slipped into the chair opposite me.

"Good because I'm not lying." I huffed. "Now it's your turn."

He breathed a laugh and leaned forward, lighting the candle with a gesture. "I mean I believe you aren't a spy. No spy would be so careless with secret powers."

"Well, that's something I guess." I shrugged. "I could use a bath. Care to leave me alone for an hour?"

His eyes followed my gesture to the tarnished tub. "I think we both could use a bath. I must stink as badly as you do."

"Ass."

"I'm not leaving. I don't think you're a spy, but I don't trust that you won't do something stupid or try to run." He tapped the table with his fingertips in a rhythm. "I will turn my back."

I couldn't hold in a snort. "You think I trust *you*?" Inside my heart pounded and memories of that kiss we shared had me denying further ideas. It was a mistake to be naked in the room with him; of that I was certain.

"I've already seen your body," he reminded me in a bored voice. "I controlled myself then and I can do it now. I'm not a beast."

"Debatable," I muttered. But the itch to remove the grime on my body was undeniable. "Fine. Sit and face the fire."

"Would you like me to fill the bath first?" he asked. I couldn't tell if he was being serious. When I balked, he continued, "It'll be much faster if I use magic."

"Oh. Okay." I stepped back, hugging myself as he strode toward the tub, which I realized had no faucet. In the wall to the left was a hole I hadn't noticed before. Rivven swept his arm past it in a fluid motion, and within seconds a rush filled my ears. Water shot out of the opening and spilled into the tub.

When it was nearly full, he made the same motion in the opposite direction and the water stopped, flowing back into the wall. I gaped at him as he stared at the surface for a minute, his eyes glowing again. Then he dipped a finger inside, testing it.

"You're welcome," he quipped as I stared in disbelief.

"You can control water and fire?" I squeaked, dipping my own hand into the hot bath. He hadn't even used flame, just heated it with his eyes. *Who is this man? Or rather who is this sorcerer?*

"You are an observant one," he said, turning and sitting before the fire.

I waited a moment, then undressed and slipped inside the warm water with a sigh. Beside the tub on a small copper dish sat a chunk of soap. At least I hoped it was soap as I pried it up and began to lather. Surprisingly, it smelled of patchouli and tobacco. Not so different from Rivven's scent. Relaxing back, I cleaned every crevice and hair on my body, dunking below the surface to rinse it all off. When I emerged, shoving my hair back from my face, Rivven was standing beside the tub, holding open a huge white cloth for me. His eyes met mine as I let out an exclamation and crossed my arms over my breasts.

"You said you'd turn your back!" I yelled.

"I did. Then I turned back at some point." He grinned.

"Pig."

He shook the towel. "It's my turn."

I rose and snatched it from his hands to wrap it around myself as quickly as possible while careful to splash as much water toward him as I could. Then I stepped out and tossed my wet hair back as I passed, smacking him with it as he laughed.

"Feel free to watch me in retaliation, little spy."

I spun on him, so angry I could barely stammer words. "You said you believed I wasn't a spy."

"I like that the name bothers you," he admitted, dropping his shirt to the floor. "Besides it suits you." With a wink he undid his pants faster than I could look away. "I am impressive, I know, but you don't have to gape."

Skin burning from several kinds of heat, I shot my gaze up his perfect body to his face and swallowed.

Enjoying my reaction, he made a few fluid hand motions. Behind him, the bath water rose and spilled over the side of the tub, cascading into a metal grate set in the floor. Moments later, a rushing sound signaled the arrival of fresh water, pouring in like a small waterfall to replace it.

I set about drying off as Rivven busied himself in the steaming bath. But when I bent to retrieve the clothes I'd left on the ground, his wet grip stopped me.

"There are women's clothes more your size in the armoire," he said.

"Won't the bitch be mad I stole her clothes?"

Rivven let go of my wrist, head snapping back like I'd slapped him. "How did you know they belonged to Elora?"

I rolled my eyes so hard my head hurt. "She nearly murdered me because she thinks we're betrothed, so that was my first clue."

I stomped over to the old, beaten cabinet and yanked it open. I selected a dress, since apparently the elf didn't believe in pants. With the door half shut to shield me from Rivven's gaze, I shimmied into it. Despite my petite stature, she was thinner than I would be even if I were a skeleton. My hips stretched the fabric, and my breasts tugged the low-cut bodice even farther open. I didn't want to know what my ass looked like. I was used to hiding my body under a cloak and men's clothing. My whole life had been spent trying to blend into the shadows. At least the garment was a dark, midnight blue, which was why I selected it.

By the time I emerged from behind the door, Rivven had dried off and pulled on a new pair of tan, tight-fitting pants that hugged his ass and massive thighs. He'd filled a copper basin and was using a switchblade to shave his face. Apparently, he'd already hacked off half his hair as well, so it hung in wet waves that teased the bottom of his ears.

He turned when he felt me looking and his gaze flew to my body, mouth hanging open.

"You've already seen it, remember?" I said with a snort. But I smiled internally knowing I was able to garner that kind of reaction. I'd never thought about finding a partner, even just to fool around with. I never considered how attractive I might or might not be. My life had been filled with avoiding and fearing others and their motives. I'd dedicated my time to training in combat and protecting my sister. The occasional fleeting thought of finding someone else was dismissed as soon as it came up, flooding me with guilt for the desire to separate from Leuruna when all she had was me. It wasn't like we had any healthy couples to look to as examples anyway.

"You look..." Rivven finished with his face and cupped water over the skin he'd revealed. "Presentable when dressed appropriately."

"Gee, thanks." I sauntered over and tipped his chin up, pretending to examine him. "I prefer the scruff. It matched your personality better, wild man." I slapped his baby soft cheek lightly and went back to sit at the table.

When Rivven joined me, I tried to pretend he wasn't still shirtless. Not that the front didn't gape open on their damn shirts anyway, but at least the *idea* of being dressed had been in place. Now, he simply flaunted the rises and dips of each muscle in his arms, chest, and back. As he turned to retrieve a couple of glasses and a pitcher from a cupboard behind him, I noticed something I hadn't before.

A sigil was inked over the back of his shoulder which had probably been covered by hair, an anchor crossed with a curved sword like the one that now rested, propped against the bed and still in its sheath. When he set the wooden cups down and began filling them with a dark liquid, I remained silent.

He drank deeply from his, then refilled it.

"I need a brush," I said when he started pouring a third.

With a deep belch, he rose, retrieving one for me with a wooden handle. He bowed with a flourish and handed it to me.

"You're already drunk," I told him as I yanked it through my hair.

"Just relaxing. You'll never do it that way." He snatched the thing from my hand and moved around behind me to press a palm down on my head when I tried to stand, keeping me seated.

To my surprise, he began gently working the bristles through one small section at a time. It felt so good that I relaxed and closed my eyes.

"It's not poisoned you know," he said as I started to drift off.

I jerked up, but he kept working out tangles behind me. I was thirsty. So, I took a taste. The wine was surprisingly sweet and tart on my tongue. I could see why he'd downed so much so quickly as I did the same.

By the time he'd finished with my hair, I was convinced we were on a ship of some sort, tossing back and forth on the waves.

Groaning, I stood, holding on to the table to keep from tumbling to my ass. "Make it stop moving."

Rivven steered me around until my nose hit his chest.

"Ouch. Your pectorals are too hard." I was a whiny drunk, apparently. Come to think of it, I drank ale all the time, and I'd never been as affected as I had been by this mystery wine. I poked him over the heart as I glared up at where his face had blurred into two. "You did this on purpose."

He held my upper arms, which I still appreciated, since if he hadn't, I'd probably be sprawled at his feet.

"You can't hold your liquor. I think you better lie down. In the morning, we will discuss our next move when Galan arrives." He stooped for a moment and then I was lifted into the air, clinging to his shoulders.

"Who is Galan?" I asked then hiccupped as he tossed me on the bed. "Is that another elf you're fucking?"

Rivven pushed me down by the shoulders then pulled a blanket up over me. "He is Tromodian, and I have not had the pleasure. Though I'm sure he would be interested if you offered. Now sleep."

I scrunched up my nose at his order before turning over on the most comfortable mattress I'd ever felt and slipping into a deep sleep.

This time the mirror was closer than the last, and Rune was dressed in one of the fitted, restricting gowns Father sent servants to dress her in when she made court appearances. Her hair was twisted up into a complex braid that wound around her head in layers. Our fingers touched, causing the glass to ripple as before, hers behind white lace gloves, mine bare.

"Where are you going?" I asked.

Rune averted her eyes. "Father has ordered me to practice with Serano so I know how to behave appropriately."

"You know how to behave." My brow furrowed. Why wouldn't she meet my eyes?

"How I am to behave when I meet my future husband," she clarified. "Things like how to curtsy and smile and speak kindly and when spoken to and—"

"I get it." I cut her off, but the fear that there was more to her "training" sent a shiver down my spine. If I pressed, she might leave though, and I wanted to talk to her.

I missed her.

But when she finally turned and I saw my own eyes reflected back, red and swollen and filled with unshed tears, something inside me broke.

"You don't want this," I said. I already knew that, but seeing her like this...

She shook her head slowly. "But I must do what father asks. He is right to want an heir."

"You're his heir!" I hadn't meant to say it with such anger, but why couldn't she remember who she was? She was the most powerful wielder in Centos.

My words made her wince, drawing back inside herself and looking down as though it hurt to see me as much as it did to meet Father's eyes or Serano's.

"*Maybe,*" I said softer, "*you'll like whoever wins the Imrati. It could be someone handsome and obviously he'd have to be talented.*" I pictured Rivven bowing before her then standing and striking my father through the heart.

"*I don't want to marry. I...I don't want to...to be touched the way a husband touches his wife.*" Her admission was barely audible. It was a lot for her to be that vocal about her fears. And I understood them from her perspective. She knew so little of the world and its ways. At least I'd had chances to see things from the shadows.

"*If he is a good person, it will be enjoyable. I've seen some women who like it.*" I thought back on the occasional trysts I'd walked in on between guards and palace servants. Often, they ended quickly, but both parties seemed passionate when it was consensual, and though I was no expert, I could tell the woman liked it. I'd more than liked it after all when Rivven kissed me.

"*It isn't that. I don't want...never mind.*" Rune's momentary frustration ended with a mix of melancholy and resignation.

"*You won't have to worry,*" I said, and she snapped her gaze back to mine. "*Technically, the winner of the Imrati chooses the betrothed, and the winner this time will be choosing no one.*"

Rune's confusion turned to laughter then back to confusion again. "*No one would do that, Nyah.*"

"*I would.*"

EIGHT

I woke with a gasp, springing up in bed. Beside me, Rivven lay sprawled on his stomach, one arm slung over the blanket resting on my thighs. The first thing I did was make sure I was still clothed. Finding the dress undisturbed, I attempted to calm my breathing and slipped out from under his grasp, making him stir for a moment then roll to his back with a grunt. Once I was certain he was still asleep, I shoved on the slippered shoes I'd found at the bottom of the cabinet and crept to the door. It was ridiculously heavy and hadn't been oiled in—well, ever, judging from the painfully loud creak as I tugged.

Wincing, I had it almost open enough to slip through when a large hand reached above me and shoved it closed again.

"Damn it to hells," I cursed, flipping around so my back was to the door as Rivven leaned over me. A shadow of his scruff had already started growing back, and even with his fiery glare, he looked stupidly handsome. Okay, maybe because of that glare.

"Going somewhere, little spy?" he challenged.

My shoulders slumped. "I was trying to." I crossed my arms as my head thrummed with pressure and pain.

"Were you heading back to report to the false king? Or were you planning to challenge Elora to a magic duel?" He smirked. "You'd lose by the way. She's an elf."

If it were anyone else, we were discussing I'd want a demonstration of elven magic. As it was, I couldn't help but picture stabbing her through the heart.

"If I were going to duel someone it would be with a sword, and I assure you, I would win." I pressed a hand to my mouth and shoved past Rivven to the grating before losing the contents of my stomach.

Gentle hands held back my hair as I puked my guts out. When it was over, he knelt beside me with a cup of water.

"Thank you." I swished some of the water in my mouth before spitting it out. I guzzled the rest.

"So," Rivven said, offering a hand up, which I ignored as I climbed to my feet. "You aren't good at drinking, but you are quick on your feet and good with a sword—or so you claim."

"I am," I said, head held high.

He nodded. "You aren't a spy, yet you know inside secrets of the kingdom, such as the invocation of the Imrati trials, And you had no trouble watching me and my men from a distance for a prolonged period, nor avoiding my traps."

I remained still, letting him work out whatever conclusion he was headed toward. He circled me as he thought, and I remained focused on the rumpled bed where he'd apparently lain beside me.

"You say you have something the king wants yet carry nothing. Which means," he paused, "you are referring to either information or ability for which he wishes to use you. Assuming you are not lying that is."

"I already proved I'm not. I passed your stupid test remember?" I growled through my teeth.

"Then you demonstrated fire wielding," he said, stepping so close, I took a counter-step back.

"I told you I have no idea how—"

He waved my words away. "Of course, he wouldn't teach it to you if he knew you had it. He'd be giving power to someone who might oppose him. No. I believe he wants to use your abilities for himself. We just have to figure out where they're from and what he plans to do with them. Then they can help us take him down."

I let out an exasperated noise and sat hard at the table, rubbing my forehead and letting my hair swing to shield me from Rivven.

He leaned over me, working at the knots in my shoulders, and once again confusing the hells out of me.

"You said you hate him," he whispered by my ear.

"I do," I admitted. "But it isn't that easy."

"Doing the right thing is never easy. But it's always worth it." Rivven straightened. I heard him walk around the table to take the other seat.

I peered up through my fingers at him. He sat waiting, arms crossed. I opened my mouth to speak, and a knock sounded on the door. Rivven made a shushing motion and moved to the door with such speed and grace, I was stunned. He managed to pick up his sword on the way, tucking it behind him as he cracked open the door.

In seconds, he'd thrown it wide and tossed his sword back on the bed. Elora entered with a large tray featuring a kettle, mugs, and a platter of bacon and eggs.

My stomach rumbled.

"Thank you," Rivven said, taking it from her and setting it on the table before me.

"You seemed too busy to go get any food or supplies last night." She shot a look at me, sizing me up and darkening slightly when she saw her dress stretched over my fuller figure. "So that's what she has that I don't."

"Excuse me?" I rose to my feet.

"Breasts," she said with a sigh. "I guess men will be men."

"Elora," Rivven warned, voice low and menacing. "Respect."

She huffed and shrugged her slight shoulders. "I respect those who earn it." With that she turned and left, the door shutting behind her on its own.

"I'm sorry," Rivven said, sitting back down. "I hadn't realized she would be the jealous type."

"Well, from her perspective you probably left here acting like she had reason to expect you to return sometime for her company." I started piling my plate. She might want to poison me, but not Rivven. His cock was no good to her if he was dead.

"I—" Rivven cut off his retort with a swallow that made his throat bob as he stared off into nothing, probably realizing for the first time that he'd led her on. I shoveled in some bacon and chewed as I watched understanding and regret light his eyes, instead of the usual fire.

"Then you show up introducing another woman you actually intend to marry. Which means you never meant to marry her." I poured myself some tea that smelled of citrus, rose, and coriander then clutched the warm clay mug between my hands, enjoying the warmth.

Riven sank low in the chair as I watched him over the lip of my drink.

"I screwed up," he admitted. "I thought we'd been on the same page. No expectations. I clarified when she started leaving her things here, and she said she understood."

"Sometimes, people have unspoken or unacknowledged expectations," I offered, feeling slightly bad for him since I'd seen it play out before at the castle. More than once a serving girl had fallen for a guard, whispering to her friends that she'd make him change his mind—but he never did.

"You know a lot about women and relationships," he said, reaching for some food.

I snorted. "Maybe because I am one."

"And the relationship part?" he pressed, shoveling some egg into his mouth.

Averting my eyes to my plate, I poked at the food with a fork made of twisted copper. "I've seen enough people screw up that I get it. But no. I don't have a relationship with anyone."

"Back to discussing the evil king," Rivven said through a mouthful.

"Must we?"

His stare was his answer. I grumbled and took another gulp of tea. "Fine. You want to use me somehow to get to him? Therefore, you want to do exactly what he would."

"I am nothing like him." The vehemence with which Rivven spoke caught me off guard as he swept his plate from the table and stood glaring down at me like a rabid animal. For the first time since he'd captured me, I felt true fear. He must have seen it in my expression, because he softened and sat back down, rubbing a hand over his face.

"Guess I know how to get your undivided attention if necessary." I clenched my hands in my lap so he wouldn't see the tremble in my limbs.

"My apologies," he said. "You certainly are good at garnering my attention."

I blushed, attempting to hide a small smile at that knowledge. "Look," I said, staring into my tea. "I am not opposed to helping you so long as I don't have to go near him. But before I spill all my secrets, it's only fair that you explain exactly who you are and why you're planning this suicide mission."

Rivven's hands slammed onto the table, forcing my gaze up. He leaned across, eclipsing the space between us and capturing my attention. My breath caught as his eyes darkened, tiny flickers of flame igniting behind his pupils.

"My name is Rivven of the Fallow clan." He paused as though waiting for my reaction.

Normally, an introduction wouldn't mean much since I already knew his first name. But the Fallow clan—that was the name of the last family meant to rule Tromodia. *Or at least that's who it was supposed to be.* It was Castor Fallow, destined for the throne that was originally betrothed to Rune's mother, the next queen, and only child left of those in charge at the time. Since only men were allowed to rule in Tromodia's tradition, they'd been engaged by their parents since birth. But she'd left him for my father—Balram—gods knew why, politics aside. Castor came after Father and met his death by the evil king's hand.

Castor hadn't had any sons. He'd been meant for the queen and had stayed faithful. The Fallow clan was supposed to take over and rule at her side. So where did Rivven come in?

"I don't understand," I whispered. "Castor was the last of your line, wasn't he? How are...who are you?"

"You know his name?" The pain in Rivven's voice startled me. I'd yet to hear him show any emotion other than stoicism, anger, sarcasm, or intensity—if that was an emotion. I wasn't sure.

"I know the history that's hidden. Most people let it remain in the past, but sometimes that past feels more real to me, more hopeful than the present." I hid my fists on my lap beneath the table. Rivven had earned a bit of the real me when he showed he was human after all.

He nodded, taking in the information. "He was my uncle. I am his older brother's son."

"So...you're a prince?" I asked, smirking. He had no clue that I was technically a princess, so his title meant little to me.

"No." He looked away, but I couldn't miss the way his muscles strained and tightened. "No. My father died by the hand of an assassin sent by the false king. They didn't know my mother was pregnant with me. She hid it. And the rule of Tromodia fell into disgrace. Our beautiful lands have splintered into factions where poverty and greed now reign. Go to the docks and you'll find thieves and pirates, like the men I hired who attacked you. Rarely a noble sailor or fisherman other than those that gate keep and sell the fish for inflated prices."

Rivven stood and leaned against the wall, looking at me, but the way his eyes glazed over, I was certain he was seeing something else. Somewhere else. "I have trained my entire life, first to be able to fight off an assassin should one find me, and then, to take revenge for the state the false king left my people in. To take back what is rightfully ours."

"You mean, m—the evil king married Tenara to take over Tromodia, then killed off the men in your family to ensure no one could oppose him?" I asked, standing.

"Unfortunately, yes. And worse, I believe his sudden demonstration of air wielding, which happened shortly after, means he stole it somehow from Tenara." Rivven's eyes narrowed on me as he took a step forward. "I wonder—"

"What?" I snapped, not liking the way he was staring at me, like I was a shiny sword or trinket and not a person.

"If he knows you can wield fire magic, he'd want your power for himself. He'd try to siphon it out of you somehow as well, if that's even possible."

A sick wave crashed over me as I pictured his scepter and how he'd been using it to steal magic from his own daughter. I fell back into my chair, shoving the plate away. "It is. I've seen him do it."

The last thing I wanted was to be in the same position as Rune. *Is that what she hid in me? Has she somehow inherited more than her mother's air magic and father found out? But how is it possible she carries so many different types of magic?* I'd never heard of such a thing—not even in the history books I'd scoured so many times. I'd always allowed her space and never pressured her, too afraid I'd cause her pain of which she'd had enough. But maybe I should have pushed harder. Why was she so damned closed off when it came to talking about her power?

This time when I tightened my fists, it was to conceal tremors of pure frustration.

"I need to stay the hells away from him."

"We need to use you as a lure," Rivven spoke at the same time.

"Listen." I stood, swallowing back the bile that threatened to rise in my throat. "You haven't seen what I have. You should understand though based on what he did to your family. That man is sick and everything he touches is cursed. I'm probably cursed." I laughed hysterically, sounding like a mad woman. "Don't curse yourself too. You seem like a decent enough guy. Go back to Tromodia and lay claim to a section of the land. It's not everything but—"

"I don't care to rule," Rivven bit out as though I'd insulted him. "I want revenge." His eyes lit again. But I was already getting used to it, so it had less effect on me than before.

"Well good luck with that," I said with a smile. "I can't risk him getting his hands on my power." He didn't need to know it belonged to Leuruna. No need to bring her into this, no matter my complicated feelings.

"Nyah, I will keep you safe." He grabbed my shoulders to prevent me leaving, and I supposed to reason with me, though his desperation increased the pressure of his grip, I pulled back, rubbing my arms.

"You can't promise that. Not with his power. Are you going to force me as your prisoner? Or are you going to let me make my own decision as you promised to do if I was telling the truth? How good is your word, Rivven of the Fallow clan?"

Rivven dipped his head, taking a step back. "I have one more thing to tell you, and then you can decide for yourself."

"Go ahead." I doubted whatever he had to say could convince me otherwise.

"I have more power than just the fire and water from my father's Tromodian side. My mother isn't human. I'm part elf and I can wield some of her people's magic as well."

NINE

I groped for the edge of the mattress and sat down. "You're half elf?" I hadn't even known they existed until we came here. Not outside of books anyway. It made sense that he would be welcomed by them. "You don't look it," I added weakly.

"My mother is from the mountain elves, an entirely different society. Larger of body and a bit heartier than the desert and forest dwellers."

"There really are different elven kingdoms?" The idea fascinated me. I wanted to force him back in the chair and question him all day. Or... "Is there a library where I can read about your history?"

Rivven's mouth snapped shut as he cocked his head at me. "Do you mean to say if I'd told you I was half elf from the beginning, you wouldn't have given me such a hard time?"

I shrugged. "If I believed you then. Probably not." I patted his scruffy cheek, then stood on tiptoe to dig through his hair in search of his ears.

He batted me away, laughing. "They're only slightly pointed. Most people don't notice."

"Amazing." I bit my bottom lip and reached up again, going slower this time. He tilted his head just enough for me to run my fingertip over the top of his ear. Sure enough, the tip was harder than the cartilage of my own and curved into a rounded point.

He cleared his throat, grabbing my wrist. "That's enough," he said in a rough voice. His copper skin darkened along his cheek bones.

"Sorry." I pulled my hand away and tucked it behind my back, wondering if I'd accidentally prodded an erogenous zone of some sort. "What powers do elves wield? Does it also depend on the environment? Do they worship different gods?" Some of my millions of questions erupted. There hadn't been nearly enough details in any of our books.

"Let's take a walk and I'll try to answer your questions. But, Nyah," he warned as he pulled on a fresh tunic, "I'm starting to think the seer's message wasn't about invading Centos."

Pausing on the way to the door, I looked up at him in surprise. "You mean you don't want revenge?"

"On the contrary, I plan to get it, but I think the destiny I was supposed to find on my path by leaving when I did was…" He scratched at his jaw. "Well, you. The timing was too perfect. I think we are supposed to work together."

That was a lot to lay on a woman. But I couldn't deny the draw I felt toward him. The gods had done stranger things, but we had to clear the air if we were going to work together. "You owe me for treating me like a spy and tying me up."

"I make no apologies for acting with caution," he said evenly. "I've never met anyone who managed to escape the walls of Centos. The only person I ever heard of leaving, aside from the king, was the assassin sent after my father. That is, until those guards came after you in the Night Forest."

"I'm sorry about your father." My shoulders slumped as I regarded the situation from his point of view. "I would give anything to have a decent father, even for a little while. I guess that was stolen from you too."

Rivven reached out and tucked a strand of my hair back behind my extremely human ear, and my heart sped up. I'd never been touched in such a tender way by anyone other than my sister. At least, not that I could remember.

"It's possible your father was from Tromodia," he said gently, his voice pulling me from the haze. "Killed for his magic. Did you say you were raised in the keep?"

"Yes, in the keep." I averted my gaze. I couldn't admit that the man who'd murdered his father, and nearly destroyed a once thriving kingdom, was my own flesh and blood. I'd hate me as much as I knew he would if I admitted it. "I tried to stay away from others, keep outside their awareness."

"He went after you?" Rivven asked, tugging open the door to the stuffy little room so that we could explore beyond his apartment.

"His advisor witnessed the power, and I ran. I barely escaped, and I'm pretty sure he's going to have more people looking for me. To be honest, I'm surprised we made it out of the Night Forest so easily. The forbidden lands would mean nothing to the king, if he thought he could retrieve me." Another truth I could offer.

"I meant what I said. I will protect you, Nyah. Any enemy of the king is a friend of mine. I've already given you my word."

"I appreciate that. But even if you're right, and we were supposed to meet, it can't be just to hand me back over to him and the danger." I wound my way down to another level of Elvenloft to explore a marketplace filled with wooden carts rimming the boardwalk. "I'd rather avoid the bastard, no offense. Running toward certain death or torture isn't something I'm accustomed to. No matter how good I am with a sword. I'll help you, but not in that way."

Rivven grinned. "If what you say about the Imrati tournament is true, and the king will be leaving his kingdom to award the winner the powerstone, then you won't have to step foot in Centos ever again."

I noted he'd avoided promising I would never see the king again. It was a thing with Rivven, maybe an elf thing for all I knew, to speak truths that twisted or excluded important information. I let it go for now. He was the closest thing I had to a friend, and I certainly had no clue how to travel the world out here without him. It would be ten times more difficult without a knowledgeable guide, even if he was a self-righteous pain in the ass sometimes.

"What are these?" I picked up a plump yellow fruit from a nearby stand, feeling its hefty weight in my palm.

"You don't have *pilas* in Centos?" Rivven's voice rose in surprise.

I cocked my head as I sniffed it, and my mouth immediately started watering at the sweet, citrus scent.

The elf behind the cart reached to snatch it away before I could take a bite, but Rivven caught his wrist, stopping him. As soon as Rivven tossed a coin at the slender, russet-skinned man, who caught it in his opposite hand, all seemed forgiven.

I sank my teeth into the tender flesh of the *pila*.

Closing my eyes, I groaned in appreciation as the juice spilled over my chin. When I swallowed and opened my eyes again, both the man at the cart and Rivven were staring at me wide-eyed.

"What'd I do?" I asked around my next bite.

"I've never seen anyone eat a *pila* in quite that way before." Rivven grinned and dragged me forward with my prize still in hand.

"What way?" I asked.

"With so much...pleasure."

I couldn't stop the blush from creeping up my neck. "It's just so good. We don't get much fresh fruit and vegetables in Centos. We take dried herbs to make up the nutrition and occasionally get some imported for the keep, but they aren't fresh like this." I lifted the half-eaten gem in my sticky hand.

"I suppose when dark magic blocks out the sun, that's what happens," Rivven mused. "Ah, here we are."

We stopped at another section of the vibrant market nestled between two larger carts. Both overflowed with diaphanous fabrics of just about every pattern I could imagine, hanging on racks and stacked in colorful piles.

I finished off the last bit of *pila*, leaving a pit that I sucked on, then tossed in a compost bucket stacked between the vendors. Rivven watched me as I slowly licked every bit of juice from my fingers. I found I enjoyed making him uncomfortable.

"What's all this?" I asked, wiping my sticky palms on my hips. I didn't care much if I soiled Elora's clothing.

"You'll need appropriate outfits to travel back to Tromodia with us," he replied, clearing his throat "Go ahead and pick out a new wardrobe. You'll need some training gear, travel wear, and dresses for formal occasions."

My eyebrows lifted. "And how am I supposed to pay for all that, your highness?"

The cringe the nickname elicited cemented his new moniker. Retribution for "little spy" was at hand.

"Consider it repayment for tying you to a tree overnight when I thought you were a spy." He tugged more money from his pocket and handed it to me.

I didn't want his money or the strange clothes that would keep drawing attention to me. As it was, the stares I was getting from other strolling patrons and merchants made me feel far too exposed. It was strange that Rivven's attentions didn't make me feel that way. On the contrary, I enjoyed his eyes on me.

I didn't want to think too hard on that, so I focused on sorting through the wares on the closest cart. He wasn't wrong. I did need appropriate clothing, no matter what I did from here on in, and perhaps if I chose my own things, I'd garner less attention instead of more.

"Wait, you said come with 'us.' Who is us?" I asked, perusing the closest pile of useless satin shirts that would not serve to cover anything important. Let alone keep me warm.

"I sent a messenger falcon for Galan the first night we met. He should be here soon. It's only a couple of days ride from Tromodia." Rivven lifted a lace gown that had more holes than fabric and eyed me.

Snatching it from him, I set it back in the pile. "And who is Galan?"

"A friend." Rivven smirked.

"Wait. You sent for him that night? I thought you were taking me back to Centos to kill the kin—" Rivven's hand was over my mouth before I could finish.

"Do keep our private business...private, darling." He sighed, then released me. "I never intended to bring you with me to Centos. If you'd been a spy, then you were a liability. If you weren't, well, you'd still be a liability."

The truth settled over me like ice pouring down my spine. *He'd played me?* He'd made me believe I had to *convince* him not to take me back there, when his only intention had been crossing into the desert?

"You are an arsehole, your highness," I snapped.

I turned away before he could respond, stalking through the racks and pulling every black item I could find from the sea of silk and color. When I had an armful, I shoved them at Rivven and slapped some coins into the waiting palm of the grinning elderly elf woman with thin white hair and crinkled skin.

"Morbid, but acceptable," Rivven muttered, handing them to the woman to fold and put in a sack. "You know color won't hurt. I realize you come from the Night Kingdom, but you aren't stuck there anymore."

"Can I use the rest to buy something else?" I asked, ignoring his comment.

"I don't see why not. But first, you'll need appropriate footwear and a traveling cloak."

Doubting I'd have enough for anything decent, I frowned. But I had an idea in my head, and I wasn't going to give up easily. I followed Rivven to yet another area, and this round, I took my time searching, until I found a pair of dark brown leather boots perfect for travel and combat, and black slippers—both at the cheapest price possible. Then, I picked out a simple wool cloak, black, of course, with a hood and single clasp of bronze, ignoring the rich furs and ornately detailed trims of others, which remained too attention grabbing for my taste.

Once I piled all my goods into Rivven's arms, I grinned and ran off with the remaining amount. He cursed as I hurried through the now crowded market, zig zagging deftly, until a glint of silver told me I'd reached my destination. A glance over my shoulder proved I'd managed to lose my shadow, at least temporarily.

Greedily, I perused the wares displayed on black velvet and stone. The stories seemed to be true. Elves were master craftsmen and forgers, each weapon making my heart pitter-patter with want more than the last. Complex yet streamlined designs curled around silver blades of all sizes and shapes among the plethora of weapons available.

When I saw it, I stopped cold. It was almost as if a pulsing glow surrounded the elegant sword. Maybe it was the way the thin, tapering blade caught the light. Or perhaps it was the welcoming shape of the carved grip. Whatever it was, I reached for it, surprised by the precision of balance and weight as I swung it gingerly, testing its feel.

When the presence closed in behind me, I spun, tip of the blade a breath shy of Rivven's throat. He stayed still, but aloof as I withdrew and pulled it toward me again, laying the flat of the blade in my hand. A pattern was etched inside—a combination of strange runes and vines that wove delicately up and down then around to the hilt.

She wasn't Stealth, but damn was she beautiful.

"You're trained," Rivven noted.

"There are many things you've underestimated about me." I winked, then turned to address the merchant. "How much?"

"Fifty *sollions*."

I balked. I had less than half that left in my possession after my other purchases. I refused to beg Rivven for money though. I'd just have to find a way to work for it. Or...I could sneak back at night and steal it. I'd leave the remainder of my money, of course. I wasn't heartless.

But Rivven stretched over me and handed the man his price without a word. Then, he added a bit more and said, "She'll need a back sheath as well. Leather and comfortable. We have a long journey ahead."

If he wanted to spend his coin on me, I wasn't going to stop him.

By the time we left the market, I was happily munching on a roasted pheasant leg as Rivven hefted several burlap sacks filled with my new possessions. We'd chatted the rest of the time as I openly questioned him on everything I'd ever wondered about elves.

"If your magic doesn't come from the gods, where does it come from, and what are the rules?"

Rivven chuckled, pupils bouncing as he tried to follow my excited movements. I couldn't help but dance around him. This whole world he'd introduced me to was a wonder.

"You have to remember I was raised in the human world. But as I understand it, elves have a special connection to the ether, so they draw their magic from the same source as the gods. Humans have no direct access, so they rely on their gods' benevolence."

I slapped my palms against his massive chest, bringing him to a stop halfway up the stairs to the level of his apartment. "What's the ether?"

He stared pointedly at the spot where my now clean pheasant bone was pressed between his body and my hand. I removed it sheepishly.

"The ether is like a shroud of energy that overlays everything in the world." He met my gaze, and I watched mesmerized by the embers dancing in his irises.

"Can you see it?" I asked, eyes wide.

"I can. Though I wonder if perhaps what I experience is only a fraction of what a full elf does. Nevermind the gods."

"What does it look like?"

"It's like..." Rivven drew a breath as he leaned in, swathing me in his cedar scent. "Like the stars fell to earth and swirl around anything that holds magic or power. You have a sparkling waterfall of light that draws my attention and everyone else's here. It made me wonder what power or enchantment you carried from the start."

I swallowed, trying to imagine the ghostly aura of the stars streaming over Rivven. It was already nearly impossible to look away.

"Come on," Rivven broke the spell between us and I scurried after him.

"Thank you, for today," I said, when he dropped my things to open the heavy door of his apartment.

"You're welcome," he answered, an amused grin on his stubbled face. "Now if you don't mind staying put, I will go pick up a few more items that are needed."

"I suppose," I agreed, surprised he was willing to trust me on my own, despite my appreciation of the time we'd had. Poor decision on his part but far be it from me to protest.

Hesitating as though he sensed my thoughts, Rivven muttered something under his breath and walked out, shutting the door closed behind him.

TEN

The damn door was locked, and no amount of shoving and jimmying was going to open it. He probably used some crazy elf powers to keep me prisoner. And the worst part? If I challenged him about it, he'd just point out that I tried to escape, so it was justified.

Fine. It wasn't as though I had a plan of where to go or what to do. Besides, maybe running away wasn't the right answer.

I sorted through all my new goods and went about discarding the ill-fitting Elora dress in favor of some soft tights and a wraparound tunic that fell over my hips. Frowning at the V of skin in the front, I hooked my new leather harness over my shoulders and around my waist, cinching it. Then I practiced sheathing and freeing my new sword. It felt like an extension of my body already.

As I lunged and parried with an imaginary enemy, it grew even more natural and graceful than I ever had with the armory sword I'd stolen so many years ago. I loved Stealth, but it hadn't been crafted for my hands. But this? This was meant for me. I was sure of it. I couldn't explain it, except to say I couldn't imagine anyone else wielding it. I wondered if somehow the elf that crafted it did so for me. Magic had done stranger things.

The next order of business was to fish out my new brush and braid my hair, so it was out of my face. I coiled it at the nape of my neck and pinned it in place. Finally, I tugged on the supple leather boots that hugged my calves and sighed happily. The woolen cloak covered my sword without blocking access to drawing it. I felt more like myself than I had in days.

By the time Rivven returned, I had rolled up my remaining belongings, ready to be packed.

"You've been busy," he mused, setting a sack of food on the table as he eyed me up and down. He then freed two leather bags with long straps from his shoulder and tossed me one.

"What's this?" I peered inside the empty satchel.

"It's for your belongings so we can travel." Rivven began stuffing his own things inside the new bag as I scoffed.

"This won't fit half of what I bought."

"It will," he insisted. "It's crafted with elven magic. There's always room for more. Just be careful not to put anything too heavy inside. The weight doesn't disappear, just the bulk. And that new harness for your sword? That'll meld to your body, so no one sees it either. You have the element of surprise that way."

Humming, I began filling my new bag with my ready clothing. True to his word, everything went in easily.

"So...when Galan gets here, we set out right away? For Tromodia?" I asked as Rivven pulled out a netted bag filled with pila fruit.

"Knowing Galan, he'll want to rest for a day or two. He isn't always welcomed in elven villages, so he enjoys when I sponsor his arrival." Rivven kicked off his boots and crossed his feet over the top of the table.

I snagged the bag of fruit out of the way and sat opposite him. "So, he didn't pass the test with the black spike?"

Smirking, Rivven stood again to fill some cups with mead he'd bought. He tugged the cork out with his teeth before pouring. "The black spike, as you refer to it, is a screening measure. And no, he didn't pass."

"Was it painful?" I asked, leaning forward to accept my drink.

"No." Rivven averted his eyes as he drew deeply from his cup then set it down. "It shouldn't be. I truly hadn't realized Elora would react the way she did to you."

I downed some of the mead then stood and picked up the discarded dress from the floor. After wrinkling my nose at it, I tossed it into the fireplace.

"She wouldn't want it with all that *pila* juice on it anyway," I said, sitting back down.

"There's a thing called a wash basin," Rivven said.

We both laughed. It might have been the first time things felt easy between us, and I liked it. But guilt threatened to choke me. Rune was trapped as always, maybe further gone than ever, and so desperate, she had put this strange magic in me. And here I was, laughing and drinking with an almost king and a new wardrobe.

I set the cup hard on the table, letting my mood darken the lightness between us. Strained was better. Safer.

"What?" Rivven asked, setting his own cup down far more gently. He sat up then, putting his leg back on the ground and leaning toward me despite my cold attitude.

Drawing a deep breath, I looked him in the eyes and squeezed the wooden goblet. "I'm going to enter the Imrati and help you kill the king."

The only sign that he heard me was the rise of one bushy eyebrow. I sipped my mead and waited. *I've made up my mind.* I wasn't sure if the dreams were real, but I'd made a promise and it felt right. I could either run and hide for the rest of my miserable life with guilt as my only companion, or I could do something useful and put my training to work. Maybe if the gods looked favorably upon me, I would find a way to save my sister and put her on the throne.

"I was planning on entering," Rivven said finally, stroking the side of his cup with his thumbs. "The general plan is to win, earn the betrothal to the princess, and then, when I'm close enough, strike down the evil king."

"You've heard about the princess?" I asked through a constricted throat.

"I did a little research just now. I wanted more information, since I know you were telling the truth. I'm still trying to figure out why the king's suddenly running the trials now after keeping the powerstone for himself for so long. But I'd be a fool not to use it to my advantage. He's in such a rush he may well make a mistake with his security, allowing me to get close. The date's been set for solstice. That's less than a month away."

I nodded, having wondered the same about my father's motives, but I couldn't tell Rivven everything. "He'll recognize me...from the keep. He wants the magic in me. I'll have to disguise myself." I still hadn't mentioned the fact that I was his daughter. I wasn't sure that would be a good idea with Rivven's easily changed moods. The fact I hated the king should be enough to trust me. That and we both had reason not to want him getting his hands on my—Rune's power. Watching the light go out of Balram's eyes with my new blade thrust through his heart was such a beautiful thought, I grinned.

"I doubt the king will allow women to enter," Rivven said, watching me. "If he means to extend his line..."

I shrugged. "The winner only names the betrothed. I know it's a technicality, but it's enough. He'll be looking for magic wielders though. Strong ones. So that's what the trials will be geared toward."

"Are you sure you want to do this?" he asked, voice softer than I'd yet heard from him. "You don't have to. I would accept help with suggestions, like the one you just made. Information and insight. But bringing the magic you hold so close when he wants it so badly—I hate to agree with you, but I'm not sure it's a good idea."

"You don't think I'm capable of winning?" I narrowed my eyes and squeezed my cup tighter.

"That's not what I said. Though I think you need some more training if you mean to win. Until now, your instincts have been to run as far from him as possible. What changed?" He drained the rest of his cup and sat back, tilting the chair with him.

"If we work together, then we have a better chance. Whoever wins can name you. And if one of us is eliminated, we can look for an opening before that even happens." I ignored his last question, hoping to convince him of the logic in having both of us in the contest.

"I will be the one to kill him either way." Rivven's jaw clenched along with every visible muscle in his body. His eyes glowed.

Standing, I leaned over the table, close enough to feel the heat emanating from him. "We both have good reason to want to end him. If I have the opportunity first, I will strike. I make no promises otherwise."

Slowly, his gaze drew upward to meet mine. I refused to flinch away, no matter the wrath and deep lines of his furious face. "What did he do to you other than try to take your power, little spy?"

For a moment I remained still, a million and one non-answers filtering through my head. But it was important for Rivven to understand how personal this was to me. So much more so than he could ever imagine.

Do I trust him enough to tell him the truth? This one decision could drive a wedge between us before I could even begin the journey. One way or another I would accomplish my goal, but it would be easier with an ally —especially one with Rivven's powers and resources.

I dropped into my seat, back and neck so stiff that I felt like a brittle branch ready to snap.

"My father," I began, staring down at the remnants of the drink that now soured in my stomach. Any buzz dissipated with my words. "You assumed he was dead, but he's not. He ignores my existence. But I have the better end of the bargain."

"I didn't ask—"

"Let me finish." I looked up quickly then down again, my fingers twisting in my lap. "I have a sister. She gets all the attention, but it's a far worse situation for her because he is an evil man who delights in abuse."

"I'm sorry," Rivven said, softer again. The man was the epitome of fire and water, complete opposites that might rise at any moment to overtake the other.

"Don't be. The thing is, I'm a bastard child. I don't even know who my mother was, and that's how I'm treated. The only reason I stayed at the keep was to be there for my sister. Not that I was ever brave enough to stand up to him for her." The last thought brought tears of bitterness to my eyes. I hated myself for my weakness. For my fear. *What does my life matter when I've spent it hiding?*

Rivven rose and came to my side, kneeling next to me. Still, I refused to look at him. Not even when his fingers found mine, gently prying my hand from its clenched partner and folding it between his—large, rough, and warm.

"You see, the king wanted my sister's power. She is a true sorceress. And he, well, he's been siphoning it from her, bit by bit, using the crystal in his scepter. I've seen him do it with my own eyes, hidden behind the curtains while she suffered." My voice caught, but I forced myself to go on. "And then the day before you found me in the woods, he tried so hard to break her open and get it all that she..." I turned to face him, tears free falling freely now. I hardly cared. I didn't deserve them or the look of pity on his face.

I stared at our hands, at his dark copper skin. He waited, silent, as I swallowed and steadied myself.

"She put it in me somehow," I whispered. "Her magic. And I ran. The royal advisor and the guard came after me, but I made it past the wall."

I waited, expecting him to ask who my father was, to pry the knowledge out of me. But instead, Rivven guided me into his arms, sliding me onto his knee so I could lay my head in the crook of his neck, where his now substantial stubble scratched lightly at my skin. His warmth and the security of his arms around me seeped into my body. I let go, sobbing against him as he held me, unmoving until I emptied myself of tears.

When I quieted sometime later, he turned his head, sliding against my cheek and pressing his mouth to the top of my head.

"Just because your sister had it worse, doesn't mean your suffering was invalid."

I gasped a little, still pressed into him.

Then I sat up straighter, wiping my face, and he rose with me. He offered his hands, steady and sure, and helped lift me to my feet. For a moment, he kept his grip on my arms, as though unsure whether I could stand on my own.

I wasn't sure either.

"I can't imagine how a man could give his daughter over to a king to do with as he willed. Your father rivals King Balram himself for the title of most evil. Perhaps we should kill them both."

"I have to rescue my sister. And the only way to do that is to see the king dead." I fueled the words with all the vehemence I'd released, ignoring his assessment, which was far too close to the truth.

"I will see to it. And I agree to your terms." Rivven released my arms and tilted my chin up to face him.

"My terms?" I asked, trying to steady the trembling in my body.

"If you have the opportunity first, you may make the kill. But know I don't intend to let that happen."

I nodded, sniffing.

Rivven's forehead touched mine. His warm breath wafted over my chest and ripples of desire sparked to life unexpectedly, as though he'd sent an ember floating down to dry kindling. I sucked in a breath at the intense sensation. I'd never been this open—this intimate—with anyone. Even with Rune, I never shared my guilt for fear of her trying to absolve me of it.

His large hands slid up my arms, leaving tingling, oversensitive skin in their wake. I moved my head against his, forehead to forehead, sharing breath even as mine sped up, reveling in the intensity of whatever was happening. One palm slid to my cheek, and I leaned in, nuzzling into the touch. His other hand slipped over my shoulder and down my back where he tugged me closer until our bodies aligned, hard muscle to pounding heart.

I'd taken a chance on opening up, and I wasn't upset with where it had taken me. Feeling raw, bold, and overwhelmed with Rivven's proximity, I never wanted him to stop. I wrapped my arms around his shoulders, trying to keep him close. Tilting my head to look into his eyes, I found them filled with flames once again, but this time, it was the kind of fire I yearned to devour me.

I needed...more. But more what?

Memories of the kiss we'd shared when he'd shut me up in front of Elora floated through me. Yes, that was the more I longed for.

Just as I rose onto my tiptoes to reach for him, a knock erupted at the door.

Rivven released me and I fell to my feet as he backed away several steps, staring at me wide eyed and panting. I stared back, pressing a finger to my lips where I'd longed to connect with him.

The knock sounded again, each bang making me wince.

Rivven spun and strode to the door as I attempted to straighten myself out. When he threw it open, a man stood on the other side, leaning against the doorpost. Golden hair framed his face and green eyes crinkled in a way that promised mischief. Silken robes of emerald draped over him with golden embroidery, and though his chest also peeked through, showing a glimpse of a beautiful body, it wasn't as muscled as Rivven's. By the smooth glow of his skin, I imagined he did far fewer physical tasks and honed it mostly through exercises done in the comfort of the indoors.

He and Rivven embraced, slapping each other on the back as though it were some sort of mutual greeting ceremony. I watched the stranger with curious reservation as he entered and eyed me, making me feel so naked, I had to glance down to be sure I still had my clothing on.

"You didn't tell me you'd have a welcome party waiting," he quipped, taking a step closer. "I would have hurried."

"You were supposed to hurry anyway," Rivven said, stopping him with a grip on his shoulder as I backed up into the mattress. "And this is Nyah. She will be joining us."

"You must be Galan," I said carefully, unsure of our new companion.

"At your service, M'lady." Galan bowed with a flourish, winking as he raised his head. Then he straightened and sauntered to the table, inspecting the open bottle of mead before swallowing some. "I thought you hired a merry band of thieves, Riv. I can't blame you for changing your mind though. I'd prefer the company of a beautiful woman as well."

"They didn't work out," Rivven grumbled, stepping between us. "Nyah is from Centos. She has information on the king. She is how I learned of the Imrati."

"Hmm." Galan swallowed another mouthful, made a face, and set the bottle on the table. "Yes, well everyone in the civilized world knows now. So if you weren't busy running around in the Night Forest, you'd have heard anyway."

"I'm more than an informant," I said, crossing my arms. The weight of my new sword remained a steady support at my back. "I'm going to enter the Imrati along with Rivven."

"Is that so?" Galan sat in the seat I'd previously occupied and cocked his head to assess me again. He tapped his upper lip, which was as clean shaven as Rivven's was last night.

If Rivven's arm hadn't shot out to prevent it, I'd have had my new weapon pointed at his throat to demonstrate some of my other useful skills. As it was, my hand stayed gripped around the hilt behind my shoulder while my body tensed, abdomen pressing against Rivven's restraining motion.

"You should know by now not to judge by appearances, Galan." Rivven neither moved to release me nor looked my way. "Next time I won't stop her from showing you what she's capable of."

"Apologies." Galan stood and reached a hand toward me.

I growled, making Rivven sigh.

"Please try to get along. These next few weeks are already going to be intense enough as we prepare." He dropped his arm, and I released my blade, but still didn't take Galan's hand.

"I really am sorry," Galan said with a pout. "I do tend to come on strong sometimes. It was a shock to hear of Rivven wanting to bring a woman along if I'm being honest. He spends his days so serious. Always planning, training, plotting, and never trusting anyone at his side. Well, present company excluded, of course. I'm also surprised someone as lovely as you agreed to stick to him. After all, fun isn't exactly something he knows how to do."

Rolling my eyes, I glanced at Rivven, who indeed had gone quite serious. "You seem to think women 'as lovely as me' are for fun. The last man who acted on that belief is carrion in the Night Forest."

Galan's eyebrows shot up as he backed away palms out. "No offense intended. I can see why Riv seems to appreciate your company. You two are cut from the same cloth."

"Let's get to work," Rivven said, gesturing for me to sit in the other seat as he took a spot on the edge of the mattress.

I swallowed, thinking how close I'd come to losing control with him just minutes earlier. Perhaps I owed Galan a favor for interrupting what could have been a huge mistake. I had witnessed many couples finding each other and invariably torn apart for some reason or another. And it wasn't fair to Rune, who was stuck with our father. I had to spend my time focused on rescuing her. Then maybe...

"You're deep in thought," Galan noted, catching my attention. They'd been chatting about the specifics of registering for the Imrati among other details as I'd drifted into my reverie.

"I'm thinking about how the king must be stopped and how much I'm going to enjoy seeing the life drain from his eyes."

Galan peered at Rivven who watched me with a subtle smile on his lips. Lips that were more addictive than mead.

"She's perfect for you." Galan raised a glass at us and drank deeply.

"I'm going to go for a walk," I said, rising. "I'd like to see more of Elvenloft before we go, while the two of you plan the logistics."

Half expecting Rivven to protest, I made my way slowly to the entrance. But instead of trapping me or insisting on staying with me lest I escape, Rivven simply traced my movements with his gaze as I opened the door. Warmth flooded my belly as I met his eyes before closing it behind me.

Somehow things had changed. I'd gone from prisoner to partner in crime, from spy to...I didn't know what I was to him, or what I wanted to be, assuming I got the chance to *be* anything. Even the thought of prioritizing what I might want felt foreign and wrong while Rune was still captive.

I sighed. Using my new found freedom as a distraction.

My march down the boardwalks and levels of the city started at a harried pace as though I was trying to outrun something. But as I reached the second to bottom level, I slowed my stride. Here were living quarters, succulent gardens, and playgrounds where children swung from bars and laughed with shrill and careless voices.

My feet came to a stop to watch a small girl with pointed ears and wild, dark hair leap across a make-believe obstacle. She blocked a friend's fake assault with a wooden sword. That's probably what I looked like at her age. But when I searched my mind, a growing sense of panic filled me as I came up empty.

I hadn't thought about my childhood in well...I couldn't even remember the last time, and now that I had, I found the memories eluded me. Like far off wisps of smoke, they were impossible to hold on to. Somehow, someone had stolen parts of who I was like ripping pages from a book. The idea of it made me lightheaded. The harder I tried to pry open my mind, the more my anxiety rose, and the closest thing I could grasp was a memory of being a fourteen-year-old girl, standing in the hallway outside of my sister's room with the urge to run.

Icy fingers of dread slid along my spine as I backed away from the raucous children. Their screams and laughter suddenly overwhelmed me, too loud to accommodate. I threw my hands over my ears, trying to wall it off as my pulse thundered in my temples.

I ran into something and spun, sinking into a fighting stance, but thankfully, not drawing my sword on the tall elf facing me. He was thin and wiry, spectacles resting on the bridge of his long nose.

"Are you alright, miss?"

"I—yes. I'm fine. Thank you. Just a bit lost."

"Oh." He smiled then, relief washing over his delicate elf features. It was a wonder Rivven had come out so massive, when all these elves seemed so willowy. "Perhaps I can help then? What were you looking for? This level is off limits to outworlders. For protection of the vulnerable, you understand."

A glance back at the playground showed that most of the kids had stopped their games and gathered around the edge of the boardwalk to gawk at me. Some looked curious, others frightened.

"I didn't mean to scare anyone," I said, relaxing. "I'm so sorry. I'll just be going." I rushed past the man to the nearest staircase.

"Wait. Miss, what were you searching for?" he asked from behind.

I paused. "I guess I wanted to go outside for a bit." The truth was I didn't think he could point me toward wherever my lost memories were hiding.

"Are you sure? The desert isn't a friendly place."

"Just for a few minutes," I clarified. "I need some space to think."

The elf nodded like he understood and pointed me upstairs. "Topmost platform is where you'll find the curtain. Be sure the guard knows to let you back in."

"Thanks." I smiled and offered my hand. "I'm Nyah."

"Trenton." The man shook and grinned. "It's a pleasure to meet you. I've never met an outworlder before to be honest. Just seen some at a distance. I don't mean to be forward, but I'd love to find out more about you. For scientific purposes, of course." A deep blush worked its way up his cheeks, reddening them more than they already were. "I'm a historian. Research and learning are my passions."

I grinned. "I'd like that. I'm fascinated by the subject. I'd love to learn more about your kind as well." Maybe making friends wasn't as hard when you didn't live in an oppressive, soul sucking place.

"How about tonight? I'd be happy to treat you to dinner at my favorite eatery, the Dusty Rose. Fourth level outside the marketplace. Say at moonrise?"

As long as romance wasn't his purpose in inviting me, I didn't see the harm. The more I could learn about the elves and the rest of the forbidden lands, the more information I'd have in my arsenal to work with to free my sister. That was how I should be spending my time.

Still, I thought about Rivven, and the idea made me squirm for some reason. I pictured him and Galan and decided I was happy for an excuse to stay away from the cramped room while they plotted. I still wasn't sure I cared for Galan much. But it would be easier to give him an honest chance, if I could keep some distance.

"Sounds nice. Thank you." I turned to go and leaned over the last flight downward, curious as to what lay beneath.

"Nyah, don't." Trenton warned. "It's not safe. Only the elders and the guards go down there."

"Why?" I peered over the railing again, but all seemed quiet. The guards I'd noticed when we'd arrived were nowhere to be seen.

"The door to the deep is there," he whispered, checking behind him to make sure the children had gone back to playing and lost interest in us. "That's where the beasts of the Deadlands dwell. You know, Valley Serpents and *scarlions* and such." He shuddered. "The things that hide beneath the sands outside."

"I see," I agreed with another glance. But I didn't. Trenton looked far too pale to hound with questions. So instead, I turned toward the steps leading upward. "See you later."

Trenton relaxed, gripping the wooden rail. "I look forward to it."

ELEVEN

To my consternation, Galan was the only one in the rooms when I returned. He leaned back in Rivven's chair sipping his wine when I entered.

"Hello again, Nye." He tipped his goblet toward me, but I glared in response.

"My name is Nyah," I said, rummaging through my new belongings.

"Yes, but Nye is so much easier on the tongue. That's what nicknames are for. So friends don't have to put as much energy into formality with each other."

"What shall I call you then?" I asked, forcing some fake cheer. "Other than Galan or arsehole I mean?"

He laughed uproariously at what he assumed was my joke. "Oh, you are a fun one. You may call me Gray if you like. It's short for Gray Fox, which is my moniker back home in my village."

"Oh?" I selected a satiny black jumpsuit for my outing this evening. "And why is that?"

"I am known as an excellent tracker as well as a wily business partner. With my sparkling personality I can talk my way into or out of just about any situation you can think of."

"I see. Well, Gray, I am in need of some privacy to get ready for dinner tonight. So, if you would be so kind as—"

"Dinner?" He stood up, eyes gleaming with interest. "I didn't know we had plans?"

I snorted. "We don't. There are other people that exist."

"Indeed. Well, I shall be intrigued as to how Riv takes this news." He winked, set down his goblet and moved to the door.

"It has nothing to do with Riv," I retorted, though something in my gut twisted when Galan mentioned him. *Why would it upset Rivven? I'm not his prisoner any longer. He trusts me.* Would he think it was a romantic dinner? Surely, he wouldn't assume that...

"As you say, Nye." With that, he left the room.

I hurried over to lock the door, then I set about washing up in the basin and making myself presentable. With every passing minute, my mood soured until I was huffing and tossing things as I used them, grumbling about men and their assumptions about women.

The moment I'd shared with Rivven played on a loop in my mind, waking my body to wants and wonderings that confused my feelings even further.

When I decided I was pleased with my hair pulled up on the sides and loose behind my shoulders, I strode to the door and threw it open, only to find Rivven with his hands crossed and one leg up against the doorframe as though he'd been waiting.

"Did I lock you out?" I asked, confused.

Straightening to his full and substantial height, Rivven glowered at me, drinking in my appearance from head to toe and back up again, stoking whatever fire he'd imbedded earlier. I shifted uncomfortably, wishing he would speak.

Except I had Trenton waiting for me. *Right.*

"If you aren't going to say anything, then at least move aside." I attempted to shoulder past him.

Grabbing my arms, he stopped me from passing and leaned down to sniff me.

"What are you doing?" I asked bewildered.

"You're wearing perfume," he said at last. "Lilac and orange blossom."

I swallowed. "Very astute nose. It was the scent I picked from the vendor."

"Your natural scent is nicer," he said, releasing my arms. "It's more of a moonflower and angel's trumpet combination. Both poisonous but lovely."

My mouth parted, yet I had no response. *Was that a compliment or a barb?* I couldn't be sure, so I cleared my throat.

"Um, I didn't realize you knew plants so well."

Riven shrugged. "It's something one learns with an education in magic."

A flush warmed my cheeks. I hadn't been trained in magic. Nor had it occurred to me that normal wielders would go to school for such things. As a princess of any other realm, I supposed I would have been raised with tutors in magic and history, but not as Balram's daughter. No such lessons existed. Another of my father's controlling whims, presumably to prevent his people from being able to overthrow him.

For the first time, I felt pity for my father. With all his great power came paranoia that someone would take it away. Someone like him.

"I...have to go." Yet I remained still, not wanting to leave Rivven's orbit. Was it a royal thing? Did he, the legitimate king, exude the air of a man who was so important that his very aura drew one in like a black hole?

"I heard you have dinner plans." The tendon in his neck jumped.

"I—" I paused and shifted my weight. "I see Gray isn't much of a secret keeper."

"Was he supposed to keep this from me?"

"No. I don't mind you knowing." I wanted Rivven's jealousy, which was a ridiculous, childish truth that sent a wave of shame over me. I had to forget the feelings he'd unleashed in me. I had to stuff down any wonderings about the future. We were partners, but not that kind of partners. We would work together to kill the king and free Rune. This was all just ridiculousness on my part.

"You can't go."

"What?" I snapped out of whatever strange headspace I'd been occupying and straightened.

"I'm sorry, but you can't."

"You are not my captor any longer," I said, glad I had my sword strapped to my back beneath my cloak.

"No, but I am your betrothed. At least as far as these people know. And if they find out that isn't the case, then we are both in trouble."

I forced a harsh laugh. "What are they going to do? I think Elora would be thrilled to find out we aren't a couple."

Rivven grabbed hold of me again as I made to pass him by. I wiggled, but he held firm with his damn giant hands.

"I mean it, Nyah. Elves take truth seriously. They will try to kill us if they find we've lied to get you inside the city."

Stilling, I thought through his words. "Why didn't you tell me this sooner?"

"The last thing I expected was for you to leave my presence for the first time and seduce someone."

"Seduce!" I couldn't control the rising of my voice. But I shook my head and took a breath. "There was no seducing. It isn't even a romantic meeting. Besides, we're leaving soon."

"Yes, tomorrow. Galan wanted to stay longer, but we have limited time to train before the Imrati."

"Trenton is waiting for me," I admitted. "I just wanted to learn more about the elves."

"Why not ask me?" Rivven said, stepping closer so that his body was nearly touching mine.

"I just...I met him when I was wandering and he's a historian." I shrugged my shoulders as best I could in his grasp. "You said yourself you were raised with humans."

"Have I upset you somehow?" Rivven lifted me and set me on the inside of the door, then closed it behind him as he walked me backward into the room.

"Upset me?" I squeaked the words. "No. Well, other than tying me up and assuming I was a spy and acting like I had no choices in my life anymore? Not really."

"Hmm."

"Hmm what?" I snapped looking up at his stubbornly beautiful face. Then I grinned. "You haven't shaved again."

"So?" he asked, stroking his near beard.

"So, I told you I liked the beard better. Now you're growing it."

"Coincidence."

"If you say so."

Before he could retort, the door swung inward once again and an out of breath Galan entered, face ashen.

"What's happened?" Rivven stepped in front of me, I wasn't sure if it was to protect me or to exclude me, but either way I wasn't pleased.

"They're coming. We have to get out of here. Now."

Rivven turned and rushed to shove things into his satchel as I rounded on Galan.

"Who's coming?" I asked.

"Your dinner companion must have told someone," he answered. "The Elvenloft Council is coming to arrest you both."

"How long?" Rivven asked from the other side of the bed.

"Maybe five minutes."

"This is insane." I grasped the bag Rivven thrust at me. "They're really going to arrest us for lying about a private matter like our relationship?"

"Elves are not human. They are quite strict when it comes to rules and honesty. What you and I think is insane, they may embrace," Rivven explained.

"Elves will be elves," Galan agreed, holding the door open as Rivven ushered me out. "Carn is waiting outside. He refused to leave without us."

"Who's Carn?" I asked from between them as they peered around the boardwalk before hurrying forward.

"Stop!" Elora's voice screamed at us from halfway up the stairs to the exit.

"By Xylon's flames," Galan swore under his breath. "It's never simple with you, Riv."

"No need to bring the god of the seven hells into this," Rivven muttered, shoving me back the opposite direction. Besides, this is all on Nyah."

"I had no idea such wild rules existed," I exclaimed as we rushed forward, darting around and between people. "You could have warned me."

"Riv probably thought you wouldn't be interested in anyone but him.

He is quite the lady's man." Galan's teasing proclamation seemed to darken Rivven's mood more than the situation. His eyes glowed and he grumbled so low it almost sounded like an animal instead of human speech.

"Stop, Rivven. It's her I want. I'll let you pass." Elora's words carried above the confusion of the crowd and the thundering of our feet as we ran to the marketplace level.

"Bitch!" I yelled back, but Rivven's grip on my arm prevented me from turning around to face her with my sword.

"I can't protect you if you run," Elora said as Galan leaped over a wagon full of vegetables.

"They're coming the other way too," I said, freezing in my tracks. I could see the tops of several heads bobbing their way toward us at excessive speed.

Galan turned from the other side of the cart and freed a glittering golden rapier. "I'll hold them off."

"No." Rivven pulled his sword. "I'll stall with Elora. Take Nyah and get to Carn."

"No." I grabbed his hand. "I don't trust her."

"Go," he ordered.

"No," I said again. "We're all going."

"Come on, sweetheart." Galan lifted me from behind and climbed nimbly over the railing. We dangled on the edge of the third level from top.

"Let go!" I yelled, wanting to beat him with my fists, but clinging for dear life for fear of falling to my death.

The next moment, Galan jumped, his emerald cloak billowing out around us as we went into freefall. Screams tore from my throat as the bottom of my stomach dropped out. But a buoyant wind pressed up against us so hard that our descent slowed.

"Relax. I'm an air weaver," Galan said. When I looked at his face, his smug expression angered me even more.

But I've done the same haven't I? Or close to it. When jumping from the citadel.

I blinked. This was at least part of the magic Rune had shared with me. I knew it came from her mother the air wielder. It had taken me to safety when I'd been desperate to escape Centos. Maybe I could finally find out how to use it.

"How do you do it?" I demanded as we floated toward the very bottom of the city. Exactly where Trenton said was forbidden.

Galan laughed, but my expression cut it short. "I just...call to the air and focus on my intention I suppose."

"Right." When we passed the second to last level where I'd met Trenton earlier, I deemed it close enough to be safe and shoved away from Galan.

Spreading my arms I fell backward, calling to the wind and ignoring his colorful exclamation. *Soft landing*, I willed. Then I felt it. The same buoyancy I'd sensed with Galan pushed against my back and my heart leaped.

I was doing it. I was flying.

Then I hit the sand, hard, knocking the breath from my lungs. But it was soft enough that I didn't suffer any lasting damage and accepted Galan's hand up a moment later.

"Next time a little warning," he said. "I didn't understand what the hells you were doing."

"I'll warn you, if you warn me before jumping off railings," I countered then looked around. To the left were the enormous double doors fashioned of giant logs and trimmed in gold.

"That's the council's quarters," Galan explained. He steered me to the other side where a dark corridor wound out of sight. Flickering light from sconces teased the path. "And that's the way to the—"

"Deep," I finished, recalling what Trenton had taught me. I stalked toward the passageway with him in my wake.

Twelve

When we reached the entrance, Galan yanked a torch from the wall and pressed a finger to his lips. He mouthed the word *guards* and once again pulled his rapier. I followed silently.

This was more my territory—sneaking up on some guards. The familiarity of it was a strange relief as I freed my sword and stuck to the shadows hugging the walls. This was where my preference for dark clothing came in handy. Galan's flashy outfits, on the other hand, would make a great distraction. I'd have to remember to thank him later.

Sure enough, on the final turn, an enormous round steel door loomed ahead flanked by two elven guards in leather armor, donning silver helmets and gleaming swords of their own.

"Halt," one barked, raising their weapons at Galan.

"I would if I weren't in a hurry," my companion said with obvious regret. "But I am, so I'd appreciate it if you'd step aside. I hate to hurt anyone."

Both guards attacked at once.

Galan darted to the side, kicking one to the floor with a well-placed boot to his rump. The other he blocked with his rapier, and surprisingly, the thin sword held against the thicker one, bowing but slightly under the strain.

I sprung forward, running for the door, only to find a strange control in the form of a chunk of quartz on a slanted podium.

Open.

I willed the crystal to turn, trying the same approach as air magic. As I set my hand on the stone, the loud screech of metal assaulted my ears. Sand tumbled from the edges as the doors opened on an even darker tunnel that seemed to feed through the sand itself. *Of course.* The deep was so named as this exit was buried beneath the desert.

There wasn't much choice. Either back, and fight the whole damn city —or out. We'd have to take our chances without. I joined Galan's fight, parrying just in time to save him from being stabbed in the back by the guard he'd sent to the floor earlier.

"Door's open," I called over my shoulder as Galan fought at my back. "Just stab him and let's go."

"I don't want to kill anyone," Galan said through the clanking of metal.

I sighed. "Then wound." I feigned to the right and dropped to my knees, stabbing upward to catch the guard I was fighting right below the shoulder joint. He dropped with a cry of pain. I winced.

"You should've let us through." I kicked him to the floor as I held onto my blade. He slid off the cold metal, releasing it.

When I turned, I found Galan releasing the body of the other guard from a chokehold. The man sank to his knees and then the ground.

"He's just unconscious," Galan said.

"I don't really care," I answered and rushed through the tunnel.

Galan scooped up the fallen torch and joined my side with an appraising look. The sand gave beneath our feet, making it far more difficult to hurry as we moved up the sloping passage. The groan of the giant door shutting behind us made my jaw clench.

"I wish you a painful death in there," the guard shouted at us. His laugh turned to coughing as we were swallowed by the darkness. Only the torch Galan held gave any reprieve. Yet, it cast more moving shadows in a shallow circle, not far enough forward to provide any semblance of light.

A combination of apprehension, and the difficulty of the gradual climb, had us moving cautiously. I recalled the strange names of the beasts Trenton had mentioned, and the shudder they'd evoked. Swallowing, I glanced at Galan the Gray Fox, wondering if he was as uncertain as I was. His narrowed gaze fixed ahead as if he could will himself to see beyond the dancing light of the torch.

I bit my lip, afraid if I spoke, I'd attract the attention of some horrifying monster, sure the cravenbeast from the Night Forest would be nothing in comparison. Despite the punishing upward angle of the path, I'd managed to find a decent pace, adjusting to the give of the sand.

Galan's arm shot out to stop me.

Holding my breath, I readied my sword and waited. Straining, I picked out the soft sound of scratching further into the tunnel. Clicking and tapping followed.

Galan leaned over my ear and whispered, "Scarlions."

It was entirely unhelpful as I still had no clue what those were. I didn't dare whisper back. Instead, I waited as Galan held the torch to the sides of the tunnel, ducking as he felt along the wall of sand. It had to be magic holding up the tunnel as the thin grains collapsed into sheets of dust when he touched them. We'd have been buried alive without it.

Focusing on the clicking and scratching as it grew louder caused panic to grab hold. Galan dropped to his knees and stretched with the torchlight. He waved vigorously for me to hurry,. He'd found a smaller tunnel, serving as an offshoot from the main one. It wasn't big enough to travel through, but it was enough to offer shelter if we curled inside.

He ushered me in first then squeezed in beside me. With his knees to chest and his head ducked in he couldn't have been comfortable.

"Put out the torch," I whispered as softly as possible.

"They're sightless," he muttered back.

Small mercies. I hated the thought of being trapped down here in complete darkness. Though I nearly changed my mind when the first of the trio of scarlions emerged. It took all I had not to gasp or scream when the pincers, big enough to snap a full-grown man in half came into view, followed by the head. No eyes, only antenna that quivered as it searched ahead by vibration and a bug-like beak that looked as horrifying as the pincers.

The thing just kept coming, six long legs scuttling through the sand on points, lifting and plunging into the ground in turn to keep it moving at a good pace despite the give. The exoskeleton was near see-through white and covered its grotesque body. Finally, a curved tail with a wicked point on the end emerged, dripping with a dark viscous substance I had no doubt was poison.

Galan and I could have lain head to foot and not been as long as the creature. When two more joined it, I swallowed hard. We remained still, the only movement that of the flickering flame Galan held aloft. The beasts paused, clicking pincers and twitching antennae. The front scarlion swung its tail over its head, and the two behind it scurried along the sides of the tunnel, one just missing our hiding spot. The other skittered to the ceiling of the tunnel, defying gravity.

Just move on, I prayed to whatever gods could hear me.

The front one swished its tail again then began walking forward, back the way we'd come. The one on the side by us followed, dropping to the floor a moment later. But the last one disappeared outside of the torch's flame and high above our vantage point.

We waited, hoping it would follow its friends into the tunnel, but only silence greeted us. If my legs were this cramped, I was sure Galan had to be close to losing feeling. Carefully I tapped his hand with a finger.

Slowly he shook his head. But the longer we waited, the closer the torch came to burning out, and being in the dark with that thing was even worse than facing it. Maybe it had scurried back up the corridor where it came from and was too high to see it. Or maybe it had found another side tunnel like the one we were in but big enough for it to fit. Or maybe it was sleeping.

We couldn't just stay here forever. We had weapons and magic.

Still, I followed Galan's lead and remained as silent as possible, until another sound made us both turn toward the inside of the tunnel we huddled in. *What else?* It had to at least be smaller than the scarlion to fit in here. But small didn't always equal safe—even I knew that.

Galan's face twisted as he quietly cursed with every expression I'd ever heard and more. He grabbed my wrist and met my eyes with what I read to be a *we act now* expression. My favorite kind.

He unwound his body, climbing from our spot gracefully into a crouch and holding the torch as he peered upward. The scarlion dropped from the ceiling above, making him spin around to face it, sword out, as I joined him on the ground.

One giant pincer snapped at him, but I slid beneath and thrust my sword into one of the creature's joints. The thing emitted a shriek as dark grayish blood oozed around me. Galan yanked me from beneath as it flailed.

"Watch out for the stinger," Galan shouted, forgoing the silence, since it obviously knew where we were.

We both ducked and rolled to avoid the swing of its deadly tail. It was that exact moment something slithered from the side tunnel to join the battle. I snatched the torch from his hand and waved it toward my feet, revealing an enormous serpent. Its mouth was open with several rows of jagged teeth the size of my arm.

"Valley serpent," Galan shouted.

"What do we do?" I asked, scurrying backwards into my companion. He lifted me to my feet as he blocked another tail attack with his sword.

"Run?" he asked as I swung at the snake thing that struck toward me, forcing it to the side.

"Hard to run in this sand," I countered, backing toward the angled path we'd originally been on.

"We're close to the surface. I can feel the air currents." Galan pierced another joint on one of the scarlion's legs. "If we can get out of the tunnel, we'll be fine."

I didn't see how that could be true, but I was willing to try f if it gave us a chance. I danced away from another assault by the serpent, which hissed out some sort of liquid. I brandished the torch and caught a glimpse of green mucus sizzling against the sand. *Great.* It spit poison or acid or something.

"Do the scarlions have any natural enemies?" I asked, rolling away from the tail.

"Not underground, which is why we need to get to the top."

"What's up there that can kill them?" I pressed, darting toward the serpent as the scarlion whipped its massive stinger.

"A dragon," Galan shouted as I ducked, letting the tip sink into the snake's body.

Of course, a dragon. I conjured up an image from an illustration in a book I'd read as a teenager and focused with everything I had, hand outstretched. "Cover me," I demanded as I shut my eyes.

Claim it, Rune had said. Fine.

I claim your magic.

My *magic.*

The sound of Galan's blade clashing against exoskeleton answered. I willed with all I had for the illusion magic to take shape. Galan's yelp had me springing my eyelids open, but I smiled at what I found.

I did it. I'd conjured a small black dragon that filled the interior of the tunnel between us and the other beasts. It roared impressively as I grabbed hold of Galan's hand and tugged him up the path.

"Where the hell—"

"I did it. I got lucky." My sister must've transferred some of her other magic also as I'd hoped, and I'd watched her enough through the years to learn a thing or two. "It's illusion magic from Centos, so we have to hurry because when they get brave enough to strike at it, it'll fade."

With that knowledge, Galan used his sword as a kind of walking stick to help propel himself forward, and I followed his example with my own. The torchlight dimmed as the fuel at the top ran low, but another source of light found us from ahead, up the steepest bend of the tunnel. It was so bright I had to shield my eyes.

"The sun," Galan said reverently as he hurried forward.

Clicking and scratching noises rose from behind. When I glanced back, not one, but all three of the scarlions scurried up the incline toward us at double their usual speed.

"I think they're angry." I didn't add that the wicked sting we'd seen it land must've killed the serpent. That only made them seem scarier.

"Come on." Galan grasped my hand, making me drop the torch and our feet lifted from the ground. I joined him in willing us forward as fast as possible. The sun rushed toward us as we flew up the tunnel.

"Carn!" Galan yelled as we burst through to the surface and into the sky, three scarlions snapping at our feet.

I thought we'd made it out of reach when something hard whacked our sides, sending us sprawling into the hot sand. I tumbled to my back in time to see the tail that struck us readjust so its stinger glinted in the sunlight. It hovered above Galan where he lay sprawled on his stomach and dazed beside me.

Holding out my sword, I did my best to prepare for the crushing blow, but a shadow engulfed the view above me. An enormous beast, the color of flame and coal, soared across the sky. It snapped its massive jaws over the scarlion, sending entrails and blood spurting over us like a rainstorm.

Rolling to my side with my arm sheltering my head, I caught my breath and then scrambled to a standing position. The lizard-like animal was chomping its meal and the other two giant bugs disappeared below ground once again. Galan joined me a moment later as I continued to stare at the scaled creature. Its forked tongue slid out to lick the mess left from the meal off his face.

"Ah, Carn. I'd like you to meet Nye."

The beast roared into the air and flopped on his stomach, nose about ten feet from where I stood. I barely reached its shoulders when it lay flat. Swallowing my apprehension, I took a tentative step forward, but Galan lay a hand on my wrist, lowering my sword.

"He's friendly, but if you point your sword at him, he'll probably roast you."

Nodding, I sheathed my weapon and glanced at Galan for approval before approaching the beast. His scales glinted in the light, throwing sparks ranging from yellow to orange to almost red interspersed with the ash color beneath. One large green eye followed me as I reached up a hand and gingerly touched an orange scale bigger than my head. It was hard but also satiny to the touch and warm but not too hot. I stroked its side, enjoying the feel of the scales slipping beneath my palm and stopped when I thought he'd roared again. But I realized after a moment it was more of a purring sound. I continued.

"You better cut that out before he likes you more," Galan said, climbing on one of the creature's legs, then up his back near the neck.

He reached for me, and I accepted a hand up, using my newly found wind magic to help lift me. When I landed, I noticed the leather saddle that sat behind the lizard's neck. It had been camouflaged by the dark spines that stood out in a row on either side of it, each as thick as the trees back home. It was doubtful we'd be easily spotted from up here.

"What is he?" I asked, taking a seat behind Galan.

"Carn? He's a Sand Dragon. No wings, but he can jump far enough, and he breathes fire."

I was sitting on the back of an actual dragon. Not an illusion conjured from a storybook or a fable. *The real thing.* It felt like second nature and a dream all at once. I should have been terrified, but maybe it was the fact it saved us from the scarlions. Or maybe just that in the last few days my entire perception of reality had been tested. Either way my heart raced with excitement.

It was everything I'd ever dreamt of—exploring the unknown, traveling beneath the sun, and the company of others that acknowledged me for who I was. *But who am I?* What kind of person was I if I let myself revel in the moment while my sister suffered? I sighed inwardly.

"Is Carn his full name?" I asked, pushing the dark thoughts aside for another time. "Or is it a nickname like you give everyone else?"

"Riv named him Carnage, but I thought it a bit rough for such a good fellow." Galan leaned down to scratch behind Carn's neck. "He'll take us to the mountains, and from there, we'll travel through the gates of Lehon to Tromodia."

I was about to ask about the gates of Lehon and why Carn wouldn't go with us when a shout in the distance had me snapping my head around.

Rivven ran full tilt across the sand, followed by at least ten elves on smaller lizards of their own. I thought he had a good head start at least; well, that was until the arrows started flying in an arc over his head.

"Go, Carn!" Galan yelled, kicking the saddle.

With a roar, the Sand Dragon reared onto its hind legs—making me grab hold of the side of the saddle—and leaped. He landed between Rivven and the elves, forcing them to a sudden halt where several fell from their steeds.

"Hurry," Galan shouted back at Rivven.

When I turned, I found the large man clutching his side with one hand, blood pouring between his fingers. An arrow protruded from his ribs. The other hand gripped Carn's scales as he struggled to climb toward us.

Without another thought, I called for the wind to lift him and carry him up to us. It set him gently behind me, and I fell to his side, examining the wound.

"You're full of surprises, little spy," he rasped between unsteady breaths.

I barely noticed the fire pouring out of Carn's mouth toward the elves as I sucked in my bottom lip.

"I don't think they hit anything vital." Rivven dismissed me, but the sheen of sweat on his forehead told a different story.

"I need to pull it out and get it clean before you die of infection," I said, already gripping the shaft.

"If you pull it, I'll bleed to death instead," Rivven argued as I fought to balance on the now running dragon.

"What do you recommend then?" My voice pitched high with desperation.

"I'll find a healer at the gate," he said, and then his eyes rolled back in his head. He grimaced, hand covering mine on the arrow.

"They're designed to cause more damage coming out," Galan said, joining me.

I released my hold and sat back, horrified. With all the power my sister gave me, there was none that would heal. That kind of magic belonged only to the gods. Or maybe those that could see the ether that Rivven had described. That was the best form of magic, I realized helplessly.

"There has to be something we can do," I said to Galan as Rivven's head lolled to the side. "Look at the amount of blood he's lost."

"He's had worse. Careful, Nye, or I'll think you care for him."

"I do," I insisted. "Of course, I do. Why wouldn't I care if he died? That's horrid."

Galan's eyes twinkled. "Would you care as much if it were me with a wound?" He pouted, sticking out his bottom lip.

I shoved him hard. "This is serious."

"Just trying to lighten the mood." Galan rubbed his arm where I'd pushed him as the seemingly endless desert flew by around us.

"Are there healers at the gate?" I asked, watching Rivven's copper complexion tarnish with a green tint.

"He isn't looking good, is he?" Galan asked, crawling over to his friend's side. "This isn't...they wouldn't have..."

"What?" I dropped to my knees again and leaned over where Galan was examining Rivven's side.

Without answering, he carefully pulled up Rivven's soaked shirt, gathering it so it didn't disturb the arrow. Beneath the blood where the thing disappeared into his toned muscle, a ripple of blackened skin crawled outward like spider legs, bubbling beneath.

"What is that?" I breathed.

"Poisoned tips." Galan's face went taught with anger. "They use scarlion venom from the stinger. But they're expensive weapons. The idea that they'd use them on Riv is ludicrous. They save those for true enemies."

I was too focused on the idea that there was deadly poison in Rivven's wound to respond. My heart lodged in my throat as tears slid down my cheeks, fast and furious. Black tendrils of poison leached outward from the wound, stretching farther with every passing minute.

"What do we do?" I asked.

Galan remained silent, staring daggers at the spot.

I shoved him again. "How do we stop it?"

"The only ones with that kind of magic are the mountain elves," Galan said. "And they would resist helping him."

"Why?" My hands fisted so hard, my nails cut into the skin of my palms.

"Because his mother didn't leave on good terms." Galan met my eyes. I was surprised to see the glassy look of unshed tears in them. "I'm sorry, Nye."

"No." I shoved him again and he let me, going limp as I took out my rage on him. "I won't accept that. He's still one of them. They should help him. They *have* to help him."

"We can try," Galan agreed, but he neither looked, nor sounded hopeful.

"Carn," I said, voice thick with determination. "Can he get us to the mountain elves?"

A roar answered me as Carn leaped into the air. The mountain range I'd always stared at from the top of the citadel grew closer and closer as he bounded forward. From here, I could make out the jagged outlines of each peak, and the snowy tops grew more defined. Trees and brush dotted the landscape all the way up. The tallest peak rose in the distance, disappearing beneath clouds, but Carn veered toward the smallest one, still an enormous height. I had to crane my neck to see it.

Riven mumbled some words, catching my attention. I leaned over him, ear to his mouth as I placed a palm on his chest.

"Gate," he whispered. I wasn't a hundred percent sure he wasn't just speaking in his sleep.

"First, we have to get you healed," I said, trying my best to be reassuring.

"No," he whispered, pained, "gate first. Have to register...Imrati..."

"What's he saying?" Galan asked, joining me.

"He wants us to register at the gate first," I repeated, incredulous.

"Oh," Galan winced.

"What?" I pressed as our trajectory turned vertical and I nearly fell onto the shaft of Rivven's arrow.

"There's a registration deadline for the Imrati. His evil highness didn't allow much time between the announcement and signing up. Clearly, he wants to limit the participation."

I pressed my eyelids closed. "When is it?"

"Sundown. Today. So approximately...six hours from now I reckon."

"How long will it take to get up the mountain?"

Galan tipped his golden head back as Carn leaped from landing to landing on our way up. His shoulders slumped. "Too much, if you figure in the time it'll take to heal our friend."

"We must do this." I stared down at Rivven. We had to get in the Imrati or I'd lose my best opportunity to help my sister. I'd promised, if only in a dream. But I couldn't let Rivven die just so I could reap revenge on my father.

"Can you register for all of us?" I asked.

"I think identification is required," Galan answered, stroking his smooth face. "Blood usually. Yes, that will work." He rifled inside of his emerald cloak, now filthy with layers of sand, blood, and who knew what else from our journey. Then he pulled out two small vials and handed one to me.

"What's this for?"

"Put some of your blood in it," he instructed as he bent over Rivven to collect some of his spilled blood in the other.

I freed my sword, swiped the edge across my palm, wincing at the sharp pain, then squeezed my fist over the vial until it was half filled. I sheathed the sword, stoppered my blood, and dug in my bag for some cloth to wrap securely around my wound.

"Excellent." Galan snatched the vial from me with a grin. "Leave it to the Gray Fox to get it done. You get our man healed."

"I will," I promised as Carn's jolting pace came to a halt.

"I believe if anyone can other than me, it's you. I must say you've made an impression. Now, get off so I can get back down and register us all. When you finish, Riv will take you to the borderland on the other side of the mountain at the gate. I'll be there waiting."

Galan floated Rivven's unconscious form to the snowy ground, and I followed with my own magic. The air up here was thinner, but fresh, and I'd probably used too much power as every muscle in my body ached with fatigue. But I didn't care. I'd managed more than I ever could without Rune's magic, and I'd keep going until I knew Rivven was going to survive.

Still, when Carn and Galan disappeared down the mountain, my heart lurched. What would happen if I couldn't find help? Or if they refused? It didn't matter. Failure wasn't an option.

Even if I had to hold a blade to someone's throat, I'd see him healed.

THIRTEEN

Finding the mountain elves was not a problem. They found us, emerging from the snow. Bright silver spears glinted in the sun as they pointed them at our hearts. Far larger than the desert dwellers, these elves' muscular physiques and taller stature made a better case for Rivven being related. Like their kin, they had pointed ears, but darker, thicker hair than the desert folk, and more pronounced cheekbones. Apparently, the cold didn't bother them since their clothing left little to the imagination. More worrisome than the weapons leveled at us were their expressions, as cold and menacing as the surroundings.

Leaning protectively over Rivven, I glared at the closest elf who'd stepped forward near his feet. Her hair was wound into a complex braid with bits of what looked like shaped ice crystals dispersed within. Her icy clear eyes narrowed into slits as she fixed her gaze on me.

I had to get this right, yet it was the one thing I was absolutely no good at. Talking to others. I swallowed the dryness in my throat.

"We've come to ask for aid. My companion is half mountain elf and in need of healing. He was hit by a poison arr—"

"Enough." Her sharp command echoed from the rocks and stopped me cold.

My angry breath burst out in clouds of steam as I attempted to control my temper. Insulting her was probably not going to help save Rivven. I waited, continuing to stare back at her. I refused to cower. That was going too far.

"I know who he is," she said after another moment. She relaxed, setting the bottom of the spear in the snow beside her like a walking stick. The elf leaned against it to inspect Rivven. None of the others moved.

"Then you'll help?" I asked, unable to keep the desperation from my voice.

"His mother was banished from our land when she chose to mix with a human sorcerer. He is the product of that unseemly bonding." She curled her lip, and I noticed tiny points on her incisors.

"You can't blame him for his parents' actions." I straightened though still on my knees. "I know I am not *my* father. Rivven is a good man. He is of your blood. Help him."

The elf cocked her head as though considering my words. "You are brave, human. Surely you know none who have ventured into our lands have ever returned."

Tittering broke out among the others in the circle, but I kept my eyes on her.

"His life is worth the risk."

Her eyebrows rose at my response. "I see. And what can you offer me in return for healing?"

This had to be an improvement, if she was asking for payment. But what did I have that she could use? "What is it you want?"

"I doubt you have anything to offer." She bent over, still clutching her spear. "But since you show bravery and concern for one of our blood— banished or not—I am giving you one opportunity to make an offer I may agree to."

No pressure then. I nodded, wracking my brain as she watched me. I doubted they needed magic, and even if they did, me doing some tricks wasn't enough. But maybe if they hated humans, they'd hate the worst of them more...

"This man, Rivven, and I, share the sworn task to assassinate the evil king." I stood then, forcing her to straighten as all those around us whispered. Still, I remained focused on her. "If you heal him, there is a good chance that we will succeed."

"What makes you think you can succeed where everyone else has failed? Especially with a half-human who lays dying at our feet?" she challenged.

"I was raised in the king's keep and have something he wants very badly. Rivven..." I gestured to the unconscious man, so pale and covered in sweat even in the snow, "...trained his whole life for a chance to kill the king. Soon there will be an opportunity outside of Centos, where he is vulnerable. If we work together, me with my knowledge of the king, and him with his skill, then we can do this."

The elf considered this information, and I held my breath. Then she leaned forward and spoke. "And why are you sworn to do this task?"

Inhaling deeply, and knowing the elves' feelings about deceit, I decided to speak the truth. "The evil king is my father. I hate him more than anything. I will succeed at ending his reign of terror and oppression to free my sister, the true heir, who he keeps a prisoner."

For a moment, my announcement was met with silence, save the howl of the wind as the elf stared at me with an expression of stone. Then, as I debated trying to overpower her and force someone to heal Rivven, a smile curled her lips. She pounded her spear twice in the ground.

"Take him to my cave. I will heal him."

My sigh of relief was drowned out as all around us, spears lowered, and whispers turned to shouts, some excited, some angry as several people lifted Rivven and walked him toward a path through the snowy cliffs. I moved to follow but was stopped by the elf's grip on my arm.

"I want his head."

"Excuse me?" I gaped at her.

"The evil king of the humans. If you manage this assassination of yours, you will bring me his head so that I may dance with it on a pyre."

"I...I will see it done," I said, and she smiled, pleased.

"Very well. Come. Join us for dinner while your mate recovers." She moved off toward where they'd disappeared with Rivven so fast it was difficult to keep up.

"He's not my mate," I called after her, but it was either lost to the wind or she didn't care.

The cave felt more like a cavern outfitted with all the comforts of home—a roaring fire at its center and soft animal skin rugs of thick white fur. I sat anxiously upon the rug, watching as the elf murmured over Rivven's wound, slowly passing a hand over the spot.

"*Ayeisha*," she cried as she yanked out the arrow, causing his entire body to jolt. I started to rise, but she dipped a hand in one of several nearby bowls and pressed a handful of mashed berries and leaves to the wound.

The blackened skin had spread to cover most of his torso, creeping up his neck toward his face and down to his hip where his pants rode low. His shirt had been cut off long ago, and his glistening chest rose and fell in an erratic rhythm, sometimes taking far too long between breaths. I refused to look away.

This is my fault. If I had just kept to myself or never left the room, I wouldn't have met Trenton and agreed to dinner. I couldn't believe such a seemingly innocent thing had led to this.

A male elf tried to hand me a plate of food, but I couldn't stomach the thought of it. It wasn't that it didn't smell amazing. But my insides were in turmoil. When Rivven ate, I would too.

"Sinsha is the best healer in the known worlds," said the elf kneeling beside me as he set the untouched plate at my feet. "He will be good as new soon."

"Thank you," I whispered, still not looking away.

I felt him rise and depart, but I was far more interested in the way the poison seemed to recede, retreating from Rivven's throat and abdomen and growing closer to the origin site. Sinsha continued chanting and passing one palm over his sternum as she pressed yet more pastes of various colors and consistencies from her bowls onto the wound

A wind howled through the cavern, making the fire bow and flicker as I hugged myself against the cold. Finally, Sinsha sat back on her haunches and rested her hands on her thighs. She looked over at me.

"We must let him rest now. He will recover."

"Thank you," I said, voice cracking.

"Eat. Your aura is weak." She stood and strode over to a basin near a pool of water to wash up.

I glanced at the plate, which was more of a bowl filled with a stew of meat and hearty vegetables. Cringing, I peered over at Rivven who'd settled into a far more even and restful sleep, sun-kissed skin glowing again with its normal color. I couldn't make out anymore black spots, but his wound was covered with a mound of berry-colored mush, so it was hard to tell what was going on beneath.

"He lost a lot of blood." I eyed his body.

"Magic has a way of recovering what was lost," Sinsha said, joining me and accepting another bowl from an elf that appeared again from nowhere. Or maybe I wasn't really paying attention to anything but Rivven. He'd come so close to dying.

"Please. You are my guest." Sinsha gestured at the bowl before me.

I reluctantly picked it up and took a bite on the silver spoon they'd provided. My eyes widened with surprise. "This is amazing."

"We know the herbs that grow here well," Sinsha said, clearly pleased. "Humans rarely bother with what grows in deserts or mountains. They don't care to look beyond their own noses."

I couldn't disagree when I'd spent my life until now cooped up in a kingdom of oppressive darkness and fog. My heart clenched as I took another bite, chewing. Rune would be amazed at all the different places and people and things I'd come across on this journey. She had to be free so I could show it all to her. To see her smile or blink up at the sun, it would be a dream come true for both of us.

When she took over the rule of Centos, she would be a benevolent queen, opening the borders and no longer hoarding magic. She could bring the people together and start trade between lands—maybe even elves and humans.

Before I realized it, my bowl was empty. I blinked back the heavy fatigue that fought to take over after so much adrenaline and exertion—both magical and physical.

"Sleep. You are safe here. You can both be on your way tomorrow." She rose to leave. "Just remember, you owe me a head."

I curled into the warmth of Rivven's body beneath the furs and sighed. Soon, I drifted into a deep and dreamless sleep. When his arm fell heavily across my chest, I blinked open my eyes to find him sleeping peacefully a breath away. Sitting up, I scooted back, throwing off the blankets and pressed a hand to his now healed side, still sticky from Sinsha's remedies.

He stretched, roped muscles straining beneath his copper skin. By the time my gaze reached his face, he was still and awake, watching me with parted lips.

"You're better," I breathed, throwing myself over him and settling my head against his chest.

His arms surrounded me and as he spoke, his breath moved the hairs at my temple.

"Did you enjoy looking me over while I slept?"

I pushed away, smacking his infuriatingly hard chest as I did so. "You should be thanking me for saving your life, you ungrateful bastard!"

Rivven grinned, amber shards sparking in his eyes which only served to fluster me. He loved being able to get under my skin. I stood and crossed my arms, glaring at him.

"Where are we?" he asked, standing more slowly and looking around at Sinsha's enormous home.

"The Cloud peaks," I answered, rubbing my neck. "With Carn's help, I brought you to be healed. The arrow that got you was poisoned."

Surprise wasn't something I'd become accustomed to seeing on my companion's face, but it was there, clear as the Deadlands beneath the glaring sun as he gaped at me then examined his side where only a faint discoloration was visible.

"This is impossible," he said finally. "We have to get out of here, little spy. They'll kill me when they find out who—"

"I would not heal you only to slit your throat, Son of Miyal," Sinsha said as she crossed the cavernous room. "Yes, I know who you are."

Rivven stood still as a rock formation and just as expressionless as he watched her.

"Sinsha approves of our mission." I broke the silence when it felt too heavy and long to hold. "I've agreed to bring her King Balram's head."

Rivven's fiery gaze turned on me. I squared my shoulders and lifted my chin. "It's a small price for your life."

The glow of his irises faded, and he swallowed, nodding. "Thank you both." He looked at Sinsha. "May I have a few minutes with my friend?"

Sinsha smiled curtly and left the cave. The moment she disappeared, Rivven rounded on me, backing me into the table where I'd eaten the evening prior.

"Do you have any idea how dangerous it was to come here?" he seethed, his chest pumping like it was trying to grow larger.

I gripped the wooden edge behind me. "I didn't care."

"Clearly. But you need to care, Nyah." He grasped my face between his palms, forcing me to look at him. "I accepted long ago that I might die on this quest, but I will not allow innocents to be hurt on my behalf. That is important to me. That is what sets me apart from...from him. Do you understand?"

I did. More than he could imagine. The trouble was, I was no innocent. The king's blood ran through my veins. Maybe I wasn't like him, but the fact I'd lied to protect myself, the fact I hadn't cared to spare lives the same as Galan had when we fled, the fact I'd never stood up to my father or tried to protect my sister, who was innocent.

I didn't deserve or want Rivven's protection or devotion.

Prying his wrists away, I stiffened. "I hate to deflate your oversized ego, but my choices are just that, mine. I alone own the consequences."

Once again, his eyes sparked but calmed so quickly I might have imagined it. And despite his clenched fists and white knuckles, he backed away a step.

"These—my mother's people are known to be reclusive," he said, staring over my shoulder. "There are rumors that my mother never addressed, which say they kill and consume those who stumble upon their land, whether accidental trespassers or not."

I had no words.

"They found the idea of my mother's pairing with a human so abhorrent that they threatened to disembowel her if she dared come near the base of the mountain again, let alone climb it." He stepped back into my space, swathing me in his scent and his presence. "And somehow you, a carrier of someone else's magic, born to an uncaring father in the evil king's keep, somehow convinced them to not only spare the abomination their exiled produced with a human, but to heal me as well. Do you understand why I am suspicious?"

"I—" My mouth dried up, so I simply nodded. "Do you think perhaps there was more to your mother's story than she shared?"

Rivven's brow raised.

"I mean, maybe it wasn't about her being with a human, but what they thought of him in particular?"

"Are you questioning the character of my father?" He walked me against the table again until his body pressed into mine and the whole thing tipped off the ground. "The elder brother of the heir to the throne of Tromodia?"

I swallowed. "I can't imagine anyone worse than my own father. Or the king," I added quickly. "I meant no slight to your father. I just...if they don't trust humans that's one thing. Perhaps they fear us. But maybe if they meet individuals who don't embody the stereotypes? People like us." I gave up, unable to find the words, and lowered my gaze.

"You have a good heart, Nyah." Tilting my chin back up to face him, Rivven's expression was far softer than it had been since he awoke.. "I overreacted. You saved me, and it doesn't matter how or why. Thank you."

"I couldn't let you die."

"You could have." He leaned in.

"Not when it was my fault you were shot and poisoned," I argued.

He straightened, stepping away again, and a pang of longing replaced the feel of his body against mine. "You felt guilty?"

"No. Well, yes. I can't believe the desert elves poisoned you just because I made a dinner arrangement with someone, but—"

Rivven's laughter shut me up. Face burning, I released my grip on the table behind me and straightened. "What's so damn funny?"

"It turns out they weren't chasing me entirely because you made a dinner plan. They weren't happy when I mentioned it and likely would have booted us for that alone. But I'm afraid this is about you, Nyah. They wanted to turn you over to Balram."

"What?" Since when did elves obey my father's wishes? The rest of Centos considered them a myth. "How?"

Rivven pulled out a seat before dropping into it. "You were right about him hunting you. He sent messengers. Every village, whether human or elf between Centos and Tromodia is looking for you. He's offered to pay handsomely, including easing up on the taxes he demands in return for his benevolence." Rivven's features hardened around the last word.

"You ran rather than turn me over?" I grabbed for another seat, unable to trust my legs.

"I'd die trying to keep him from having what he wants." Rivven lowered his gaze to the tabletop. "Especially you," he muttered.

"We...we have to meet Galan and Carn on the other side of the mountain," I said suddenly. "Galan went to register us for the Imrati, and he doesn't know. He may be in danger if Elvenloft put out word we were traveling together."

"Trust me, Galan is in no danger. Lies fall from his silver tongue like silk from a spider. It seems you brought us to the one place where Balram dare not send a messenger." Rivven narrowed his eyes, considering me. "We must find a way to disguise you before we leave for the gate. You won't be safe otherwise."

"What about you?" I asked. "They know you helped me."

Rivven snorted. "They'll be looking for you, not me. I'm sure they thought me dead. I would have been if it hadn't been for your quick thinking and stubbornness."

I wasn't sure, but I thought his expression softened again, something almost sad and heavy behind it. Tentatively, I reached out and took his hand. The corners of his mouth turned upward until something behind me caught his attention. He straightened.

"Thank you for your hospitality," he said as he stood, bowing slightly. "May I ask one last favor before we continue on our quest?"

"We do no favors, Son of Miyal. Speak your request and we will come to an agreement." Sinsha moved gracefully to join us, long hair pulled back, revealing her pointed ears, possibly the only part of her expertly honed body one could label delicate.

Rivven's nostrils flared, but he relaxed. "Nyah requires a disguise. The evil one has spies everywhere hunting her."

Sinsha regarded me, before speaking. "Our magic won't disguise, but I believe I can help in another way if Nyah is willing."

I stood to meet her gaze. "Whatever it takes to make it to the Imrati and kill the king."

Fourteen

It took hours, but Sinsha knew who to call to help. They succeeded in changing my appearance so much that I no longer recognized my own reflection. I stared into the full-length mirror set before me. It was crafted out of a sheet of pure ice and smoothed with magic on one side to reflect the surroundings.

Something I hadn't realized was Sinsha's age, but now that her full-grown daughter, Kendara tended to me, I understood the woman had to be at least twenty years older than she appeared. Kind and outgoing, Kendara had put me at ease as she and some other elves worked on me. Listening to her tell stories of the Snow Bears and Ice Weasels that hunted on the mountain distracted me enough I barely noticed as they cut and dyed my hair lighter while turning my skin darker.

"We will present you to your mate as soon as you are dressed," Kendara said, brushing more makeup along my cheekbones.

"He's not my mate," I said again. The thought forced a blush that had nothing to do with the bronzer she applied.

"Of course," Kendara amended in a tone that said she didn't believe it. Before I could contradict her, she added, "Oh, Terra, come in."

I turned to find another young elf, tall and slender with toned arms and stomach visible between short layers of fur and skins. Glancing back and forth between them, I wondered if there was something more than friendship budding, and I smiled.

"You've brought the clothing," Kendara said, standing to take a bundle from Terra. Her long fingers brushed the other elf's, and the two of them froze for a moment before Kendara cleared her throat and unraveled the outfit.

"That's different," I said, noting the bright blue linen jumpsuit that crisscrossed with see-through cutouts down the torso.

"We don't have a lot of choices," Terra said in a raspy voice. "This belonged to the last outworlder who visited. You don't want to look like us or there will be too many questions."

I stared at the jumpsuit again, finding no evidence of blood. Still, I was afraid to ask what had become of the owner, especially whether she'd been *consumed* as Rivven mentioned earlier. Instead, I swallowed back the lump in my throat and tried to force a smile.

"Thank you. It certainly looks different from my normal attire, so it's a good disguise." Though with all the makeup and bright, showy clothing, I'd likely garner far more looks than my usual black. I thought about insisting that I stick to the shadows as I was used to, but decided if Rivven and Sinsha agreed, it was likely they were right, and this was the best course of action.

It was strange, feeling the cold air on the back of my neck without the heaviness of a braid hanging over it. But I approved of the deeper color in my skin and the gold tones in my hair gave me a healthy glow.

When Terra left and Kendara helped me into the outfit, I hummed softly.

"What?" she asked.

"Nothing. Just seems like Terra is a lovely person."

The material was loose around my waist, but Kendara grabbed a length of thick dark ribbon and wrapped it around my middle several times, cinching it as I watched the red in her cheeks deepen in the mirror.

"I agree," she said as she worked.

When she finished, Kendara backed up with hands on her hips to take in the final product. Then she knelt and tugged the pant legs down over my own leather boots, covering me to the ankles. "Okay, you're ready. Let's go show your *not* mate." She spun me around and half pushed, half guided me across an open field of snow to the gaping maw of her mother's cave.

When I entered, Sinsha and Rivven were seated at the same table, eating from a platter of snails and various root vegetables in an array of colors. They glanced up in unison. Rivven's gaze drank me in from head to toe and back up again in a way that left me feeling practically naked.

"The clothing is really for a bigger person, but it'll pass," Kendara said, turning me by the shoulders so they could see the back and sides as well. "She no longer fits the description at the very least."

Rivven pushed away from his meal and stalked toward me. He reached for a piece of short-cropped hair and slid it between his fingers. "I miss your long dark hair," he said in a low grumble that sent a burst of electricity to my core. I bit down on my lower lip to prevent the gasp that tried to escape.

"Nonsense, she's beautiful," Sinsha argued.

"I never said otherwise," Rivven snarled then turned back to me, the ghost of a smile on his lips. "I just miss the length that's all. But this suits you, Nyah."

"Thanks." I shifted my weight, uncomfortable beneath his attention. "It's cold. Let's go find Galan."

With a nod of agreement, he reached behind me and threw a thick white fur around my shoulders. I started to protest, but his expression stopped me. Then he handed me my sword in its sheath and spun me toward the door.

"Our scouts will lead you down to the gate," Sinsha said, grasping my arms in farewell.

"I look forward to seeing you again when you deliver the head of our enemy."

"Right." I gripped her back, then followed the others outside where an enormous bear, whiter than the snow stood on all fours. His snout was higher than Rivven's head with long, wicked tusks protruding on either side. On his back a tan saddle was strapped down with a bench and some loose furs. To the sides and rear of the beast were two even bigger ones with elves already mounted, reins in hand.

I gestured and flew to the empty bench with Rivven, landing softly on the leather seat. He leaned down and tucked the furs over our laps before gathering up the reins. From this vantage point, he looked every bit the impressive elf warrior the others did, broad shoulders supporting a thick fur cloak. Only his skin, lacking the reddish hue of the other mountain elves, an obvious difference.

With another slight bow of his head, he jerked the harness, and the bear loped away from the camp, flanked by the others. Before long we broke into a sprint, the animal moving faster and more agilely than I'd expected as we followed a steep and rocky descent down the opposite side of the mountain.

It took less than two hours to wind over the path, and when the snow bear stopped shy of the last bit of dirt, Rivven set the reins aside and leaped off. He landed lightly on his feet despite his size. Then he reached up his arms as though offering to catch me.

Rolling my eyes, I used another air current to float down beside him.

"Don't do that in front of anyone," Rivven warned as the elves and bears turned to depart. "Lesson one of training for the Imrati, never give away your secrets. The element of surprise may be crucial."

"So, act like a defenseless damsel?" I asked, batting my eyelashes.

Rivven gave me a sidelong grin. "Yes. Then they won't expect you to wield your weapon or your body the way you actually can."

I'd meant it as a joke, but what he said made sense. So as much as I hated the idea, I decided to follow his advice. Helpless, it was.

The minute we stepped off the mountain path, civilization seemed to appear from nowhere. Hordes of people bustled in and out of a giant rectangular stone gate. Guards in some sort of green uniforms sat lazily on either side, watching the passersby. Here women seemed to favor flowing gowns or skintight pants with hardly an in between state. The men wore shirts and vests that closed over their chests, unlike the ones Rivven tended to sport. I noted his was closed up to the last few buttons this time though.

The furs on our backs were suddenly cumbersome and too warm, but I didn't want to lose them as they might come in handy in the future. Rivven grabbed my arm and motioned for me to remove mine so he could stow them behind a boulder at the base of the mountain. I complied, but I wasn't thrilled with leaving them there until he drew a swirling set of runes on the ground and the pile of white faded into gray. It blended with the boulder so well, I never would have known they were there without seeing them vanish.

"I thought you didn't have earth power and used your earth spell for the wagon in the wood," I murmured as he joined me at my side.

"I always have a backup or two." His palm settled on the small of my back, surprising me, yet the warmth and strength of his touch had me leaning into it.

We passed by the guards with a nod and through the giant gate. Spread before us, the village opened into a bustling market square ringed by brick-and-mortar buildings and streets wide enough to fit several horses side by side.

The buzz of overlapping conversations made me want to cover my ears and retreat into the shadows between the stalls. But Rivven's hand provided a lifeline as he steered me through the center of the square—until he paused, nearly making me trip. When I glanced up to complain, the cause of his distraction became clear.

A wooden platform had been erected, and a crowd gathered around it. Above their heads, the words, *Vote for the Imrati Champion* flashed in magical blue flame, floating in the air. The sea of people sent up a sudden roar as they clapped or thrust arms in the air, cheering. I flinched, but after meeting my gaze, Rivven tugged us forward, around the outskirts to get a clearer view of the stage.

A beautiful woman in a sparkling sea-foam blue dress that hugged her body stood smiling so wide, I wondered if it hurt. Beside her, about ten men stood, all shirtless and flexing their muscles for the crowd. They ranged in size from wiry to nearly Rivven's stature; some had ink etched on their arms and torso, while others had so much hair they looked animalistic.

The woman raised her hand, and the gathered crowd fell into a hush.

"I'm sure you already have a favorite. I know I do." She winked as another cheer burst around us. The most muscular of the men flexed again, and I couldn't hold back a sneer. He reminded me too much of Rufus and the other guards. Perhaps, it was the arrogant look that said he knew he was the best specimen of the group.

"What is this?" I whispered to Rivven.

"This is the chance for those who've signed up to show off a little, and maybe make a bit of coin." He leaned down to whisper in my ear, his hot breath sending a shiver over my body. "The people love the Imrati and likely are thrilled it's back. It's always been a time for celebration."

My father had kept it from them for too long. And now that he'd set it in motion, even though he seemed to be rushing it, the people were finding a way to rejoice. But...

"What will the winner get?" I asked, sizing up the big one who had just flipped an opponent onto the wood with a loud crunch. The sprawled man didn't get up.

Rivven shrugged. "Bragging rights. It doesn't matter. We should go find Galan."

"Give me a minute," I said, already darting toward the foot of the stage.

"Ny—Starla!" Rivven called. But I had hoisted myself up and strode over to the woman in blue.

"I'm entering the Imrati as well." As I spoke a silence fell over the gathered people like a blanket. "I'd like to wrestle him." I pointed at the large man whose lips curled like a cravenbeast ready to lunge.

"I don't want to hurt you, little lady," he said, once again flexing for the audience.

I didn't want to be the center of attention, but if it would allow me to feel like I'd shown up Rufus for once, I was game. I smiled politely, striding up to him to run a finger down the center of his chest.

I could have sworn I heard Rivven's low growl from the crowd at my feet, but I just blinked up at the man in front of me as flirtatiously as possible. It wasn't easy since he smelled of sweat and ale.

"Maybe she just wanted a touch," the woman behind me said.

Even as the crowd laughed, I struck. I slipped one foot forward, bending into a lunge that forced his weight up and over my shoulder. The resounding crash hadn't finished echoing before I'd turned with the tip of my sword to his jugular.

He raised his hands in surrender, even as his face contorted in rage. The crowd roared with approval. I backed up and leaped off the side, disappearing into the fray.

Rivven grabbed my hand and snaked us through the nearest carts until we were well hidden. As he rounded on me, I still couldn't hide my pride and glee.

"Low profile, I know," I said, halting his tirade. "But he reminded me of someone in the keep, and I couldn't help myself."

On the other side of the cart we hid behind, the voice of a young boy sang out. "Look! It's a power crystal. Can I have it, Mama, please?"

"It's not real, Caltar," a woman's voice responded.

"But I can pretend to win the Imrati. You want me to practice for when I'm older, right? I'm gonna win the real thing someday."

"Let's go." Rivven tugged me once and led us across a dirt street to some buildings where the sounds of the celebration faded. When I tried to say more, he simply stared straight ahead, the tendon in his neck jumping. I decided to celebrate my win in silence.

Slowing to a stop, I glanced up at a wooden sign hung by iron joints that creaked in the wind. It read, *Tavern at the Gate*, which I supposed was an accurate description—if not very creative. I was about to ask why we were stopping here when Galan's voice floated loud and clear beyond the swinging doors.

"I cannot be held responsible for your stupidity."

Rivven's jaw clenched yet again as I glanced up at him. I wondered how often Galan caused trouble, and how many times Rivven had lectured *him* on keeping a low profile. *Like me.*

I followed him inside in time to see a giant of a man leaning over Galan at a table in the corner. Several others who sat around them scooted back. Cards were strewn over the surface, along with a small pile of golden coins gathered in front of our companion.

"Is there a problem here?" Rivven asked, tapping the shoulder of the angry man Galan had called stupid. Height wise, they were equals, but girth? The other man had quite a bit on Rivven. Although, most of his bulk didn't appear to be muscle.

"This arsehole cheated me out of a week's worth of wages." The man thumbed toward Galan who was busy scooping his winnings into a coin purse.

"I didn't force you to wager anything," Galan argued.

Rivven's hand was the only thing that stopped the giant from attacking. My own itched to grab hold of the sword on my back, but I forced myself to stay still.

"What's your name, friend?" Rivven smiled.

"Tarfin," the giant grumbled.

"How about I buy you a drink, Tarfin?" Rivven offered.

The man growled. "After I beat a lesson in manners into this one." Then he lunged.

Galan darted out of the way a second before a meaty fist hit his face and Tarfin crashed over the table, scattering cards and the other occupants. Wood splintered as the legs wobbled beneath his weight and the whole thing went down with Tarfin on his stomach.

Cringing, I danced out of the way of a half-drunk ale that toppled in my direction.

"Time to leave," Galan whispered, snagging my arm and retreating through the door.

"Fuck," Rivven yelled from behind us as we dashed through the maze of streets and buildings, until Galan ducked into an alleyway with laundry hung out to dry across the thin opening above us.

He pressed me to the wall with an arm as he leaned out, listening. Once satisfied, he released me and spun to face us, a too-happy grin tugging at his lips.

"Low profile?" Rivven seethed at him with an expression that would have made me shrink. But Galan just laughed and hefted his full purse.

"I had to do something to entertain myself while you two were playing in the snow. Life's too short to be bored."

"Did you register us for the Imrati?" I asked, stepping between them.

"Of course. We are all three registered. Interestingly, you don't show up under your blood. You are an unknown and unregistered individual, Nye. As if you weren't intriguing enough."

A glance at Rivven showed his face soften into a thoughtful expression, but panic seized my insides. My father had never added me to the registry? *I guess I never truly existed to him.* Then again, perhaps it was because he didn't want his own blood known. Not many could wield blood magic. In fact, as far as I knew, it was both outlawed and extinct, but much had been kept from us about the real world, so who knew if that was true?

"It seems he was planning to make you disappear without anyone noticing," Rivven said, and though his voice was gentle, the tremble of rage sang from somewhere beneath. "He kept you and your sister close so he could harvest the Tromodian magic you inherited from your father."

My mouth dried up, which seemed to happen a lot around Rivven. He was right, of course. Balram had been doing so with Leuruna since she was a child. The guilt of keeping the truth about my bloodline from Rivven turned my stomach.

"What name did you give?" Rivven asked, turning his attention to Galan.

"Starla of Tromodia. I always fancied that name."

"You registered me under a false name?" I asked, shocked.

"They are after you, so that's best." Rivven turned his attention back to Galan. "Good work."

"I believe in being discreet," Galan said, and I gaped at him. He was anything but.

"The king will recognize me," I blurted. "Change of hair and all or not, surely he'll realize who is competing."

"By then it will be too late. Even he cannot disrupt the Imrati. There won't be a single person who won't turn on him." Rivven shrugged. "Imagine how nice it will be to rub your talent in his face."

"And if I'm eliminated early? He'll come after me." I hadn't thought this through enough. I wanted to fight for Rune and my freedom. But the thought of him getting ahold of me turned my blood to ice.

"Then I suggest you train hard and don't allow that to happen, little spy."

FIFTEEN

"Why isn't Carn coming?" I asked for the third time since we set out for Tromodia.

"Dragons are not allowed in the city," Galan answered as he leaned out the window of the carriage he'd purchased with his winnings. It was as inconspicuous as he was, which was to say, not at all. With bright red and gold paint adorning the sides and giant wheels, it attracted far more attention than I was comfortable with. Judging by the glares and grunts coming from Rivven since Galan showed up with it, I suspected he felt the same.

Seated on top next to Rivven, I spied the hilly terrain blanketing the way to Tromodia, now northeast of us. Pine trees and golden oaks rimmed the wide road, so flat and packed down that there were barely any bumps. It had to be a major route between the gate and Tromodia, but I had yet to see another traveler. Then again, we headed out in the middle of the night. Our big, gilded wagon, hooked to two spotted horses large enough to take on the snow bear we rode down the mountain, wouldn't stand out at night, Galan had argued.

Luckily everyone was so busy running around like chickens in the city that they wouldn't have looked twice if we'd been standing on our heads. It made the argument that Carn would cause havoc far less convincing.

"Why couldn't he come around and meet us here?" I pressed, folding my arms. I liked the giant lizard and was hoping to see him again.

To my surprise, Rivven turned to me, reins in hand, and sighed. "There are traders and hunters in Tromodia that would try to skin him and sell him off in pieces. It wouldn't be fair to bring him there. Besides, he's happiest in the desert, not by the ocean."

I settled as he returned to watching the road. He was protecting his dragon. Not that I doubted between us and said beast, we couldn't fight off any poachers. But the idea of protecting him was...nice.

"Will anyone go after the horses?" I asked after a bit.

"No. Though they may try for the whole ridiculous rig. It makes us look like an easy mark."

"I heard that," Galan called out the window. "Don't you want to come down here and rest on the satin pillows with me, Starla? I'm much better company than that brooding hunk of man."

I snorted, unable to stop it. "No thanks. Take a nap while I keep his highness entertained."

"You can both eat a Kromar as far as I'm concerned," Rivven muttered.

Another snort burst from me as I pictured chewing on the foot of a wooden troll—yet another storybook creature I assumed might be real, knotted branches and all.

"You know I bought this rig as a tribute for the forest elves, right?" Galan's sudden presence startled me as he climbed in beside me, sandwiching me against Rivven's side.

"I could have given them coin," Rivven countered.

"Another group of elves?" I asked, intrigued. So far, I was more of a fan of the mountain elves than the desert dwellers. "Will they be friendly or try to capture me?"

"I misjudged the desert dwellers. I didn't think Elora and her kind would cater to a request from the evil king, yet they clearly did, so I can't be sure," Rivven said, bolstering the horses to pick up their pace. "It'll be a good test of your disguise, I suppose."

"And if they are looking for me? How difficult will it be to get past them?" I asked as the trees opened to rolling hills covered in clovers in the near distance. The scent reached me at almost the same time as I spotted it, and I inhaled deeply. Strangely, it felt familiar somehow, even though the only clover I'd ever seen was dried and sold at the market on occasion in Centos.

"Very difficult," Rivven muttered. "Keep your mouth closed and head down when we reach the outskirts."

"We'll be almost there once we crest the other side of these hills," Galan added helpfully. "It's just a short sprint to Tromodia. We'll catch sight of the ocean soon, over to your left."

I followed the direction he indicated, squinting but unable to see the elusive sight yet.

"What's it like?" I asked.

"The ocean?" Rivven turned toward me and raised a brow. "I forget you've never seen it. It's breathtaking. Churning waves frosted with white foam when Darvol is angry, and bright blue ripples when he's calm. And the smell..." Rivven inhaled deeply as though tasting it. "It smells like freedom."

"It sounds wonderful," I whispered, awed at how the hard lines of his face seemed to fade as he described it. *This man belongs to the sea.*

An arrow whistled overhead and Rivven tugged at the reins, guiding the horses off the path to the left. I'd already unsheathed my sword by the time the next volley came. I knocked one away from Galan, who was gripping the side of the seat to keep from falling off as we jostled and leaned with the quick change in direction.

Galan grabbed the shaft of another that had found the side of the carriage and yanked it free of the wood.

"No poison," he reported as we crashed into the trees, forcing us to duck. "Always look at the bright side, Starla."

"Jump," Rivven ground out as we bumped down into a ravine.

Galan grabbed my hand and using his own air magic, leaped up and across, setting us in the Y of a golden oak where he blended in. Rivven had jumped as well, but he'd gone forward, landing on the back of one of the horses and bringing his sword down on the shaft attaching the steeds to the carriage.

The entire thing smashed into the trees below us, splintering into pieces. By the time I looked back at Rivven, he'd already freed both horses from the mechanism and was executing a dive, tuck, and roll across the ground, landing in a crouch with his sword in hand.

With no time to catch our breath, the sounds of feet rushing down the ravine announced the arrival of our attackers. Galan swore under his breath as the first figure appeared, followed by a dozen more.

They were small in stature, maybe hip high to Rivven, but they moved quickly, short swords no bigger than large daggers clutched in their hands. Their skin was the color of the soil by the tree roots and their clothing matched the leaves and bark so much so that they blended in easily. Long, dark hair flowed behind them, revealing pointed ears which gave away their identity.

"I don't want to hurt you," Rivven shouted as they surrounded him, coming to a stop with sharp weapons.

A male nearest him laughed. "I doubt that'll be an issue. Typical human trash, thinking you can best us because of our size."

"It's not your size, and I am not human." Rivven slowly lifted a hand and pulled his hair away from his ear.

"Halfling," the elf muttered. "I suppose we can't eat ya then. Fine. What'd you bring as tribute?"

Straightening and lowering his sword, Rivven glowered and pointed toward the wreckage that was the ostentatious carriage. "That."

The small man scratched at his beard as he assessed it. "Well, that's a darn shame, ain't it?"

"If you hadn't attacked first, it might've been in one piece," Rivven said.

"And where are your companions?" the elf asked, searching for us.

"What companion—"

"Don't play me a fool. We saw them well enough when we shot you off the road."

"Majesty," a female elf squeaked at the man. "If the others are human, make him leave one."

"Good idea," the one, who was apparently the king of these people, stated.

"No one's eating anyone," Rivven announced, raising his sword again part way. "Let us pass. The horses that were attached will make fine steeds or fetch a good price at market."

"Where are they hiding?" the female elf demanded, ignoring Rivven's offer.

I climbed from the tree, missing Galan's attempt to grab me and dropped beside Rivven.

"I'm here. Now accept the horses as tribute and let us through." I ignored the idea that they might eat horses, if they ate humans, and hoped they would opt to fetch a good price as Rivven suggested.

Murmurs erupted among the elves, and I pointedly did not look at Rivven, knowing he'd be grinding his jaw at my appearance. But I saw no reason to delay the inevitable. Besides, there was still a chance they only saw one other person and Galan could remain hidden.

"Lovely human," the king chirped, bowing to me as he dropped his sword to his side.

That was...unexpected.

"Thank you," I said, looking around as the others eyed me and shifted.

"I expected a soldier, not a lady. Forgive my suspicious nature. You will join us for the sunrise ceremony," he announced with a shout, and the others yelled their agreement.

They gathered around behind us to herd Rivven and I out of the ravine and toward the clover covered hills. As difficult as it was not to look back, I forced myself to avoid giving Galan away. Something still didn't sit right with me, and it never hurt to have a backup plan.

We climbed one hill, but on the other side, a door camouflaged by clovers opened to admit us into an underground village, much like the desert dwellers had hidden theirs. We descended a set of stairs carved into rock and dirt, ending in an open cavern where stalagmites and stalactites jutted from the natural landscape like menacing teeth, all coated in phosphorescent moss. The moss seemed to cover nearly everything, illuminating the space with an eerie glow.

A maze of caves of varying sizes twisted around the outskirts of the enormous area, which held rows of tables and benches, as well as cascading floral decorations made of white lilies with elongated petals and bunches of tiny purple and red Fairy Eyes. To the right, along a curving wall, a large stage had been set up. On it sat two thrones, covered in moss, except for the seats, where giant red mushroom caps cushioned the surface.

A massive firepit flared to life before the stage and between the rows of tables. A ringing shout rose up among our...were they captors or friends? I wasn't sure anymore. A glance at Rivven proved no help, since he always looked like he was ready for an attack. They'd let us keep our weapons, which I thought was a good sign.

"Put some seats up here for our guests," the king demanded as he climbed on the highest throne, legs dangling from the enormous chair.

Bodies and hands surrounded us, more or less shoving us up the steps and onto some cushions thrown at the base of the king's throne. I'd have had trouble fitting into anything but his own seat, and I had no doubt Rivven would have shattered a smaller chair with his weight.

"Prepare for the feast," the king shouted and clapped his hands. Most of the elves scurried off into the various pathways and caves, presumably to start cooking.

Sitting cross-legged, arms draped over his knees, Rivven angled his body so he could keep both the elf and the open area in view. I noticed he'd also managed to block me partially as well.

"Why are you attacking travelers?" Rivven asked. "You never used to do more than demand payment for passage. What's changed in the last moons cycle since I've been through?"

The king stroked his bushy beard and considered Rivven with beady black eyes that reflected the moss lighting's green glow.

"You are familiar." His non-answer had Rivven's shoulders draw even tighter, back rod straight. "What is your name?"

"I have none," Rivven said. "I am a traveler and ghost among my people. You may call me River."

Interesting.

"My name is Starla," I offered, earning a glare from the ghost.

"A lovely name for a lovely woman," the king said with a wink.

"Thank you, your majesty." I did my best to smile in an attractive way and bat my eyelashes. If he liked me, I'd use that to our advantage. "But why *are* you attacking travelers? You gave us quite a fright."

The king's countenance changed. His head lowered and his shoulders sagged. "Humans rode through here about a week ago. When we stopped them at the barter point, instead of offering as usual, they ruthlessly attacked my people. Almost half of our tribe was slaughtered with no cause, men, women, children, it didn't matter."

"I'm so sorry," I said, getting to my knees and resting a hand on his arm. "Who were these horrible people?"

"They were dressed in armor, like soldiers of old. But we did not recognize the insignia they bore. They claimed to be the new rulers of Tromodia. Thus, we've declared war." His small eyes, visible above his beard, glistened with unshed tears and determination as he beat a fist on the arm of the throne.

"We are not like those who attacked you," I said softly. "In fact, I too am running from soldiers like them who were sent after me."

Clearing his throat loudly, Rivven shifted behind me. He didn't like me telling the king, but I couldn't blame the man for being leery of humans after such a betrayal.

"They defiled my queen in front of me," he admitted, pain lacing his words. His arm stiffened beneath my touch. "Then they cut off her head and trampled her body with their horses. You...you remind me of her a bit."

I gasped with the horror of what he'd witnessed. He'd been acting downright easygoing with us, considering what he'd been through. My heart ached for him. At least that explained why he'd relaxed around me.

"There is no ruler of Tromodia," Rivven said, calling back our attention. "They lied to you, your majesty."

"I don't care where they were from. If they are an example of what humans have become, then all those like them shall die by my sword."

"But I am human." My statement seemed to coincide with the tendon in Rivven's neck jumping. "You see, I mean no harm, right?"

The king patted my hand where it rested on his arm. "Do I? Or did you have no choice when we surrounded you?"

I pulled back, stunned.

"What would you have done if you'd been with them? Watched? Laughed? Participated in the atrocities?" He leaned toward me, speaking softly, the sparkle of a dare in his small eyes.

"I'd have fought with you," I answered. "My whole life I've seen evil decay the world, and I am done sitting by while it happens."

"Then it is a shame you weren't there."

I looked to Rivven. *What did that mean?* But he stayed silent, tense as always.

"Your highness?" I asked.

That was when the others started returning, filing into the great room with an enormous cauldron of delicious smelling vegetables and seasoning. They placed it on a bar and hoisted it over the fire.

"We drink!" the king shouted, jumping to his feet.

This man was giving me whiplash with his changes in countenance. He made Rivven seem level-headed.

A pretty young elf with chestnut hair rushed up the steps, carrying a tray and three goblets. The king's cup was encrusted with jewels, which he lifted.

Everyone stared as she offered us the other two drinks. Rivven remained still, but I glanced between the king's watchful eyes and the audience waiting to see what I would do. If I refused, I'd show no trust. Perhaps that's what they were waiting for.

Hand trembling, I grasped the tin goblet in my hand and sniffed it. A cloyingly sweet scent filled my nostrils, and I tipped some into my mouth. A surprisingly tart jolt joined the overly sweet notes, and I swallowed with a smile. Everyone cheered and the king and the others drank from theirs. I took another swallow and Rivven snatched his and took a sip.

"Come and dance with my people," the king said, gesturing for me to rise.

I grinned and stood. *I made the right choice.* I accepted his hand as he walked me down the steps and into the fray before the fire where the stew filled the air with an aroma that made my stomach grumble. Whatever they drank was strong as I felt lightheaded while I swayed to the music of woodwind and tin drums. Small bodies joined me, moving around me in a dizzying motion.

Glancing up at Rivven, who stood on the bottom step above the fray, I grinned. The moss-light made his copper skin glow where his shirt parted. I swiveled my hips, heat rushing through me as I motioned for him to join me.

He stepped into the swarm of people and strode up to me still stiff as a board. I threw my arms around his neck and pressed against him as I moved. The world seemed to spin around us as though we had our own pocket of time. His heart thrummed against mine in a sporadic rhythm that belied his stoic exterior. I wondered in that space between beats whether he was as confused as I was by my feelings. All I wanted was to get closer—so close that I couldn't tell where I ended and he began. As I pressed into him, I became hyper aware of every inch of space where our bodies met.

"Dance with me," I mouthed, staring up into his fiery eyes. Was the flame inside him or a reflection from the fire behind me?

Gripping my waist, he stilled my movement, but everywhere we connected seemed to ignite with sparks of heat like he'd used his power. I could no longer hear the drums as much as feel their pulsing beat inside of me as I began to move against him. Then, just as I was giving in completely to my instincts, a cool weight settled over me as though liquid marble had been poured through my limbs.

My mouth dropped open as the edges of my vision turned black, and my body froze in place. All at once, I went limp against him. A roar filled my ears as hands tugged at me and my clothing, but Rivven scooped me over his shoulder once again. I heard the *shwing* of his sword being drawn as he spun around, creating a buffer as he backed toward the fire. I stared at the dancing flames as they blurred in and out of focus.

"—in the pot and we'll let you go." The king's voice felt far away.

The heat from the fire was too close…too much. I coughed as Rivven backed further toward it.

"Since when do you eat human flesh?" Rivven demanded.

"Since they destroyed my people. My queen!" the king roared.

Wait. They want to put me in the pot and eat me? I was the only human here…

The flames rose along with the fear of my realization. Those bastards used a potion in the mead. I'd foolishly believed they'd been testing my trust. I never should have given them the opportunity. How was Rivven staying on his feet? I tried to crawl my way up his back so I could stand, but I ended up making it nowhere.

"I know who you are now, *River*," the king of the forest elves said. "You are the one responsible for leaving the humans of Tromodia to become what they have. Your weakness as a leader drove them to this! Drove us to this!"

Rivven's grip tightened painfully on my thigh, and I cursed. The king had hit a nerve. I tried to say it wasn't his fault, but the words refused to come. Silently, I cursed myself for allowing this to happen. I loathed the feeling of helplessness more than anything, and it was my own fault. I should have known better than to trust so easily. I was such a fool. He'd been lying when he said I reminded him of his queen. He was acting so strangely because he was trying to lull us into relaxing and following along.

The first clang of metal on metal reverberated through my body as Rivven swung, bouncing me roughly. He moved with sharp, sure movements, and the meager contents of my stomach threatened to resurface. Even he couldn't survive an attack of so many.

A gust of wind whooshed through the cavern, growing in intensity until the flames of the great fire bowed. Rivven stumbled forward, dropping me to the ground. I stared up at his magnificent body, utterly in awe as he dove over me, sheltering me. His sword planted point first in the dirt beside my face.

The storm filled the room, whipping Rivven's hair around his head as the others screamed. The sounds of bodies flying and thumping against the ground joined the howling anger of the wind. Rivven lowered himself against me, clutching the sword hilt and me as the great gust tried to drag us both toward the fire.

After what felt like an age, it stopped, and a pair of boots landed near my head. My gaze trailed upward to find Galan swaying and pale like he'd been trampled by a cravenbeast.

"Time to go," Rivven said. And he was on his feet with me slung over his shoulder again as we dashed free of the cavern. The few elves left standing, cowered and rushed around in a panic, not paying us much attention as we fled.

"We have to get to the border," Rivven yelled. But between Galan's weakened state and my potioned arse, he would be hard pressed to get us all there.

That's when I saw the horse. Even upside down it was gorgeous. One of the giant beasts that had been attached to the carriage waited, grazing lazily on the clover of the nearest hill. Rivven tossed me over its back on my stomach. Soon Galan joined me, and Rivven climbed on behind us. It wasn't comfortable, but it worked as we headed toward the last hill and the final path toward Tromodia.

Sixteen

We crossed the border and found a soft patch of grass beneath the protective shade of a willow. Its leaves and branches fell like a curtain over us. Galan laid passed out on the other side of the trunk, where Rivven arranged him as comfortably as possible, leaving him with a pat on his shoulder.

I watched as he returned to my side and lay down, head propped on his elbow as he regarded me with a deep sigh.

"Are you hurt?" he asked, but I couldn't read his emotion. Was he angry or worried? *Both probably.*

I pushed my head from side to side making myself dizzy again. I probably had a few bruises, but as far as I could tell it was nothing serious. I liked how his scent of cedar and tobacco muted everything else when he was this close. Homing in on his full lips, I wished I had the strength to reach up, pull him down, and feel them moving against mine.

"I'd love to hear what you're thinking, little spy. You don't hold back when you're sober, so I can only imagine what you'd be saying right now if you could."

"Arsssssshole," I managed to get out.

He smiled like it was the best compliment he'd ever heard. "No points for originality, but you get good marks for effort."

I narrowed my eyes, or at least I thought I did, but his gaze fell downward to my breasts. *Is my clothing ripped or something?* I strained to feel anything, only to realize I was so cold I was trembling. The next thing I knew Rivven lay flat and gathered me against him, pressing his warm, hard body along mine. He let out a small breath as his body grew hotter, almost stinging against my skin. I wriggled uncomfortably, but he held me in place.

"I think it's the aftereffects of the potion they dosed you with. The second I felt the dizziness, I turned up my body heat and burned it from the inside. I'll have to teach you to do that I suppose."

His words distracted me as my body defrosted against him. Soon my fingertips began to tingle, and I pulled them clumsily up between where our chests mashed together. "C...c...cold."

Rivven gathered my hands in his and lifted them to his mouth. His hot breath encapsulated them as he stared into my eyes, his amber flecked with his internal fire. It felt so good I moaned, and the corner of his mouth jerked up.

"Have you learned yet that it's better to stay quiet or hidden and follow my lead?" he asked as the heat penetrated deep in my bones, waking sensation everywhere we touched. I was sure he felt my heart pump faster, if not the way my nipples hardened against him as though they'd been taught to respond to the anticipation of his touch. The smug expression he wore said he was probably aware of my thoughts as well.

Why did my irresponsible body have to choose this man? Desperate to wipe that smirk off him, I did the only thing I could think of and pushed with all my strength, succeeding in rolling him onto his back and landing on top of him. I let my face fall onto his, resulting in a clumsy yet forceful kiss.

His arms reached around me, holding me in place as I managed to suck in his bottom lip. It had looked as lush and juicy as pilas fruit and tasted even better. As my rhythm and skill increased, he responded with a satisfying groan that made me pull harder. He nipped back at my upper lip, and I gasped a little, pulling my head up slightly.

"You are under the influence of a potion," he said during the reprieve. "I can't—"

"Yes, you can," I said, only slightly slurring my words as I reached down and set my palm where the length of him pushed against the material of his trousers.

"Fuck, Nyah." His eyes rolled back, but he firmly set me on my side again, extricating himself so he could stand.

I watched silently in fascination as he paced in front of me, yanking a hand through his hair, and his erection straining for release. The men in the keep where I grew up never said no when a woman threw herself at them, or another man for that matter. Did that mean he didn't find me desirable and wasn't sure how to tell me?

A sudden overwhelming sense of shame assaulted me, stoking tears in my eyes and making me sit up and scoot back against the tree trunk. When Rivven noticed, he dropped down beside me, reaching out. I scooted further away.

"Don't touch me out of pity," I said, fighting not to cry in front of him. I could barely look at him as it was.

"Pity? For fuck's sake, Nyah, I don't pity you."

As usual I had no retort for that. He didn't feel bad about rejecting me? I let my head fall back hard against the wood and squeezed my eyelids closed.

"Nye, look at me." He grabbed the sides of my head and forced it toward him, but I kept my eyes shut tight. I felt his forehead connect with mine. "I don't know what just happened, but I think you have the wrong idea in that head of yours."

Sniffling, I peered through my lashes a tiny bit to find his eyes so close to mine that I thought the tiny flames inside might burn me alive. "What idea is that?"

"Do you think I rejected you because I'm not interested?"

I blinked. "Always answering questions with questions."

"For the record I'm trying to control myself. I don't want you to think I took advantage of you when you were under the influence of magic...or as a captor. If you choose to join with me, I want you to know it was your free will, your choice."

"You are infuriating," I said as he sat back on his haunches. "But for some damn reason I'm attracted to you and I...I want to know what it's like to lie with a man. With *you*. But I don't want your guilt either." I studied my fingers as I twisted them in my lap, the potion all but gone from my system.

"I would think it was obvious that I'm attracted to you."

I chanced a glance then realized he was referring to his erection. Heat rushed to my cheeks. His brows furrowed, accentuating the scar hovering over his eyebrow.

"Wait. You've never lain with anyone?" he asked.

I prayed for the ground to swallow me whole, but it didn't, so I managed to shrug. "I guess I never had the opportunity. I was always looking over my shoulder and protecting my sister. I spent my time either hiding from the king's presence, teaching myself to fight, or with her."

The enormous sigh he heaved seemed to deflate him so much that he collapsed fully to the ground, throwing his head back and stretching his long legs out before him. "Gods, I am not equipped for this. Give me a hoard of evil doers to fight and I will jump in with a clear head, but emotions? I'd rather be boiled alive."

"Sorry to be such a burden ever since you've kidnapped me," I spat, standing up. A quick glance showed Galan fast asleep on the other side of the tree for which I was grateful. If I'd woken him and he'd gotten in on this awful conversation...

"You mean since I saved your life? And as I recall, you chose to accompany me on my quest since it seems to mirror your own." Rivven stood facing me now, once again having moved so fast and stealthily that I jumped when I turned to find him nearby. Before I could retort, he grabbed me none too gently by the arms and tugged me even closer. "I won't pretend to know what you've been through, but I do know what my childhood was like thanks to the king. It certainly changed my destiny for the worse."

"We're both products of selfishness and pain. Lovely." I looked down and away, wishing I could curl up on my side and sleep off the headache that had formed.

Rivven shook me and I grudgingly found his glowing eyes again. "Damnit, Nyah." His nostrils flared as he appeared to fight internally to find the right words. "You have a choice now, which is something you didn't before. You don't have to live for your sister or anyone else. You are free, and you should leave it all behind and run. Live the life you want and screw everyone else."

My jaw slackened as I took in the intense truth he fought to share with me. "That's not what you're doing," I said softly, lifting my hand to stroke his wiry beard he'd let grow since I said I liked it better.

He froze, a new kind of tension overtaking his body as he closed his eyes and leaned into my touch. "I'm not free," he murmured so softly I wondered if he knew he'd said it aloud.

"Neither am I," I answered, and waited for him to look at me again. "If somehow we both make it out of the Imrati and manage to kill King Balram, maybe we will be."

"I admit I've never dared consider beyond that moment. I've pictured severing his head a million times, but after—you realize I'll never be truly free though." Gently, he took my wrist and slid my hand down to my side then stepped back.

"What do you mean?" I asked, forcing myself not to make up the distance he'd put between us.

"Someone has to rule in his stead," he said then smiled sadly. "I don't know what the hell I'm doing, but at least my intentions are good."

"You won't be king," I said, confusion wrinkling my forehead. "There's already an heir. And she's good, not like...her father."

Rivven's face hardened into the mask he usually wore, all evidence of the fragile man who'd been with me moments ago gone like smoke. I noticed the way his hand curled into a fist at his side then loosened again but stayed close to the hilt of his sword. Was he seriously considering fighting me? After saving my life? After kissing me back?

My chest constricted. Why had I trusted so quickly? Hadn't I learned that no one was worth opening myself to besides Rune? Shame on me for forgetting so easily just because my body fancied a man's touch.

"Nyah," he interrupted my spiraling thoughts with carefully crafted words, like I might be a wild animal prone to attack, "the princess is part of the king's hold on Centos—on the stones. We—I can't leave her alive."

My first reaction was blinding rage, but I stuffed it down deep in my belly as my magic flared. It wasn't just mine either. It was far more intense than I was used to, and I wondered if it was somehow hers as well. Like her power meant some of her was inside of me. My protective nature blazed to life, and I considered pulling my own weapon to end the threat right here and now. But that would be stupid. Rivven was a formidable enemy and one that would be easier to dispatch if he trusted me and didn't see it coming.

Was I really thinking about how to kill the man in front of me? My stomach flipped and the pain in my chest and head intensified. *Logic. I need to think logically.* Drawing in a slow, deep breath, I forced aside the power thrumming behind my skin and around my heart. I sat, leaning against the tree again and gathering my knees to my chest. He would not strike someone who wasn't defending themselves. This much I understood about Rivven.

He squatted beside me again, making me feel like we were moving in circles, but I stayed quiet, observing him. I was committed to helping him kill my father. I'd given him the Imrati as a suggestion. But by doing so, I'd put my sister, the one person I wanted to protect with my entire soul, in greater danger. She'd given me her power. Now, she'd be even less able to defend herself than she had before.

All my miserable life I'd trained with the idea of defending her, yet I'd failed once again. I'd never confronted our father. I'd never stopped him. Now, when I thought I finally had the courage to do something about it, I'd led another danger to her feet. All I wanted to do was fix the mess I'd created, but when I thought about killing Rivven to end the threat, I wanted to vomit.

I'd have to convince him. It would be better for him not to rule if that wasn't what he wanted. But gods help me, if he wouldn't see reason, I was going to do whatever it took to protect her if it came down to it. My own convoluted feelings be damned.

Leuruna was innocent. She wasn't a monster, though she was weak, and it was her weakness that I hated because I now knew it was a mirror of my own. Fear or not, danger or not, I was determined to change the script.

"Rivven," I said after a long pause. "I need you to understand something. I grew up alongside the princess Leuruna. The way he treats her…it's horrible. It's worse than you can imagine. She's as much a victim and a prisoner as I was—more so."

Rivven's sharp intake of breath was the only thing that gave away he'd even heard what I said. I stared at him for a time to make sure he was truly listening before I continued.

"She hates him as much as I do."

Rivven's tongue darted out to wet his lips as he settled beside me in the grass, hands nowhere near his sword, which I found a relief. Yet, I wouldn't forget that he'd thought of it, even in preparation to defend himself. It was the first place his mind had gone even after coming so close to—no I wouldn't go there. I needed to keep my head on straight. For Rune's sake as well as my own.

"How is it you were allowed to grow up so close to King Balram's only heir?" he asked carefully.

My gaze snapped to his as I realized my mistake. The only way that might have happened was if I'd been her handmaiden, which she wasn't even allowed. But Rivven knew as well as I did that the king would never have overlooked two potential sources of powerful magic growing up together, sharing private conversations, and potentially plotting against him. No, part of his abuse was keeping her isolated. But I could still tell a partial truth.

"I learned to sneak," I said, hugging my knees tighter and staring straight ahead, lest he see I hid more than I admitted. "I was a shadow in that castle, climbing trees and turrets, staying silent and unnoticed. I learned at a young age to come onto her balcony from the outside, and we would talk late into the night. I'd slip away when he came near."

"I thought you said all you did was train, hide, and think about your sister. What of her?" Rivven asked, leaning in.

My chest was too constricted, my head throbbing. Tears fought to squeeze from the corners of my eyes as I held tight to myself in a ball, unable to respond or move lest I lose what control I had. The lie hovered in my mind, I only had to calm myself enough to speak it, but...

"Nyah," Rivven said, covering my hand with his using slow, controlled movements. "What aren't you telling me? I'm not going to hurt you."

All the turmoil inside me focused into a sudden sharp burst of anger. I jerked away, glaring at him. "You sure about that, your highness? You sure seem ready and willing, dare I say eager, to assassinate the whole damn kingdom right along with the evil king."

Rivven swallowed, remaining still, eyes locked on me. "Who is your father, Nyah?"

I was so tired of living a lie. I wanted Rivven to know the real me. I needed to find out who he really was and if he didn't know me, how could I expect to know him ever? The lies dried up on my tongue and the truth burst from my chest like a flame meeting dry kindling.

"Balram is my father as much as he is Leuruna's," I admitted, the words bitter but strong. "If you wish to kill me now, fine. But I will fight you to spare my sister and do not underestimate me."

I stood then, ready to pull my sword, despite the heaviness in my still clenched chest. Rivven stood too but made no move to attack.

"You were never a spy. You were a runaway princess. And that's why he wants you and your power so badly. That's why you have Tromodian power. The queen. She passed it on to you. You withheld the truth because you knew I'd kill you if I realized who you were," Rivven said, but the words weren't angry or biting. No, they were almost...pitying, and he'd told me he didn't pity me. More lies.

"No." The word came out harsh and acidic. "She was not my mother. Leuruna and I share only a father."

"Then the magic's not yours at all, is it? It's all your sister's. She sent it to you and told you to run."

I said nothing, just waited as he reasoned out his next move. I remained ready.

"He wants the Tromodian power so bad he'd kill his own blood to get it." The hatred in Rivven's eyes wasn't aimed at me. Still, I stiffened. "When he demonstrated Tromodian powers, it solidified his hold over the other kingdoms. I never understood how he'd gotten it. And now he wants more."

"It's because it was never his," I said as my stomach twisted. All those times I'd seen him touch the crystal to Leuruna's forehead, watching her drained of energy as it grew brighter and deeper purple replayed in my mind.

Rivven began to pace. "He drained it from the queen, then from your sister when he used her up," he ground out. "And now, he sees your sister is a dead end. Unless he can find a match for her to produce yet another heir to move onto when she's no more than a husk."

The truth of it, stated so bluntly out loud, forced a lump to form in my throat. I grew dizzy. Something had happened to force our father's hand to do this. *What the hells has he seen or done?* He was trying to siphon all her power before he let her out of the walls. But that meant that something triggered the need for a grandchild. Something that meant Leuruna wouldn't be around forever and that he needed a new source...

"We can't let you near him," Rivven said, but I barely heard him through the buzzing in my ears. "We have to keep you safe. We'll hide you in Tromodia. You won't go anywhere near the Imrati."

"I'm going to the Imrati, Rivven," I said slowly, confidently, as my head cleared. "And make no mistake, I am going to kill the godsdamned king."

Seventeen

Everything changed over the few restless hours I'd chased sleep. Rivven's presence pushed me away, like a buffer had been created around him. I found it difficult to look at him, even when I sensed his eyes burning into the back of my head. Something had shifted when he reached for his sword last night. I felt hollower than before, when I'd held the secret close to my chest. Despite him knowing the truth now and seeming to understand, I no longer felt his presence as a safety net. Instead, I wondered painfully whether he saw me as a means to an end now. Or worse as representative of proof that everything the king touched withered.

Here I was another wounded soul—collateral of the whims of Balram. It was how I'd built my identity, but now that I'd seen so much of the world outside of Centos, I no longer wanted to define my life by my father's cruelty. I wished only to escape it along with my sister to find and explore our own desires. Sadly, until now, I'd thought perhaps Rivven would be part of that future, beyond the assassination, when I would have the opportunity to give my entire focus to whatever—or whomever—I wanted.

I'd expected Rivven to lose trust in me when he found out who I was. Ironically, it had been the other way around, as I'd lost some of the innocent trust I'd so blindly placed in him. All I could see was his hand reaching for his weapon. All I could feel was a pain in my chest like he'd carved out my heart. It might have been a silly reaction, but there it was, impossible to ignore. It hurt far worse than anything my father had done because I hadn't expected it.

The certainty that Galan could feel the chasm that had grown overnight between Rivven and I was reinforced by his lack of gloating about saving our arses from the cannibalistic elves with his air powers. Instead, he remained silent as we marched onward toward the sea. It appeared he too had secrets, like the extent of his abilities.

"Grohier is just over the next hill," Galan said, throwing an arm over my shoulder and making me wince. "You'll love it, Nye. I might be biased, but my city is the best in Tromodia."

Rivven overtook us without slowing his pace. The set of his shoulders was so tense, I imagined his muscles would protest later. Galan followed the trajectory of my glare and hummed softly, arm still slung over my own tense shoulders.

"He's probably scented the sea air. It's been a long time for him to be away," Galan said, nodding to himself. "He'll relax once he gets an ale or two in him and we're settled in the boat."

I stopped walking, causing him to jerk to a halt in confusion.

"Boat?" I repeated.

"A vessel that floats on water." Galan spoke as though I were a child. I smacked his arm, hard.

"I know what it is, but why are we going on one?"

"It's a houseboat. It's Riv's home. Didn't he tell..." It was Galan's turn to narrow his eyes at Riv's vanishing back. "No, I supposed he didn't."

Rotating my neck, I released a few cracks that I rubbed after. "Great. A floating house." Swearing under my breath, I picked up my pace as I crested the last hill.

I could feel Galan's smirk at my expression, but I couldn't help it. The scene that spread before us was something out of one of the library's fairy tale books I'd devoured as a child. It reminded me of Rune's favorite story of Illio and the place he'd lived before he'd frightened everyone into subservience. I wondered, not for the first time, if the story of the gods dividing up humanity's magic after he created the Shadow Hand was real or fiction.

The colorful town, filled with humble wooden buildings painted red, blue, and white, backed up to the largest body of water I'd ever seen. Blue, in brilliant hues from light to jewel, flowed farther than my eyes could see, meeting the horizon and putting even the brilliance of the sun-filled sky to shame. It was far from still, always moving, lapping at the white sand behind the boardwalk like a hungry beast. Its roar matched the image.

"She's beautiful, isn't she?" Galan whispered then inhaled deeply, his chest pushing forward so far, I thought the button on his turquoise shirt would burst.

Sniffing, I caught a whiff of something salty and sour, different from the ozone smell of rain. Not unpleasant...just...unique. I supposed to them it smelled like home.

"What's wrong, Nye?" Galan asked, noticing my face.

Perhaps, I wasn't very good at hiding my emotions. Not like I thought I'd been, anyway. No one had bothered to pay attention before, and now both he and Rivven could read me far too easily.

The problem was I'd thought of home, and I had no such nostalgia or longing for it. Nor for the cloyingly sweet scent of rotting vegetation that belonged to my father's kingdom. All I wanted was to go back, somehow get Rune out, and bring her here to show her what the world should be like.

"Just remembering something," I mumbled, then hurried along the curling path toward the village below.

By the time I fell into Rivven's shadow, he'd reached the edge of the boardwalk nearest the water. This close the city wasn't quite as idyllic as it had seemed from the top of the hill. Paint on the buildings was chipped and faded in places, some overridden with graffiti. Parts of the walkway had collapsed, making it mandatory to watch where I stepped. I cringed when Rivven's weight caused a normal enough looking spot to bow beneath him with a creaking, cracking sound.

He didn't falter, just kept striding past boarded-up storefronts and closed doors. He aimed for an alleyway that trailed down to a small pier where several beat-up boats bobbed, tied to rusted posts.

Zeroing in on the one at the end of the short pier, he leaped across the small chasm where it struggled to free itself from the rope and disappeared inside a dark square shaped opening.

I took in the supposed boathouse, most of the white rubbed off to the point that the natural wood showed beneath. It looked about as long as if Rivven and Galan had lied down feet to head plus a bit. The large round wheel let me know where the front end was as much as the slight point before it. A strange image of Rivven popped in my mind, muscles straining as he steered the enormous helm, a carefree expression I'd never witnessed lighting his face. I shook myself, hoping it wasn't as difficult to balance on the thing as it looked. I took the same leap Rivven had over the edge of the vessel and onto the deck.

I threw out my arms just in case, but even though the sea beneath caused the whole thing to be in constant motion, I found I could manage more easily than I'd anticipated. I grinned and peered into the dark opening he'd disappeared down. Stairs led the way to where a light bobbed in and out of view with the rocking of the boat. The steps narrowed with no railing but closed in paneled walls framed it.

Following the trail, I ducked beneath a low hanging frame. I entered into a living space crammed with a small bunk bed that looked far too short for Riv's long body on one side and a table and two rickety chairs on the other. A lamp swung from above, the sole source of light. Rivven must have lit it when he'd come down here. On the table, papers and parchment were spread along with quills and bits and pieces of some sort of mechanism, but I had no clue what. Before me, toward the bow, and where I judged must be below the big ship's wheel, was a thin door. Assuming that's where he'd gone, I approached.

I'd tell him I was going to stay at an inn somewhere. No sense in making us both uncomfortable. He owed me nothing, and I owed him the same. Maybe both of us trying to use the Imrati to kill the king would mean we'd have double the chances.

Why I was so damned nervous to tell him, I had no idea. Maybe it was merely the queasy feeling of being inside the small space as it moved on the water. Throwing open the door, I stepped through.

The tiny washroom confronted me with little space between a small toilet, single sink beneath which Rivven's clothing was bunched into a crumpled mess, and a narrow, vertical cube where Rivven stood completely naked below the spray of a small waterfall. Unaware of my presence, he let the water flow over his head and shoulders all the way to his feet, where it swirled down a series of tiny holes to disappear.

For a good minute, I gaped at the sight before me. He was pure muscled perfection, honed into a deadly fighting machine. Even the white scar I hadn't noticed in the Night Forest that first day marring his hip and thigh, it seemed to add to rather than detract from his beauty. And then there was his cock...

I fixated on the way the water trailed over it in a semi-hard state, dripping onto the floor. I couldn't help but wonder what it might feel like in my hands or taste like in my mouth.

Swallowing, I started to back out and wait. But his familiar deep voice stopped my retreat.

"Might as well stay and finish the show," he said, and it was hard to tell if he meant it as a punch or a joke. Either way, my cheeks burned.

I leaned against the now open door and tried to look annoyed as he finished cleaning off and waved away the waterfall. It disappeared through a cut in the wall near the ceiling.

Rivven shook out his long hair like an animal after falling in a stream, spraying me in the process, then groped for a soft-looking cloth that hung over the edge of the sink. He rubbed it over his face and head, then patted down his body, finally tying it around his waist where the low V dipped, pointing right toward the now hidden treasure I'd discovered.

"Couldn't wait?" he asked with a wicked grin as he stepped up into my personal space, eating the distance we'd kept all morning.

"I'm going to stay at an inn," I announced, daring him with my expression to argue.

He shrugged. "Probably more comfortable. But how do you plan to pay, little spy?"

"I think you can stop calling me that, now that you know exactly who I am." I hurtled the words at him as he pushed past me into the main room where he opened a trunk in the corner and began digging out fresh clothing. "And I don't know. Maybe I can offer to work in exchange."

"Should I call you by your title?" he asked when he came up for air with a pale-yellow shirt.

"Please just use my name." I hated the idea of him referring to me as a princess.

"Very well, your highness."

"That's *your* title," I threw back at him, red faced from anger now instead of embarrassment.

"Not if your sister is in charge. I get to float off to sea after I kill Balram, the royal bastard. She's your problem then."

"*Excuse* me?"

Rivven dropped the towel and pulled on some fresh pants right in front of me. But I stared hard at his face, refusing to take the bait so he could tease me and avoid the conversation.

"You want me to spare your sister," he said, shirt on but open over his chest as he approached to take my arms in his hands.

"You won't kill her. I promise you that," I said, fighting the urge to shove him off. "I'll see you dead first."

At that he tilted his head, and I couldn't identify the emotion that passed quickly over his face. "She's been used and abused by your father for her whole life you said."

My throat thickened but I let out a strangled, "Yes."

"She's broken," he said sadly, and I nodded, swallowing hard. "Nyah, please tell me how then can she rule? Truly rule? With all honesty, is she capable?"

I thought of Leuruna in one of her catatonic phases after she'd been drained by our father. The way she disappeared inside of herself when things became difficult. I thought of the way she couldn't look at him, the way she dressed like a child, the way she never left the palace.

The tremble in my chin began before the wave of dizziness swallowed me. As though it felt the precariousness of my thoughts, the boat rose and fell in an unsettling wave, tossing me into the table where I grabbed at the wall and slid into one of the chairs.

Rivven waited, watching me, but if I spoke, if I admitted it, did that strengthen his resolve that she was something in the way to be eliminated? *Get it together.*

"You're looking for another excuse to kill her," I said, but the words carried too much fear, too much heaviness, and they lacked the bite I'd intended. No, it came out as an earnest plea and not what I'd hoped at all.

The understanding in his eyes made me bristle as he sat in the other seat and leaned across the table. "I'm sorry I said that."

"I'm not. I'm glad I know where I stand." I looked pointedly past him where his sword and scabbard leaned against the trunk.

"I'm not going to kill you, Nyah." He smirked when he said it.

My head snapped up. "No, you're not, but you seemed to have no problem with the idea last night."

Leaning back, Rivven's face lit with surprise. "Is that what this is about?" He laughed, and it was too loud and obnoxious in this stifling space.

I stared, not answering until he stopped showing amusement.

"I overreacted. Okay? I've had the pleasure of those I trusted turning on me before."

"You trusted me?" I asked.

"I still do." He reached out and set one large, warm yet calloused hand over mine lightly like he was afraid I'd yank it away. "You saved my life on that mountain."

My heart twisted. Damn it hurt when he was so earnest yet kept acting in such conflicting ways. How could he still trust me, if he was ready to pull his sword on me?

"I want your word you won't kill her," I said. For some reason I believed he would not break a vow. It didn't mean I'd trust him exactly, but I would feel better.

Rivven grimaced. "I do not intend to kill her."

"That's not quite the commitment I was looking for," I said. "I mean it, Rivven. I want a promise or I'm going to the inn to find work. I'll do this on my own."

"While I'm sure you'd make a fine whore, somehow I don't see you being happy in that capacity." His words shocked me.

"Not that kind of work."

"That's the only kind you'll find a ready need for I'm afraid." Rivven stood, words bitter and posture stiff. "With no unifying ruler, Gahair is not the city it used to be. In fact, if you choose to go to the inn, make sure to keep your sword handy. All you'll find are pirates, thieves, whores, and the like."

"Guess you fit in perfectly then." He whipped around to face me, and

I continued, "A deposed king turned assassin who turned his back on his people instead of taking his rightful place."

For a fleeting moment, I wondered if he would snap and strike at me. But as my words seeped into his skin he stiffened instead, taking a rigid step forward.

"I get that you're angry." He bit off the words, but it was clear I'd gotten through that thick skull of his. Some small part of me regretted it, but I shoved that away because the rest of me wanted to lash out, to scream, to fight. And...and...Rivven was the only person I'd ever felt safe enough to truly let loose on.

It was then Galan entered, nearly tripping down the steps with a huge smile on his face that disappeared the moment he saw us.

"I stop at the inn for some information and the two of you look like you're about to burn the city down."

Rivven's jaw tightened, muscle twitching. The thin line of his mouth refused to open as he locked his gaze on me. He wasn't going to tell Galan. He was offering me a choice.

"I thought the inn was dangerous," I said, hand on hip.

"Not for me," Galan bragged. "Lou, the proprietor knows me well. I'll have the best room, overlooking the sea."

"You mean she'll share her own bed with you," Rivven corrected never taking his eyes off me.

Galan shrugged. "Same difference. More entertaining. We should start training at daybreak though. It seems the Imrati will be run differently this year."

"What do you mean?" I asked, both Rivven and I moving toward him.

"According to the gossip, contenders will be picked up at one of several rendezvous points and taken to a secure location. Only those invited or registered will be allowed to witness the trials. It seems the evil king is indeed paranoid. Can't imagine why."

"Where's the closest rendezvous?" Rivven demanded.

"Right on the beach. At least you don't have to worry about travel time. We have two and a half weeks to train, not nearly enough. We'll need every second of it."

"How do we know what to train for?" I asked. To my knowledge, past

Imrati involved a random mix of mental and physical tests, and the only similarity among all the trials was the danger involved.

Three trials would take place. One for each god and goddess, therefore, one for each major kingdom and their own indigenous magic. Since the prize, the powerstone, was to be passed to a new victor every few years, it made sense. But my father had held onto it for too long, creating an imbalance never meant to be. The Imrati was a contest of magic— about magic. Those who couldn't wield were still allowed to enter, but they stood a very low chance of survival. Even less chance of winning.

"We don't know, and that's why we need as much time as possible," Rivven answered. "You can have the top bunk, Nyah. If you are hungry, there's still a bit of meat in my satchel. I'll see you in the morning."

"Where are you going?" Galan asked, saving me the hassle as Rivven brushed by him on his way to the steps.

"I've been gone a long time. I owe Sharlyne a visit." With one last glance my way, Rivven snatched up his scabbard and bounded up the stairs that looked far too fragile to hold him.

Galan turned to me with an accusatory look. "What did you do to him?"

"Me?" I demanded. "Blame his stubborn royal ass." Using a single rung of the ladder, I climbed into the top bed and pulled the blanket over my head where I waited until I heard Galan sigh then leave before coming up for air.

One question rose to the top of the whirlpool of questions and doubts threatening to drown me.

Who is Sharlyne?

EIGHTEEN

Sleeping on a boat was easy. The gentle rocking motion lulled me into unconsciousness far faster than intended. Or maybe I desperately needed the rest. Either way, I rose again in the same position I'd drifted off in, body stiff and heavy.

I leaped lightly to the floor and poked my head above the surface to get my bearings. The first light of dawn teased the horizon line across the water, a gentle swirl of pink coiling up toward the darkened sky where both moons sat round, fat, and pale silver.

Only the rush of the water greeted me, and I decided I had time to wash up and change. Unfortunately, though, I lacked the water wielding Rivven possessed, so I opted to take a dip in the ocean.

The sand was warm and soft on the soles of my feet, a welcome surprise. The first slow slosh of water that ran up and over my toes was even warmer. With a smile, I chased its retreat, splashing into the heavenly bath. Every ache and bruise on my body sighed in relief as I submerged and pushed off the sand. I swam out to where the land sloped far below me. The water itself was crystal clear, revealing a hidden world of brightly colored coral and fish. There were so many, I consciously had to avoid running into them as they swam in small schools in and around the reef.

I broke the surface, gulping in air and in a much better mood as I faced the never-ending length of the ocean. The sky had brightened to a warm orange mixed with bright pinks and yellows as it pushed away the dark and revealed the pale blue of the morning sky.

Somewhere close by birds called, announcing the arrival of the sun. It was the most incredible scene I'd ever witnessed. A tear rolled down my cheek, melding with the ocean water, far too small to have any impact. Yet, when it hit the surface, a wave swelled from the depths, lifting me higher before carrying me closer to shore.

I was much further out than I'd anticipated. The beach and pier were now nothing more than small toys in the distance. Was that…Rivven and Galan? Two figures waved their arms above their heads.

I lifted my hand to wave back. *Guess they're eager to start training.* I sucked in a breath and dove, propelling back toward the shore. I didn't get far, however, as my path was blocked by a bare-breasted woman, long sunshine hair floating around her like a sheet of velvet. Stunned, I drew back, forcing myself upright as I floated beneath the waves. I took in the sight as I tried to understand where she'd come from.

When she twisted, I saw the rest of her. Where her waist began to dip toward her hips, scales started feathering over her skin. They grew thicker and larger, shining iridescent green even beneath the surface. She had no legs, only a fishtail.

I headed for the surface to get some air, and she popped up right in front of me. Her eyes were too large, her nose two nostrils on a flat face, and her teeth were small and pointed when she smiled. But somehow, she remained beautiful, if inhuman. Her skin glistened a pale green in the now bright sunlight, and her hair glowed with an unknown light.

A mermaid? Of all the creatures I'd read about in the library, and all the art and stories from the museum, the mermaid was the one I'd least considered likely to be true. Then again, the being before me looked nothing like the attractive humanesque female typically depicted. I supposed men saw what they wanted.

After about a minute of floating there, she opened her mouth and emitted a terrible sound. I threw my hands over my ears and nearly sank below the surface again. Upon seeing my reaction, she snapped her mouth closed, appearing offended.

Offshore Rivven and Galan pumped their arms and legs hard against the water as they swam toward us, still too far away. When I glanced back at the mermaid, she was so close her chest grazed mine, though thankfully mine was wrapped in a simple undergarment.

She smiled again, revealing those disturbing teeth. When I opened my mouth to speak, she grabbed me and yanked me under. We hurtled toward the sea floor where the coral twisted into a maze.

I wriggled, kicking my feet to try to get leverage or stun her into releasing her ironclad grip. But two more mermaids rose up to meet us in a blanket of bubbles. They took hold of me from all sides as I thrashed against them, unsure how long I could hold my breath. My heart pounded in my ears and my lungs constricted as instinct over, desperate to free itself.

They pulled me toward the coral, and I managed to free one hand. I reached toward the surface where Rivven's face appeared as he dove after me. We locked gazes and a wave of calm washed over me.

My heart warmed in my chest as the magic inside me rose. But what good was fire beneath the ocean?

Rivven parted the water before him and it propelled him at me, faster than anyone could naturally swim.

Reaching for my own old, tried-and-true power, I shoved all three of the beings away, forcing them to release me to float in place. The original mermaid, still right in front of me, bared her teeth and snapped at me just as the tip of Rivven's sword crashed through her chest with a burst of dark blood clouding the water.

We both gawked at it before he yanked it out and she floated backward, wide eyes staring at nothing as she seemed to reach for me.

My chest burned as I kicked for the surface past Rivven who floated, sword ready to take on the others if they decided to be brave. Lights burst into my vision as I kicked harder, chest cramping with the need to draw breath. I wasn't going to make it. I couldn't hold it.

A burst of pressure shot beneath my feet, propelling me faster than a viper's strike. Breaking the surface, I gasped for breath, coughing, and choking as I fought to pull more air inside my burning lungs. Galan grabbed me, pulling my back against his chest and wrapping an arm around my front to keep me from sinking again.

Once my breathing calmed to a slower wheeze, I stilled. *Where is Rivven?* He couldn't stay down there forever. He had to breathe too.

"Let go," I rasped, and Galan did so I could spin toward him. "Give me your sword," I demanded, already reaching for it beneath the water.

"I don't think that's a good idea," he said, smirking. "Let Riv—"

But I'd pulled his weapon so smoothly he hadn't noticed, until I held it up clutched between my hands.

"Nye," he warned, face darkening.

I blew him a kiss and dove, sword outstretched before me.

Rivven was wrestling for his own weapon with one mermaid while trying to keep the other off his body. Blood floated from a deep wound on his arm. As I approached, I realized my error—it was several deep punctures.

It bit him!

It twisted away from his reach and ducked low, opening its mouth to take a bite from his thigh. I plunged Galan's sword through its side, right between its ribs and into its heart.

Free of the second threat, Rivven used his left hand to punch the other beast until it released its hold on his sword. It bared its teeth but backed away rapidly as we both held blades toward it. It turned and swam, disappearing into the coral forest.

Grabbing my waist, Rivven pulled me against him as another burst of a jet stream rocketed us both up to the surface. Galan snatched his sword back from me, then started swimming toward shore without another word.

Rivven's waterspout carried us back to the beach at a slower pace. The energy of it sputtered out as we reached the shallows, and I tucked his arm over me so I could help half-lead him from the water.

"That was a lot of magic," I said, collapsing beside him on the soft sand.

"You seem to keep getting into dangerous situations that call for it," he grumbled.

"They really ought to put warning signs on the beach." I glanced around as if more monsters lurked. "Danger, mermaids, swim at your own risk or something."

"No one around here is ignorant enough to need the sign," he said after a long moment.

"You know I've never been here. I had no idea." I shoved his stupid shoulders then made a face when he winced and clutched at his wound. "Sorry."

"It's good for him," Galan said, joining us, somehow completely dry. "Training wounded will help. There could be similar circumstances in the Imrati. Now stand up, you two."

We did, and a wind whooshed around us, settling when we were dry as well and I became painfully aware of two things. The first was that Galan had used his own powers to dry us all off and second, I was still in my undergarments.

Neither man made a comment as I silently pulled my training garments out of my satchel and dressed. Although, I caught Rivven's eyes on me more than once—at which point he'd quickly look away. I smiled inwardly.

"What do we start with?" I asked, stretching my limbs.

"I've been studying the past Imrati to find patterns," Galan said with a wink. "The Tromodian trial almost always has to do with a physical championship. It's varied between weapons and no weapons, brute strength and agility, or even stamina. Typically, there's a foreign terrain that could be anything from an empty plain with nowhere to hide to rocky hills with treacherous footing to desert to—"

"In other words, it could be anything," Rivven commented, arms crossed. "Helpful."

"Who decides the nature of the trials?" I asked, interrupting them as I scrubbed my hair with a cloth to finish drying it.

"The gods do," Galan said. "Or rather they send the instructions to the holder of the powerstone, and they set it up."

My heart sank as I dropped the cloth to the ground. "So, King Balram has control of the trials."

"That's true, but would he defy the gods directly?" Rivven asked with sincerity, gaze seeming to search inside my soul for the answer.

"If he thought he could avoid retribution, absolutely," I said, fists on hips and feet planted wide. "And when was the last time the gods intervened here? They haven't exactly done anything about the fact he held onto the powerstone passed in the Imrati for so long."

"Until now," Galan said.

I knew nothing of what happened to prompt his actions. The assumption he was planning to force Leuruna to marry and provide another magical heir to drain over time still sickened me. *But why now? And why was the drawbridge up that night he'd announced it?*

"What's going on in that head, little spy?" Rivven asked in a low voice, stepping close enough for me to smell cedar and tobacco. But I hadn't forgotten his reaction the day before. I refused to give him any more information that could betray my sister.

"Just trying to understand Balram's motivations," I said then pulled my sword, causing him to take a step back. "Let's do this."

Conversation fell away as we sparred. Rivven's strength, coupled with his skill, made me feel clumsy and weak for what may have been the first time in my life. But my agility and balance challenged him a little. With Galan I was far more evenly matched with sword play. But the most useful bit of the morning might have been watching them fight.

Galan anticipated Rivven's moves, or at least seemed to, as he used Rivven's momentum to score a few crucial seconds to strike. But when he called on his air powers to throw Rivven off balance, Rivven responded by summoning a wave up the shore and sending Galan to the ground where his weapon was knocked from his hand. Rivven was on top of him before he could recover, and despite the way his hair whipped around as it pulled from the tie he'd gathered it into, Galan yielded.

"You didn't try that with me," I said, leaping from the rock I'd been seated on. I bit down the wince that tried to escape when I landed on sore muscles. "Adding magic, I mean."

Habitual magic was not something common in Centos. It was a silent rule that the king was the only wielder. Only Leuruna, and therefore myself, made use of our abilities, and when I thought about it, never in his presence. My brows furrowed at the realization.

"You aren't ready," Rivven said.

"The match would end too quickly," Galan added with another wink that made me want to smack him.

"Try me." I freed my sword. "As a matter of fact, let's all spar together. It isn't just one-on-one in the Imrati, is it?"

The men exchanged a glance and lunged simultaneously. I summoned the air magic that had become like second nature to me and executed a perfect backflip up onto the rock where I'd been seated earlier. Caught off guard, both my opponents stumbled, and I used my good old trick to shove them onto their stomachs. I pounced, landing with one foot on the small of each man's back, my sword at Rivven's neck.

"Surrender," I demanded, feeling rather smug—at least until burning pain shot through the sole of the foot planted on Rivven's back.

I screeched, yanking it away and a gust of wind shoved me so hard it felt like hands slamming against my back. I flew forward, twisting just enough to land hard on my shoulder. Before I could recover, Rivven was on me, the weight of his body pinning mine in place. His hands circled my wrists, tugging them up over my head as I wriggled wildly beneath him, trying to free myself—but to no avail. He was too damn huge and heavy.

"Keep moving like that and this will turn into something else entirely," he whispered in my ear.

I stopped struggling for a minute, panting, but feeling the truth of his words as his cock pressed against my stomach hard enough to bruise. Then, an idea struck me—I smiled.

"Like this?" I whispered back and focused my motions in a far more purposeful way than my previous flailing, bucking my hips as I wiggled against his length. When he caught his breath, loosening his hold a fraction, I shimmied upward until our bodies were better aligned and rubbed my core against him.

Instead of completely distracting him as was my intention, a wave of electric desire surged through me, and it took everything I had not to gasp and moan.

"Are we still sparring or do you two want some privacy?" Galan asked, and Rivven was off me in an instant.

Sitting up, I glared at them both. "I almost had the upper hand," I complained.

"It's a good tactic," Rivven said, refusing to meet my eyes. But a ruddy color rose beneath his copper skin. "If a larger man pins you in the trials, that's a valid way to distract him enough to stab him."

"Now I wish I'd been the one to take you down," Galan said, offering me a hand up.

"Very funny. We all know the rules are to use whatever innate abilities we have." I brushed the sand off my black outfit.

"Let's break for food and work in the boat this afternoon," Rivven said, recovered now and grimacing as usual.

"What are we working on?" I asked, glad for a rest and some nourishment.

"Magic studies," Rivven answered as he gathered his things. "I want to know the exact extent of your powers."

I swallowed at the knowing look he shot me. He meant he wanted to know the princess' powers. And I wasn't sure that was such a good idea. At the same time, I knew I needed training, if I was going to wield the magic Rune sent me. I'd need it if I was going to kill my father and defend my sister.

"Are there any magic instructors in this city?" I asked, following them onto the boat, where instead of going below deck, we stayed on top and sat on white benches near the bow.

"We'll be your instructors," Rivven said then disappeared below deck only to reappear moments later with a large basket. "Between us we are adept at three of the four elements, and you seem to have propensity for two, air and fire."

The scent of something warm and sweet drifted from the basket as he set it before us and removed the cloth from the top. This time, I did moan at the delicious aroma as he lifted a freshly baked loaf of braided bread from inside. He broke off large chunks and handed them to Galan and I before diving back in for a knife and a tub of something white and creamy looking.

"Whassat?" I asked through a mouthful of the most amazing bread I'd ever put in my maw.

"Cheese." Rivven tugged the remainder of the giant piece from my mouth. He spread a large helping of whatever type of cheese that was on my bread, then he handed it back.

I eyed it suspiciously, upset that he would ruin something so divine. But I sniffed, then darted my tongue out to taste it. In seconds, I was devouring the creamy sweet combination and reaching for more. It turned out he also had fresh Karonberry preserves and Pilas in there.

After a glorious meal and a full skein of water, I lay back on the bench staring at the cerulean sky and a few puffs of clouds floating lazily overhead.

"Get up, it's magic time," Rivven announced, shoving my legs off the seat, so I had to sit up straight.

"Fine. Teach me how to set your boots on fire," I groused at him.

He had the audacity to chuckle. "Tell you what, if you learn enough, you'll eventually be able to match me at sparring. That'll feel pretty good I'd wager."

"And if you're my teacher, how am I ever supposed to best you? You'll know all my moves, plus whatever you haven't shown me."

"She has a fair point," Galan said, picking his teeth. "We should hire Lou."

"That would be like announcing to the entire town she was here. It's a terrible idea." Rivven turned on Galan, but my interest was piqued.

"Wait, a second. I have a disguise and a fake name. What's so bad about the idea if this Lou person is a good teacher?" I demanded, standing.

I debated asking whether we should consider Sharlyne as a teacher, still curious who Rivven had run off to visit the night before. But I stayed my tongue, not wanting to distract from the idea of a true magic tutor when for all I knew this Sharlyne woman wasn't even a wielder. Though I'd have bet she was good at wielding her female wiles. Visions of Elora from the desert elves mixed with the new name, causing me to glower.

Instead of speaking, Rivven ground his teeth. I grinned, liking the way the mention of this Lou person upset him for some reason.

"Galan, take me to Lou," I said, still staring at Rivven.

"I'm not paying for it," Rivven said, folding his arms as though his decision was final.

"I have plenty, don't you worry, Nye," Galan said, offering his arm.

With that, Rivven disappeared beneath deck, and I let Galan lead me along the boardwalk. A few more people milled about in the daytime, mostly dressed in either lurid or ragged clothing—sometimes both, as though they wanted to pretend to be rich but hadn't had money in some time. No one met my eyes with more than a furtive glance as they scurried around. Galan seemed not to notice as he paraded us forward then up a hill toward some larger homes and buildings.

The grounds in this new area appeared better kept and cared for. I caught sight of a man, back glistening with sweat as he hacked at a set of bushes in front of one home. The skin of his shoulders was darker than the rest of him, reddened and leathery from the sun.

Instead of taking me to a home, Galan turned a few more corners and aimed for a large, three story building painted yellow with white trim. A gaudy sign hung above the door, proclaiming it to be the *Shipwreck Tavern and Inn*.

Boisterous laughter spilled onto the walkway as we approached, along with merry music. When I hesitated at the door, Galan simply tugged me through with him, bursting into a well-kept dining area filled with barrels that supported table tops and wooden seats with red velvet cushions. A bar sat along the far wall, and to the left, a stage rested with a big scarlet curtain, currently the backdrop for an enormous instrument being played by a man with a white beard. He swayed back and forth, fingers dancing over a combination of strings and keys that sent sound shooting from a row of uneven pipes standing above them.

Galan led me to the right where a staircase rose to the second and third floor rimmed with railings. At the top of the first landing stood a woman. She wore a deep purple gown with flowing sleeves and a corset so tight that her breasts threatened to pop out of the top. Her long red hair was pulled back in a cascade of curls, and her beautiful face was painted with brightly colored makeup. She grinned at Galan and gracefully sauntered down the steps, letting her long fingers trail over the banister.

Looking away was impossible. I had no idea what her age might have been as she carried herself with the maturity of someone who'd been around for some time. Yet, her skin was smooth without so much as a single line or wrinkle.

I realized with some embarrassment that her sea-blue eyes had caught mine staring, and she now watched me with amusement as she reached the last step. She paused there, slightly above where we stood.

"What trouble has the gray fox brought me now?" Her voice was soft, yet deep and melodic as she continued to take me in.

"Louvalia, this is Starla. Starla, Lou. I have taken it upon myself to mentor this young orphan whose goal is to enter the Imrati. And by that, I mean I wish to hire you."

"I doubt she'd have any trouble doing what I do, but I have no idea how that would help in the Imrati," Lou said with a wink.

I glanced toward Galan whose grin made him truly look like a fox. "She needs a magic tutor. A good one," he said.

"Magic can't be learned. It's innate." Lou's entire countenance changed as she stiffened and held the railing so tight her knuckles turned white, standing out against her tawny skin.

"I think you'll want to hear her story," Galan said, flipping a golden coin I hadn't seen him holding before. "Perhaps, in private?"

The corners of her mouth tightened, but she nodded behind her and turned to lead us up the stairs. We followed into one of the many rooms to find a large four-poster bed, a window with a small balcony, an armoire, and a desk with a mirror and another velvet lined chair. With the door shut behind us, the music from downstairs faded, but a pounding on the wall behind Lou caught my attention. The rhythmic knocking seemed to shake the small painting of the sea on the wall, but neither of the others acknowledged it.

"What's your story?" Lou asked, hands clasped before her and eyebrow raised.

Galan opened his mouth to speak, but Lou cut him off. "Tell me yourself."

Licking my lips, I took in Galan's shrug then turned to Lou. "I was kidnapped by pirates as a young girl." I had no clue where that came from, and I think it surprised her as much as it did me. But I kept going. "They made me work and told me for years I'd better be as valuable as my parents claimed—or I'd be fish food."

Pausing here, I noted that Galan remained almost impossibly still, but Lou's attention was on me. Since she wasn't mocking me yet or throwing us out, I continued.

"When we stopped here, Galan and Rivven saw them threaten me. The captain had given me an ultimatum, either show my magic or be used up as I should have been at the beginning. I tried, and I guess they noticed that not only did my hands spark with fire, but when the captain reached for me, I sort of...flew from the boat."

"You have more than one element," Lou said finally.

"Rivven and Galan fought them off and saved me," I said taking a deep breath for both dramatic effect and to steady my nerves. "And well, I entered the Imrati with them to make some gold. I learned a lot about fighting by watching my captors and practicing when they slept. But I don't know enough about my magic."

If the pirates in the story were the king and his guard, it was almost the truth. I waited with a dry mouth.

"And what do you get out of it, Gray? You do nothing out of the goodness of your heart," Lou challenged.

"I'm hurt." Galan put a hand over his chest in mock pain. "But if our girl wins, then I have a direct link to Centos and whatever riches await me there."

"Very well," Lou said as the pounding on the wall finally ceased. "Leave her with me. She can stay here for two weeks and train. And don't you or that animal you hang around with bother her. She needs to focus."

Galan bowed low and opened the door to leave. I worried what I'd gotten myself into and reached to stop him, but Lou cut me off.

"Payment up front."

Galan froze, spun around, marched to Lou, and handed her a small bag heavy with coin. He caught my eye as he passed by me and winked before leaving and shutting the door behind him.

I spun back to face Lou who was shutting a drawer on the desk. I opened my mouth to ask what was next when a new pounding started on the opposite wall. She smiled as I glanced over at it.

"Busy day for the girls. Pay it no mind. Now, sit please."

I dropped onto the corner of the enormous bed and folded my hands.

"Now, tell me the truth. Who are you and why are you here?"

Nineteen

"I don't know what you—"

"I'm not the gullible fool Galan seems to take me for. But there has to be a reason if he wants me to do this. What's the real story? If you tell me the truth, I might not kill you."

"Kill me?" I scoffed, standing and drawing my sword. "You'd threaten me when you've been paid to help me?"

"Settle down." Lou made a squeezing motion with her hands and my arms flew to my sides, bound tightly by invisible air currents. The same pressure shoved me flat on the bed and threatened to choke me.

The face of my captor loomed over me as I struggled to breathe with the weight of what felt like a dragon sitting on my chest.

"I don't *actually* plan to kill you. I just wanted to see how you'd react. You reached for your sword instead of your power. We have a lot of work to do."

The pressure lessened, but I didn't try to sit up. "Do you believe me?" I rasped.

"Hells no. You looked at the wall like you had no clue there were people fucking on the other side. If you'd been taken by pirates years ago, they'd have taught you about all that. Don't get me wrong, I'm glad for your sake that didn't happen. But I *do* want the truth. I think you owe it to me if I give you weeks of my time."

Whatever remained of the air that held me down dissolved. I did sit but didn't lift my sword. Instead, I drew a deep breath. "I'm a runaway princess and I want to kill my father, the evil king, before he can drain my sister's power. She gifted me some of hers to keep it away from him, and I don't know how to access all of it—or even the extent of it. I am entering the Imrati so I can assassinate him and rescue her."

Lou watched me for a heartbeat of silence. I held my breath. But only the slight lift of her delicate eyebrows gave away any hint of surprise. Now that was something I'd pay to learn how to do.

"That's better. Now stand up. I'm going to take a look at what's in that heart of yours."

I rose, sheathing my sword and standing still as she circled me. When she got back around to the front of me, she raised two glowing white hands and set them against my chest. I gasped as something inside of me responded, a warm burst shoving from inside my ribcage to meet her.

The glow around her hands changed, turning crimson and hot. Yet, instead of burning me, it felt comforting as the pressure inside me doubled, burning back in response. Next, the color turned to blue and a wave of nausea overtook me as I swayed forward. I would have fallen if she hadn't been there, still braced against me and holding me up. Before I could ask, the color changed again to green, and this time, my balance returned, rooting me in place as a steady beat bounced against her palms—much like what had happened to the walls. This time it wasn't fucking though.

When she drew back, I dropped onto the bed again, setting my own hand against my heart.

"What was that?" I whispered.

Lou dropped into a seat at the desk, and for the first time since I'd met her, she looked a bit unsure. "You have all four elements within you in a seemingly unlimited supply. I've never seen anything like it."

"All four?" I repeated. "No, I've only ever shown fire and air."

"They're in there." Lou straightened. "And there's something else too. But it's everywhere. It's like you're made of some other type of magic. I've never felt anything but Tromodian elemental power. I don't know what it is and that I cannot teach you. I wield all four elements as well, but not in unlimited supply."

That had to be the innate magic of Centos. But I wasn't a powerful wielder like my sister. Besides, I didn't know if she could survive if she'd given me everything. So that meant what Lou felt had to be something else. *I won't share this with her... or Rivven.* If I learned to wield the elements, maybe I could use the same principles to unlock whatever it was.

"Tell me about the times you used your abilities. What was happening at that moment and how did you feel?"

I thought back. "I was being hurt by someone when the fire came out," I said, remembering the desert elf and her jealousy. A smile broke over me when I pictured her clutching her burnt hand. But then I recalled how she and her people tried to turn me over to my father and had nearly killed Rivven, the man she supposedly loved.

"Hmm," Lou grunted while examining my wrist. "And the air?"

"I was running and tried to make an impossible jump to escape being captured."

"Both times you were in danger and the element made sense in response. Air would help you make the leap, and fire would lash out at something causing pain."

"Then what will bring out the earth and water? I had trouble in the ocean before and nothing happened," I said as the pounding began on the opposite wall again.

"Interesting." Her eyes sparkled. "That's exactly what we need to find out."

Goose flesh prickled my arms as I hugged my naked body, shifting awkwardly from foot to foot while Lou filled a steaming copper tub. I'd hesitated when she instructed me to undress but decided she'd probably seen far more if she was running a brothel. At least I wasn't here for *that* sort of work. I complied, and as soon as she moved aside, I climbed into the warm water. The soreness in my muscles—buildup I hadn't even realized I'd been carrying since that morning— eased as I leaned back with a sigh.

"Comfy?" Lou asked.

"Yes," I agreed.

"Good. Hold your breath."

"Wha—" I sucked in some air and clamped my mouth shut just as the water rose above the edge of the bath and swirled around my head. Wildly, I tore at the stuff, trying to pry it from my face, but it followed my every move, drowning me even as I stood and tried to climb from the tub. Slipping, I slid back down inside.

"Focus!" Lou yelled, and I could hear it even through the water. "Clawing at it won't help. Your hands will pass straight through."

I stopped struggling for a frightening pause as my lungs cramped. It was like being trapped by the mermaids all over again. I closed my eyes and shoved with my mind, mentally screaming, *Get off*!

The water surrounding my head shot forward, releasing my face so I could gulp in air as it splashed into the tub and all over the tile below. I remained sitting, clutching the sides of the copper basin and gasping for breath as water ran off my hair and over me.

"Good," Lou said from the doorway. "Again."

I tried to protest, but the water was back so fast I barely had time to suck in another breath. *Bitch*, I thought, *you should try dealing with this.* When the water flew from my head, instead of falling, it rushed over Lou's beautiful face. Her eyes widened and her coiffed hair floated up behind and above her like a scarlet fan. She pushed with her hands at the air, and I fell against the tub with a painful jolt to the back of my head as the water crashed over me again.

"Ow," I complained, gingerly testing to be sure I hadn't cracked my skull open. When I looked again, her makeup had run in dark rivulets over her cheeks, circling her eyes in streaks of black. Her hair was flat, wet, and ruined, and she stood gasping for breath. But even though she looked like a woman who'd taken a beating, her eyes flashed with malice, and I knew she wasn't letting this go easily.

But I was ready. When she sent the water at me for a third time, I shoved with all my might, sending it back at her like a fist slamming into her chest and knocking her to the floor. I stood and climbed from the tub, unsure what to do next, yet certain she wasn't done.

Instead of water this time, she wrung her hands before her, sending a whirlwind of air around me. I tried to get a feel for the currents, but they were moving at such speed and power it made me dizzy as it lifted me into the air and across the bedroom. I hurtled toward the window which flew open at the last moment, and the cyclone spit me out, nothing below me but grass and dirt twenty feet down. It felt like the universe paused as I hung in the air, flailing my limbs.

I managed to catch a natural wind current and flew away from the house, landing in a tall tree at the other end of the yard. A wolf call made me turn to find a man leaning out of another window, no shirt on and a petite brunette woman behind him.

"A naked flying woman. How much for an hour with her?" he yelled.

The small woman behind him smacked him hard upside the head. Then Lou's voice answered from the open window I'd flown out of. "Back inside now."

I hesitated. But I'd just unlocked another power, even if it was under less than desirable circumstances. Anyway, where would I go naked, wet, and penniless? Certainly not back to Rivven so he could make fun of me. No, I wanted to do whatever it took to be able to win when I next sparred with him, even if it meant putting up with Lou.

With another steadying breath, I launched myself back through Lou's apartment, shutting the windows behind me. I landed softly on the ground near her and fidgeted. I was half afraid of what she'd do but also ready with fire burning a line from my heart to my fingertips.

You've got some spunk. That's for certain." Lou smiled and relaxed, patting my cheek. "Let's get you dressed. We only have a couple of weeks, and you need to be able to face an invincible king."

TWENTY

Six days passed by fast, as if a current had pulled me out to sea. I felt just as lost. All I could do was tread water, or in other words, follow along as best I could with Lou's lessons, which meant always being ready for a random attack. Not that anything quite that drastic had occurred. It took me almost forty-eight hours to understand it was due to the limitations on her powers. She needed time to recoup.

The hours in between were the most difficult. The more I tried to avoid thinking about Rivven, Rune, and the Imrati, the more it all seemed to stir in my mind. Lou and her "girls," as she called them, worked late into the evening, and I barricade myself in my room to avoid the raucous noises from the tavern below. Hoots, screams, and whistles rose above the music. I knew the stage was being used by some of the women that lived here and did more than just perform privately. Despite the smidge of curiosity niggling in my head, I did my best to shut it all out and focus on reading one of the Tromodian books I'd found on the library shelves downstairs.

A library wasn't something I'd expected to be in a brothel, but then again, I'd never been in one before. *Well, not a true one.* The prostitutes in Centos lived on the streets and dealt from the back of abandoned homes and shops as well as the dark alleys.

I hadn't corrected Lou when she'd assumed I was naïve. I may never have done the deed, but I'd witnessed plenty of guards and servants. It was something difficult to avoid when they had no compunction about doing it in drafty halls and stairwells. I'd even run off men who'd taken things too far while in the village when a woman screamed for help. Once, a man had pressed a filthy hand over her mouth and bent her over a barrel of trash. I'd looked right into those terror-stricken eyes and rushed out with Stealth, slicing off his hand at the wrist.

The man had run screaming, blood spurting from the gaping wound as the woman shrieked and fled from me, hiding behind other barrels. After that, I'd stayed clear of that alleyway.

In this house though, Lou ran a fair business. I'd learned quickly that the patrons not only respected her, but feared her abilities, which she'd show off—lighting a cigarette with her finger or blowing a kiss at a man and mussing his hair. I hadn't missed the way the patrons swallowed and stiffened when she did that or the smirk on her face when she demonstrated this on the first day as I'd dried off and pulled on clothes.

The clothes were another matter. She'd insisted I wear some of her girl's dresses so I fit in, and no one would question who I was. I'd agreed grudgingly, clarifying that if a man put hands on me, I'd kill him without a second thought. She'd shaken her head as she fixed her hair and makeup but assured me her clients knew to keep their hands and mouths to themselves, unless they'd cleared it with her and prepaid. When a girl was in training, she'd said, no one was allowed to paw at her unless she approached them.

Lou and her girls—I counted six in total—slept in daily, which I supposed made sense considering how late they worked. But no matter how noisy they were, or what hour my mind quieted enough to slip away into unconsciousness, I always woke just before dawn, wide-eyed and heart pounding. I tried to convince myself it was for fear of an attack from Lou. But repeated dreams featuring an assassin switching between the faces of my father, his advisor Serano, and Rufus, his Captain of the Guard, plagued me.

Arguing about wearing my sword beneath my clothing didn't change my mind or my habit. I wasn't letting it out of my sight. In fact, I used the quiet dawn hours in the courtyard below to practice my drills as I had in

Centos. I'd wear the training clothes I'd arrived in and workout until I was covered in a sheen of sweat—and the sounds of voices and clinking glasses wafted from the kitchen. Then I'd rush back upstairs, wash my things, and dress for the day.

On the fifth day, I'd chosen an emerald green dress with a slit up the side and layers of ruffled petticoats showing. It landed mid-calf above my laced boots and squeezed my ribs so hard I thought I'd pass out. The effect was to push the tops of my breasts up so high I was surprised they didn't hit me in the chin when I sat. But it wasn't like I stood out among the six workers or even Lou herself, so I decided to look at it as part of my training. I may not be comfortable or unconstrained during a trial and still expected to do battle.

On the way downstairs, I noticed Lou glance up. I braced. Sure enough, she shot a gust of wind at me that I easily redirected with a wave as I hurried down the remaining steps. Two girls were with her, sitting at an otherwise empty table near the bar and sipping from teacups. They looked over at me, one curious, the other with pursed lips, like she was holding back a complaint.

"Good morning," I sang, mostly directed at the scowling girl in the purple and black dress. Her long raven hair was tied up with a ribbon and streamed in a silky puddle down her back.

"Maybe for you, but my head is ready to split open," she muttered.

Maybe it wasn't me that had caused her expression. I relaxed a bit, feeling guilty for my assumption. I searched my memory for her name and came up with Mina. The other one I thought was Persy, or something like that.

"There's a plate for you here and a cup of tea with milk like you prefer," Lou said from the counter. "Bring it over without getting up."

The rolling of my eyes was immediate, but I stopped quickly. I sighed and focused on the plate and tea. Both items wobbled as they rose from the bar top, spilling a bit of liquid on the polished mahogany.

"One at a time," Lou barked, which made me unreasonably angry.

I narrowed my gaze at my breakfast and floated it over before me, setting it gently on the table between the two girls where I took a seat. Without looking, I flicked my fingers, and a dishtowel rose from the bar and smacked Lou in the chest.

"You don't mind wiping that up do you?" I asked sweetly as I sipped at my lukewarm tea. Without a thought, I tapped it with a nail. It warmed up perfectly.

Persy clapped as I blew on the now steaming drink, but Mina groaned, setting her head in her hands.

"Wish I had a healer for you, sweetheart," Lou told her. "But I can't afford one for every time one of you decides to take a sailor up on drinks all night."

Mina's slight shoulders trembled as she burrowed further into her palms. The anger I'd felt earlier flared again. She'd been doing her job, and she found it easier to live with if she was a bit drunk.

A wave of cold doused my skin, raising the hair on the back of my neck and arms. *How the hell did I know that?* I swallowed hard and considered the woman before me. My fingers twitched.

"Mina?" I said quietly, setting down my fork. "May I try something? To help your headache?"

Mina peered between two fingers warily. "As long as it doesn't hurt."

Closing my eyes, I thought of the ether as Rivven had described it then focused on the energy I pictured pulsing from her body. It was like someone shot me between the eyes with a slingshot. I stifled a gasp. Reaching up with my hand, I pictured a dark line of pain connecting the two spots on our heads and tugged. In my mind it came loose, and I tossed it away into a small fire I'd conjured. Then, I opened my eyes.

Embarrassment flooded through me. My face burned harder than when Rivven teased me. But just as I was about to run up to my room and refuse to return, Mina lowered her hands and blinked at me, mouth open.

"How...how did you do that? It's like all the pressure and the stabbing pain just released."

I sensed Lou stepping closer over my shoulder.

"Did you just *heal her*?" Persy squealed, slamming her hands on the table and making her blond curls jiggle. "That's like extinct magic. At least for humans. Wait, are you an elf?"

Before I could reply, Lou grabbed her by the earlobe and yanked her from the chair with loud protests. Her eyes teared up as the madame dragged her to the side door by the courtyard.

"She's not an elf and it wasn't healing magic, you ninny. It's an old custom from the northlands. A trick of the mind. Learn the difference before some fast-talking pirate convinces you to take a voyage with him and sells you to the slave trade."

With that, Lou tossed the crying girl out the door and slammed it shut.

Mina and I sat gaping at her, and as Lou strode toward us, I focused on my companion. She straightened in her seat, visibly shaking with fear.

Faster than I could think I shot up and stretched out my arm, stopping Lou from approaching any closer. "She isn't going to tell anyone," I said with far more confidence than I felt.

I let Lou's scowl slide off. It didn't affect me like it did her employees. Maybe since my livelihood didn't depend on her. It was vice versa, though I shoved away the disturbing thought that the money wasn't coming from me.

I had no money or survival skills for after the Imrati.

It wouldn't matter once Father was dead and Rune was free and in charge. What I'd do beyond that wasn't something I was ready to think about.

"I swear nothing out of the ordinary happened this morning. That strong tea must've cured my hangover. Lovely. Now I should rest up for a busy night." Mina rose from the table with a too wide smile, barely glancing at me and rushed up the stairs.

Slowly, I lowered my arm and sat back down to finish my now cold plate of eggs and fruit. I was suddenly starving.

"Next time you want to try something new, I suggest you be more careful about who else is around you." Lou snatched a berry from my plate and popped it in her mouth.

"And next time you feel like taking from my plate, which was paid for with Galan's money, I suggest you ask if you want to keep all your fingers," I replied sweetly, batting my eyelashes at her.

Her face drained of color and her nose scrunched, twisting her normally beautiful appearance. I tilted my head, waiting to see if she'd strike while angry. Instead, she took a few minutes, breathing and watching me chew.

"Look," I said after swallowing the last bite. "I'm not trying to cause you trouble. But I'm also not here to work for you. You were paid to teach me to wield, and you're doing well, I think."

"So glad you approve of my methods. But while you are here under my roof and my care, you will follow my rules. I don't need trouble, and word on the street is that the king is searching for you." She held up her hand when she saw my expression. "I only know because you shared the truth with me. I'd like to keep it that way for both our sakes. He may be offering good payment, but I'd be a fool to trust the god of the seven hells at his word."

A hard lump formed in my throat, even though I'd drained my tea. I felt like a stupid, hardheaded cravenbeast for my behavior and assumptions. She may have been harsh with her girls, but she'd done it to prevent them from spreading the word about my whereabouts or putting the pieces together themselves.

"Thank you," I whispered, no longer able to look her in the eye.

"Starla, sometimes you have to do things you aren't proud of to prevent worse. That's a lesson I hope you learn from me instead of the hard way. Even if it's not about wielding."

The corner of my mouth pulled into an attempt at a smile of appreciation but felt—and probably looked—more like a cringe.

With a heavy sigh Lou yanked out a chair then sat beside me at the table. The scraping of the legs against the tile floor made me wince. I'd been considering running up to my room to process what had happened.

"When I first came to Gahair I was an orphan," she began, waiting until I lifted my eyes to hers to continue. "My parents died in a dragon attack on our farm. They hid me and my brother in the cellar, but Palner didn't stay put. He thought since he was a fire wielder he'd be safe. He wanted to be a hero."

The corner of Lou's mouth tilted up, then quickly changed direction, creating a deep divot trailing downward as her eyes glassed over. I believed she was seeing it play out in her mind. Curiosity chased away the shame and anger. I leaned forward. I wanted to know more about this normally closed off woman.

"I watched, peering through some holes in the boards. I used to think my big brother was a god. The dragon's snout filled with flames, and my father aimed his pitchfork at its belly as it reared up. My mother screamed and Palner charged, covering himself in a skin of fire. Seeing him, the dragon turned and let loose. The pitchfork bounced off its scaly armor as my brother disintegrated before my eyes. The smell of burnt flesh filled my nostrils. The dragon was more powerful."

The horror of watching her family being murdered by such a beast sent a chill from the top of my head to my toes. My fingers twitched with the urge to reach out and take her hand, but the way her fist was balled up, knuckles white, made me rethink the move.

"My instinct was to run to my brother, to try my own feeble magic against the thing that took him." She looked at me then, sea-colored eyes sharp and hard. "One look at my mother's pleading face and I stayed put. Do you know why, Starla?"

I shook my head unable to form adequate words.

"Because I knew I would die, and my mother wanted me to live. I fought my instincts and listened to the advice I could hear in my mind. I'm alive today and grateful for that."

Swallowing down the lump in my throat, I busied myself with my last gulp of cold tea. "Think before I act," I choked out, meeting her gaze. "And sometimes you have to do something that's against your instincts because it's a better choice."

"Go get your sword and let's see if you can combine your combat skills with your magic." Lou patted my hand, stood, and began clearing the counter.

Rising, I considered admitting I had my sword already strapped on me but ran upstairs instead to change into my training gear. Just to be safe, I put the dress over it all. This time maybe I'd ask before ignoring Lou's wishes.

By the time I'd returned and stepped through the courtyard door, Lou was waiting, leaning against the tree I'd flown to that first night. Next to her stood a man I didn't recognize, tall and muscled with a broadsword at his hip and a patch over one eye. His remaining one ogled me, a light shade of brown that reminded me of Rivven's. Yet nothing else about this man, aside from his build, seemed similar. Where Rivven's body language was careful and rigid, this man's was loose and confident. While Rivven's appearance remained gruff and wild, it still held a level of grace. This man's stature was one of someone used to hard labor and an itch to move.

I didn't like him.

"Starla, this is Fiorge. Fiorge is an old and trusted customer of mine. He was one of the first to bring his crew here when we opened, even though at the time people didn't like that I'd opened in the middle of town proper instead of the harbor."

She waited like I was supposed to say something, so I managed a "Hello."

"Fiorge is a water wielder, one of the strongest I know," Lou continued, setting a hand on his grimy shoulder and rubbing it. "He has very specific tastes as well. Ones I don't normally cater to here. But for Fiorge I try to make an exception, if the girls are well compensated and no permanent harm comes to them."

My eyebrow rose at this information she shared so publicly. Not that anyone else seemed to have a window open at the moment. Still...

"Today I thought we'd do a little experiment," Lou announced with a grin and a wink at Fiorge. "Let him get his aggression out beforehand with you, and then he can have a nice time with Persy."

"I see," I said, though I liked him even less. Now that I'd seen her threaten Persy to prevent her from talking about my abilities, I thought I also understood why she'd send him in with her after our sparring match. I liked that even less. Especially after I'd kick his ass and make him angry.

It was unsettling to think the girl might tell someone what I could do, and I understood Lou's philosophy. But I'd rather take my chances with word of mouth with so little time before the Imrati anyway. My father couldn't do anything once it started, or he'd risk backlash he couldn't afford. It was better than risking Persy's well-being. Especially with this man.

I began unlacing my dress, which made him grin lasciviously, showing off yellow teeth. Lou moved away, planting herself at the door of the kitchen and giving us a wide berth. When I'd dropped my garment to the ground, revealing my training gear, I reached back and unsheathed my sword with a satisfying sound. I planted my feet in a ready stance, glad I'd tied back my hair, so it wouldn't be a hinderance; though I wished it were still long enough for a proper braid.

Water was his power, and that was fine, especially since there wasn't much around here. Brute strength I'd dealt with before. Likely he was as cocky as they came, which would serve me well. But I didn't trust Lou not to throw something additional at me when she saw me winning too easily. I'd have to be on alert.

"You are a pretty little thing," Fiorge grunted, freeing his weapon as well, but remaining aloof. "It'll be a shame to leave any scars on ya."

"Can't say the same about you," I remarked with a smile.

"Smart mouth too." He laughed. "I do love teaching ones like you to behave. I'm beginning to like this idea more, Lou. Maybe you'll let me bring her up to the room after."

"She's not of age," Lou lied. "You'll have to wait for that. Next time you pull in though, I'd say she'll be ripe and ready."

Fiorge licked his lips as he approached, and I couldn't hold back the wave of disgust that flowed over me. Would it be so bad to stab him through the heart and be done with him? It'd be a favor to women across the world.

If I did that though, I'd probably cause quite a bit of trouble for Lou and those she cared for. Maybe I'd have a talk with her about denying him access though, despite the higher pay. At least, unless the girls agreed without duress. Avoiding a worse future by sacrificing now was one thing, but forcing others to sacrifice was another entirely.

"Are you going to leer at me all day or fight?" I challenged, not wanting to make the first move.

"Want me that bad, do ya?" With another laugh he lunged forward, swiping the tip of his sword toward my stomach.

It was too easy to dodge and dip, striking beneath his extended arm. One good jab to his side, and I somersaulted past and back to my feet behind him, forcing him to spin around, off balance to face me. I thrust again, but this time he countered, barely catching my blade with his and stumbling a few steps.

He wasn't laughing anymore. Instead, he held up his hand and pressed it to his wound. His face reddened to match the color of the blood on his fingers. A growl issued from his chest as he attacked full force this time. I spun, ducked, and dodged, enjoying the way he became more and more off balance.

"Enough!" Lou shouted from the doorway. "You're supposed to be practicing magic, not acrobatics."

Her words distracted me enough for my opponent to tackle me to the ground with a roar. Without a second thought, I used the air currents to flip him forward above me, over, and onto his back with a thud. I stood and circled around as he reached into the air and squeezed his hand into a fist.

Below the earth rumbled, shaking so violently I threw out my arms for balance. *What's happening?* He yanked his arm down and my feet sunk into the soil, burying me halfway up my calves. I flailed, pulling with all my strength but unable to budge. He stood, dusting himself off and snatching his fallen sword from the ground.

"You said water," I ground out at Lou, who wore a smug smirk as she leaned against the doorframe then shrugged in response.

"No one's going to announce themselves or their abilities before attacking you, sweetheart."

My gaze snapped back to the filthy pirate now standing with his sword pointed at me. Thankfully, I still held my own and swung it, connecting with his blade as he approached. He stopped, but a dangerous leer spread across his face. It reminded me too much of the one worn by the Skipper —the only other pirate I'd had the displeasure of meeting in the Night Forest. Rivven had hired him, but luckily, had not hesitated in lopping off his head. It was a moment I'd avoided thinking too hard about until now.

Sudden, frenzied anger burst through me at the memory of that helpless feeling. The way my legs were trapped beneath the ground reminded me of being held against my will. Emotions swirled in intense waves of heat and nausea as flashes of memory assaulted me. I no longer knew where or when I existed as Fiorge's face morphed into Skipper's, then shifted into...into Serano, the evil king's advisor.

Where did his face come from? Cold dread and unbidden fear stole my breath. I fought the lightheadedness threatening to pull me under and escape the onslaught of—not memories exactly as much as the feeling, the understanding that I'd been trapped and hurt before. And the fact that no specific memory came to me froze me with terror.

Fiorge disarmed me before I could gain control of myself, and I was only partially aware of him lunging at me. But instead of the cold steel of his sword pressing against my skin to demand my surrender, there was a pinch of pain as he squeezed my breast.

The next thing I knew, Lou grasped his wrist, prying him off me. Their voices blurred, going at the wrong speeds as tremors shook my body.

"Starla," the word formed and echoed as though it had been yelled in my ear. It was the sharp slice of pain that sluiced over my face from Lou's slap that chased the fuzziness from my head.

Gasping, I grabbed hold of her as the earth slowly pushed me back up to the surface, regurgitating me like an unwelcome guest.

Twenty-One

I barely noticed Lou leading me inside and up the stairs to my bedroom, where she helped peel off my boots and tugged the blankets over my shivering body. Was I cold?

The next thing I knew, she was sitting beside me, gently brushing my hair back from my face, an unreadable expression in her eyes.

"I've seen this sort of thing before. Who hurt you?" she asked when she was sure I was listening.

Licking my lips, I considered, somewhat shocked by the question. The answer wasn't easy because I didn't know how to make sense of what was happening. What *had* happened?

She sighed. Her words landed soft despite the hardness in her features. "Hells, I've felt it or something like it myself. Men are nasty, horrible creatures."

"What?" I asked as I tried to sit up, but she put a hand on my shoulder.

"Sound funny coming from someone who trades in sex?" She laughed, but it was humorless. "Better to control them using their cocks and make a bit of coin, than let their cocks control them and break us."

"What are you saying?" I knew, but I wouldn't let the thought in. She had to be wrong. I had no such experience. Rivven had stopped it from happening.

This time the look on her face was clear—I didn't like it. My jaw clenched and my teeth ground together. There was no reason to pity me. "What happened to Fiorge? I'm surprised you didn't wait 'til the fight was over."

"I told him to leave the property. He knew my rules and he disrespected me by disrespecting you."

My throat grew thick as I struggled to find the right words. Eyes stinging, I still felt confusion over what had happened.

"It'll help if you talk about it." Lou's voice sounded older somehow as she spoke. "Well, usually it does. I can't promise since everyone is different. Just know you aren't alone." Maybe it was the slight tremble in her words or the way she was treating me like a breakable object when she hadn't hesitated to throw me through a window less than a week prior.

After a long while of silence, she patted my hand and stood to leave.

"The thing is...I can't remember." My own words frightened me as she spun around. "I don't understand what I saw or felt."

Lou nodded, sitting beside me again. "That happens sometimes too. What's the earliest thing you remember?"

The panic of being unable to recall my childhood when I'd seen the elves on the playground returned tenfold, bursting the wall I'd built around it into shards. It wasn't right. The understanding that I'd been the one to steal my own memories blinded me with a combination of fear and anger. Dizzy, I gulped down air, trying to fill my lungs when they felt like they were already packed with earth.

"Slow breathing, hon. That's it. Here."

I glanced to the side as Lou produced a flask from inside her bosom and unscrewed it. Normally I would've laughed at her, but I just let her tip it to my lips and swallowed the liquid. It burned its way to my stomach, filling me with heat and taking the edge off.

"My earliest memory was about ten years ago, age fourteen, I guess. I was exploring the palace, hiding behind furniture and sneaking around." I stopped, recalling. It was as though it was all new. Had I also not been allowed out of the rooms like Rune? It didn't make sense to me.

"I'm going to push you now, Starla. If this comes out during the trials, you'll risk ending up dead. Now try to go back from there. What was happening before you went exploring?" Lou asked too gently.

My face screwed up as I attempted to force the memory, but the furthest back I could get was standing outside Leuruna's room, facing away from it. I shook my head. It was the same thing I'd come up with by the playground, and it made me want to hurl something across the room.

"That's alright. Why don't you rest for a few hours? It'll come to you. We can try something else to unlock your earth wielding." Lou patted me again and left, shutting the door quietly behind her.

I stared out the window as light rain began to fall, pattering against the glass in a hypnotic way. Before I knew it, my eyes had closed. I started to recall the fight with Fiorge, smiling at the way I'd handled him, until he forced me into the ground. It wasn't just that though. It had been the look on his face that matched Skipper's.

Going back, I thought about how they held me naked, forcing me toward the tree trunk for him. Then Rivven's sword came down, killing the bastard. But I'd felt it in that moment too—a base fear, the urge to fight and flail. The feeling of overwhelming helplessness.

That last thought brought back Serano's face, the leer that matched the others. His dark eyes filled with promise, and...and that feeling of helplessness as his hand settled over my breast through my gown.

What in the seven hells? He'd never shown an interest in me. I'd only ever seen him with Leuruna or my father. He was a sorcerer, interested in magic, fucking attracted to magic from what I could tell. I tried to force more memories, tears sliding from my eyes and wetting my pillow. But nothing more came. Nothing but the other memory of when I was fourteen exploring the castle.

If that had happened, why couldn't I remember? Why hadn't I remembered when Skipper attacked me? I'd gotten some good swipes in at that fight too, but it hadn't been enough. They'd overpowered me. If Rivven hadn't...

But he did. Just like he'd saved me in the ocean when my water wielding hadn't surfaced yet. The realization hit me that maybe that time in the forest those men hadn't gotten far enough to trigger whatever this was I now recalled. Rivven had saved me from more than just that fate. *But not forever.*

I hated it. I loathed the idea that I wasn't strong enough to not only protect Rune, but myself. Not then, not in the woods, and not today.

The hot tears flowed harder, soaking more than the pillow, but now they were a force of anger and frustration. *I will not be powerless anymore. I refuse.*

Rising, I forced away the head rush and ground myself, feet planted at hip width as I raised my arms spread beside me. Before me the window flew open with a gust of rain and air. I turned my face up, reveling in the feel of the cold water pelting my skin. It was strong, harsh, and oh so real.

Inhaling, I drew the droplets into a circle before me, wind still rushing around me. Then I flung my eyes open, and the circle morphed into the shape of an arrow. I scanned the courtyard and found the space empty— no surprise in the rain. Still, I glared at the spot where I'd fought Fiorge earlier. The arrow flew and struck the ground where a ring of fire surrounded the spot I imagined he'd stood. Finally, I glanced up at the tree, and one thick branch bent forward like an arm. The smaller ones trimmed with leaves reached out, flexing like fingers as it pressed against the flames, smothering them by rubbing them into the ground. I jerked my head once, and the tree lifted, rearranging itself into its normal state. I blew slightly, closing the open window, and cutting off the sound of the outside.

My face was wet, but my tears had subsided, and something hard had been erected in my chest. I wasn't tired from the use of magic. I wasn't even confused or angry anymore. Instead, I felt a strange kind of quiet power. I could identify it now—exactly what my sister had put inside of me. It thrummed with want inside my veins, and it was more than just Tromodian power from the queen or Centos' magic of the senses. It was something else. Something old that belonged not to my sister or me but had been placed in our care.

I didn't know how she'd gotten it in the first place or kept it from our father. But I did know one thing that I was certain of. I was going to use— no *allow* it to help defeat the evil that had taken over our land.

TWENTY-TWO

Exhaustion was my constant companion as I pushed myself to what felt like inhuman levels during the remaining days of my training. If I stayed consumed by that focus, then the memories—or the lack of them—would stay at bay. Still, one unwelcome thought continued to hover just outside my concentration. The disappointment that Galan, and more so Rivven, hadn't come to check on me.

The simple truth was, I missed him. I missed his infuriating protective instincts, his warm calloused hands, his damn intoxicating scent, his stinging humor—and most of all the way he would look at me when I spoke, like I was the only thing that mattered in the world. I even missed arguing with him. And after having some distance, I'd cooled enough to realize that his intention to kill Rune had been born of logic. He hadn't had the information about her true nature. I'd withheld it. And that was on me.

I wanted to show him my progress and pictured knocking him on his ass, then climbing over him as the earth restrained him. The things I imagined after that—well, I kept those locked in a secret place in my mind and heart.

It was Galan who came to collect me at the end of my weeks of training. By then, I was satisfied I'd learned all I could from Lou. And though my feelings about her were mixed, I had a healthy respect for what she did and the way she protected her girls.

While the two shared words and jokes, I said my goodbyes to the girls, taking special care to give both Persy and Mina a hug. It nearly stunned me when they both squeezed back so hard, they almost knocked me off my feet.

On the way back to the docks, Galan asked many questions about my stay but was suspiciously quiet when it came to stories of whatever he and Rivven had done to train while I was gone.

"Was it worth my money?" he asked finally, after I'd evaded the details the fifth time he reworded the question.

I snorted. "Yes. Though you may not like being handed your ass, I'm fairly certain you'll appreciate watching me lay Rivven out flat."

The quick way he turned his head toward the water wiped the easy-going smile from my face.

"Galan? What aren't you telling me?" I stopped and grabbed his arm to make sure he gave me his attention. "Why didn't Rivven come with you to get me?"

A light wind blew all the stray wisps of hair from my shoulders as he tightened his lips into a thin line. I waited, arms crossed, for the truth as I tried not to let my internal panic show.

"He left early for the Imrati."

I blinked. That wasn't what I expected. I knew he'd wanted to train me himself and not involve Lou, but was he that upset that he left early? And...

"How? I thought there were rendezvous points?"

Galan's expression lightened. I supposed he was glad I wasn't making a big deal of Rivven's desertion. But inside, I could barely keep track of the tumult of feelings that roiled around like boiling water.

"He traveled south along the coast so he'd enter in a separate area than we would. He didn't want any suspicion about you two working together, if either of you were recognized."

We resumed walking as I puzzled it out. "Why would there be an issue if someone recognized him? He'd have every right to challenge for the stone after the assassination of his uncle and father." After all, they'd been in line to inherit the throne, until Balram had them both murdered. It should have been Rivven that sat there now.

Galan threw an arm over my shoulder. "What do you say we take a break from training and get a drink?"

Apparently, I wasn't the only one avoiding a sensitive subject. "I think I've had enough of a tavern atmosphere for a while. Thanks, though. Unless—where am I going to sleep?" The idea of the bunk on Rivven's boat was appealing after all the noise and chaos of Lou's place. And as much as I appreciated that Galan was still there, I needed some alone time to process Rivven's unexpected departure.

Galan cast me an inquisitive look. "Riv's boat is still available. He warded it to allow you to come and go as you please. But if you're asking to share a room with me, I will happily rent the finest."

Rolling my eyes, I threw his arm off my shoulders. "The boat will be perfect. Go enjoy yourself, Galan."

With a salute, he left me at the small pier where Rivven's houseboat rocked in an easy rhythm. The first thing I noticed when I climbed down the steps into the living quarters was how his scent permeated every inch of space. After being apart from him for so long, it felt like dunking myself in a vat of memory and emotion. Dazed by the onslaught of feelings, I walked over to the chest where he kept his clothing and knelt to open it.

I was angry at him for leaving without saying goodbye, but that seemed such a silly reaction, I almost laughed. Rune would think that way, but I wasn't a child and, of course, he would do everything he could to help us reach our goal of assassinating my father. I was being petty and selfish.

Gods, I couldn't believe I'd come to the point of making my dream a reality. *Soon Rune will be free. We both will.*

I held one of Rivven's shirts to my nose and inhaled. Something low in my belly fluttered like I'd swallowed a bunch of moths. Oddly, my shoulders relaxed as I felt safe. I wiped a stray tear from my face, set his clothing on the soft rug, and lay on my side, curled against it.

The slow swaying of the boat lulled me into a drowsy state. I hadn't gotten much sleep the night before. I'd worked as a bouncer for the first time—invited by Lou—and I was even allowed to wear my normal clothes. Every time a man ignored the rules and touched without permission or payment, I was the one who got to remove him and make sure he wouldn't return—or at least would think twice about it. I'd used all the elements in various ways with the ease of breathing. It was hard to believe I hadn't just *felt* how to use it when Rune had given it to me.

Did she know how to use it? The secret part? Where had it come from? These were the questions that ran through my mind as I drifted off to sleep.

Rune's reflection grinned at me as I lay my palm against hers, causing the ripples to spread outward through the glass.

"You seem different," she said.

"I think I am. Being out in the world, meeting people from other places, it changes you. But not in a bad way."

Rune's smile faltered, sending an arrow of guilt to my heart.

"Don't worry, I'm going to free you soon so you can experience it all too," I assured her.

"I can experience it through you, Nyah. I don't have to go anywhere."

That shocked me. Surely, she wanted to? "You won't have to worry about Father much longer. We have a plan."

"We?" The word came out panicked, her gaze dancing around as though a hidden intruder lurked in the shadows.

"It's okay, Rune. Just a friend. He's going to help. But you will be free. I will win the Imrati and name you, so you can decide your own fate. Then I'm going to kill Father."

Rune's face paled, and she looked back over her shoulder as she shushed me.

"Is someone there?" I asked, alarmed.

"No. But saying such things out loud...I don't want you to do this. I...he's our father."

"He's evil. He's been hurting you your entire life." I yanked my hand from the mirror in disbelief. "How can you not want him dead?"

Rune swallowed, eyes owl-like. "Dreaming of it and doing it are two different things. I can't rule. I can't, how? What would I do? Oh, Nyah." Tears slid over her face as if a faucet had been turned on.

"Calm down. You don't have to do anything you don't want to do anymore. But you'd make the best ruler, Rune. You have a good heart."

She smiled, seeming finally to look at me again. "Thanks for saying that."

"I mean it. Rune?" I asked, averting my eyes to where my fingers twisted together.

"Yes?"

"Where did this magic come from? There's so much, and not just from your parents either." Even though having powers from both sides was unheard of.

"I suspect father did something when I was born," she whispered, staring down at her hands. "I think he used the stones, but I'm not really sure what it was, or how, or why me and not himself."

I inhaled sharply. It sounded like something he'd do to her first to make sure there weren't any problems. But if it worked, why hadn't he done it to himself too? I supposed I should be glad he didn't, or he may have had no more use for her. But I decided not to say that.

"Is this real?" I asked suddenly.

Leuruna's eyes searched mine, flitting back and forth so fast I became dizzy. "Of course it is. We're connected."

I nodded. I had one more question. But I didn't know how to ask it. And I didn't want to risk sending her into a catatonic state.

"I had a memory," I said carefully.

She cocked her head.

"What's the first thing you remember?" I asked in a rush.

Leuruna was visibly taken aback but tapped her lip in thought. A smile spread over her face then. "I remember...before Mama died, she took me out in the garden and showed me all the different flowers. A bee flew out of the pink soralias and I hid against her chest. She soothed me and explained that if I treated the bee with respect, not only would he leave me alone, but I'd see so much more beauty in what he did to make our kingdom more magnificent. Now I sometimes pretend I'm a bee and can spend my time flitting from blossom to blossom."

That was not what I expected.

"Nyah? What's wrong?" she asked, furrowing her brow.

"It's just, I can't remember anything about my mother or my childhood at all." I tried to keep the tremble from my voice, but I couldn't. I did try to force a smile though. "And when I tried really hard, well, I remembered

something I never...I mean it couldn't...I don't think it happened." The lump in my throat grew as I stumbled over the words, making it harder and harder to speak.

"What did you remember?" Rune's voice turned sharp and serious, which made me jerk back.

"I saw Serano's face," I whispered then stopped, twisting my hands.

When the silence grew too heavy, I glanced up expecting to see she'd withdrawn. Instead, there was an empty mirror.

I sprung from the floor with a gasp, still hanging on to Rivven's crumpled shirt. The material was wet with tears, and I tossed it onto the table, backing away and scrubbing my arm over my face.

Thinking about what that might have meant, I searched for something else to focus on. I rushed up the steps, intent on practicing, when I spotted a group of people with weapons drawn heading down the pier. I slipped back into the shadows and watched.

They stopped at a neighboring boat where a man was sitting on the edge with a fishing line in the water.

"Have you seen this woman?" a man asked, producing a sheet of parchment.

"No one that attractive around here," the man said with a laugh.

"She may have changed her appearance slightly. Take a better look." The tall woman with a deep voice asked, shoving it at him again.

The man frowned, clearly displeased. "I said no. Now move on so I can fish in peace."

The woman yanked his head back by a chunk of greasy, dark hair and pressed her dagger to his throat. "Take another look."

The man snatched the paper, now crinkled from where she'd gripped it along with the dagger, and she took a step back. He swallowed as his gaze traveled over the image that I couldn't see but was certain was of me.

"No." When the woman flinched toward him, he put up his hands. "I'm sorry."

"Have you seen any new women about?" she asked. "In the last few weeks?"

The man scratched his head. "Riv brought someone on his boat a couple of weeks ago. But she was gone after a day. That's not all that

unusual though. He has prostitutes over now and again. And that seer...
what's her name? Sharlyne I think it was."

Sharlyne is a seer? I recalled Rivven having followed the word of a seer
who he said he trusted. And he'd mentioned needing to see a Sharlyne
when we first arrived. That had to be her.

"This Riv, you say he brings home women often?" the woman
pressed.

"When he isn't traveling. He got back again a couple weeks ago,
maybe. Just about when he got that latest whore."

Sure, I had to be a whore just because I joined Rivven on his boat.
Arsehole.

"Where's his boat?" they asked.

Shit. I slipped back down the steps as he pointed out where I was. I'd
have no trouble dispatching the three of them, but I didn't need to attract
a lot of attention now. There were few hiding places, however, as I
searched around frantically.

You have illusion magic, I reminded myself.

When they inevitably searched the area, all they'd see was a pile of
clothing where I huddled beside the chest.

"Those were some serious wards," one of the men said as they poked
around me. "Good thing we have the skeleton key spell."

"Quiet, Berle. Someone hears you been buying black market spells
from elves, we'll all get thrown in a cell."

"There ain't no one here. It was probably just a whore."

"Looks like someone searched it though. Wonder what this Riv has
that someone wants," The woman who'd threatened the fisherman said
staring straight at me.

"It don't make sense," Berle said. "The wards were still up."

"Let's go interview that seer and ask for the bitch's whereabouts," the
woman said, clearly done here.

"We don't got money for that," Berle said following her toward the
steps.

"We aren't paying." She set a hand on the hilt of the dagger at her hip,
and they disappeared from view.

Well, hells. Now I had to go save a seer and ask her a few questions
myself.

TWENTY-THREE

Instead of trying to find her myself, I decided I'd let the mercenaries do it for me. Following them and avoiding prying eyes was something I could manage without much trouble. As it turned out, we didn't have to travel far, just up the boardwalk and down one more street that dipped toward the shore. They asked a few passersby along the way, and it was fairly easy to locate Sharlyne.

The shop in question was a tiny, with peeling paint around a smudged window that might've been pretty once upon a time. A single eye was painted on the door above the knocker, and Berle appeared genuinely intimidated by it. But the large woman shoved past him and reached for the heavy iron piece.

The door swung open before she could touch it. A petite woman with large, light brown eyes, smooth copper skin, and messy dark hair tied in a scarf stood in the doorway, looking at them.

"May I help you?" she asked in a voice like a gentle breeze, breathy and sweet.

The woman held up the parchment beside her. This time I could see a crude sketch of my face on it. They didn't have a picture of me? That was somewhat helpful. I strained my eyes to see the words, but it was too hard from this distance.

"Not her," the big woman said.

"Are you Sharlyne?" Berle asked.

"Yes."

"Where is she?" the man that wasn't Berle asked, snatching the paper and thrusting it against Sharlyne's chest.

She inclined her head, examining the picture.

"I have never met this woman."

"You're a seer," the woman said, freeing two daggers so smoothly I wasn't sure if she used magic. "So, take a look and give us the answer."

Sharlyne's big, owl-like eyes focused on the woman, and I got the impression she wasn't the least bit impressed. One side of my mouth quirked up, and though I'd drawn my sword, I leaned against the wall of the alleyway across from them to watch.

"I'm afraid I cannot help you." Sharlyne turned, but the bigger woman caught the door with a fist. One dagger held just above the seer's head.

I leaped from the shadows, but by the time I sprinted the short distance, Sharlyne had twisted the woman's forearms. The daggers clinked as they bounced against the ground. The two men spun as I ran at them with a cry of distraction. I sent a burst of wind from my left hand, knocking Berle into the wall, where he crumpled into a puddle on the walkway.

The other man I grabbed by the shirt and pressed against the window of Sharlyne's shop, my blade at his neck. When I turned my head, I found the large woman unconscious at Sharlyne's feet. The seer watched me curiously.

"You're her," the man said when I spun back to him.

"Too bad you recognized me. Now you have to die," I said, sounding far more confident than I felt. Suddenly, the thought of dispatching this man in cold blood—though clearly not a good person—made my stomach turn.

I felt a light touch on my shoulder and glanced down. Sharlyne had set her hand there.

"You don't have to kill them," she said in her soft voice.

"Sadly, I do, or I have a problem."

She shook her head somberly. "They will not survive to tell anyone. But it doesn't have to be by your hand."

Damn it to hells. I knew Rivven trusted this woman's word, and I had a suspicion who she might be to him. But even if I wanted to, it would be foolish of me to leave this to chance. These people were looking to turn me in.

"Sorry to have to do this but—"

An arrow zipped past me and impaled the man I held right between his eyes. I released him, dumbfounded as he slid motionless to the ground. Sharlyne grabbed my hand and pulled me inside her shop, shutting the door quickly behind us and locking it.

"Who—what—" I couldn't find the words.

She looked at me, hands still pressed against the door. "Friends. You are safe."

Flabbergasted, I turned to take in my surroundings. The room was draped in heavy velvet in dark, rich hues of purple and green, which showed too much dust gathered in their folds. A small table, covered in a matching cloth, sat in the center of the back wall, surrounded by shelves that held a mixture of books and odd knickknacks, including crystals and animals stuffed to appear alive.

A giant, round crystal as clear as ice sat in the center of the table, along with well-worn cards. In a basket on the floor nearby, yellowed bones lay, worn smooth by use and age. Sharlyne waited in the middle of the room as I approached her. Swallowing, I reached up. When I hesitated, she simply waited, and I took it as permission. I slipped the scarf back over her ear, and sure enough, the same rounded point as Rivven's popped out.

I smiled as I dropped the cloth back over her again. "You're his sister."

"Yes. How did you know?" she asked, curiosity lacing her words.

"You have the same eyes—well minus the fire. And a similar face."

Sharlyne smiled. "Would you like some tea?"

"Please." I sat at the table and examined the cards as she busied herself in the corner behind a curtain, where I assumed she had a stove.

My hand hovered over the ornate deck, vines twisted over the back. The closer I got, the more the skin of my fingertips buzzed with magic. Mesmerized, I touched the deck. I sucked in a breath as a card slipped diagonally from the deck and stuck to the pads of my fingers as I pulled back.

The front showed a sword held in the air, one side in shadow and the other in light. A woman's face appeared on one side, and a man's on the other, both in profile, looking at each other. As I watched, blood seemed to swell at the tip of the blade and began flowing over the front of the card.

I dropped it onto the table, shaking out my hand with a yelp just as Sharlyne set a steaming mug before me.

She smiled faintly as she took the opposite seat and reached for the now upside-down card. No blood was left on the tablecloth, but she frowned as she considered it.

"This is the card my mother pulled the night your father won the Imrati," she said, then set it down and slipped it beneath the deck. "She never explained it fully, but she knew he was evil even before that. I remember Father had dismissed those worries and gone so far as to break the circle of salt in a spell she'd crafted to prevent him winning. Too bad he hadn't trusted her more." With a heavy sigh, she sipped her drink.

"How do you know who I am? Did Rivven tell you?" I couldn't believe he'd share my secret with anyone.

"No." Sharlyne blew on her mug and sipped again.

"Who have you told?" I asked, cupping my own mug to keep my hands from going to my sword.

"No one." She smiled. "What happened out there was courtesy of the men my brother left behind to watch out for me. He doesn't like to leave me and when he does, he's serious about it. I've had more customers accidentally killed..." She sighed.

My eyebrows rose, but I said nothing as I sipped my drink. Honeyed lavender made me settle back in my seat and relax.

"I can see him doing that," I mumbled.

Sharlyne chuckled and I smiled back.

"He's protective over those he loves, but that's endearing, even if it does get annoying," she said, glancing at the window. "They probably cleaned up already. But I'm glad to meet you in person. Now I can't say I never met you though."

"Are you prevented from lying?" I blurted. It was in the stories I'd read of elves, and like so much I'd discovered, I wanted to know the truth of it.

"I can lie. But I get a bit sick when I do. I'm afraid I don't know if that's a me thing or an elf thing. Would you like a reading, your highness?"

I stiffened at the name. I'd never been called that in earnest, and she'd said it as though it was a foregone conclusion. Like a million people had used the term all my life. "Please, Nyah. Or...I guess, Starla. That's the name Galan gave me for the Imrati."

The entire atmosphere changed when I said that. The room seemed to darken as Sharlyne sat up straight, breath speeding up in sharp little bursts as her pupils expanded. She squeezed the pottery in her hands so hard, her knuckles turned white.

"You shouldn't go."

"Go where?" I leaned forward. "The Imrati?"

She nodded. "What I see...I thought you were supposed to, but I can't believe...you mustn't." Setting down the mug, she reached for my hands in earnest.

"I have to go, Sharlyne. Are you saying I'll die if I do?"

She licked her lips. "If she follows the most likely path, banished she'll be."

"Are you still talking about me?" Her speaking in the third person was more disturbing than the prophecy itself.

Sharlyne collapsed back in the chair with her fingers pressed to her forehead.

"It's so complicated. My brother needs you. If you don't go, he'll die. But if you do go..." Her shoulders slumped.

"Then I die," I said. "Well, good thing I don't believe in this shit."

Sharlyne let loose a little nervous laugh. "I wish I didn't."

"You said most likely path. That means there's one where we both end up okay, right?" I leaned in.

"I thought you didn't believe in this shit?" she asked, eyes twinkling. No, I'd been wrong about the fire not being there. The tiny specs were glowing just like her brother's.

"Either way, it's an out. As long as there's some kind of chance, then that's all I really need." I downed the remainder of my tea. "Thank you."

"Thank you for visiting me."

I stood and stretched. "May I ask one more thing?"

"Of course." She stood to meet me.

"That card? If that foretold the story of your uncle, my father, and Queen Tenara, what does it mean that I pulled it again?"

Sharlyne hugged me tight. Then she spoke into my tunic. "I hope it means that the wrongs will be righted, and balance will return. You can do that for us all."

TWENTY-FOUR

The next morning, Galan was waiting for me at the top of the stairs, just after dawn.

"Ready?" he asked, arms and ankles crossed.

"As ready as I can be." I slung the sack Rivven had given me over my shoulder, and we walked the short distance to the rendezvous spot near the edge of the village by the beach. About five others stood milling about there, all men. Several glared at me, but the rest didn't bother to glance my way. None of them looked particularly fit or combat ready, except perhaps the one that towered above the rest. He had long, straw-colored hair and dark eyes that seemed to swallow light. His clothing was simple and well-worn, but his wet shirt clung to his chest and arms, showing off the bulging muscles beneath. When his gaze threatened to devour me, I smirked.

"Fall off a pier this morning?" I asked, ignoring Galan's barely perceptible sigh.

The giant man huffed. "Just needed to cool down after my training. You here seeing off your fella? Seems like you should've left him when he said he was trying to marry the princess."

"He's not my fella. And I'm not seeing him off. I'm entering as well."

The man didn't hold back his laughter. "What's your name?"

"Starla. You?"

"Juban. I look forward to seeing you fight."

"You sure know how to make friends," Galan whispered.

Before I could respond, someone pointed up at the sky. My skin crawled as I shaded my eyes and looked up. Several objects floated across the clouds, and the closer they got, the clearer they became. But when my brain caught up, I was already in disbelief.

"A sky wagon," one of the strangers in the group said. The long, curved carriage flew across the horizon, drawn by two horses whose wings stretched double their width. One was tan, splotched with patches of brown. The other was pure white, brighter than the puffy wisps behind him. And leading them all was a third flying horse, blacker than night and larger than the others. It carried a single rider.

The rider must have been wearing armor, as the glint of the sun made it hard to look at them. I waited as they grew closer, diving toward us like arrows. Some of the men hurried away from the area. I stayed put as the enormous black horse landed before me, tucking its wings to its sides and dipping its regal head, revealing a twisted golden horn atop its brow.

The man astride the beast made Juban look like a forest elf. He was as impressive as his steed with ebony skin, shining armor shaped to his chest, and a helmet covering his head with a scarlet feather sticking out. He slipped easily from the alicorn and caught me in his ice-blue gaze. Shockingly beautiful, he reminded me of what I'd thought when I first saw Rivven emerge from the pool near the waterfall.

A second man steered the wagon from the top. He called to the group, "Everyone on board. If you aren't registered and you climb on, you will be thrown out above the deadlands."

I felt Galan press against my back. "Come on, Starla," he whispered.

But I couldn't stop staring at the man on the horse.

"She'll catch up," the man said, clearly amused. "Sometimes it takes them a minute. I *am* pretty impressive."

Despite the evidence I'd seen already of dragons and elves, I still hadn't quite believed in the third kingdom of sky dwellers.

"You're Astridonian," I said, making him look at me again.

"Perceptive and beautiful. Torvo at your service, m'lady. Are you invited as a guest?"

"I'm entering the trials," I said. "And I hate to deflate your ego, but I've just never seen a flying creature before. Men, I've seen plenty of."

He laughed loud and carefree. "Come up here and ride with me, m'lady."

"I should join the other contestants." I grinned, now watching his steed, and trying to deny the part of myself that longed to get closer to the majestic creature.

"I am a contestant as well. I happened to volunteer to help retrieve the others. But if you're scared—"

"I'm not scared," I said quickly. I nearly floated up to take a seat with him, but realized I shouldn't give away my air powers unless necessary.

That wouldn't have stopped me before I had Rune's powers. So, I grinned as he offered a hand for me, then jumped up, grabbing the pommel and hoisting myself up and onto the saddle without help.

"How does this thing work?" I asked, reaching to stroke the velvety mane.

"Like this." Torvo gave a light kick to his mount's side, and the enormous wings spread beside us. Each glossy black feather shone with a blue sheen in the sunlight. With a single powerful flap, we lifted from the ground. Within moments, we were airborne, Tromodia shrinking beneath us like a child's toy as we dipped and turned to face the opposite direction.

"Good girl, Ash. Let's show our new friend how we do it."

"She's beautiful," I said, daring to stroke a feather as she flapped her wings, raising us higher and shooting forward over the forest.

"You appreciate beautiful things," Torvo said, body coming flush with my back as he leaned in to direct the reigns. "What's your name?"

"Starla," I called over my shoulder, raising my voice against the rush of wind and the steady beating of Ash's wings. It felt as though I had to shout, even as he'd barely whispered the words.

"Named for the stars. You belong in the sky. It's a crime you weren't born in Astridon."

One of his massive arms slid around my waist, and I knew I shouldn't have, but I turned up my body heat right below it. In seconds, he yanked away with a shout.

"Ask permission," I advised.

"I could toss you off the horse right here and say you fell."

He was lucky he couldn't see my face. "Then I'll have to slit your throat before you do."

To my surprise he chuckled, carefree. "Well played. My apologies, Starla. Let me try again. May I hold you, so you don't fall off the horse when we land in a moment?"

In a moment? I glanced down but saw only the mountains to the left and the deadlands below. "I'm capable of holding on myself, thank you, Torvo."

"Let me know if you change your mind." He whispered near my ear and pulled on the reins.

Ash raised her torso until she was nearly vertical. I slid back against Torvo's chest as we raced upward. I bit back a scream as I tried to squeeze my thighs tight enough around her, but all my weight was given to the man at my rear. His arms raised beside us, gripping the reins as I tried to make sense of why we'd gone up instead of down.

We rushed toward a dense cloud, and within seconds, were swallowed by white mist. The rushing sound I'd almost grown accustomed to vanished, leaving only silence in my ears and a wall of white before my eyes. Then, just as suddenly, it passed and a breathtaking view of the top of a mountain opened before us. Like an island in the sky, it rested, the center being not the peak of the mountain, but a gleaming castle fashioned of crystal. So massive, it was likely larger than Centos.

Gently, Ash glided to the grassy plain on the outskirts of the sprawling castle. Numerous spindly turrets reached toward the sun with round bulbs at their tips. To the left, stood woods filled with tall, straight trees and to the right, stretched a serene lake, water so still it glistened like silver.

Torvo slid off the horse and offered me his hands, which I once again avoided as I leaped to the ground and dusted myself off.

"Thanks for the ride, Ash." I patted her nose, and she whinnied appreciatively.

The wagon landed nearby, and I hurried past Torvo to meet them. When Galan disembarked looking a bit peaked, I smiled and clapped him on the back.

"Group nine from Tromodia," a woman called from closer to the lake. "Sign in here for roll call and get your cabin assignment."

With a mutual look, we hiked to the line and waited to give our names and blood samples. When we'd been cleared, I was given cabin fourteen and Galan cabin seven. The woman must have noticed our unease since she looked up from her paperwork, something she hadn't yet done much of, and said, "We want people from different locations to mix."

I nodded and stalked down the winding path behind the water toward the cabins. Mine was at the end, tucked behind a few tall trees. Shouldering my pack, I pushed the door in and stopped in my tracks. The place itself was fine with four small beds, a washroom, and a compact kitchen. But what made me freeze were the two men inside, who looked up at me just as shocked as I was to see them.

"Um, greetings," I said, tossing my bag onto one of the empty beds. "I'm Starla."

The men exchanged glances. One was short with a wiry beard and prematurely graying hair. The other was more average in height and had a soldier's body with a longsword at his hip. He had a shock of red hair poking out from a cap on his head and appeared awfully young.

"Dann," the redhead said raising a cup in salute.

"You the welcoming committee?" the other man asked. "I mean you aren't exactly dressed like I'd expect. But I heard they treat the contestants well."

"Are you insinuating I'm here as a...treat?" I asked, taking a step further in the room.

Dann shied away, clearly nervous. *Smart kid.* But the other man looked me up and down in confusion.

"I'm a contestant too. I've been assigned this cabin, unfortunately."

The man's brows shot up into his hairline.

I dropped onto my cot. "I wouldn't try anything. Unless you want to lose a body part. And it might be one you'll miss." I smiled politely at him.

Dann tried to cover a laugh, which made me like him even more.

"The name's Pan, and I don't need any sass. I got enough of that from my wife. She's dead now. And no need to take offense when it was reasonable for me to ask what the hells you're doing here. You'll get offed in the first event, a tiny thing like you."

"We'll see," I said, freeing a knife from my boot and cleaning my nails with it.

"I don't know," Dann said. "My coin's on her. She seems to know what she's doing. I bet she makes it far."

"Thanks, Dann." I beamed at him. "So, who's the fourth?" I jerked my head toward the last unclaimed bed.

Pan shrugged. "Don't know yet. But judging by you, I'd guess it's an elf." He laughed at his own joke.

"If it is, you'll be dead by morning," I said. "If you insult him the way you did me anyway. Though I'm still debating if it's worth it, or if I should just let you get killed in the trials."

Pan stood, making his chair squeal as he pulled his sword.

"Whoa," Dann stood, palms out. "If either of you kills the other, you'll be disqualified and probably killed. Rules."

I shrugged. "I guess I leave it to the trials then."

Pan made a face at me and put away his weapon.

The door opened, and we all turned to find Torvo struggling to fit through the frame. He grinned at me, ignoring the others. "Well, if it isn't the Lady Starla. What luck."

"Is it?" I asked, gesturing to the bed near mine that waited for him. "If I didn't know better, I'd think you requested it."

His boisterous laugh startled the men at the table, but I'd grown used to it already. I had to admit it was louder inside a building though. "Against the rules, M'lady. No requests. No favoritism."

He reached up and removed his helmet. A cascade of silver hair fell over his shoulders, as striking as his eyes. He tossed it on the bed along with his sack and kicked off his boots.

"Gentlemen," he nodded at the others, "You may call me Torvo."

"Pan and Dann," the redhead said quickly. "The rhyme's just an unfortunate coincidence. Where's everyone from?"

"Astridon," Torvo said with a slight bow.

"Tromodia," I added.

"Centos," Pan said. I held back the cringe that threatened when he said it. I didn't recognize him, so chances were good he wasn't from the area nearest the keep or the village I frequented. There were quite a few after all.

"I was raised on a farm outside of Tromodia," Dann said with a grin. "Where are you from there?"

I swallowed and repeated the name of the only town I knew. "Gaihor."

"No wonder you know your way around a blade," Dann said approvingly. "I hear things have gotten bad there. You'd have to be tough to stay."

"I'm going for a swim in mirror lake. I like to freshen up after a long ride." Torvo unclasped his breast plate and removed his tunic from beneath, revealing layers of honed muscle like the gods themselves shaped him. Even Pan and Dann gaped at him when he unlaced his pants and stood nude before us.

The gods didn't leave out anything. The more I tried not to look, the worse I did.

"Care to join me, Lady Starla?" he asked, stepping far closer than necessary.

"I'm good, thanks." Looking up into his face helped release me from the spell as his knowing smirk stoked my anger like a torch. I wiggled my fingers in a goodbye gesture and lay back on my cot, hands beneath my head.

Though I closed my eyes, I remained aware of everything going on around me. The door shut, letting me know he left without bothering to invite the others. *Am I really the only woman in the Imrati? That seems unlikely.* Sure, Father wanted an heir, but there were ways to go about that if my sister married a woman. I thought about Kendara of the Mountain elves and her desire for the woman Terra. Perhaps placing the women in cabins full of men was a ploy to make us feel uncomfortable and drop out. That seemed likely given Father's goals, which most certainly weren't to make his daughter happy.

"She asleep?" Pan whispered.

Since I didn't hear a response, I figured Dann shrugged or nodded. The floor creaked as someone came to take a closer look. I nearly gagged when I smelled fish breath waft over my face. One of them lacked hygiene.

"I don't like it," Pan said from above. "Something's strange with this one. They probably want us to off her and save them the embarrassment."

"The rules—"

"Rules are meant to be bent, if not broken. And if we don't do it, I suspect our new roommate will take her for himself."

"What do you mean take her?" Dann asked, voice high pitched and growing closer as he crossed the room.

Not rolling my eyes proved difficult. I'd hoped to hear something useful, but this was more than expected. Best to get it over with early I supposed.

"I'll show you how since you're clearly inexperienced," Pan said.

The second I felt his hand on my shoulder, my eyes snapped open, and I jolted forward, my skull connecting with his face. Pan stumbled, hand pressed against his now broken and bleeding nose.

"Bitch," he snarled, sounding like he was sick.

"Seems you deserved it," Dann said, grinning at me. "I have six sisters and if she hadn't reacted so fast, I'd have slit your throat, mate."

I sprung up from the bed and snatched a knife, which I pointed at the man clutching his face. He backed into the wall as I strode forward, until the tip was pressed at a soft spot between his ribs. One jab upward and it would pierce his heart.

"Give me one good reason not to kill you now," I said.

"They'll throw you out for breaking the rules," he stammered.

"Self-defense," I muttered, pressing hard enough to prick his skin through his shirt.

"There ain't a mark on ya!" he spat, blood spraying on my shirt. "It's clear who attacked who."

"He's right." Dann set a tentative hand on my shoulder, and I glanced at him. The boy was pale and serious. "Let him be. He'll leave you alone now, won't you, Pan?"

"I don't want to touch you now."

I thought he meant it as an insult, but it was fine with me. I leaned in, pressing my free hand to the wall above his shoulder.

"You so much as look at me funny again and I won't hesitate to snap your neck."

He nodded quickly, and I backed away.

"How am I supposed to sleep?" I asked, taking Pan's old seat at the table where Dann joined me.

"We can take turns keeping watch," he said. "I don't mind, and I bet that other guy, Torvo won't either. He seems to like you."

Taken aback by his observation, I nodded. "Thank you. I appreciate it." I jerked my head toward Pan. "Maybe I'll tie him to the bedposts instead."

Something inside burned with the urge to run at him and sink my blade between his eyes. My fire magic swirled and rose as I pictured it. Why was the urge to strike him down so strong when I felt guilt with the thought of dispatching the man at Sharlyne's shop?

Shaking my head to clear it, I stood and retrieved my canteen to douse the flames. I'd never felt such a lust for vengeance before for anyone but my father. It disturbed me.

Pan limped into the washroom to clean himself up. He'd have to have someone reset his nose, but I wasn't planning on volunteering, even though it would be painful.

"Why'd you sign up?" Dann asked, watching me.

It was an innocent question from a boy who hadn't seen the evils of the world and was trying to make conversation. He was a good kid, and I hoped he survived the trials, though I knew the odds were against that.

"I believe that everyone should be able to choose their own partner. If I win, I will choose that gift for the princess."

Dann's head jerked back like it had never occurred to him. "Gods, I hadn't thought...if I win, I'll ask for her hand. If she says no, I will take my winnings and go back to the farm." He straightened in the seat and set his chin.

A smile crawled over my face. "I think if someone as noble as you wins, she may choose to say yes."

Dann's face burned as red as his shock of hair.

Pan returned from the other room, face swollen with purple crescents below his eyes as he glared at both of us.

"Him, on the other hand..." I said, then took a sip from my canteen as I glared at him.

Dann looked away, but I caught the smile on his face. I think we both knew Pan's likelihood of winning was low. Either he had no magic, or he was so skilled at holding it back that he let me nearly kill him. I'd been ready for more of a fight to be honest, and I itched to let loose. I wished I could talk to Galan. If only he, Rivven, and I could share a cabin. Though that would be almost impossible, based on what the woman at the registration had said. They wanted us to mingle and intermix.

The door swung open and a dripping wet, naked Torvo strode inside. He stopped at the sight of Pan then glanced at me. I shrugged and smiled. He shook his head and started pulling on his clothing.

"It's under control," Dann announced unnecessarily.

"I had little doubt the lady could handle herself." Torvo winked at me. I wasn't surprised he had surmised what had happened.

His words calmed the fire inside of me as I took them in. This may have been the first time a powerful man had seen me as I was, not the weak, helpless woman I appeared to be to many. I appreciated that so much that tears welled. I pushed them back with another gulp of water.

TWENTY-FIVE

Having been provided with uniforms representing our kingdom of origin, we were herded outside for the opening ceremonies. Overnight, the grounds had been transformed with enormous stands erected in a U-shape around the lake and the forest beyond. At the top center of the stands sat a shaded platform with three chairs, the middle one raised on a dais and fashioned into a silver throne. Upon it sat my father. Flanking him were Serano and Leuruna, the latter dressed in an enormous ballgown of silver and violet that slipped off her shoulders. Her frost-colored hair was teased into a pompadour, and her breasts nearly burst from a corset laced so tightly it must have been painful. It also explained her regal posture as she scanned the horizon, looking for all the world like a beautiful flower. But I knew that face. She wasn't truly present. Under the circumstances, it was hard to blame her for checking out.

Still, I longed for her to fight back. She had the power, but not the strength, thanks to the monster we called Father.

My disguise must have worked. My shorter, lighter hair and Tromodian pantsuit of cerulean blue, like the sea, was enough. I shoved aside the pang that came with the realization, once again, of how little I meant to my father—that he wouldn't recognize his own daughter. Perhaps he would when I shoved my sword through his heart.

"You look happy," Galan said, striding up beside me.

I glanced over to find him in the same cerulean outfit that left little to the imagination. "Have you seen Rivven?"

Galan jerked his head to the right. I followed the trajectory to the opposite side of the arc of contestants. Rivven stood a head above those surrounding him, face tilted upward, and eyes locked on the king.

My stomach clenched. I hadn't seen him since leaving for training. And seeing him there, even though he avoided my gaze, caused something deep inside of me to lurch toward him. Feelings I'd collected, nurtured during our time together, rushed through me with a fierce intensity that stole my breath.

"Sizing up the competition?"

Suprised by Torvo's voice so close, I almost jumped when he whispered in my ear. I smiled nervously at him. He had his silver hair tied back in a knot and his bright blue eyes were set on me. His uniform was crisp white and hugged his body to the point I wondered if they hadn't had a size that fit him.

I nodded.

"Smart. But it's hard to tell by appearances. Be ready for anything from anyone," he advised. Though it was such a generic statement, it hardly helped.

"I'm glad you didn't misjudge me," I said under my breath as music swelled around us and a woman in a bright red dress that sparkled in the sun appeared, facing the stands. Now that I looked, I realized the audience was small, hardly filling the space set out for them. I remembered that the whole event had been rushed and planned in a secret location. Certainly no one from below could reach the sky palace. Most of those in Centos didn't even know it existed. Still, I wondered how secure my father was being in a foreign place.

If he was worried about assassination attempts, he would be smart. At least two of us here were planning just that.

"What's that music?" I asked Galan on my other side.

"The anthem of Centos. It's the last kingdom that won the stone. Don't you recognize it?"

I lowered my voice and leaned in to whisper back. "We never played music or had much of a reason to sound the anthem considering we never left, and no outsiders visited."

When the instruments stopped, the woman in red spoke. "Welcome to the 460th Imrati trials!" It was her voice I recognized before her appearance. She'd been the one on the stage at the Gates of Lehon.

Those in the stands cheered and clapped, some stomping their feet on the wood.

"His most gracious highness, King Balram of Centos, has revived the custom, and offered the hand of his only daughter, the princess Leuruna, as the prize."

More cheers erupted as my cheeks burned. So much for acknowledging bastard children, especially ones who stole magic and ran. The woman in red curtseyed.

"My name is Zoella, and I am honored to host this year's trials. Those of you from Astridon may recognize me as the queen's favorite bard and entertainer, but I'm humbled and thrilled to be chosen to host the Imrati for all of you. The celebration will be recorded using magic and played back for those in all three territories, once the winner has been selected."

More applause as she smiled.

"Thank you! Now to introduce our contestants." She turned toward us, keeping herself open to the audience as well. "Only forty-two entered this year, far less than in the past. But judging by the determination and —," she strolled over to Rivven and squeezed his bicep, "muscle mass, I'd say we're in for a treat, nonetheless. Certainly, some favorites for the princess to root for." She winked at Rivven, but he remained stoic and poised, hands clasped behind his back. I wondered what he was thinking. Had he noticed me?

Hoots and cheers rose from the audience as she made her way past the rest of us, stopping in front of Torvo. "Yep, folks, let's hope there's some test of strength and stamina this time."

Unlike Rivven, Torvo played into her insinuations by lifting his arms and flexing his muscles to the point I feared the material would rip. I glanced up at the stands and my father's interest was held rapt by Torvo's display. Had he approved?

"No point introducing everyone until after the first trial which starts this very evening. When we've gotten down to a dozen or so contestants, we'll meet the real contenders more intimately tomorrow evening at the celebration ball."

"Ball?" I blurted out, but no one seemed to hear me over the applause. Even the contestants were clapping.

Get through the first trial and then worry about it.

"Now for his majesty's entertainment, I invite all the contestants to show off a talent. The princess will pick one winner who will receive an assist in the first trial."

The crowd went crazy, and even though it was small, it was loud enough to make me wince. I didn't recall hearing about any of this from former Imrati, though to be fair, they stopped before I was born.

Thankfully, Zoella started at the other side of the group. But even as I watched several men do everything from standing on their head to singing, I couldn't think of a single thing I could do that wouldn't cause suspicion. I wasn't about to give away my magic, as the man before Rivven was doing now, creating a whirlwind that gathered wildflowers from the long grass along the bank and carried them up to my sister.

Serano snatched them before they fell and forced a grin. Before setting them on the railing in front of Leuruna, who hadn't so much as blinked. But the air wielder who'd done it was busy bowing for the crowd.

Rivven was up next, and I watched as he drew his sword and demonstrated perfect form as he battled an imaginary opponent. When he finished, he bowed his head slightly and returned to his spot. As the next man took his place, Rivven's eyes finally met mine. I inhaled sharply.

Something crossed the distance between us and struck me straight in the heart like an arrow. It wasn't the glow of his fire, though that was clear enough, it was something like relief at seeing me here alive and well. And something more that I couldn't name. A combination of relief and fury rose within me. Relief that he cared at all and fury I thought I had tamped down that he'd abandoned me.

I spotted another woman then as she stepped out. She was from Astridon, judging by her outfit. I watched, transfixed as she flexed her back and two large, feathered wings unfolded, as bright white as her costume and trimmed in blue. Gasps rang out all around from both audience and contestants as she lifted off the ground then set herself back down, and her wings disappeared.

My head flipped toward Torvo. "Do all of you have those?" I asked in awe.

His answer was a wink. Then he leaned down and whispered, "If you want to see them, we can meet in private later."

Was that an innuendo or an actual offer? Either way, I became distracted as my turn came closer and closer. "What are you doing?" I asked Galan under my breath.

"You'll see."

That was not helpful. Had he and Rivven been prepared for this? Why hadn't they told me?

A man I recognized as the one I'd tossed over my head on the stage at the Gates stepped forward. Predictably his "talent" was flexing his muscles. I would have laughed, had I not been terrified at how fast my own turn approached.

What am I good at? Magic, fighting, and sneaking around—nothing helpful in this situation. *Hells!* Galan was next.

"You okay?" Torvo whispered. "You seem distraught. Performance anxiety?"

I blinked up at him. "I don't know what to do," I admitted.

He smiled. "Let's go together then." He held out his hand as Galan walked to the center and sang. His voice was so powerful and beautiful that I froze, staring at him as the mesmerizing melody surrounded me, calming my nerves.

When he finished, he received a standing ovation.

Everyone stared at me expectantly, and I had to force myself not to bolt. But Torvo grasped my hand and tugged me forward with him. He swung me around and caught me by the waist with his other hand, and in a moment more, we were dancing.

I'd never danced with a man in my life. I'd witnessed it a few times when Father had forced Rune to attend a dinner, but I had no idea how to move. And yet...I was doing it. Well, mostly Torvo was doing it, commanding and steering me with his powerful hands and body as he leaned one way and then another.

To my surprise, music rose around us as it had when the anthem was played, and as it quickened, so did our steps. Torvo spun me out, jerking me back toward him when I threatened to fall, and catching me. when I thought I could no longer be surprised, he lifted me, tossing me in the air and catching me, only to dip me backward so far, my chin length hair swept the ground.

The music stopped and applause rang out as I fought to catch my breath. Torvo paused before straightening and tugging me up beside him. Then he squeezed my hand and led me back to the line of people.

"Not sure what we do if more than one person wins the assist," Zoella said. "Next!"

I watched curiously as Dann took his turn, gathering some smooth stones along the way. Only when he began juggling them did I realize why. When he finished, his face was once again red, and I clapped delightedly. Maybe it was the high of having gotten through my part of the demonstrations.

When the last person went, showing off his fire-starting ability, Zoella appeared again. "Quite a talented group. Do we have a winner, Princess?"

"The princess proclaims Torvo of Astridon the winner of the competition," Serano stated after conferring with Father. He'd bent in front of Leuruna to make it appear as though she'd whispered something to him, but I knew she hadn't.

Applause and whistles came from the stands, and Torvo glanced at me with surprise, before taking a bow.

"But what of my partner?" Torvo asked as the applause died down.

Zoelle had just reached us, but when Torvo spoke, her brilliant smile faltered, and her hands stopped from clapping. It took a few moments of her blinking as she processed his words, but then she recovered and spun toward the audience.

"What a gentleman!" she exclaimed, encouraging the whoops and hollers to rise.

A glance at Rivven showed him glaring distrustfully toward Torvo. Galan simply seemed amused.

"The gentleman has won," Serano stated, bringing an abrupt halt to the chatter, "not because of the dance, but because of his assistance to the young lady."

My face burned as the crowd and contestants began chattering. It all blurred into buzzing as I fought to get control of my breathing. Torvo angled his body in front of mine, dropping a shadow over me. It was enough to help me as he raised his hands to the sky and roared in victory.

Slowly the stands emptied, and the contestants wandered off. My gaze stayed glued to Rivven, who looked as though he was about to march toward me but stopped after a step or two, then he turned and departed without a word. My stomach dropped in disappointment when he strode the other way. I didn't understand what had happened. We were supposed to be together in this, weren't we? Had I done something? Or was it because he'd thought about who I really was, what I'd confessed about Rune, and still had plans to murder her? Forcing back the tears, I pressed my feelings into determination, straightening my spine.

Soon all that were left were myself, Torvo, Galan, and Dann.

"I thought you were amazing," Dann said with an awkward pat on my shoulder.

"Your juggling was impressive," I said, then I looked up at Torvo. "Thank you."

He shrugged. "I needed a partner, and you seemed a more attractive option than the brute on my other side."

Was that all? It felt like he angled himself to protect me, but maybe it was a happy accident. Either way, I couldn't get too comfortable with him —or anyone else. I had to focus on winning these trials so I could free Leuruna.

"May I steal Starla for a moment?" Galan asked, gripping my arm.

Torvo's eyes snapped to the point of contact, and I smiled. "Of course, old friend."

With that, my other roommates wandered off toward our cabin, and Galan led me toward the trees.

"What is it?" I asked as he searched the nearby area to be sure we were alone.

"Are you alright?" He grasped my upper arms and searched my eyes.

"What? Of course." I pulled away from his too tight grip, stepping back. "I just don't have a talent and—"

"Last night," he interrupted, stepping close again. "You were alone in the cabin with three men."

"Yes, so?" I folded my arms, trying to decide if I was offended at his concern or touched.

He swallowed and looked away. "One of them was talking this morning by the lake. He said some things I didn't want to believe, but I had to check."

This was too much. I shook my head in confusion. "I—nothing happened. He tried, but I broke his nose."

"I saw that, and it lent credence to his story. I didn't doubt you'd put up a fight."

"But you thought he would win?" I folded my arms over my chest.

"It was three to one. He said they all—damn it, Nye. I just wanted to be sure you're okay." Galan's fist slammed into the nearest tree trunk, sending bark flying.

Swallowing the thickness in my throat, I laid a hand on his shoulder. "They didn't. In fact, the other two seem, well, decent."

Galan searched my face, as though trying to decide if I was covering something up. Finally, he nodded. "I'm glad you're okay. Riv would never forgive me if I let something happen to you."

A sharp laugh burst out of me along with some of my sequestered hurt. "I highly doubt he'd even notice. He hasn't so much as waved at me since I left for Lou's." The admission felt too personal, too vulnerable. It shouldn't have mattered, and now, I'd let Galan of all people know it had.

"I assure you, you matter to him. To both of us," Galan said.

Hugging my midsection, I looked him in the eyes. "I'm still going to kick your asses tonight."

"That's more like it. I was afraid you were getting emotional on me for a second."

I punched his arm. "Spar a little?"

"We should keep our moves to ourselves," Galan warned, and a light breeze tickled the back of my neck.

"Can't wait for a chance to do a little damage tonight. See you later then." Hesitating for just a moment, I leaned in and kissed Galan on his smooth cheek. I'd never done that before, but his concern for me was so touching, it felt natural.

So this was what it was like to have friends who cared about you. A small smile played on my lips as I hurried back to my cabin.

TWENTY-SIX

The first trial of the Imrati took us by surprise. Not that anyone knew what was coming, but being led on a two-mile hike to the base of a rocky mountain surrounded by a spiraling ring of thick clouds before we started, was likely not on anyone's guess list.

A gilded palanquin, held aloft by four of the king's strongest guards—including Rufus—carried two side-by-side thrones, upon which sat my father and sister. Naturally, hers was lower to the platform than his—no one could outshine His Majesty. I smirked when I saw Serano walking alongside the ostentatious litter, clearly disgruntled at not being included on top. His dark cloak billowed around him as he clasped his hands in front of his waist, sneering at everyone who looked his way.

Averting my eyes, I searched the other contestants. I couldn't be sure, but I thought Rivven might have been staring at me— he glanced away the second we made eye contact. Pushing the thought aside, I found Galan stretching his long, lean muscles, and Dann, who seemed almost jolly as he craned his neck toward the top of the rocky cliffs. If the idea was to climb it, I'd be fine—with or without my air magic. I decided not to reveal my abilities unless necessary.

I hadn't seen Torvo yet. He hadn't returned since winning the favor yesterday, and like everyone else, I was curious what it might be. In my opinion, he deserved it since he'd saved me from looking like an idiot with no talent.

Pan grumbled to a group beside me about it being too dark to climb safely, assuming that's what we were meant to do. It hadn't even occurred to me, since the ample light of the double moons illuminated the white clouds surrounding the jagged stone the same as it would have in Centos. I was used to eternal night, as were the others competing from our kingdom.

This time, my father spoke, and the second his icy voice rose, an uncomfortable silence fell over the group.

"One of you will earn not only the stone, but the ability to name the princess' betrothed. The future of my own line is in the hands of the gods now."

If only that were true.

"The first trial—"

A roar thundered over the land, shaking loose rocks from the mountainside and forcing me to throw my hands over my ears as I searched for the source.

Blotting out one of the moons, with leathery wings spread wide and talons open, a black dragon flew. Fire burst from its mouth, striking the treetops behind us. I spun as screams erupted around me. An entire redwood split in half, both sides crashing to the ground in flames. Beneath one lay a man from Tromodia. Even as my mind processed the grisly scene, he was engulfed in flames. Someone sent water flying at him from somewhere, but he was ash by the time the fire died.

"She is unhappy," my father said, continuing as though nothing had happened. "Someone has taken her egg." From beside his throne, he reached down to pull aside a drape of violet cloth. Beneath it lay an opalescent egg the size of my calf.

"The life inside can only last a few hours without its mother's fire. It has been enchanted so that she cannot see or smell it. Your task is to retrieve a piece of that dragon's hoard before then and return safely here to deliver it to me."

Murmurs broke out—some excited, some confused, some terrified. I could only focus on the egg. I thought of Carn and how sweet and protective he'd been. The royal bastard had stolen this creature's child just to enrage her?

"Bastard," someone muttered behind me, and I spun to find the other woman with the wings. "They're endangered, the dragons are."

A lump formed in my throat as a familiar winged creature cantered up beside the platform, bearing an even more familiar figure astride.

"Ah, our champion arrives." My eyes narrowed at the glee in my father's tone. So, he approved of Torvo. That alone made me question my assessment of the warrior. "The favor he has won allows him to use one beast of his choosing during the trial in any way he wishes."

The sleek black equine snorted and stomped the ground with a hoof, as if eager to show off. The memory of Ash's soft feathers and silken mane brought the ghost of a smile to my lips.

Above, the dragon roared again, the gut-wrenching sound of a mother's grief that tore through my soul as well as my ears.

"You have three hours," the king announced, "beginning now."

All around me, others burst into motion. Some ran for the rocks and began climbing. Some flew using air magic or wings of their own. Torvo pressed his massive thighs together, urging on his mount. She took to the sky with ease. When he spotted me watching, he winked then focused on his destination as they disappeared into the cloud cover.

Time was of the essence, but getting there first wasn't the smartest move. Not when an angry, desperate dragon waited. I skirted the edges of the rocky base and ducked down, confident no one on the platform was looking my way. Then I waited, watching as Galan used small bursts of air to propel himself upward with each reach for the next handhold. He was doing a decent job at making it look natural, but I could tell he needed the magical assist. Rivven had disappeared in the initial rush, and I tried to ignore the resulting pang in my chest.

To my astonishment, the minute everyone was out of view, the guards lowered the platform to the ground and my father dismounted, carrying his scepter. Rufus joined his side as well as Serano, and the three hiked back through the trees at a decent pace, leaving three guards, an empty staring Leuruna, and the egg alone.

Ignoring the impulse to act was impossible. Relying on my tried-and-true stealth abilities, I stayed low to the ground, darting between jutting rocks, shadows, and fog until I was within a few feet of the platform's edge.

I focused on the woods, calling up Rune's illusion magic, and mouthed the word I wanted to use. My father's voice bellowed from somewhere in the trees as I did.

"Guards!"

In seconds, the three remaining men exchanged looks of concern and pulled their swords, rushing off to help. I leaped onto the platform, dropping to Rune's side. Up close, I could see that she'd been dolled up to look far healthier than she really was. Beneath about an inch of thick and skillful paint was a woman thinner, paler, and hollower than I'd ever seen her. It seemed she'd sunk even further in the seat since I'd used my distraction.

Part of me wanted to take her and run. But I knew there was nowhere in all the realms safe from Father's pursuit. He needed her, and he didn't care how much it tore her apart to syphon her power. I swallowed hard and set a hand lightly atop hers.

"Rune," I whispered. It wasn't that I thought the guards would be back yet, but I knew I had only a short time with which to work. "It's me. Can you hear me?"

She blinked but gave no further indication that she had. Forcing back the tears that threatened, I squeezed her. "I promise I'm going to win this and save you."

Knowing I was running out of time, I forced myself away from my sister—or what was left of her—and turned toward the egg. The dragon breathed fire, and Father had said this offspring needed those flames to survive. I took one gulp of air before reaching for it and calling fire to my hands. The intense heat made me cringe and start to sweat, but since I'd thought ahead and used my fire abilities, the surface was not burning my flesh, and that was enough as I rose, clutching the egg carefully.

A slow, soft thrum from inside the iridescent shell pulsed against my fingers. I startled, realizing it was the baby dragon's heartbeat. The sound of men rushing through the brush urged me into motion. With a leap, I landed on the soft ground, cradling the egg. Willing more magic, I crouched behind a boulder to watch and make sure my plan worked.

The men re-emerged from the woods, swords still drawn, their faces anxious and pale. They knew it had been magic that lured them from their posts. The moment they saw Leuruna on her throne and the illusion of the egg set beside her, they relaxed. After a cursory search, they manned their posts once again.

I grinned as I made my way silently back to the other side of the mountain. With a quick glance around to ensure no one was watching, I launched into the air and straight upward. I was either stupid or clever—and only time would tell which.

When the first contestant came into sight, I decided to use more magic —at the risk of depleting my energy—and cloaked myself in an illusion that would be hard to notice unless looking directly at me. Slowing my pace, I noted the sudden increase in climbers. Apparently, their speed and abilities were fairly matched.

Scanning for familiar faces, I spotted Pan then watched in horror as he reached the leg of the man just above him, whom I recognized as Juban from the pickup site. Pan grasped his ankle and yanked, dislodging one of his competitors. Juban screamed as he fell to his death, spinning his arms as though desperate to grab onto something. I looked away, ducking my head against the egg in my arms.

If only he'd had air magic or wings he was hiding. Pan would have been in for a surprise. One thing I decided then and there was I would make sure Pan would not win this competition. He was not worthy of my sister.

Ignoring the fatigue starting to tug at me, I increased my speed and attempted to avoid staring at the climbers. As I neared the dragon's nest, it became clear that those who'd flown before me were now in a battle for their lives.

Blazing heat warped the air currents above me as I warmed my body with fire magic to avoid being disintegrated. Several bits of burnt body parts rained down, accompanied by human screams and grunts of effort.

It was too much magic for too long, despite my newfound stamina, so I dropped my illusion and landed on a rocky outcrop just below the cave opening, from which bursts of flame shot forth. I murmured encouragement as I readied to climb to the opening. All I had to do was return her baby. *How hard could that be?*

When the last of an intense bout of flame waned, I swung up onto the ledge in a crouch, holding the egg out. I didn't want to think too hard about the source of the ash on the group of men who stood panting and gaping at me. Trembling arms clutched swords and clubs, sweat shining on their skin and soaking their burned, tattered clothing. My gaze swept the cave: mostly dark, but lit slightly by the burning embers on piles of ash.

The dragon crouched, wings flared and eyes gleaming red. She was backed into the rear of her nest, where glittering bits of jewels and gold sparkled behind her. The piles of treasures created a rounded bed that, I supposed, wasn't too uncomfortable for someone with armor-like scales and talons. Movement, though slow and subtle, drew my gaze to the outskirts. I spotted Rivven edging toward the treasure while the others fought openly.

I returned my focus to the mother dragon and, as carefully as I could, I outstretched my trembling arms, offering her child back.

"Duck!" someone yelled as the beast's mouth opened, and an orb of glowing light expanded, deep in her throat. It billowed out toward me.

I closed my eyes, praying my fire abilities would protect me better than they had Lou's brother as the flames shot at me.

But instead of being incinerated, strong arms grasped me around the waist, and as the egg and I were flying, the blast of heat wafted over my dangling legs. The sensation, though painful, was not the excruciating torment I imagined burning to death would be.

I opened my eyes, but it wasn't necessary to know who had hold of me. I recognized the familiar hard press of Torvo's body from behind just as it had felt on Ash. But at present, the alicorn was missing, and I had a sudden desperate surge of hope that she wasn't dragon toast.

Torvo dropped me onto the ledge beneath the cave. I spun to find him hovering in midair, bare, broad chested with silver wings—matching his hair—outstretched to the sides. He was breathtaking, and it was difficult, even under the circumstances, not to appreciate his muscled physique on display. After all, the only clothing that remained on him was a bit of cloth tied about his hips, dangling to mid-thigh.

"Your steed—"

"I let her go the minute we reached this point," he assured me. "There was no need to endanger her. I can maneuver more easily with my own wings."

"Thank you," I choked out, glaring down at the egg, disappointed that my plan had gone so horribly wrong.

"You risked your life to return her child," he said, tilting his head.

My face burned. "I know it was foolish, but I couldn't let her suffer, and I wasn't going to let this baby die."

"A noble cause."

Detecting no sarcasm in his words, my mouth dropped open in surprise. "Still, it was foolish. I'll go back up and sneak in so I can leave it."

"I'll distract her," he offered.

"Don't die on my account," I said, lips twisting upward. But I meant it. I was glad he wasn't one of the charred piles in the cave. My heart squeezed when I remembered Rivven was still up there—and so damn close to the dragon. And where was Galan?

"I don't intend to. Only to win the powerstone and keep it safe."

I gaped at the man before me. He'd saved my life. But my father seemed to favor him. Could I trust him? Did it matter?

"And to win the hand of the beautiful princess," I said, watching for his reaction.

"I shall choose whomever she favors," he said with a smirk. "I have no interest in leaving Astridon. Besides, there are other, more worthy women."

"The princess is very worthy," I snapped, then regretted it immediately.

"Perhaps," he agreed, dropping onto his bare feet and moving closer. "But I prefer a woman who is not afraid to stand up for what's right."

I clamped down on my tongue before I could give myself away, although my shoulders fell in defeat. He was right about Leuruna. She'd had the ability to stand up to Father all along, but instead, she retreated inside of herself. I hadn't thought too hard about what she'd said in my last dream. But the idea that she wanted to spare his life after everything...

I shook my head, trying to throw off my mind's wanderings and focus on the current situation.

"A woman who knows how to fight but chooses her battles." Torvo had continued speaking, and I became aware of him again when he stepped so close I could feel the heat coming off his body. "And beauty is of course welcome," he added on a breath.

Oh. He meant...

His lips connected with mine and all thought fled for a single blessed moment. The next thing I knew, he'd backed away and flown up toward the mouth of the cave. I was left with a racing heart.

I couldn't let Torvo or Rivven die while I battled with my tangled thoughts and emotions, so I went to what I did best— I sprang into action, climbing up to the cave once more. This time, the scene was even more gruesome as several of the men had decided to engage the dragon in actual combat all at once. They'd gotten too close for her to breathe fire on them. Swinging and stabbing their weapons, dark blood sprayed all over themselves and the ground as the magnificent beast jerked her body sideways, throwing one man off as another attacked from the opposite side. Her talons found the man before her, raising his spiked club to strike again. She pierced him through the heart then stomped her foot, crushing the remainder of his body as she roared in pain.

The ground below shook, rocking me from side to side as I struggled to keep my balance. Climbers had arrived as well and were rushing to join the fight, including Pan. Rivven appeared before me as I crept closer to the hoard, pressed to the shadows. His sword was drawn, skin glistening with sweat. In his hand, he held three rubies.

"Leave," he demanded, offering one of the gems. "I got enough for all of us."

I gaped at him, unable to form words. He hadn't spoken to me for ages, and now, he expected me to drop the egg and go?

"No," I managed as a body flew past us and slammed against the stone wall, sinking to a bloody, broken puddle. "I'm returning the egg first. And...and I want to help her." As soon as I said it, I realized it was true. To me, the dragon, deadly as she was, was only in this situation because my father had forced it on her. It was too familiar to ignore. I was done not standing up for what I believed in.

Rivven's face contorted in that familiar mix of frustration and disbelief as he tried to grab the egg. But I held on tight and avoided him, since his hands were already full.

Meanwhile, from the corner of my eye, I spotted Torvo, sword drawn and eyes gleaming with menace as he took in Rivven cornering me. I turned toward him, shook my head, and then nodded toward the mother dragon.

With a moment of hesitation and a nod, the winged combatant ran full force toward the fray. Instead of striking the dragon, he plunged his sword deep in the back of Pan, who'd just pierced beneath a scale and drawn blood.

"You need to leave, I'm not playing around, little spy."

My head snapped back to face Rivven, and judging by the way he leaned back, I wondered if my eyes glowed. "You don't tell me what to do. Go on and run with your treasure. You earned it. But leave me the hells alone."

I charged past him and slid, kicking up stones and dirt to avoid the flailing of arms and beast. Landing on my knees, I crashed into a pile of coins. I glanced up to find a man hovering over me, blood coating the side of his face as he glared down, a dagger in each hand while mine were filled with the egg.

"Might as well thin the competition," he muttered raising a dagger. Before I could sweep my foot beneath him, Rivven's curved blade removed his head.

I grinned as Rivven swung toward the battle and severed a hand holding a sword covered in the dragon's blood. My chest warmed as I took a moment to watch both Rivven and Torvo defend the dragon. It became quickly apparent that the beast knew it too, as she deftly avoided bumping or crushing them while she went after the others.

"Your mom is a warrior," I whispered to the egg, exhausted from the continued use of my fire power.

But my joy faded as one of the climbers, barely burned, shoved his blade through her eye. The dragon froze for a moment then stumbled, crushing two more opponents in the process. Rivven dispatched the man who'd done it with a cry, but it was too late.

I watched, unable to do anything as the beautiful beast, now bathed in red from a multitude of wounds, tumbled to the ground and stilled.

"No." I fell on my bottom, clutching the egg with the still beating heart inside. The battle ceased, swords dropping to sides, as the weary participants staggered to the pile to collect their treasure.

Rivven and Torvo wavered, resting their weapons and breathing hard. Simultaneously, they focused on me and moved to my side.

"I am sorry," Torvo said, dropping his chin to his chest.

"Thank you both for trying." I stumbled when I tried to stand.

"Too much magic," Rivven scolded, taking hold of my arm. "Give me the egg for a bit while you rest."

"No," I insisted, stubbornly. Tears burned my eyes as I gazed at the body of the mother dragon. "I can't. I know you mean well, but I need to take care of her."

"Her?" he asked, amusement twinkling in his eyes.

I shrugged. "Instinct?"

"I'll take you back down," Torvo offered.

I wanted to protest, but I was in no shape to try and either use more magic or climb while holding the egg. Rivven nodded, eyes narrowed and lit with flame. I wondered what he thought of Torvo, but I was glad he'd at least seen the man fighting on our side. Too weak to argue or question, I acquiesced, letting Torvo scoop me up again, this time one arm beneath my thighs and the other at my back.

"Wait," I said. "Did you get some treasure?"

"Here," Rivven handed him a ruby. "I think you already have some treasure, Starla."

I glanced at the egg. Would my father kill me for stealing it? He couldn't because I was in the Imrati. I'd fulfilled the directive of the first trial by getting a piece of the dragon's hoard—the most important piece. But judging by the way my consciousness was waning, I might not be awake to see his reaction.

TWENTY-SEVEN

I blinked my eyes open to find myself alone on my cot. The last thing I remembered was drifting off in Torvo's arms. I'd used more magic than I ever had before, over a longer period as well. But it had been worth it to save the—

Springing up, my gaze spun, and I swore as I clenched the blankets and waited for the world to stop moving. Two cots had been shoved to the side, and a fire burned where they'd been, circled and supported by large stones. In the center of the flames lay the egg.

I let out a sigh of relief, and my face fell into my hands as it all came rushing back. I couldn't imagine how it had ended up in my cabin with me, though I suspected Rivven had something to do with the fire. Smiling, I recalled how he had returned, not only protect me, but the mother dragon as well, just because I'd insisted on it. I supposed that made it easier to forgive him for avoiding me, though I still wanted an explanation.

Stumbling to my feet, I found I was dressed in my own training clothes. Someone had changed me out of whatever remained of the Tromodian jumpsuit from the first trial. I doubted anyone other than Galan or Rivven would've known this was how I'd preferred to be dressed. My cheeks warmed, but I dismissed my concern, since I'd been in compromising positions around them before. And my heart told me Rivven wouldn't have let another soul do it. Though that did make me concerned about Torvo.

After checking on the egg and making sure there were no cracks and that the thrum of the baby's heartbeat still drummed on, I moved to the cabin door. The sound that crashed over me when I inched it open made me wince. Someone had put a silence charm around it, so as not to disturb those inside. Or with the intention of making sure no one outside would hear what happened on the interior.

I shuddered, recalling Pan's death with a sense of relief as my ears adjusted to the loud drumbeat and shouts of revelers. The sun warmed my face, letting me know it was now daytime as I approached the celebration. But inside, I remained cold with the knowledge that the dragon had died undeservingly, fighting for her child and her peace.

The sight of the huge campfire reminded me of the night Rivven had tied me to the tree and saved me from his hired men. But the scene was radically different as so many men danced around it, shouting, drinking, and laughing. Silently, I counted those remaining.

Nineteen, including me. We'd lost so many, and I'd wager most were dead rather than unsuccessful.

Hugging my middle, I wandered closer to the spot where I'd seen Galan and Rivven, now together as the former chugged ale.

"Here she is!" Galan announced, throwing his arms open. "I had no idea you were such an animal lover, Starla."

I sat on the log near where Rivven rested, brooding as ever. The light in his eyes danced along with the fire behind Galan, but I wasn't sure it was all reflection.

"How many times has Carn saved your lives?" I asked, snagging his drink and letting it burn down my throat.

That silenced Galan, and even his semi-permanent smile faltered at my words. "This is supposed to be a party, not a memorial." He snatched the drink back and stormed off toward where several Tromodians pounded on drums.

Rivven considered me. "Feeling better?"

I nodded. "Why have you been ignoring me?" I asked, scooting closer to him.

His eyes widened. "I thought it was obvious. If we came in looking like allies, others would seek to eliminate at least one of us."

"Ah, I see. You were protecting me."

"Yes. I vowed to protect you, and I meant it. It hasn't been easy watching from a distance—"

I laughed, cutting him off. "I didn't need your protection. I didn't ask for it. What I needed was your support. Especially after we arrived here safely."

We stared at each other for a long minute while I fought back tears at the truth of the pain I'd felt. The abandonment of the first friend I'd ever made.

"I'm sorry," he whispered. "You're right. I was so busy planning the best chance at accomplishing our goal that I didn't realize what was most important."

"And what was that?" I asked through the thickness in my throat.

"You."

My heart stopped. I was sure of it. Then, it began pounding twice as fast, as though to catch up with the missing beats. Half of my mind forgave him while the other half spouted frenzied protests that his actions had to be what mattered.

Actions indeed. I pictured the way he came to my rescue in the forest and again with the elves. The way he propelled me to safety in the ocean.

"You saved the egg," I said when I couldn't find other words.

"It'll be safe in fire. I made sure it was hot enough."

"How did you get it back?" I asked, wondering what this unpredictable man did to chase off not only Torvo but keep the egg from the king.

"You don't remember?" he asked, worry creasing his brow. He grabbed my hand; his was so hot I nearly gasped.

All I could do was shake my head in confusion. "I was out cold."

Rivven glanced around, and finding no onlookers, he tugged me up and led me into the woods, far enough that the distant drums beat like a pulse in the back of my mind. When we reached a clearing that looked out toward the palace, he sat on the soft grass and pulled me down beside him.

"Nyah, you didn't pass out until we got back to your cabin." He waited, still holding my hand as though trying to prevent me from running off.

My mouth opened and closed wordlessly as I shook my head. I would remember that.

"You went through the line to present your treasure, kneeling before them as we all did. He went to take the egg. But the princess stood and announced that due to your cleverness, you should have the privilege of keeping your treasure, along with everyone else who'd returned successfully. I don't think he liked it very much, but there was little he could do."

"She...she stood up for me?" I asked, my voice breaking into a million pieces along with my heart. "Rune? She stood up to Father?"

"She did. And for the first time, I could see the resemblance between you." Rivven smiled gently, squeezing the hand he still clutched like a lifeline.

Not only was she alive and out of her catatonic state, but she'd done what she'd never dared before all—for me. Maybe Rune could change. Maybe this plan could work.

"What happened to Torvo?" I asked, trying to focus on something else lest I turn into a blubbering mess.

"Your winged devotee?" Rivven's jaw clenched, and I cocked my head at him. "He left after presenting his treasure."

"He isn't my devotee," I said, though I wondered if Rivven was right, remembering Torvo's statement on the ledge. Without thinking I touched two fingers to my lips.

The next thing I knew, Rivven had yanked me into him, grasping my arms almost painfully as his eyes burned with flame. "He touched you?"

I shook my head, confused at his crazed reaction. "He has only treated me with kindness," I said. Despite the roughness with which he handled me, I realized I'd missed Rivven's arms far too much. And my body's reaction proved it.

"Did he...did you..." He searched my eyes for answers as I blushed.

"No. Well, he kissed me, but not like you have."

Rivven's mouth quirked up into a wide smile as he loosened his grip slightly. "And what way is that, little spy?"

"You know with...passion." Saying that word made me want to dive underground and stay there. I couldn't even look him in the eye.

"Then I will have to erase the memory of him, since he was so lacking in the passion department."

Rivven's mouth covered mine before I could respond, and I opened to him on instinct. He deepened the kiss, claiming my mouth and stealing my breath as he laid me back on the ground and covered my body with his. Using a touch of air magic, I flipped him around so I straddled him, never breaking the kiss. I'd missed the heat, the electric sensations everywhere we touched—I'd missed him.

He groaned into my mouth as my hips moved, grounding my core over his length of their own volition. His palms traced up from my waist, over my breasts and to my neck to cup my head, holding it in the best position to continue to devour me.

Clumsily, I tore at his tunic, tugging it from his trousers. He caught my wrists and flipped us once again, pinning me to the grass, so all I could do was buck against him. I enjoyed the sound it forced from his throat, and judging by the way he hardened even more, nearly bruising my stomach, I felt like I was winning whatever this was, despite my position.

He threw his head back, breaking our connection, and I immediately went for the skin at the base of his throat above his collar bone. I sucked and bit like a wild beast.

"Oh gods, Nyah," he groaned, transferring my wrists into one of his enormous hands. Then he slid his free one down to my breast and tugged my tunic aside roughly, revealing the hardened peak that yearned for his attention.

He growled before taking it in his mouth and repeating what I'd done to his neck. I arched against the ground, crying out as ripples of pleasure coursed through my body, only increasing the hunger in my core.

"Rivven, please," I begged, squirming, but not knowing exactly what I needed. Only that he was the one I wanted to give it to me.

"Are you sure?" he asked, releasing my arms and ripping my tunic open completely before gripping the laces on my pants. The heat from his hands made me want to yank them off myself so he could touch the part of me that yearned for him the most. I wanted to know what it would feel like to have his hands and mouth on me.

"Gods yes," I said as he batted my hands away.

"Good because I can't stand it anymore. You've been all I could think about since you left for Lou's." Rivven undid my laces and tugged off my pants, leaving me bare on the grass. The wetness between my thighs embarrassed me, but tiny flames issued from his eyes as he pried my legs apart and drank me in.

"Rivven, I—"

"I overreacted that night and I've regretted it ever since. The truth is, I left early because I didn't trust myself around you." He lowered over me again, nipping at my lips between words. "I was an idiot for fearing my feelings would interfere with my ability to do what I needed to. I was so close to marching over to Lou's and dragging you back to the boat with me, anyway."

"Why?" I managed between kisses.

"To do this."

He slid down my body until his head dipped between my legs, and I lost the ability to speak. He lapped along my slit, drinking me in. I shuddered against him as he did it again then thrust his tongue inside my entrance. *Oh gods.* My body was melting. I was sure of it. I was losing control as he continued his ministrations. He moved his mouth up slightly, sucking at a new spot that made me whimper. When he did it again and plunged a finger inside of me, I jerked against him, eyes rolling back in my head.

"Oh, oh gods, Rivven, I'm going to explode," I breathed as pressure coiled inside of me with each new move.

"Go ahead, I've got you," he said, slipping a second finger inside of me.

Moments later, with the pressure of his thumb and curled fingers, my release roared through me, like the fire breathed from the dragon. I screamed Rivven's name as he continued to work me to the brink of torture. When he finally helped me down to earth, my body had become no more than a puddle of shivering limbs and electric shocks.

I lay spread open, breathing hard, and all I could do was watch as Rivven leaned over me and sucked my juices from his fingers, a low growl issuing from his throat.

"I knew you'd taste amazing," he said, eyes hazy, voice throaty and deeper than normal. "But that description is inadequate. You taste like a goddess."

My voice was still missing, my thoughts confused, but I willed him to touch me, to join with me and hoped he'd read it in my eyes—the only thing in the realms I was certain of.

"I'm rock hard," he said, moving so that he hovered above me, hands pressed against the ground on either side of my head. "I need to take care of that. But I don't want you to feel you need to—"

Reaching up with arms like jelly, I pulled him on top of me and kissed him deeply, the taste of fire and my own body fueling my desire. Wanting to make sure he understood, I slid a hand down between us, and tugged down his trousers, releasing his cock which burned in my palm.

"Fuck me," he said, eyes rolling back. Then he twined his fingers through mine, forcing them away from where I wanted them, and I felt him at my entrance. "Keep that up and I won't last long enough to make you come apart for me again. And I need to hear you peak if I'm going to."

With that, Rivven slid his cock inside just an inch—and gods it felt right. I moved my hips again, trying to take more of him.

"I'm trying to take it slow, so I don't hurt you," he said, voice breaking as he shoved in a bit farther.

"I want all of you. Now," I said.

In answer, Rivven thrust himself further in, and despite my complaints, it took some time until his entire length stretched and filled me. Pleasure coursed through me. So much so that the minor pain was nothing but an echo that reminded me of that strange edge between the two. I whimpered when he slid back again to just the tip.

But in the space of a heartbeat, he was driving into me again, and another wave of ecstasy rolled over me. He began a rhythm, slow at first, then faster, and then he lifted my legs and got to his knees. This time when he thrust, I swore I disappeared and was replaced by pure bliss.

I wasn't going to make it long. When he reached down to press once again with his thumb over my pleasure center, I was blinded by the orgasm that ripped through me. Rivven called out my name—my real name—as he rocked into me as far as he could, cock pulsing with his release.

When we'd both floated back into our bodies, he stopped thrusting his hips slowly and released me so he could collapse beside me in the grass.

"How many times have you done that?" I whispered in awe. He must have had quite a bit of practice.

"You mean fucked a woman?" he asked with a chuckle. "Because if you're asking how many times I've fucked a goddess, the answer is only once, just now."

I couldn't resist smiling even as I playfully smacked his chest. "Tell me," I insisted.

"Too many, I'm afraid. But none in the last year. Not since my seer warned me the time was coming."

"I met your sister," I said, reaching over to trace the ridges of his muscles in his abdomen.

Rivven rose slightly, stilling my hands. "You know who she is?"

"I have to live up to the nickname you've given me somehow. Don't worry, I like her."

"It's hard not to," he agreed, letting his head fall back on the grass. "I suppose now I've met your sister as well."

"And you haven't killed her yet," I said, remembering the way he'd jumped to that conclusion. It was strange how, when he pulled away from me, instead of worrying more about Rune, I'd been preoccupied with the idea of him leaving me.

"I don't plan to," he said softly, brushing the hair from my face. "Not when I'm smitten with her sister." He kissed me again, this time slow and lingering.

When he leaned back, I licked my swollen lips. "And how many times have you been smitten?"

"You ask a lot of questions, little spy."

"I wouldn't be much of a spy unless I got information."

His laugh was heartwarming, and the carefree expression he wore while doing it was so different from the one he usually carried. I wanted this side of him. I yearned to see the carefree Rivven all the time.

"I've never felt this way before," I offered. "And not just the new physical experience."

His laugh stopped. This time the intensity of his gaze made my thighs wet again. "Neither have I."

Twenty-Eight

"We need to get back before sundown for the ball," Rivven announced as I traced the dips and rises of his chest, musing about another round of lovemaking.

"I am in no mood for a ball." I glared up at the sun that threatened to slip below the horizon. "Let's skip it. This is far more enjoyable."

"I'd love nothing more, but I swore an oath. We'll be free to make all the love in the world after the evil king is dispatched." Standing, he pulled on his pants, ruining my view. "For now, we must play his game. I suspect he'll give out another gift for the second trial."

"I don't even have anything to wear," I complained as he helped me to my feet.

"They supply clothing like they did for the tournament. Besides," he tugged me into his chest, catching me about the waist, "you may find I'm a better dancer than your devotee."

"Is that so?" I teased, pleased that he no longer wished to distance himself from me.

In answer, he spun me out, caught my hand, and dipped me for a kiss.

I supposed going to a ball with Rivven wasn't the worst thing I could be doing. It was likely far better than whatever Father had in store for the second trial.

"So that was the Astridonian trial," I said as we walked back through the woods. "No dream magic, but it certainly gave anyone with wings an edge."

Rivven stopped. "Actually, I think that was the Centosian trial. It was in the dark and illusion magic would have helped—had anyone used it."

"Most of our people don't dare show magic," I mused. "The king is the only one. It's an unspoken rule. But if that's the case, it accidentally gave the Astridonians a helping hand."

"Not necessarily." Rivven spun around a tree and tickled me in the ribs, making me squeal. "Getting up there first could also have been a death sentence."

I quieted, having thought the same during the trial. Still, it seemed odd somehow—and quite a coincidence that Father had chosen to "gift" an Astridonian whose wings would work just fine. But it hadn't been much of a boon after all. Perhaps it was a cruel joke. I wouldn't put it past him.

Before we emerged from the trees, Rivven kissed me. Smoothing my hair, he smiled down at me. "Save me a dance, little spy, so we can scout together."

"I shall consider it," I said, unable to hold back what was possibly the biggest grin I'd ever worn.

Going our separate ways to our cabins was difficult. A stubborn part of me wanted to claim every last second I could with Rivven now that we were together. Still, I couldn't help but feel lighter—like all things were possible. As I entered my cabin, I found a dress like I'd never dreamed of wearing laid out on my cot along with Torvo in white dress clothes that stood out beautifully against his complexion. He was nice to look at, but what I'd experienced with Rivven was so much more—and I had no doubt he too would look breathtaking in his outfit.

"Where have you been?" Torvo scowled.

"I could ask you the same. You were nowhere to be found at the celebration bonfire." I lifted the glittering masterpiece off my bed with care. The gossamer, iridescent fabric slipped over my fingers. I imagined how lovely it would feel against my skin.

"I had business to attend," he said, sitting on his cot, which made his hulking form look almost comical. "Do you plan to hatch a dragon here?"

I glanced at the fire and the egg, grinning. "Yes, I think so. Unless it waits until after the Imrati."

"Mmm. At least there is more room now that we're the only ones left in the cabin."

The news stunned me, even though I'd suspected as much when I'd seen neither hide nor hair of Dann. It made me afraid to ask, but I had to know.

"Did he fail or..." I couldn't say the word. He'd been such a nice, if naïve, man.

"He failed."

My shoulders relaxed.

"So, the king's sorcerer killed him," Torvo said.

I gasped, letting the dress slip to the floor at my feet as I blinked at Torvo. There had to be some mistake. I'd never heard of those failing a trial being murdered in past Imrati. At my reaction Torvo stood, face melting into something gentler than before as he approached me.

"I am sorry. You were present when the decree was issued, so I thought you understood. But you passed out soon after, and your friends carried you back here to rest." He cupped my face, and the contact brought me back to life.

"Thank you for telling me." Ducking to retrieve the dress, I hurried to the bathroom and with a wave, I started the water running for privacy.

I wondered why Rivven hadn't mentioned the news. Perhaps, he thought I'd remembered that part? Or perhaps, he felt it unnecessary to worry me. But it was important news, and the more I thought of the implications, the more unwelcome it became.

If father were to kill all those who failed the trials, every single one of us would be dead—save the winner. Not only were Rivven, Galan, Torvo, and I in mortal danger, there would be no witnesses left if Father was planning something. *Only those loyal to him.* I thought of Dann, the sweet, noble farm boy who could've—should have—been able to return to his sisters and family, now dead for no good reason other than my father's cruelty and paranoia.

When the cold breeze tickled the back of my neck as I weaved my short hair into an intricate design around my head, there was no doubt left about its meaning. It was a warning. Winds of change, yes, but if Father felt it too, he'd do everything in his power to stop it from ending his reign.

As I slipped the breezy fabric over my body, I inspected the outcome in the mirror. The easy grin I'd been wearing since being with Rivven had been replaced by a hard frown, but I doubted the surrounding men would be focused on that. The back of the dress dropped into a low V, farther than I was comfortable with, and the beaded straps held the rest in place, despite the matching dip in the front. It fit me perfectly, perhaps magically made by elves, so that it coated my body like another layer of skin.

The iridescent fabric gave the illusion of nudity even with the already ample amount of skin showing, and tiny delicate flowers draped in strands down the skirt to the floor just above my feet. Despite the look, it was quite comfortable as I tested out my movements. But it would still be a hinderance if I needed to fight, and that set my teeth on edge as I spread on some makeup left on the counter for me.

By the time I re-emerged from the bathroom, my appearance had changed, and my attitude had hardened. *Fuck waiting.* I wasn't going to let my father hurt anyone else I cared about. His reign of terror needed to end, and I would make sure that happened before he took any more lives, whether the remaining contestants or innocent animals.

"You are a vision," Torvo said, drawing my attention to where he'd knelt before me. "May I accompany you to the celebration?"

"I don't think that would be appropriate. We don't want anyone thinking we're a couple, or it could influence how they behave in the next trial," I said, perhaps too quickly.

Torvo rose, nodding solemnly. "In that case, I will see you there, and perhaps one dance?"

"Sure," I agreed, face flushing far too much yet again. I knew he'd see Rivven and I dance together, and I didn't want him to feel like I was lying or being unfair. It was the type of situation I'd never even imagined myself in, and when I exited to make my way up the winding road to the brightly lit palace, the cool air was a welcome relief.

Up close, the palace was a crystalline wonder, with turrets spiraling into the clouds above. The moons cast a silvery glow over the cut angles of its clear walls. It appeared delicate, as though a single tap might shatter the whole masterpiece into sharp fragments. But I knew the diamond it was fashioned from was stronger than nearly any other crystal in all the lands.

At least, that's what my library studies told me during the year I'd been desperate to study the strange power crystal our father used to hurt Leuruna. If I'd been brave enough to approach Serano for lessons in magic, I may have figured it all out far sooner—how he'd been draining her magic and using it to power his own. But the thought of studying magic on my own had never occurred to me.

No that wasn't true, I realized as I passed two female Astridonian guards with hefty spears on either side of the grand entrance. I'd avoided thinking of the royal sorcerer whenever possible.

Another flash of his face above me, his hands all over my body, prying my legs apart.

I winced hard, shutting out the disturbing image, then I was gasping to catch my breath as I clutched a side table. Now wasn't the time, and I didn't know what to do with the sudden memory. It had to be that, as much I hated the thought. *Has he done the same to Rune? Was that why she'd reacted so oddly when I brought it up in my dream?* Bile rose in my throat. I shoved it down, straightening to my full height but clenching my shaking fists.

He would suffer as much as my father then. I need only look forward to the future. The pain of the past was to remain buried there. Lou was right. I couldn't afford to lose concentration, especially during the remaining trials.

Following the crowd into the ballroom, I craned my neck to take in the enormous arched ceiling, through which the stars shone brightly. Music swelled around the space, drowning out the hum of conversation. I lowered my gaze to take in the remaining contestants, and those from the stands, all dressed in beautiful clothing fashioned from silks, taffetas, and other expensive materials most people in Centos had never had the chance to witness. But I'd seen them often enough while spying on my father's parties.

Speaking of the wretched king, he was seated at a table on a dais raised above the band. On one side sat Leuruna, in a glittering blue gown that gave the appearance of moving water. Once again, her hair and makeup were expertly overdone. Yet, her eyes stared blankly out at the swirling crowd. It was so hard to picture what Rivven said had happened, the idea that she had stood up for me and come out of her stupor, only to fall back into it again.

On her other side, Serano sipped from a jeweled goblet. His hair was slicked back as his eyes roamed the floor. On Father's other side sat a striking woman with ebony skin as dark as Torvo's and long silver hair pulled back on the sides, with the rest cascading down her back. Her gown matched her hair, catching the lights so brightly that I had to narrow my eyes to see her in detail. The gold circlet on her head stood out among all the silver. *She must be the ruler of Astridon.* Beside her sat a younger version of herself—save the circlet—wearing a flowing white gown. I assumed she was a princess of the kingdom.

"Quite the show."

I flinched at Galan's voice in my ear and spun to find him in a glittering golden suit, shining as brightly as his personality. The moment I faced him, he whistled and made a show of taking me in from head to toe.

"You clean up nicely," he commented.

"Thanks. A bit ostentatious for my taste. But it looks good on you."

"Yes. Wealth does become me." He winked. "Seen Riv?"

"No." I searched the floor but couldn't find him. My heart sank a little. I'd feel less out of place if he'd show up.

"He mentioned having to get something for you. Might be an excuse to avoid the party as long as possible. He hates these things as much as you seem to. Birds of a feather and all." Galan snatched two bubbling crystal glasses from a passing tray, held by an Astridonian man in black, and offered me one while downing the other.

"No thanks," I said. If I put anything in my stomach right then, it might have come back up.

Galan shrugged and gulped the second glass before setting them deftly on another passing tray. "There, now that I've had some liquid courage, what say I ask the princess to dance? Surely, she can't resist the charm of the gray fox."

"More like gold fox," I said with an eye roll.

"I like that." He winked and headed for the dais. I watched as he approached the princess with a wide grin.

"Enjoying the party?" This time, the voice in my ear sent ice down my spine as I turned and took a step away from Serano. I hadn't noticed him leave his spot by Rune. Warning bells went off in my head as my vision tunneled on his oily eyes.

"I prefer solitude," I said, hoping my voice wasn't trembling like my knees. *This is ridiculous. I could kill this man in seconds. Though that would derail our mission by warning the king of our intentions.*

"Mmm." Serano snatched a drink as well, and this time I accepted one from the proffered tray, hoping it might steady my nerves. "I too prefer the company of a single person, if that person is worthy of course."

He clinked his glass with mine and took a sip. After a moment, I did the same.

"What you did in the first trial...it was impressive."

"Thank you," I managed, searching the crowd in the hopes Rivven, Galan, or Torvo would come to my rescue. But Galan was indeed dancing with the princess, who seemed delighted at whatever he was saying, and neither of the others were in view.

"You did tip your hand, though." Serano waited until I turned my attention back to him, my pulse thundering in my ears and blotting out the music. "Why what's wrong, my dear? You look pale. Would you like to sit?"

"No. Thank you. What do you mean tip my hand?"

"Well, you used illusion magic to replace the egg. That and fire magic to hold on to it. Only one other person in all the kingdoms has both illusion and elemental magic."

I set my empty glass on a tray and spun to walk away, but Serano grabbed my elbow and turned me back toward him. "Dance with me."

"I'd rather not," I said, chin held high.

"Nevertheless, you will, or I'll inform the king we've found our little traitor and break you open to drain every last bit of magic from you until all that's left is a shell." He smiled, white teeth gleaming in the light like a predator who had just captured its prey.

Without answering, I let him lead me to the floor and pull me close. His fingers dug almost painfully into my back and hand as he led us around the room, his body pressed to mine. The familiar, overpowering scent of anise turned my stomach, bile rising again and threatening to make me vomit. I breathed through my mouth and tried to calm my nerves.

"Now then, I'm glad to see you are cooperative. Don't worry, as I said I was impressed by your actions, and I'm willing to bet you have no idea of the real power inside of you." Serano pulled me even closer and inhaled deeply against my scalp as though he could scent the magic. Then he continued guiding me around the floor.

"I have a proposition for you. Starla, is it? Though I doubt that's your real name."

Didn't he know my name? After what I remembered, even if it was years ago, I couldn't fathom that he didn't know me. I spent so much time hiding, but surely, he'd kept track of the king's daughter. Perhaps not though. That's how little I meant to either of them without magic.

"Starla is fine," I said, noting that we'd moved to the outskirts of the room, where grand archways rose, leading to different parts of the palace. Over his shoulder, I saw the king escorting the queen of Astridon through one of the biggest archways, her face a mixture of anger and dismay.

"Very well. Starla, since you now hold the princess' power, that makes us two of the strongest magic wielders in the realms." His fingers clutched my lower back as he spoke, regaining my attention and forcing me to arch up toward him. "I can teach you how to handle what you've been given. She was and is a fool, the princess. She's never deserved it, but someone like you—who thinks on her feet and isn't afraid of powerful men—you can be a vision. Together we can rule the lands. I have a plan, and if you agree, together we will be unstoppable." He finished in a dip that had me heaving for breath.

When he straightened, taking me with him, he smirked. "You are either with me, or I will destroy you. It's a simple decision, but being a gentleman, I shall give you the rest of the evening to contemplate my words. Oh, and don't think about going to His Highness, that would end badly for you, I'm afraid."

"May I cut in?"

I'd never been so grateful to hear Torvo's voice. Serano bowed and spun away from us as Torvo took me in his arms, far gentler than the sorcerer had handled me, but just as securely.

"Are you alright?" he asked, concern creasing his brow. "Did he harm you? I will destroy—"

"No. Please don't start anything. He just thinks I'm someone I'm not." *Not anymore.* I was no longer a pushover or a thing to be used for his or my father's gain. Mission or not, they'd both find out if either pursued such tactics.

"Is there anything I can do? You seem off."

"Yes, actually. I could use some fresh air." I almost whimpered the words. How could part of me be so angry and brave, while the rest of me acted like a fool?

Without another word, Torvo led me through one of the archways and down a corridor. It opened onto a garden filled with flowers of every color and size. The heavenly scent washed away the strong smell of anise left from Serano and whatever potions he worked with. I inhaled deeply. There were blooms here that I'd never seen before—not even in a book.

"It's beautiful," I said, trying to let the wonder of nature overtake the confusion of what had just happened.

"May I show you something else?" Torvo asked, offering me his hands.

I nodded and took hold as his wings unfolded, lifting us nearly straight upward before setting me down on a balcony of one of the five turrets. Below us spread the grounds, lake, and forests of Astridon. But beyond, farther still and sparkling like a handful of tiny, glittering stars tossed across the land, were the lights of Tromodia and the sea beyond.

"What do you think?" he asked.

"It's breathtaking," I said, borrowing the word he'd used when I'd emerged from the bathroom. When I turned back to him, he was far too close. "Where are we?"

"These are my rooms." He moved aside and gestured to the arched opening that led into a circular space decorated with rich velvets and furs.

"Your rooms? You live in the palace?"

"Yes." He laughed softly. "You didn't know then that I'm a prince? Not that it means much in our kingdom where the women rule. That's partially why I'm participating in the Imrati. My mother wishes to join with the king through my marriage. I wish to obtain the powerstone and restore balance. My worth is more than my marriageability."

"You mean the queen that was downstairs..." My head spun. "She's your mother?"

"Yes. Mine and my seven siblings. My eldest sister, Nivania, was there as well."

I nodded, realizing she was the one dancing with Galan.

"I need your help with something, Torvo."

His head tilted. "Whatever you need."

"The evil king has been searching for something," I said aloud as the idea came to me. I'd seen him leave when the second trial started, but what could have been important enough to pull him away? And then there was the moment downstairs in the palace with Torvo's mother, when he led her away from the festivities. "What would he want from Astridon? Something that would be likely in the palace. Something your mother could give him?"

Torvo's body stiffened as he thought, staring out at the world spread before us. A vein in his neck rose as he clenched his jaw and fists at his side.

"The stone."

"What? He has it," I said not understanding.

Torvo turned to face me then, blue eyes shining like dagger blades. "He doesn't have our kingdom's stone. If he's trying to collect them all..."

I grabbed the edge of the doorframe, giving it my weight. "He's taking them all, so he'll have all the magic." But removing the stones from their rightful lands—that could destroy the kingdoms they were meant for. Was that why Tromodia was falling apart? Was it more than missing a ruler? Had my father already taken the stone from them? "We have to get to it before he does!"

Torvo grinned in a way that said he'd just won a fight. "I already have it. It's in my possession, since most anyone coming to look for it wouldn't think to check a son's room and not a daughter's. Come."

I followed him inside and toward the enormous bed covered in silks, velvets, and furs. Biceps flexing, he lifted the enormous mattress and retrieved a corded bag from beneath the center then let the whole thing drop with a thud. With care, he opened it and tipped it into his palm.

The crystal was silver and blue, which reminded me of him, and it shone with some internal source of light that pulsed in his hand.

"It's incredible," I said.

Torvo replaced it in the bag and tied it up again, then gazed around the room. "Perhaps there is a better spot. Not that my mother would ever speak the location to him."

I swallowed, not wanting to offer the possibility that she may have no choice. He already wanted to move it, why worry or offend him?

"I have an idea," I said suddenly. "Bring it with us back to the cabin. When we get there, I'll show you."

Torvo tied a long black cord around the bag and put the whole thing over his neck so that the package slid below his shirt and out of sight. Then he loosened his silver locks and shook them out until they obscured even the cord.

I opened my mouth to tell him he was brilliant, but the word turned into a yawn as a wave of sleepiness overcame me. I blinked my heavy eyelids and stumbled back toward the bed to collapse on it as another yawn took over where the first ended.

"Starla," Torvo's concerned words seemed very far away as I gave in to the call of soothing darkness.

The mirror waited as usual, but Leuruna was not on the other side. Just unresponsive darkness met my eyes, even as I called her name over and over, tapping harder and harder on the glass as ripples erupted all over the surface. If I could just break through and get to her—

"Stop," Torvo yelled, and I spun around to find him standing in the darkness, staring at me.

A glance back at the mirror showed no reflection of him, only the blackness that I somehow knew Leuruna was inside of.

"Why? I have to get to her," I explained, pulling my fist back to put more power behind my strike.

But his hand caught my wrist and prevented me from shattering the glass. I struggled against him, but with brute strength I was no match for him.

"Let me go!" I screamed.

He did, and I clutched my hand to my chest, breathing hard and glaring at him. I'd trusted him. "How are you here?"

"It's my magic." He shook his head. "I can observe dreams, alter them too, but not as fully as my mother."

"Did you make me fall asleep?" I accused, my voice echoing in the emptiness.

"No. Only my mother has that power." I paused at the slight tremble in his voice.

"He drained her power," I said, realization hitting as I pictured him escorting her through the archway while I danced with Serano.

"Who can do such a thing?" Torvo's rage was barely controlled as he shifted closer.

"The king. He does it with the stone in his scepter," I said, sadness lacing my words. I knew what he felt when he thought of the man taking his mother's magic. I'd gone through it a thousand times with my sister. "It's how he controls Leuruna."

"How do you know this?" he asked more gently, focusing in on me.

"Don't tell him," Rivven shouted.

We both turned to find him approaching through the darkness, sword drawn; though I didn't know if that would do anything in a dream.

As if to answer my unspoken question, Torvo motioned at him and the blade turned into a pink flower that sagged in his grip. Rivven blinked at it in confusion.

"He controls dreams," I offered. "So don't do anything foolish."

Rivven hurried forward and pulled me out of Torvo's reach. "I couldn't find you and Galan had no idea where you went."

"If you'd been on time, you'd have known." Tears burned behind my eyes.

"I have to go," Torvo announced.

"Where?" I asked, held back from going to him by Rivven.

"I need to find my mother's dream if she's sleeping. I have to know what happened to her. Do not break the glass or you will cease to exist out there. At least as you do now." Torvo nodded toward the darkness and what I assumed meant my body in the real world. Then he backed up a few steps and faded into the black, his startling eyes the last thing to go.

I relaxed into Rivven's arms and leaned my head against his shoulder as he embraced me. "I have so much to tell you."

"Not now." Rivven spun me toward him. "If he did this, he may be listening," Rivven breathed hotly, then pulled back just enough to speak out loud. "I might be the one dreaming right now. You are absolutely stunning."

"*Rivven,*" I said, calling his gaze back to my face. "*How did you find me?*"

"*I was on my way after you, already searching, when I fell asleep. Then I just called out for you, and you suddenly appeared.*"

A gust of freezing air washed over me, snapping me out of my slumber. I sat bolt upright in the center of Torvo's bed. He stood over me, wings outstretched like some sort of avenging angel as I gasped.

"What happened?" I asked. It had seemed so real, I felt disoriented.

"My apologies, I had to wake you."

Understanding struck, and I let him help me up. He'd flapped his wings, sending the cold night air onto me.

"Better than a kick," I said, setting a hand on his chest. "Did you find your mother?"

Torvo looked away and swallowed hard. "I did. And I end the Imrati tonight. I will tear the evil tyrant apart limb from limb with my bare hands."

"What has he done?" I asked as my chest felt like it caved in.

"She is dead." His voice broke on the word, a raw wound that I'd forced him to poke at while fresh. "He broke her wings, and it would seem he took her magic as you suggested."

"I'm so sorry, Torvo. I can't believe he took her life." But of course, I could. What use was she? She'd either given him what he wanted or hadn't. As for her power, he'd siphoned every last drop. I shuddered as a tear slid down my cheek, picturing the proud and beautiful woman I'd seen in the ballroom left somewhere, wings broken, staring at the stars.

"I wanted to wake you before he comes here looking for the stone. It isn't safe, though I still doubt she revealed the location." He turned away and started toward the balcony.

"Wait," I yelled, causing him to glance over his shoulder. "Where are you going?"

"I already told you. I'm going to kill a king."

TWENTY-NINE

"You can't. Not now while you're grieving." I rushed to stand in front of him, blocking the balcony. "He'll have the advantage. I'm sure he considered that he'd be attacked for this, but it obviously doesn't matter to him."

"I appreciate your concern, but I will not hold back like a coward while my mother's killer forces himself on the dreams of our peoples. You would not let it stand either."

My throat dried like I'd swallowed the deadlands. I was a coward. I'd never stood up to him. If I'd stopped him sooner, Torvo's mother would still be alive. Leuruna would be free. Rivven and Galan and every other person here would no longer be in danger.

"Please. I don't want to lose you too," I choked out as tears streamed down, soaking into the gauzy fabric of my gown. "We're going to kill him. That's why I'm here. I already have a plan, and you can be part of it. Just please, don't do anything yet. I think he's nearly drained Leuruna too, but he needs her alive, so he hasn't killed her. But that means he has all three kingdoms' magic right now. Torvo, he's as powerful as a god."

Lips pursed, Torvo studied me for a time. I didn't move. Let him see who I truly was. I was done hiding behind disguises and lies.

"I'm Leuruna's bastard sister," I admitted when he tucked his wings away. "I escaped when she hid a great deal of power in me. And I've come back to free her and get close enough to kill our father."

Time seemed to freeze as my words hung in the air, heavy and bare.

"What have you done?"

I turned to find Rivven grasping both sides of the other doorway. He must've run up countless stairs to get to us. The look of betrayal on his face was too much.

"He was going after the king," I said through sobs. "Balram killed the queen, Torvo's mother, and I can't let another innocent person die when I can do something. If you can't live with that, then you should go, Rivven."

"Who is this?" Torvo asked, angling himself between us. "I know you are another contestant, but who are you really?"

I stayed silent, letting Rivven decide. His truth wasn't mine to tell.

"Gods damn it, Nye." Rivven released the doorway, eyes glowing with fire. "I am a man sworn to kill the rotten king who had my father murdered." He looked straight into Torvo's eyes, shaking with unreleased rage.

"Then we have much in common," Torvo said after a heartbeat. "I will help you on your quest to rid this planet of the rot of Balram the pretender."

Both men grasped the others forearm in a pact and I released a breath.

"We have to get out of here," Rivven said, glancing back the way he'd come. "I hear someone at the bottom."

"That's impossible," Torvo said.

In answer, Rivven pulled back some thick dark hair and revealed his pointed ear. "Carry her down through the window. I'll face whoever it is." He freed his sword.

"No. You're coming with us." I rushed over to tug on his arm, but as usual he wouldn't budge. *Stubborn men!*

"How?" he challenged, eyebrow raised.

"Torvo, carry Rivven. I'll use air magic." I smiled sweetly, and without waiting for a response, rushed toward the balcony and leaped, catching an air current.

If the situation hadn't been so dire, I would have laughed at the expression of both men as Torvo held onto Rivven beneath the arms and lowered him to the ground first to join me.

"Hey!" Galan shouted from high above.

I glanced up to find him hanging over the balcony we'd just escaped from. He was the one coming up the steps?

He too used air magic to join us in the garden. Still out of breath from running, he grasped Rivven's shoulder. "The king has called everyone back to the ballroom for an announcement. We have to go, or he'll be suspicious," he rasped out. "Thank the gods for the tracking spell I put on the two of you. Worth every penny."

"You put a tracking spell on me?" Rivven demanded.

"Wait. How did you find me, Rivven?" I asked, slipping between them.

Instantly, Rivven's complexion darkened. "Never mind that now. We need to get back."

"You *both* put a tracking spell on me!" I exclaimed catching up to him and Galan as Torvo trailed behind. "How many fucking spells do I have on me?"

When we arrived at the ballroom, everyone was murmuring. Some were still rubbing their eyes, as though they couldn't understand how they'd fallen asleep. The princess I'd seen so carefree earlier sat in her mother's seat, looking as though she'd eaten bad fish. Father was in his spot beside her, drinking from his goblet, with Serano next to him. The music had stopped, and only moments after we arrived, men from the king's guard moved to block every entrance and exit.

My heart wanted to run, but I refused to follow as Serano made eye contact with me in silent question. But the king set down his cup and began to speak, forcing a hush over the room.

"What is an Imrati without a little excitement," he announced. "I did try to keep this event private and secure enough to protect from those with ill intent. Sadly, it wasn't enough. I have news." He paused dramatically, peering out over the stunned audience.

"Her majesty, Queen Farell of Astridon, has been assassinated."

Whispers rushed across the room as the princess visibly fought back tears. A tiny sob escaped her lips, and my father placed a hand on her shoulder. Rage filled me. He may have looked like he was comforting her, but in truth, it was a silent threat—and it worked as she sniffled and snapped her lips closed.

"Thanks to my adviser, the sorcerer, Serano, we know who has infiltrated the sky palace. He will meet justice now before all of you."

I doubted he was planning to confess, and my heart fluttered harder against my ribs. He was planning something, and my neck prickled with fear. Then my gaze fell on Leuruna's empty seat. *Where is she? What has he done with her?* Panic seized me, but I fought to stay still as he continued speaking.

"The guilty party is in this very room," the king proclaimed, leaning on the table and stretching toward the horrified masses. "A contestant in the Imrati. No doubt he joined to get close enough to cause harm. Why I saw him earlier tonight with the princess. Imagine if he'd assassinated not just the queen but her eldest daughter as well."

Another mumble rushed over the room as the memory played before me. I reached for Galan, but it was too late. Rufus had a sword pointed at his chest as he led him before the dais.

"No," I whispered.

Rivven began to move. Torvo reached out and yanked him back, whispering something in his ear.

"Galan of Tromodia. The Gray Fox, I believe you are called. Name your accomplices."

I'd left my sword in the cabin and regretted it at once. Despite having magic to fight with, right now, the king arguably had more and years of training than I did. Worse, I had other people to protect. I swallowed my fear and started calculating which guard's weapon would be easiest to snatch and wield.

"I have none, Sire," Galan said with only the barest hint of a tremble in his voice.

"And I suppose you'd have us believe you're innocent?" Serano sneered down at him like some sort of filth he'd found on his slipper.

"Even a fox knows when he's caught," Galan said, and my attention snapped back to where he stood, and the way those around him backed up. "I am guilty, Your Highness, but I would never stoop to allowing others to gain equal fame."

"What's he doing?" I whispered during the next rush of conversation.

"Saving us," Rivven said through shaking breath.

"No. We can't let him." I yanked at Rivven's arm as though trying to wake him.

"And as I am a fox, and therefore quite clever, Your Majesty," Galan continued. "I will save you the trouble of killing me."

The next moment, a rush of wind as strong as the one I'd felt with the forest elves parted the way to the exit. Galan ran, racing through the opening as though unbothered, while everyone else remained pressed down by the air. When the spell broke, the guards rushed after him, and the rest of us ran to the windows to watch.

Galan dashed as fast as a fox pursued by the hunt, straight for the edge of the city. The guards stopped short, swords outstretched as he tipped over the edge and out of sight.

"Quite dramatic," the king said. "But no matter. If his magic is strong enough to help him survive such a fall, which is doubtful, we will recover him on the ground when he is depleted. In the interim, we are rid of the devil. Let us raise a glass to the new queen of Astridon."

Most of those present were still reeling, but several managed to toast the poor princess. Then Serano took center stage.

"Unfortunately, Princess Leuruna won't be able to make this announcement, and so I do on her behalf. We evacuated her to a safe location at the first inkling of danger." He nodded, staring directly at me.

"We have another assist to bestow on a contestant for the second round of the Imrati. And that is the ability to save the life of a single combatant who finds themselves out of the running."

A roar burst out as though everything else had been forgotten. My knees went weak. If I won the gift, Serano would ask me to save myself, so I could help him take over. But, in reality, I could save either Rivven or Torvo from death.

Both couldn't win.

Serano's pause settled over the room as he remained fixated on me. Biting back the lump in my throat, I nodded almost imperceptibly, and his smile grew, slithering over his face like a snake opening its mouth to devour its stunned prey.

"And the winner, for her cleverness in solving the first trial is, Starla of Tromodia!"

The crowd cheered and jostled me, but I barely heard or felt it as I forced a smile of my own.

I couldn't shake the thought that we hadn't rid ourselves of the god of the seven hells. I'd just made a deal with him.

THIRTY

T suspected the others at the palace were too drunk to notice the shift, but when we were escorted back to our cabins and spread out, each of us alone under the guise of providing more privacy before the second trial, it was clear we were prisoners.

Desperate to talk to Rivven and tell him what was happening, I tried to get close to him. We each had two guards, and if Torvo could keep his cool under the circumstances, I wasn't going to be the one to botch things.

Thankfully, the cabin remained mine alone, with the egg still resting safely in the fire. I relaxed at the sight of it, unharmed. Torvo's things had been moved elsewhere. The guards stationed outside my door said that the next time I'd see him or Rivven, it would be for the trial.

Lying awake, I thought back on all that had happened, but the worst of it remained the unknown fates of Leuruna and Galan. Serano's attentions stayed a close second, and I shuddered, huddling further beneath my blankets at the memory of the way he clutched me to him and his horrid scent. Still... he'd given me a gift, whether knowing it or not, and I would take it.

Eventually, sleep did claim me, fitful though it was.

I dreamed of sword fighting with Rivven and stabbing him through the heart. Watching the life drain from his eyes sent me to my knees. The blood rushing over my hand was warm and far too real. But even as I screamed and wept, losing control of my body, the lifeless corpse before me morphed, becoming my father.

Slowly, I recovered. My body trembled as I rose, staring at his face, blood trickling from the corner of his mouth. Overwhelmed with confusion, I backed away and met a warm, hard body behind me. I spun to find Torvo, gazing at me with too much compassion in his eyes.

"Did you...are you really here?" I asked.

"Yes. I came to talk." He shifted his weight, glancing behind me at the body on the ground. "I shouldn't have interfered, but the pain you were feeling..."

"Thank you," I whispered, looking down and finding his broad chest.

"Do you love him?" Torvo asked.

"My father? I hate him," I said too quickly.

"No. Rivven of Tromodia. Do you love him?"

Words failed me as I turned the question over in my mind. Even as I protested, saying, "No, I...I don't know..." something in my heart stirred. Was it possible? I had long ago fallen for the brash, brooding, avenging king, but was it love? How could it be, when we fought for our lives and the safety of the kingdoms?

"Why did you tell me not to smash the mirror?" I asked, changing the subject so I'd no longer have to think about such a fragile, far away thing as love.

"Mirrors in dreams, especially those controlled by others, are doorways housing what we've hidden from ourselves. If you smashed through—well, I've seen others lost to themselves because they weren't ready yet, and I didn't want to lose you."

He was wrong. It had to be Leuruna behind the blackness that I was trying to get to. Wasn't it? If the king had put us all to sleep to test his newfound abilities, then perhaps the mirror was different than I'd seen before. My shoulders slumped. Maybe I could find Rune then and where they'd taken her. I just had to look for another mirror...

Torvo mistook my body language and pulled me further into his arms. I couldn't deny the comfort I found lying my head against his smooth warm chest. I doubted I'd ever turn down a hug. I'd received such little warmth from others until recently.

"What do you suppose the next trial is?" I whispered against him.

After a while, he tilted my chin up to face him. "I don't know. But it will be difficult. We may not all make it out. We certainly won't if we see this through to the end."

"No. I won't let you die. Or Rivven. Please don't think that way. I can save whoever is eliminated."

"If we are not killed in the trial."

My weakness made a reappearance even here in my dream as I shuddered, chin trembling.

"It's okay, Starla. I will make sure one of us wins. That is your plan, right? To win and get close enough to kill him."

I nodded, unable to answer. It seemed like such a flimsy plan now. So many things could go wrong, especially with the king empowered with so much magic. If Rivven and I died, and Torvo was victorious, even if he never managed to kill the king, at least he would make a kind husband for Leuruna.

"Promise you will avenge my mother if I do not make it," he said, shaking me.

"On my honor, I will do my best."

In answer, Torvo lowered his head, covering my mouth with his. Shocked, I pushed away, pressing my fingers to my lips, eyes wide.

Emotions somersaulted inside me, robbing me of coherent thought.

"I have my answer then. I will see you tomorrow," Torvo said and faded from sight, leaving me with an empty feeling, even in my dream.

The world around me darkened, swathing me in blackness. I spun, trying to find someone, anyone. And there in the distance was the glint of the mirror I'd craved. I ran to it, pressing my hand against the glass as Leuruna did the exact same on the other side.

"You're alive," I breathed.

"Only in my mind. Outwardly, I am weak. But by the end of the tournament, I will be well enough."

"Do you know what he's done?" Tears streamed in what felt like a never-ending river. "He's killed their queen. He's drained her power and yours. He's searching for the stone of Astridon."

"Then he will find it," Leuruna said, eyes glassy as her own twin rivers ran down her pale cheeks. *"He always wins, Nye. Haven't you learned yet? I tried to send you away to live the life I dream of, but you came back instead, like a caged bird that doesn't understand freedom. And now there's no escape."*

"I am not a bird. I am a warrior, and I will never go back. I will fight until the death to see you freed."

"You don't understand," she said, and I'd never seen her so frustrated. So angry. Then her head whipped around as did mine. *"He's there. Wake up!"*

My eyes snapped open to the flickering light of the fire dancing on the walls and casting shadows around the room. For a moment I just lay there, listening. I couldn't hear anything other than the crackling of the flames beneath the egg, but I could feel his presence. And then the smell...anise sharp in my nose.

Rolling to the side, I snatched my sword and swung, stopping him with the point to his bare chest and breathing hard.

His eyes flashed in the darkness. I almost believed he'd swat the blade aside without a scratch, but Serano stayed still. "Not the best way to great your future king, my dear."

"Why are you in my room?" I asked, willing my voice not to tremble.

"I've come to discuss our plan, of course. I have information you will want."

Slowly, I lowered my weapon to my side, but kept it clutched in my hand just the same. "And why are you half naked?" I demanded.

"This is how I sleep. What a dirty little mind you have. I approve. But for now, we must use our time wisely."

Suppressing a gag, I waited as he sat on the side of the bed.

"I hope you aren't having second thoughts about our agreement." He put a hand on my leg beneath the blanket. I stiffened. "You should know that crossing me would not go well."

"So you've said."

He grinned, the whites of his teeth almost glowing in the light of the fire. "And I meant it. My threats are not idle. If you work with me, the king will fall, we will claim our rightful place on the thrones of all three kingdoms, and you will have more power and wealth than you've ever dreamed of. However, if you cross me, you will watch everyone you care about die a slow and painful death before I help the king drain you of your life-force."

"You don't know anything about me. How would you know who I care for?" I challenged, although the picture he drew had caged me already.

"The princess, for one, since she felt comfortable enough to gift you her power. Then there's the friend you joined the Imrati with. He didn't get as far as he'd hoped when he leaped from the edge."

Serano drew a circle in the air and a picture formed of Galan stripped and beaten, laying on a rock floor in some sort of dungeon. Angry scarlet whip marks covered his bare back as he curled in on himself.

"No!" I couldn't help the response, even though I knew it confirmed that I cared for him.

"Oh yes. And far worse will await the Gray Fox if you don't cooperate."

"What do you want me to do?" I asked, fighting the tears, yet again. A hopeless cause to try to keep my own weakness at bay.

"Whatever I ask without hesitation." Serano's hand slid up my thigh, and I tensed again as he laughed softly. "Not yet. Not that. But the more you protest, the more I want to throw caution to the wind and take you, my sweet. There will be plenty of time once you are my queen though."

He rose and began perusing the room, stopping to stare at the fire—at the egg. "Did you know that baby dragons imprint on the first person they see when they hatch? This will be a definite boon for us. Perhaps, I will help it along a bit."

"Don't touch her," I snarled, leaping from the bed with sword in hand.

Serano simply paused, raising an eyebrow at me. "One more being to add to the list of those you care about." He tsked as he circled back to me, seemingly unafraid of my weapon as he clasped his hands behind his back. "Enough games. Put it down."

I swallowed, glanced back at the egg, and set the sword on the floor at my feet.

"Good. Now sit."

Glaring at him, I sat at the edge of the cot and watched him pace.

"You will do your best to make it through the next challenge. I will share with you some information that may help. If you do find yourself eliminated, you may use your gift and wait for me in the forest. If not, you will be one of only two contestants in the final duel. And that is exactly what it sounds like. No weapons. The winner of course will be the brute Torvo as he is a magic carrier and prince of this land."

"My magic is stronger," I argued.

"Ah, but the king plans to use the power he stole from the queen to put you to sleep and act as though Torvo did it. You will not win. He is the one the king has chosen."

The information had me clasping the edge of the mattress hard. Of course, the king had fixed the tournament. That meant they hoped for Rivven to die in this round. I vowed silently not to allow it.

"He, along with quite a few others, seem smitten with you," Serano continued. "Not that I blame them. But you will encourage Torvo's advances and feign weakness to keep him near you tomorrow. You'll see why soon enough. But the key is as soon as the trial begins, you must make it to the smallest island in the center of mirror lake. Do you understand?"

I nodded, already mulling it over in my mind. I had to get a message to Rivven somehow, to let him know where to go tomorrow.

"Good girl." Serano beamed at me. "We'll smooth out the barbarian in you soon enough. But it will serve you well in the Imrati. Remember, we want you to lose, but not until the final trial when I will take pity on you and take you as my concubine."

I shook in ire, ready to grab my sword again as he chuckled.

"See? Plenty of time for that later. It will give us reason to spend time together in private and plot the king's demise while he is distracted with breeding a new magic receptacle."

He was talking about my sister and Torvo like prize cattle. It took all I had not to vomit. "You'd better go," I spit out, unable to look at him. "The sun will be up soon, and no one can find you here."

"Oh, the guards outside already know I have an interest in you. Though their shortsighted minds can't comprehend more than the physical. Still, I will leave now. Do not fail me. Go directly to the island."

With that, he spun on his heels but paused before opening the door.

"And do try to look ravaged as I leave. We must keep up appearances. Here, let me help." With a wave of his hand, I was naked. Before I could correct my position, he'd thrown the door open and stormed out, the two men outside peering in at me as I tried to grab a blanket.

With a gust of wind, I slammed the door in their faces and looked down to find my clothing still on. It had been an illusion, of course. But quite a strong one. Had his vision of Galan been accurate? I prayed to the gods it wasn't, but I couldn't take chances with his life.

We would kill both the king and Serano and then we'd find Galan. We'd all make it through this. *We have to.* I dressed for the trial, trying my best not to think about the probability Galan wasn't powerful enough to make it to the surface kingdoms and escape.

THIRTY-ONE

B y the time we were summoned to the second trial, I was dressed,
armed, and ready. Everyone else's demeanor matched my own, as
those around me forewent the smiles and chatter for severe
expressions and distrustful glances. The stands were in the same location
as the opening ceremony, and I noted the population now far sparser.
Those who'd come to see their loved ones—and watched them die—were
either dismissed or more likely dispatched themselves. The chill wind
passed over me, sending shivers down my back.

"Welcome to the second trial!" Zoelle said as we all lined up in an arc
that was less than half of what it had been that first day. Upon closer
inspection, I noticed dark circles beneath her eyes and stray hairs sticking
out from her formerly perfect tresses. To her credit, she managed to keep
up the sunny act as though nothing was amiss. Probably healthiest for her
survival prospects, though if my father wanted no witnesses, she was
marked anyway.

Rivven had somehow made it to my side this time, and when I scented
his campfire smell, I wanted to dive into his arms for comfort. Instead, I
stayed focused on the stands where Leuruna sat paler than ever beside my
father. Had they tied her to the chair to keep her upright?

When the applause sounded, as low as possible I murmured, "Island in center," and hoped he heard.

By the way he straightened slightly beside me, I guessed he had and pressed my eyes closed for one blessed moment in thanks.

"Today's trial may prove to be a bloody one!"

Those in the stands cheered. But had they? Or was it an illusion my father or Serano had fashioned to make it look like this was still enjoyable for anyone?

"Your majesty, would you care to explain the rules?" she asked politely.

Father stood, staring at us. "Today you will use whatever is at your disposal to remain in the center of the magic ring. Simple enough, I think. Oh, and the perimeter will continue to shrink until there is only enough space for two inside."

All around me, contestants set hands on weapons and eyed those closest. I looked to Rivven and he nodded, hand on his hilt as well.

"You may begin!" With my father's proclamation, a sizzling pop surrounded us, cutting through the forest and to the stands with a visible edge of fire. Even as I watched, the circle began to shrink inward, herding us like sheep toward the desired destination.

It was big enough that the center would not be clear for some time, but I already knew where that was thanks to Serano's visit. I grabbed Rivven's hand and ran. Ducking beneath sword fights, and dodging rocks and punches, we rushed toward the lake.

Several men with Astridonian jumpsuits ran for us by the shore, swords and mace drawn and swinging. Clearly their strategy was to eliminate as many competitors as possible before things got too tight.

"Go. I'll cover you," Rivven said, stopping to draw his weapon.

I didn't want to leave him there as I scanned the area, seeing far too many people edging toward the lake as well. Perhaps the ideal location was more obvious than I'd thought.

"Go!" he yelled over his shoulder. Before I could decide what to do, strong arms grabbed me about the middle.

Torvo had hold of me, and jumped in the water, just avoiding the swing of an axe.

We emerged a few feet out as bodies splashed, sending ripples across the smooth surface, like my hand touching the mirror. The crystal water clouded with blood that burst forth in smoke-like clouds as some sank and others floated.

"Swim," Torvo demanded, standing chest deep and clutching a broadsword in both hands.

"You swim!" I yelled, splashing him. "You giant overprotective men need to stop trying to save me and help yourselves!"

Torvo glanced over his shoulder at me, amusement on his face, even as he dispatched a man from Centos that waded toward him swinging an axe. Probably the same axe that almost decapitated me moments ago.

"I cannot get my wings wet," he said simply then turned back to the approaching onslaught.

He'd carried me when I needed aid, so it was my turn to help him. Time to use some magic. I was "Tromodian" after all. So it shouldn't be that much of a shock.

Focusing on the buoyancy of the water, I swayed, rocking my body and causing a larger wave than this lake had likely ever seen. Torvo cried out as he rose with it, the new tide carrying both of us toward the center island at a pace no one would be able to match. When we were deposited on the shore of the island barely big enough for two of us to stand hugging the palm tree in the center, Torvo stared at me wide-eyed.

"You said you were from Centos," he accused.

I shrugged. "I told you the princess gave me her magic. That gift included a lot I wasn't expecting. Now, all we have to do is fight off everyone else and get Rivven over here."

"Are you certain this is the center?" Torvo asked.

"Yes."

"But only two—"

"We'll worry about that when we get him here," I insisted, attempting to ignore the impossible nature of the request. "In the meantime, help me keep everyone else off."

We ended up with our backs to the tree, hands linked together from behind and searching in every direction—including up. Though those that circled above—whether by air magic or wings—had not yet decided if it was worth the fight for the island, it remained unclear where the circle would move. Whenever someone approached by water, I sent them far out with another wave in the opposite direction, as soon as I was sure it wasn't Rivven. The longer it took to spot him, the more worry threatened to erode my resolve.

Please, I prayed silently to Reevka, the goddess of Centos. It had been many years since she'd responded to her people's prayers, but I had to do something.

When I opened my eyes again, another giant wave crested above the lake, and I braced to battle strong water magic. But as the body surfing the top became clear, my heart nearly burst with joy. It was Rivven gliding toward us, only small cuts and scrapes marring his copper skin.

The wave lowered, losing strength and speed as it approached, the fiery line of the circle now visible at the lake's edge. Rivven dropped beyond the island and treaded water, staring up at me and shaking his head.

"How do you know they won't move it?" he asked, even though it was now clear to everyone that we were in the exact center. "It's the sort of thing he'd do."

"Because I had a visitor last night that told me they want me and Torvo to be the last standing. He told me where the center was."

"Who visited you in the night?" Rivven's voice lowered with menace as Torvo's wings spread and he took flight to meet those in the sky who'd decided to risk it. Or maybe they'd become too tired to stay airborne.

"Serano," I said as he climbed onto the island. My chest warmed with embarrassment as I recounted the story I'd been wanting to share with him since the previous night. When I finished—omitting only the memory that had begun to haunt me, as I couldn't quite bring myself to say it out loud—I silently begged for Rivven to say something, anything. But he remained quiet, hugging the tree and looking at me with rage-filled eyes.

"I'll rip his throat out," he choked.

"We can use this to our advantage," I said, trying not to allow my emotions into the words.

"We will not use you as leverage or bait, Nyah. He will die along with the king. Do you understand me? I will not stop until they are both lifeless."

Throat too thick to speak, I simply nodded as bodies crashed into the surrounding water, raining down from the sky.

I'd been too distracted while talking to Rivven. Too late, I noticed the approaching group of five men, combining their water and air wielding to approach beneath the surface in a much subtler way than before. Heads popped out of the water all around, as they were lifted in the air above us, ready to strike.

"Watch out!" I screamed, flying into the air with a leap and clashing blades with the man who swung at Rivven's head.

Below and behind rose grunts and the clash of metal as another man joined my fight, both floating in the air along with me. The blows we exchanged were no training hits; these were born of desperation as the circle closed in toward us, moving faster than before.

I fully wielded my magic now, throwing bursts of air toward one assailant as I dodged and parried with the other. The sounds of fighting below continued, and if that was the case, I knew Rivven was still alive.

The man I'd thrown with a burst of air tried to do the same to me, but thanks to my training with Lou, I felt the change in the current a split second early and pulled the water from the lake in a spout, surrounding him much as she had me in the bathtub that first day. With a cry of determination, I pressed one hand down, keeping him below the surface, and ducked around the back of the other opponent.

By the time he spun to face me, he found four identical versions of me floating before him, blades raised. The hesitation my illusion caused was enough distraction for Torvo, having finished his battle in the sky, to dive and slice through the man's chest, spraying me with blood.

I released the drowned man in the lake to float to the surface with the other bodies, as my three doppelgangers faded into nothing. Torvo continued to the island where he joined Rivven in a fight against one final foe who seemed to have made it to the bitter end.

Lowering to float behind him, I swung my weapon. A second sword appeared in the assailant's hand as he met mine in midair and went for Rivven with the other.

"Bitch, it's time for you to die," he announced, raising a sphere of fire around me. My fire abilities surfaced, keeping me safe in the heat, but I'd used a lot of magic again, and it was starting to take its toll as my clothes disintegrated to ash and bits of skin in random places stung with burns.

Through the thick flames I saw Rivven's face grow ashen as he abandoned his attention to his own fight and sent a wave to engulf the sphere. Steam issued all around as I yelped with the pain that lanced through my extremities. I fell into the blissfully cool water, now filled with at least a dozen lifeless bodies. Arms once again wrapped around me, but this time I recognized Rivven's embrace. When we surfaced, inside the shrinking circle, I watched as the last man's skewered body drifted into the edge, disintegrating as it passed through.

"Quick on the island," Torvo called, clinging to the tree with one arm and reaching toward us with the other hand.

"Take her," Rivven said, handing me off like some helpless babe.

But I was too weak to fight against either man's strength as Torvo hauled me up onto the sand and clung to me.

"Get up here!" I screamed at Rivven who spun in the water to face the encroaching doom of the barrier. "We can make room. I can climb the tree."

But Rivven just looked at me, giving me his full attention and not the death approaching at his back.

"They won't allow it. You know that, Nye. Finish the mission."

"No." I shook my head vehemently, not caring that my weakness was showing, or that I was laying my true feelings out for everyone to see. "I won't let you die."

"You aren't letting me," Rivven said with a haughty laugh. "It's my choice."

"Fuck that," I said, forgetting my useless struggle against Torvo's immovable tank of a body. I glanced up toward the distant stands, knowing they were listening to the drama unfold for entertainment's sake. I screamed, "I use my gift for Rivven of Tromodia."

Behind Rivven, the circle stopped then sparked into a wall of flame before dying inches from his body. He spun in the water, searching, like he couldn't believe it had worked.

Torvo's hold loosened. I sunk to the small bit of land, sobbing as a boat approached from shore filled with the king's guard.

I couldn't stop, no matter how Torvo tried to comfort me, as they hauled Rivven onto the boat. His eyes stayed on mine until they faded into the distance as the announcer's voice magically boomed over the lake.

"What an exciting second trial! Emotionally satisfying for sure. The winners are Torvo of Astridon and Starla of Tromodia!"

Numbness struck me as Torvo helped guide me to my feet. My entire body tingled, as if it had fallen asleep, while he lifted me into his arms and flew us back to shore. When I was escorted to my cabin, I collapsed on the bed and let the exhaustion overtake me as the guards closed the door.

THIRTY-TWO

W hen I awoke this time, there were no sounds of revelry. And as I cracked open the door, I found a half dozen guards instead, standing stoically and heavily armed. They didn't look at me as I slunk back inside and sat on the floor near the egg. My stomach twisted in knots as I considered what had transpired.

Rivven was alive. I'd used my gift for him, which meant they had to honor it. At least that's what I told myself, even though we'd now dwindled to just the three of us, as far as I knew, apart from the king's inner circle.

He had to know it was me by now. *How can he not?* As for Serano, he was probably livid and plotting the most painful demise he could for me. I'd also inadvertently landed Rivven on his list of those I cared about enough to torture to keep me in line.

Perhaps that was more proof that they'd keep him alive. The thought sent a cramp through me, doubling me over as I retched air. I hadn't eaten in what felt like days, and I'd expended so much energy—magical and otherwise. What was the point in keeping up my strength when I already knew the outcome was fixed?

At least I'd be dead after the final round and wouldn't have to deal with the aftermath. That thought sent a hollow laugh ringing from my chest. *Once a coward, always a coward.*

No wonder I felt so alone. Even Rune had chastised me, angry that I hadn't taken her gift as an opportunity to run. But how could I? Would she have done the same, if she'd had the chance?

Rivven and Galan were in dire straits—assuming they both still survived, which was far from guaranteed—and the only one left that I could trust at all was Torvo, who I knew hated the king and would likely also end up as dead as the rest of us.

Dead. Dead. Dead.

Here lied the end of our ridiculous rebellion, Burying my head between my knees, I heaved once again, bringing up nothing.

I didn't know how long I stayed like that, cramped on the floor, when a sound from above roused me. Peering up, and half expecting to find Serano there to scream and inflict pain, I was shocked to see no one.

It wasn't until the second crackling and tapping sound that I noticed the thin line zigzagging up the side of the egg. I watched in awe as tiny talons the size of dinner knives poked through the shell, grasping the broken sides to pry them apart. Out popped the most adorable onyx face, tiny snout and shiny scales covering its skin. Small yellow eyes searched around as they finished emerging from the ruins, a tiny copy of its mother with small, bony leather wings and a tapering tail ending in a barb.

Our eyes met, and I grinned through my never-ending stream of tears. Out of the flames she hopped, landing in my arms on top of my bent knees.

"Well, hello there," I said, through sniffles of self-pity. "You're beautiful."

A gurgling chirp emerged from the dragon's throat as if to agree, and then it nuzzled against me, burrowing into the crook of my neck. When I felt the heat, I turned up my own. I swore she sighed contentedly.

"What should we call you?" I asked, wondering if this miracle would also be taken from me, or if I'd have the courage to help her. I thought about Carn and the way Galan gave everyone a nickname. "How about Ven? Short for vengeance."

Ven popped out long enough to lick my face with a forked tongue, then started nosing at my chest. I realized with a start that she was looking for mother's milk. *Shit.*

"Wait here," I instructed, setting her by the fire and rising. I rushed over to open the door again and called for the closest guard, who looked annoyed at my insistence.

"The dragon hatched," I informed him. "It needs milk, I think."

The other guards snickered and turned away as he grimaced at me. "And what do you think I am a fucking cow?"

Before I could retort, Ven slipped past my feet and latched onto the man's calf, piercing his armor with her baby fangs. He opened his mouth to scream and lifted his leg to kick her off, but before he could manage either, he froze stock still.

I glanced down at the baby, confused, until I realized she was sucking fiercely, blood dripping from the corners of her mouth. Throwing a hand up to cover my own exclamation, I shoved the man inside and shut the door as she continued to suckle.

Apparently, baby dragons drank blood. I repressed another gag as she worked, and the guard grew paler and paler, wondering if I should intervene. After about ten minutes, she released her hold on him, backed away, licking her snout and jumping around like a happy toddler.

The man's body loosened, and his eyes slid shut. I bent to check his pulse and found a faint beat against my fingers. I squatted before Ven who seemed quite pleased with herself.

"I take it you have paralyzing venom. Glad you didn't try to feed from me, little bloodsucker." I rubbed her head playfully, and she let out a purring sound. "Though I hope I don't get in trouble for feeding you on the king's guard." She narrowed her saffron eyes at me, and I giggled. "It was worth it."

I led the dragon to the small window at the back of the cabin, above the table where Dann and Pan had sat that first day. Both now gone. Shaking off the sadness for all the needless lives lost, I set the dragon on the sill.

"Go on," I tried to shoo her. "Be free."

Ven yawned and hopped to the table, settling into a nap with her tail curling around her adorable body. I sighed, remembering Serano's mention of baby dragons imprinting on the first being they saw. At least it was me and not him, I reasoned.

When the time came to meet once again, I tucked Ven into my blankets like a nest and kissed her head. "Stay here no matter what happens. Got it?"

She snorted, and a tiny puff of smoke emerged from her nostrils. I took that as confirmation and paused at the door to be sure she wasn't following me.

My half dozen guards—the one Ven had fed from having been replaced at some point without mention—escorted me in what felt too much like a death march to the palace and into a throne room, where my father perched on the highest chair. Fashioned from diamonds and other glittering gems, a pair of carved wings spread out in either direction behind him. My sister sat at his side, silent, her eyes locked on me. I couldn't return her gaze, knowing I'd let her down.

Serano sat to Father's other side, hands clasped on his own glittering chair, cold eyes also set on me. As Torvo was marched up beside me, I kept my gaze lowered, unable to face any of them.

"Bow before your king," Serano commanded in a bored voice.

I did without looking up.

"You've made it to the final trial," the king said.

I wondered where his announcer went—or if she was still alive.

"I bestow blessings on each of you and commend you for your bravery, strength, and intellect. However, only one can claim possession of the powerstone and choose my daughter's betrothed."

At last, I raised my gaze to lock onto my father. He'd already planned my death, but it was time to stop cowering and start meeting my fate with head held high. Whatever Rune had wished me to do, I had chosen of my own accord, and I was proud to have come back for her, whether successful or not. At least I tried, when she never had.

"Your eyes," Father said, pausing as I glared up at him. The moment passed as he glanced sideways at Leuruna, who remained still, then cleared his throat. "We will take a short recess during which I will confer with my advisor. Then, the final trial will commence."

Grasping his scepter, Father led Serano from the room, their cloaks swirling behind them as they strode away. I looked back at Rune, who seemed to focus on something over my head, a determined set to her shoulders I'd never seen before.

I wanted to shout at her to do something—anything—other than just sit there. To fight, and I'd fight with her. But I remembered how she protested when I suggested killing Father. I remembered how she'd dreamed of running and hoped to give me that "gift". White-hot anger infused every inch of my body as the fire inside me rose, heating the air around me enough to make the guards back up.

Control, I told myself. I had to save my magic. There could be a chance to use it to help those I cared about later. But I continued to stare daggers at my sister, hoping she'd see how her disappointment was mutual.

I still had the one secret ability I hadn't dared try. I'd assumed it was part of the old magic she'd hidden so deep when I first discovered it at Lou's. But I thought I understood better now that I'd met Torvo. The element of surprise might just be enough, but I'd have to wait for the right time.

Minutes later my father re-entered the room, Serano walking in his shadow, visibly shaken. When they reclaimed their seats, I noticed angry marks burned onto Serano's wrists that peeked out from his sleeves. Had he confessed his plans to the king? Had he thrown me to the wolves and pleaded for mercy?

"The final trial," the king began, "is hand-to-hand combat. You may use whatever resources are available to you. The last person left standing wins. You may do whatever you deem necessary to break your opponent." He said this directly to Torvo. "Show no mercy, and no one will fault you."

I swallowed hard. He knew who I was now; he'd recognized my eyes. And here he was, telling the giant man beside me to torture and kill me. I supposed I should have expected him to have no grace for his own daughter when she'd tried to take a stand.

The king motioned to Rufus, who gestured beyond an archway. A group of guards dragged in a barely conscious Rivven. He slumped in their arms as they pulled his sweat-soaked, bruised, and bloodied form to the feet of the king, dropping him to his hands and knees. Only half-torn pants remained on his body, and his muscles shook as he tried to keep from collapsing to the ground.

A gasp escaped my lips. When I moved as though I may run to him, two guards blocked my path with long spears.

"Is this the man you would choose to betroth to my daughter should you win?" the king asked, his voice sickly sweet.

"I..." I had no answer. But it made sense. If I named him, he would not only live but be close enough to strike. I nodded, swallowing back the tears and frustration that wracked my body.

I hated my father. The absolute revulsion I felt in his presence ate at my soul like a disease, until all I wanted to do was rip his heart out.

"When your opponent wins, you will rejoin my court," Father said, standing and pointing a shaking finger at me. "And your punishment, to start, will be to watch as this man begs for death."

Striking like a snake, the king kicked Rivven in the ribs, sending a resounding crack echoing through the sparkling throne room. Rivven slumped to the ground.

Leuruna turned to me then, flicking a glance at Rivven and back to me. The pity I saw on her face broke something inside. It was like a dam breaking, as a tide of pure rage and pride surged through me, lighting up my insides like the brightest star in the night sky.

"And when I win, you will have mercy on my opponent and release him unharmed," I said, loud enough to echo as well.

"Very well." The king laughed—truly laughed at my pronouncement —as he took his seat. "Begi—"

"Stop." Torvo stepped forward, his guards moving with him. "I forfeit."

My mouth dropped open as the king's hateful glare zeroed in on him.

"I'm afraid, though a noble sentiment, once you have joined the Imrati only the gods themselves can release you from your obligation," the king said, adding a touch of false sympathy to his words. "Consider it a blessing I have not demanded you fight to the death."

"Then I will not lift a hand. Starla may slay me without interference." Torvo raised his head and puffed out his enormous chest, beating against it with one fist in promise.

My father's staff banged against the diamond floor of the palace, making me wince and silencing all. He rose again to face the winged prince who continued to meet his eyes, unafraid.

Torvo had done what I'd wanted to do all along. He'd stood up to my father. But judging by the look in his eye, the king would not let this go unpunished.

"*Starla,*" he began in a menacing tone, "is a runaway. Did you know?"

Torvo shifted, but puffed up further, daring my father to strike.

"You did. But I doubt you know everything. I'm sure she hasn't told you who she really is."

Movement on the ground behind the king had me holding my breath, praying no one would notice Rivven as he slid toward my father. When Serano glanced that way, I cast an illusion to make it appear as though he remained on the ground, unconscious.

"She is your second daughter," Torvo said proudly.

My father paused and laughed again. "Second? I have only one."

His pronouncement that he disowned me was hardly shocking, and yet some part of me crumbled at the words. Casting a second illusion, I pulled my sword and tossed it to Rivven, while we remained still to those surrounding us.

"Then who is she?" Torvo demanded, as Rivven rose shakily to his feet, bringing up the blade, ready to strike.

"She is the one and only princess. She is Leuruna. She is the one you will marry."

Rivven froze, sword raised as he glanced back at me in confusion. I shook my head in denial. *What is my father playing at?*

"Tell them," he commanded, still staring at Torvo.

Leuruna rose from her throne as though a thousand pounds of boulders weighed on her tiny frame. She bowed her head and said, "It's true. The one you call Starla is a shadow hand. The same as Illio created in the stories. She is merely my illusion."

The words rang in my ears like nonsense as I struggled to understand them. My illusion magic dropped. Rivven remained frozen, sword raised, as Rufus spurred into action, disarming him. He didn't so much as fight back as they shoved him to his knees. He simply gaped at me in shock.

"No," I kept saying. I repeated it over and over again, louder and louder, as though that would make it true. Make them all listen. But even Torvo stared at me, dumbfounded.

I backed up, the guards around me mirroring my steps. "That can't be true. I have thoughts, feelings, memories."

But do I? Panic seized me as I tried to recall anything beyond that moment outside of her hallway at fourteen. Moment by moment, I saw myself sneaking and observing others who seemed to ignore my presence. Was it possible they hadn't ever seen me because I wasn't there from their point of view?

Confusion, sorrow, and helplessness warred within me as I sunk to the ground. Things were happening around me—a whirlwind of movement and yelling, and I had no idea who said or did what. All I knew was I needed it to stop.

I needed to speak to my sister.

"Sleep!" I screamed, unleashing the magic I'd withheld.

My head buzzed as everyone in the room, except me and Leuruna, collapsed into a deep slumber. Then I turned to her, watching as she walked to the spot where I knelt on the floor.

"It isn't true. Father made you say it," I accused, knowing somehow, somewhere, the truth waited like the shadow of death itself.

She crouched beside me, shaking her head sadly. "I wish that were the case, Nye."

"How?" I asked still struggling to comprehend it.

"Serano came to me at fourteen, when father deemed it time to learn what would be expected of me as a wife and queen." Her voice broke, but she squared her shoulders and continued, "Father meant for him to explain things, but he took it too far, insisting that if I were to feel the pain of joining now, I'd be better able to please my future husband. And when father found out, he accused me of manipulating his favored sorcerer."

"But I remember Serano raping me," I said, voice small, as I pictured his hands prying at my legs, his too strong smell assaulting my nostrils.

"I know," she whispered. "I'm so sorry. I didn't think you would, but that was the moment I created you. It wasn't even on purpose. It was just a sincere wish to be free to roam the grounds, free to fight back when abused, free to be who I was inside." A tear slid down her cheek as clear and perfect as the diamond palace around her.

"He was on me, and then the next thing I remember is being in the hall," I admitted. "But how could I exist for so many years without knowing—"

"The strongest magic is wielded through emotion," she said, picking at the fabric of her lavender gown. "Do you remember sleeping?"

Sleeping? What a strange question. And yet—when I tried to conjure up a bedroom, all I could find were hours late into the night talking with Rune or sitting on the citadel and staring at the moons. Wishing for freedom, but knowing I couldn't leave her behind.

I shook my head, roughly brushing away the tears on my cheeks.

"When I gave the rest of my magic to you that night," she said softly. "It brought you fully to life. The greatest illusion ever created. I fooled even you."

That was when they saw me. It was the first time anyone reacted directly to me. And... "It was the only way you could escape and keep the magic from Father's hands."

She sighed deeply, standing again and looking around at the others. "But you came back. I suppose in a way it was inevitable. You are a part of me."

I stood as well, grasped her hands in mine. "Then come with me. Let's run away now while they sleep."

A slow, sad smile spread over Rune's face as she looked wistfully toward the doorway. "You should know by now that running isn't the answer. It seems these men care for us. We cannot leave their fate to our father. Besides, there is nowhere to truly run."

"Then kill him now. Or let me. It's time to end this." I reached for the sword now lying at Rufus' feet, but Leuruna stayed my hand.

"We cannot kill him."

I recoiled in disbelief. "I can't believe you would stand by him after all he's done."

She shook her head. "It isn't that I'm protecting him. Mother...she used to visit me in dreams, after she'd taken ill. Her image and words were always fuzzy and broken, but before she died, she told me something. She said he mustn't die until all the stones are recovered and rejoined. I don't know why or how, but she said if he did, all would be lost."

I slumped, defeated. Hearing her speak of these things I had no memory of hit harder than any of the other evidence thus far. I'd been at home in the shadows all this time—because I was one.

"You fooled Serano," I said through my tears. "He thought I was real, and you'd sent me your magic. Even Father didn't figure it out until now, did he?"

Rune nodded, reading my body language with a somber face. She backed up, arms spread as she reclaimed her seat. "I'm truly sorry that you had to find out like this, Nye. You are the best of us."

All around people stirred. Torvo was the first to awaken, followed by the king, Serano, and the guards. And finally, Rivven, whose side had already started to purple from my father's kick.

I spun in place, feeling lightheaded and strange. Torvo gaped at me. Rivven looked stricken. I glanced down at myself, unsure what was happening and found that I'd become transparent like a ghost.

"No," I begged, spinning toward Rune. "Please." I needed more time. But even as I stumbled up to her throne, I continued to fade, feeling like one of the air currents I'd learned to catch in order to fly.

My sister's face was set, yet sad as she watched. In what I understood to be my last moments, I spun to find Rivven. It was his face I wanted to stay with me if I had enough substance to carry anything along.

"I'm sorry—I didn't know," I whispered as a sheen of light swallowed me. Without knowing if he heard or believed me, I added, "I love you."

Thirty-Three

Rivven

She vanished, evaporating into particles of light like an illusion. But I could not have made love to an illusion. I could not have fallen in love with an illusion. She hadn't disappeared. She'd simply changed.

Or perhaps I was a madman who'd lost his last speck of hope. She'd said she loved me as she dispersed into the air. Could an illusion love? The pain in my body was nothing compared to the pain in my heart. The part of me I'd kept locked inside a steel box since losing my father had cracked open, and all those feelings long buried were sharper than the sword that had been taken from me.

I hadn't meant to fall for the woman I suspected of being a spy. But she'd wheedled her way into my psyche with her stubbornness and bravery. The way her lip curled when she spoke of the king—or when she was annoyed with me. Sometimes, I would needle her just to provoke that very response because I wanted to see it. She was naïve as spring rain, yet carried a burden few could understand unless they'd suffered at an early age, as I had.

We were kindred spirits. Or so I thought. But she had indeed been a spy, though inadvertently. For even if she still existed inside the princess, half of her was now a stranger to me. And because I'd trusted her, let her in, I was a prisoner of the man I despised. Likely, I'd die soon, but I welcomed it, unsure if I could bear much more.

King Balram stormed over to his daughter, grabbing and shaking her so hard her head snapped backward.

"Where did you get this power?" he snarled. "How have you hidden it from me?"

"It was I who put everyone to sleep," Torvo announced, stepping forward, but meeting the guards' crossed swords before him. He'd been disarmed at some point. "When she gave the command, I put everyone to sleep."

The king released his daughter, and she scrambled back to her chair, eyes wide. The same eyes. Nye's eyes. I looked away as the king marched up to snarl at Torvo.

"Then why did you not take advantage of the opportunity to kill me?" he demanded.

Torvo recoiled as though shocked. I wouldn't have thought him to be so good at dramatics.

"Sire, why would I? Now that I know what she really was, thanks to you, I win the Imrati. My opponent is gone." He gestured around the space that, though filled, remained too empty. "I am promised the hand of the princess and the stone. Why jeopardize that?"

The king relaxed, straightening his tunic and pulling back his staff. "And why did you listen to the princess' command?"

"We had a pact, Your Highness, and I honor my word. She—or rather her illusion— promised if I did so when she commanded it, I could hide this safely." From beneath his shirt, Torvo lifted a small bag on a cord. He removed it and tipped the bag into the king's hand after a few seconds of hesitation.

You fool, I thought. *You're trading the stone of your people for his trust and her life. But you don't even know if she's still in there or if only the princess is left.*

Yet even as the king's eyes lit up and he clutched the stone in his palm, I relaxed slightly, knowing his ire was no longer aimed at his daughter. I remained the only one with access to my people's stone, which he would never get his hands on. I wasn't giving up on my quest. I couldn't let Nyah or my people down. I'd turned my back for too long. I might have been a prisoner, but I was closer than I'd ever been to the man who'd taken everything from me—from everyone.

"And you decided against it?" the king questioned Torvo, tucking the stone behind his back and out of reach.

Torvo straightened to his full height, a foot or so taller than the king—maybe even taller than I was. "As I said, whatever is yours will someday be shared with me. I'm not sure what you know of my people, but I have lived as a second-class citizen as a male, even as a prince. This is a far easier path to the power and greatness I crave."

The king nodded with a knowing smile. "I am proud to call you son then, Torvo of Astridon, and betrothed of my daughter, Leuruna."

The guards beside the Astridonian prince relaxed as the king spun toward Serano. The sorcerer had been watching quietly, stealing occasional glances at the princess, which she did not return.

"Prepare for the return to the Night Kingdom," he proclaimed.

"Your Highness," Serano said silkily, bowing low as he rose. "What shall be done with the prisoner?"

The king looked at me then, meeting my eyes, which I knew burned with the fire of hate he'd stoked so long ago. I filled them with promises of death, since as long as I took breath from the world, I would seek to destroy him.

He smiled, sending unspoken promises right back to me.

"He will be our guest in the Night Kingdom. We have much to discuss. He will be a tricky one, so make sure he is unconscious on the way."

"Yes, Your Majesty." Serano bowed lower.

The king clapped his hands together then spread them wide as he addressed all those present.

"A successful Imrati after all! But it is time to focus on the next momentous occasion. Let us make haste in returning home. We have a wedding to prepare for."

To be continued...

Thank you for reading! Did you enjoy? Please add your review because nothing helps an author more and encourages readers to take a chance on a book than a review.

And don't miss more of the *Sisters of Magic and Shadow* series coming soon. Be sure to sign up for her newsletter at lizzygayle.com

Until then, discover THE BINDING STONE by Lizzy Gayle. Turn the page for a sneak peek!

You can also sign up for the City Owl Press newsletter to receive notice of all book releases!

Sneak Peek of The Binding Stone

The magic is palpable. It tingles as it radiates up and down my arms. My eyes snap open the moment I feel it.

I let the power drift over and through me, soaking it up like a human does sunlight. My fingertips crackle with it. Voices become clear now, and sounds assault my ears like daggers after the blissful silence of nothingness. I prefer to sleep. When I do, there is no need to think. Or remember.

Whoever dares disturb my century-long slumber will suffer my wrath. That's a promise.

"Really? Only ten?" The voice of a young man attracts my attention.

He is close, but my senses remain dulled from my sleep inside the gemstone, so I choose to be cautious, staying invisible to human eyes. His voice, warm like honey, soothes the edges of my anger. But some qualities can be deceiving. I know from experience.

"Jer, remind me not to bring you along when I buy a used car," comes the voice of another young man. "Your haggling skills need some serious work."

I stand in the center of a modern marketplace. It is small but cluttered, centered in front of a brick house with several people milling about the lawn and walkways. Whatever time I'm in, the women wear far less clothing than I remember. Near the outskirts of the unkempt grass, I spy a girl who is closest in appearance to me. A small child tugs at her arm, but the woman is distracted. A smile pulls at the corners of my mouth, and I quickly change from the draped fabrics of my last master's time, mirroring her outfit. I nod in approval. I'm going to enjoy this century.

Now to locate and destroy the source of the threat. It is not difficult. I follow the same girl's blushing gaze toward the honeyed voice I'd heard before.

"I'll take it."

He stands a mere table's width from me, and it is clear he is indeed the One. His aura glows like none of the others. A rainbow of iridescent colors pulsates and bleeds around him like a force field. This is too easy.

A gasp draws my attention. It's the young mother, frozen in a state of horror. I've seen that look before, so I follow her stare to find the toddler examining a flower growing in a crack in the concrete. A machine of some sort zooms toward her, so big it will surely crush the child in seconds. Time slows as I raise my fingers and invisible hands lift the young one out of harm's way, setting her securely back near her mother. No one has seen, save the woman who will likely never again be so negligent.

Focusing on the rainbow aura, I raise my hands. All it will take is one blast, directed at the handsome man busy handing a piece of green paper to an elderly woman. He will cease to exist. But I feel it as I let go, and even before it bounces harmlessly off his aura, I know. So I scream. It is not as though anyone can hear it. Not yet.

"Never figured you'd go for the whole bling thing," says the one with glasses and a dull, human aura. "Try it on."

I watch helplessly as Jer slips the ring on his middle finger. The large opal in the center gleams a little too brightly, and I tug at the choker around my neck, running my thumb along the matching stone. I hope the ten-paper is worth more than it appears. Why must I care so much for the innocent after all these years? If I'd let that machine crush the child...

No. I am not, nor will I ever be, one of the human Magicians. It is what sets me apart, and the only thing that may make up for some of my past sins. The ones that were within my control.

"Great. Can we go now please?" It seems by his rush that the friend does not like it here. I cannot blame him. My nose wrinkles up as I scan the rest of the market—a few scattered tables covered in odd objects, dusty boxes stacked and interspersed between them. Most things I don't recognize, but it all looks like junk to me. So how did I end up here? Just one more indignity to add to the list.

I trail behind as the two boys move away and down the wide street. The homes surrounding the market are similar to each other, yet closer together than in my last master's time. It saddens me to find far fewer trees and greenery to balance all the brick and mortar surrounding us as we walk.

The chilled wind carries the ozone-tinted scent and humid feel of a body of water nearby, which pleases me. It is refreshing after my sleep. I let my bare arms stretch out behind me, allowing goose bumps to prickle along my skin. A few buildings away, the men amble up the uneven brick walk, scattering fall's last crisp leaves from the single maple tree in front, before bursting inside the four-story rectangle. I've seen worse. Although I'm certain this "Jer" will be upgrading soon. I continue following them up creaking metal steps and into a small room, containing a sagging, cushioned seat big enough for two, a square table and chairs, a well-worn bed, dresser, and a desk.

"Do you think it's real?" Jer's friend inspects the ring.

"I don't know, Gabe. There was something about it. Like I couldn't put it down."

Of course not. You sensed the power. My power.

I suppose I should reveal myself. If I do not, the stone will force me, and at least this way I can have a little fun with the friend.

I loosen the invisibility and freeze Jer's friend before he can touch the ring. I will teach him not to touch things that do not belong to him. I grin and let my eyes glow green with power so there can be no doubt as to my nature.

My new master's reaction is immensely satisfying. About to sit in the chair near the desk, he spies me and misses, falling to the floor with a *thud*. His face is pale, his eyes huge as his gaze darts between me and his friend. I would not be surprised if he fainted. Instead, he licks his lips and clears his throat.

"Hel...hello?"

Well, that's different.

Don't stop now. Keep reading with your copy of THE BINDING STONE.

Don't miss more of the *Sisters of Magic and Shadow* series coming soon. Until then discover THE BINDING STONE and more from Lizzy Gayle at lizzygayle.com

A thousand years of servitude left Leela more than a little jaded. Betrayed by the man she loved only begins her lessons on the wickedness of humanity.

Her hope for freedom for herself and her fellow Djinn from the magical stones that bind them has dimmed to a barely-there glimmer.

But it hasn't yet been extinguished.

When the young, handsome, and idealistic Jered inadvertently becomes her new master, Leela wonders if his tenderness and concern may be real.

And despite her years of suffering, her heart begins to open to him. And the chance at romance.

As she inches closer to trusting Jered, the past and the enemies that come with it, resurface, threatening the small spark of happiness in Leela's long life.

After a millennium of pain what—and who—is Leela willing to sacrifice for freedom?

Escape Your World. Get Lost in Ours! City Owl Press at www.cityowlpress.com.

Acknowledgments

It takes a village to make a book, and you, dear reader, are at the top of my thank you list. Without you, there is no point.

Thank you to Tina for not only believing in me but backing that up with amazing edits and hours of work. Thank you to the rest of the team at City Owl. You guys rock. Thank you to Leslie for your insight and time. Thank you to Heather for championing my work as well.

Thank you to Kelsey and Maria for your amazing art and ability to bring my characters to life.

Thank you to Shona and my family for your support of my work and all my ups and downs.

Thank you to my characters who come to life in my mind. Thank you to my community on social media and in person for your support and interaction that keeps me going. And thank you again dear readers for sticking with me on my wild rides. I truly hope I've succeeded in taking you for an exciting ride away from your worldly troubles.

About the Author

LIZZY GAYLE loves paranormal so much, she lives it. She is both an author and a psychic. Between mothering her three kids, attempting to understand her rocket scientist husband, and consistently attempting to declutter her home (that she is convinced is a secret portal to a clutter-creating dimension), she does her best to use her creative gifts  and share them with you. Lizzy is a people person so if you contact her, it will make her very happy and she will likely answer while possibly including pictures of her bunnies and/or bird. She has also been known to write Young Adult under the name Lisa Gail Green.

www.lizzygayle.com

facebook.com/authorlizzygayle

instagram.com/authorlizzygayle

About the Publisher

City Owl Press is a cutting edge indie publishing company, bringing the world of romance and speculative fiction to discerning readers.

Escape Your World. Get Lost in Ours!

www.cityowlpress.com

facebook.com/CityOwlPress

x.com/cityowlpress

instagram.com/cityowlbooks

pinterest.com/cityowlpress

tiktok.com/@cityowlpress